# THRONES OF TIME

## GENERATION 3: THE EMPTY THRONE

Copyright © 2020, CM Robles
Illustrations by CM Robles

**Cover artwork by:**
CM Robles

◀ + − | ≡ ⊥ ⋃ ʔ ⊓ ⊏ ≡ | ⊏ ᔐ ⊓ ⊤ ⊥ ≡ | · Z | + − | ᗰ · ⊤ ▶
◀ + − | = ≡ ⊓ ʔ | · + | · Z | + − | ⌐ − Z ≡ | + − | + ᔐ − Z ≡ | ᗰ ᔐ − ᖺ
ᖺ ⊥ ⊓ < ≡ | ⊏ ᔐ ⊓ ⊤ ⊥ ≡ | ᔐ ⊓ ○ ○ ≡ ⊤ ▶

Robles, CM
Thrones of Time: Generation 3: The Empty Throne/ by CM Robles

For more of the Nova-Storm Chronicles, visit thronesoftime.com

*Dedicated to:*
*Braedon Robles*

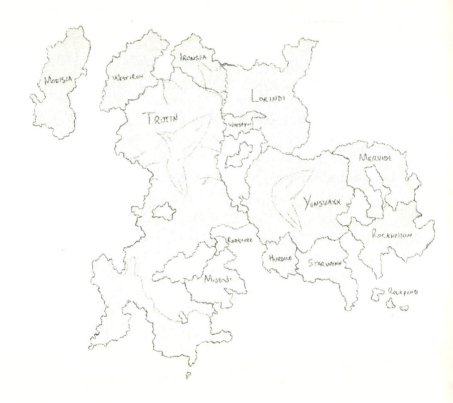

# Part One

Pg.1 / Evelyn

Pg.30 / The Last Quodstella

Pg.48 / Halloween Terrors

Pg.68 / Terrors of the Tundra

Pg.88 / Phlasma

Pg.110 / The Flying City

Pg.134 / A Savior

Pg.142 / The Sentinel's Sanctuary

Pg.151 / Modius

Pg.165 / The Raptor Cavalry

Pg.180 / Vacation on Amalga-5

Pg.187 / The Flawed Prophecy

Pg.202 / Suriv

Pg.215 / Home too Soon

Pg.234 / Tomas 'Rex' Dapar

Pg.242 / Destined Departure

Pg.249 / Kranthar's Curse

Pg.262 / Adam Jaminski

Pg.281 / The Beginning

# Part Two

Pg.318 / The Last Sarran

Pg.326 / A Rêve Stone Through Time

Pg.342 / Family of the Extraverse

Pg.367 / Cosmic Brothers

Pg.392 / Power Shift

Pg.405 / The Gateway

Pg.437 / The Ilsian Kings

Pg.448 / Death

Pg.457 / Cosmic Sisters

Pg.462 / Camp Vistor

Pg.480 / Life

Pg.502 / The Fall of Nidus

Pg.516 / Possession

Pg.548 / The Calcurus Warriors

Pg.573 / Doomed

Pg.607 / In Search of Hope

Pg.628 / Reunion of Ghosts

Pg.638 / Before the Storm

Pg.643 / Thrones of Time

Pg.713 / The Empty Throne

❖ ❖ ❖
# PART ONE
## THE PARADOX CHILD
❖ ❖ ❖

## ❖ Chapter 1 ❖
# Evelyn

"Box. Find a new Sentinel, ensure the universe's safety. Give them time. I failed," the Sentinel spoke with her final breaths as her phlasma ghost weakened.

"Affirmative." The box glowed, and it flashed away.

Time watched over the Sentinel's Army, trying desperately to figure out what to do now that the Sentinel was gone, the universe was still ending, and the Multiverse was in critical danger because of it.

Celestae turned to face her and spoke, "You know the truth. You know what is really happening. This is not the Sentinel's fault. She died trying to fix what she thought she caused. We cannot keep ignoring the truth."

"It is the Paradox Master's fault," Time admitted.

"Not that one." Celestae gestured towards the Paradox Master. "Not the human." Celestae rose from his throne. "Time, you know what must be done. He and his followers must be stopped."

"We cannot save the Multiverse," Time responded.

"Then who will?" Celestae's voice raised.

# October 29th – 1982
# Palm Springs, California

"It's me! Why does no one know that it's me? Am I really that hard to remember? I just want to be recognized! Is that really too much to ask? Honestly!?"

Thunder cracked over the distant purple mountains, shooting through the slow falling sprinkle of rare rain across the desert valley. The distinct smell of the musty creosote filled the air.

The crashing thunder interrupted seventeen-year-old Evelyn Sanchez's ranting. The high school junior's walk home in the normally dry desert was more uncomfortable than it had to be on the overcast October day.

## ❖ CHAPTER 1 ❖

She thought her frizzy brown hair was bad enough as it was, but the rain didn't help. She preferred heat to rain any day.

"Eve, can you *please* stop talking to yourself, I just wanna listen to the rain." Her half-brother, Andrew Hall, complained as he did most other walks home from their school.

"I was talking to *you,* thanks for paying attention, loser."

Andrew was two grades lower than Eve, a freshman, and he followed her everywhere. Most of the kids at the school didn't believe he was related to Eve in any way; his skin was much darker than hers and he looked nothing like her. Though that didn't bother her, the more she could distance herself from him, the better.

He was popular around the school, and well known as the immature, rowdy one; the complete opposite of Eve. She could admit, though, that it hurt to not be recognized for her academic achievements while her half-brother was well renowned for his subpar behavior.

"I can't believe you're the one who got cheered on today for just touching a stupid bug and no one batted an eye at me. I was the first to finish our test today *and* get everything right. Also, who gets the name Evelyn confused with Jaylinn? They aren't even close! We don't even have a Jaylinn in our class! Am I invisible?"

"Eve, no one cheers nerds. Plus, who's gonna cheer for you anyway? No one knows who you are! Now stop talking, the thunder's nice. We don't get it all the time. Cherish these moments!" Andrew held out his hands with a smirk as he twirled in the rain, then pushed out his leg in an attempt to trip his half-sister.

"Shut up butthead, you know I don't like the lightning, okay? I've told you this. Talking calms me." Eve stepped over Andrew's leg, as used to it as ever, and adjusted her backpack on her shoulders. She tried to speed ahead of Andrew, mumbling to herself. "Oh! And another thing!" Eve yelled as another thought popped into her mind.

Andrew rolled his eyes in an over dramatic manner.

"While we're on the subject of unrecognized talent, you agree that I should've totally gotten the part in the play, *right!?*"

"Totally," Andrew mumbled half-heartedly.

"Janet can't even sing! I can act!" Eve yelled. Her brow furrowed as she marched on. "And sing!" she seemed to add as an afterthought. "I should've gotten the part…"

## ❖ CHAPTER 1 ❖

"Maybe you would have if you were any good at it," Andrew quipped.

Eve smacked him in the back of the head with her notebook. Just then, lightning cracked in the distance, but at the same time the two of them heard a closer sound, like the explosion of an old mechanical flash powder camera. In the same moment, Eve felt a small shake in her bag and she hesitated, just outside their home.

"What're you doing? Come inside, it's pouring," Andrew complained while holding the door open for Eve.

"Just a drizzle." Eve ignored the shake. She stepped ahead and walked in past Andrew with a slight shove.

"Hey, you're home later than usual," a tired voice said from the kitchen. "How was school?"

"Sorry Mom, Eve was just being slow, *as always*," Andrew teased. "School sucked," he answered.

"It was fine." Eve slid her bag off her shoulders, ready to sit down on the living room sofa.

"Ah, Evelyn." Her mother, Laura Sanchez, stopped her with her voice, "Trash. It needs to go out."

"But Mom, it's pouring!" Eve complained, slinging the backpack back on over her shoulder.

"Just a drizzle." Andrew snickered. He plopped himself down on the sofa and began to open his backpack.

"Ay, you too bucko, didn't do the trash last time, there're two bags." Laura raised her voice to be heard over the sounds of her preparing dinner for three.

"Ugh! Fine." Andrew followed Eve out too, picking up his bag on the way out. He pulled a hoodie over his short, curled hair to keep from getting too wet, as the rain was picking up.

Eve dropped the trash bag outside when she felt her backpack shake again. She let out a startled shriek as her backpack fell too.

"Way to go, butterfingers." Andrew walked past Eve.

Eve stared into her bag, something in it was glowing purple and the bag was shaking.

"What in the world…" She held her hand out for the backpack. In a fraction of a second, a small purple laser shot into Eve's heart. Lightning struck and Andrew stumbled back. He shielded his eyes. When the dust settled and the smoke cleared Andrew stood up, and he looked towards Eve, right where the lightning had struck.

Eve held out her arms, admiring them. They were lit aflame with phlasma, a bright burning purple flame, twirling

## ❖ CHAPTER 1 ❖

around her arms slowly and calmly. She took a deep breath, gasping.

Internally she was beyond afraid and confused, but she was too awestruck to do anything but stare.

"Eve... what the *hell* is that!?" Andrew yelled.

The flames flared and small sparks of lighting shot from her fingertips as Eve stepped back in delayed surprise and shock.

The phlasma vanished quickly afterwards. Eve's backpack was near destroyed from the lightning strike, but she seemed completely fine and untouched, other than her hair sticking completely up and shooting off in crazy directions.

"Dinner!" Laura called for them.

Andrew stared at Eve wide-eyed, not knowing what to do.

Eve shooed him towards the door with her hand movements and shuffled her way along back to the house, leaving what was left of her bag behind. She pressed her hands against her head and tried to flatten her hair down again.

"*Eve, what just—*" Andrew started to ask in sort of a loud whispering voice.

"*Shhh, I don't know,*" she said, her voice like a whisper, but wanting to scream. Eve couldn't think straight and the only prevailing thought in her mind was hunger. Questions would have to wait.

The burnt and soaked remains of Eve's backpack shook until a small object flew out from it. The box with its relatively new red shell, floated above the burnt bag, paused for a moment, then whirred along and followed Eve into the house as quietly as it could manage, staying close to the ground to avoid being seen.

It cloaked itself in invisibility and waited.

Eve and Andrew sat down for dinner.

"Sloppy joes again, huh?" Andrew tried to make normal conversation, his eyes shifting nervously and his voice wavering. He stared at Eve as if to confirm he was being as unsuspicious as possible.

Eve raised her eyebrows at him.

"Honey, you asked for it," Laura reminded him.

"Right." He ate nervously, to avoid conversation.

"So, Evelyn you said school was fine? Anything interesting happen today?" Laura asked as she served macaroni to them.

Eve stared silently at her food, frozen with lingering shock. Andrew kicked her under the table.

## ❖ CHAPTER 1 ❖

She shook herself and spoke, "Normal," was the only word she could think to say.

"Wh—" Laura shook her head, confused, "What? Normal? That's not even an answer to the question I asked."

Andrew cleared his throat in an over-the-top manner.

Laura stared at him, extremely confused.

He stopped and folded his hands in one another, then smiled at his mother.

"Alright..." Laura looked back to Eve. "Still talking to Melissa?" she asked, trying to ignore the strangeness.

"Uh huh." Eve poked her food, staring at her fingers. They glowed with a faint purple light.

She shook her hand after she felt a burning sensation. Andrew watched as her hand flared into a pillaring inferno of purple when Laura's back was turned putting the macaroni bowl away. Laura turned around to Eve sticking her hand into her macaroni.

"Evelyn, are you alright? What's up with you guys today, you seem off?"

"Yeah, I'm fine, actually now that I think about it, I've got a *ton* of homework, can I eat in my room tonight?" Eve spoke quickly, her hand still firmly in her bowl. Andrew stared at her, chewing slowly.

Laura hesitated. "Sure…"

"Cool. Thanks. Bye." Eve stood up and carried her food quickly with her to her room.

"Hey, Mom?" Andrew asked after a few moments passed.

"Yes." Laura begrudgingly answered his question before it was asked.

Andrew stood up and carried his food with him to his and Eve's shared room, shuffling along as quickly, but as not suspiciously, as he could. The box floated across the floor, following them.

Eve slammed her door shut.

"What's going on with me!?" She held her hands up to her hair, instantly regretting the decision, as her hand was covered in macaroni. She made her way to her in-room bathroom and began to wash her hands and hair. "This is crazy, this *can't* be happening! Whatever's happening! You saw it too, right!?"

"I don't know *what* I saw, but it was cool!" Andrew commented. "You survived a lightning strike, I think!" he said. "I couldn't tell if it hit you but that was close!"

### ❖ CHAPTER 1 ❖

"Shh!" Eve shushed him, turning off the sink and getting a towel to dry her hair. "Mom might hear, she'll freak out."

"If I tell everyone that you survived a lightning strike, I think they might cheer for you. Do you want me to tell people? It's not as cool as touching a bug, but still, might get you some points. Oh! Or maybe we can skip school because you're super weird." Andrew laughed.

"What was that stuff?" Eve questioned herself as she stared in the mirror, subconsciously checking if she was actually awake.

The box dropped its cloak and lifted into the air, "I can answer that," it spoke, floating and spinning in place.

"Woah!" Andrew stepped back. He took a bite of his sloppy joe. "Radical."

"Andrew what's going on out there?" Eve could hear the new voice in the room, but not see it.

"It's a magic floaty talking Rubik's cube!" Andrew stood up and approached the box. It floated back and away from him.

"This isn't the time for games, Andrew." Eve turned around and saw the box, floating in her room. "Oh."

"I'm the box," it chimed, whirring its core.

"What did you do to me?" Eve asked it. She noticed the purple glow shining from within through the circles on each face. She made the connection that the box must've been what shot her from her bag.

"I infused you with phlasma powers," the box answered quickly and to the point.

"You did what to give me what? Why?!" Eve paced around the box, staring at it, trying to figure it out. She lowered her voice to not be heard by Laura.

"Powers?" Andrew questioned.

"The Sentinel gave me special instructions to find a replacement for her. And so, I did," the box answered.

"What's a 'Sentinel'?" Andrew asked, sitting on his bed, and finishing his food.

"*The* Sentinel is a person; a person who protects the universe from itself with a time machine, an army of powerful friends and allies, and powers like the kind I've awoken in you."

"Woah! A time machine!?" Andrew laughed. "Like the Omni? I gotta tell Kurt about this, he's always going on about that show—" Andrew was suddenly filled with even more excitement, something he didn't even think was possible. He was beginning to forget the reality of the situation.

## ❖ CHAPTER 1 ❖

"If you base what you know about time travel on fiction then you've got a lot of things to learn." The box spun around. "But the Sentinel died. In the future, at the end of the universe, in a different dimension at the hands of a clone of her, after witnessing the death of her wife.

"She died before she could make sure the past was safe, she was too busy protecting the future, and so she needed a successor. That would be you, Evelyn Sanchez," the box explained, whirring between the two of them.

"What? Why me? How am I supposed to protect the past? I don't have a time machine!"

"This is the past. I was built in 2072 by the Sentinel's first incarnation," the box elaborated.

"What are you?" Eve stared at the hovering box.

"I'm the Sentinel's time machine. A broken time machine, at that. I need to be recharged. Your powers cost energy to produce."

"You don't look broken. You also don't look like a time machine," Andrew said. He stared at the box for a bit. "Hey, wait a minute, is phlasma that fire stuff?" Andrew asked, still somewhat awestruck. "That is kick-ass! Eve! You're cool now!"

"You seem to adapt quickly to new situations." The box spun, complementing Andrew. "Good job."

Eve sat down on her bed and held her hands to her head. "This is a lot of stuff to process all at once. So what, I'm supposed to protect the universe? From what? Aliens?"

"Non-Earth life, yes, if that's what you mean." The box whirred. "There's a lot more to it than that."

"Aliens exist!?" Andrew exclaimed. "I was right! Kurt owes me like ten bucks now. Eve, didn't I tell you that aliens—"

"Andrew will you *please* shut up." Eve closed her eyes as tightly as she could. Her head was pounding, swarming with thoughts. She opened her eyes wide and exclaimed, "What am I supposed to do about school?"

"*School*? That's the first thing you worry about?" Andrew scoffed. "You've become basically a superhero and you're worried about what you'll do about school? Dweeb. You suck the fun out of everything, no wonder no one likes you."

"Andrew, I had plans for the future, okay? I was excited about school because I knew where it could get me! Now I'm just finding out that plans have changed and you're telling me that it's cool so I should just go with it?"

## ❖ CHAPTER 1 ❖

"Why did you want to be a teacher, again?" Andrew asked.

"So that I could teach the future generation and influence kids," Eve said, matter-of-factly, as if she had the answer rehearsed. "So, they'd turn out better than you," Eve added as a sarcastic afterthought.

"I would've done it for the summer break, but whatever," Andrew mumbled to himself before getting to his point. He shook his head then said to Eve, "Teach the future, huh? Influence the kids? Cool. Rad. Solid." Andrew looked at the box, then to Eve. "What kids?"

"What?" Eve asked.

Andrew held Eve's shoulder and shook her. *"What future?"*

Eve pushed her head back and squinted her eyes at Andrew. She darted her eyes away as a thought crossed her mind. Andrew was making sense. That didn't usually happen. "That doesn't make any sense," Eve said.

"Indiana Jones was a kick-ass teacher. You could be like him! Like if he was a super dweeb who thought he could sing and act but also happened to have fire powers! That's you, Eve. Dweebiana Jones. Save the future, dummy. Can't teach if reality breaks, or whatever."

❖ EVELYN ❖

Eve pursed her lips and thought about it for a bit. She glanced at the box. As she did it shifted nearer to her. She shuffled away and added, "And what about Mom? I can't let her know." Eve dropped her body onto her bed, shaking the mattress. "She's been through so much already…"

"Then you need a secret identity or something. What'd you say that person was called? The Sentinel?" Andrew asked the box.

"You are Sentinel now, Evelyn." The box spun around.

"Why did the other Sentinel choose me when she died? What's so special about me?"

"She didn't choose you. You were chosen a *long* time ago." The box spun, its lights dimming in and out.

"What for?" Eve sat up. "Why me?"

"For reasons I cannot explain. Not now. You've been given a lot to process."

"I don't even know *how* to even *begin* to try to protect the universe!" Eve groaned and sighed. She was obviously annoyed. She darted her eyes quickly to Andrew. "You tell no one about this. Got it?" she demanded behind her teeth.

"You sure? Think of the cool points—"

"*Andrew!*"

## ❖ CHAPTER 1 ❖

Andrew shook his head and cleared his face of his happy-go-lucky expression in favor for a super serious one. He dragged his fingers across his mouth, as if to zip it shut. He tossed away an invisible key. He put his fists on his hips and declared, "Your secret's safe with me... but only if I can be your sidekick." Andrew smiled, dropping his super serious facade.

"You're not—" Eve rolled her eyes, "UGH! I'm not a superhero! That stuff isn't real. This? This is real. Take it seriously." Eve looked to the box. "What do I need to do to get this over and done with?" she asked.

"I would teleport you to a location for you to begin, but like I said, I'm broken. I can tell you where you need to go." The box flashed its lights. "The man you need to see is in this state."

"California's a big place, I'm gonna need something more specific than that." Eve stood up and paced around.

"Monterey." The box followed Eve.

"That's up north, right? On the coast? That's gotta be hours away!" Eve complained.

Without hesitation Andrew began packing a bag, stuffing it full of comics and snacks. "Road trip!" he exclaimed.

"Andrew how are we gonna drive to Monterey? Mom won't let us use the car, not in a million years, and I don't even know how to drive!"

"You drove us to the store," Andrew reminded her.

"Yeah, once!" Eve exclaimed.

"Okay, so here's what we do." Andrew began pacing with Eve, "We steal the car—"

"No." Eve shook her head.

"Then you drive it to Monterey."

"Nope." Eve kept shaking her head.

"Bada bing bada boom." Andrew finished.

"That's it? That's your plan?" Eve chuckled. "No!" she let out in sort of a playful drawn-out way, both in awe of Andrew's relaxed nature and overwhelmed by all the information being thrown at her.

"Aw, come on, why not?" Andrew asked.

"*Because-we-could-get-in-trouble!*" Eve annunciated the phrase to Andrew to get the message across to him.

"*But-you-have-crazy-kick-ass-purple-fire-powers!*" Andrew annunciated the phrase the same way Eve did hers, in a way to mock her back. "And a time machine just said that you have to, so, I mean go ahead, don't listen to me, but you should listen to that." Andrew pointed at the box as it spun.

❖ CHAPTER 1 ❖

"Why should I? What if it's a prank? How can we trust it?" Eve pointed out.

"A prank that gives you superpowers!?" Andrew laughed. "Sign me up!"

"Shut it!" Eve yelled; her hands flared with phlasma.

"AH!" Andrew stepped back.

Eve shook her hands of the flames that startled her.

"Quiet in there!" Laura yelled from the living room.

"Sorry!" Andrew and Eve both said at the same time.

Eve turned her attention to the box and pointed it down. "Listen you freaky lamp, I don't know what you did to me, and I don't care why you did it, I don't have to be a Sentinel. Not doing it. No." Eve stood by her bed, crossing her arms.

"Aw come on, really?" Andrew drooped his shoulders. "You got me excited for nothing." He looked to the box. "Can I do it?"

The box whirred its core and glowed a bit brighter, spinning toward Eve. "Evelyn Sanchez, you don't understand. This is not a request. You *will* be the next Sentinel. You *are* the next Sentinel. You *have been* the next Sentinel."

Eve stood still for a moment, pondering. She looked at Andrew, who was obviously excited. She glanced out of her window and watched the rain fall as lightning thundered over the mountains. She closed her eyes and shook her head. "What's in it for me?" she asked the box.

"Nothing."

"I won't do it. I can't do it. You have the wrong person. I'm only seventeen."

"The universe is broken. You would break it more if you did not fulfill your purpose. The future would crumble, and the death toll would be infinite," the box said, "Though I do not mean to use fear tactics to convince you, I must, as I am merely conveying the full and honest truth."

Eve shared a concerned look with Andrew. She closed her eyes, and sighed.

"We'll leave in the morning," she said begrudgingly.

"Yes!" Andrew jumped up excitedly.

As Eve and Andrew were ready for bed, they slipped under the covers of their beds and waited for morning to arrive. Andrew fell fast asleep, without a worry, excited for what was to come. Eve couldn't sleep.

She rolled over, and over, and over. She grasped at her blankets, her mind racing. She didn't know what to do. She'd

## ❖ CHAPTER 1 ❖

glance across the room and see the box floating idly and glowing dimly in the corner of her room. She'd turn away.

The morning came quickly, and Eve had hardly slept. The two of them snuck out of their room as quietly as they could and approached their garage.

"Mom's gonna hear us leave," Andrew whispered.

"Shhh." Eve opened the door leading to their driveway. She unlocked the old run-down rust bucket, and she and Andrew stepped in. The box whirred by Eve's shoulder. She took a deep breath, and started the car. She pulled out of the driveway.

As she turned onto the road, she heard that same familiar mechanical flash again. She ignored it and drove off towards the mountains, away from the rising sun. She made it pretty far before realizing, "I have no idea where I'm going."

The box whirred and presented a hologram to Eve, displaying a map with interactive directions.

"Woah!" Andrew leaned forward from the back seat to see the navigation. "That's bad! Eve, are you seeing this?"

"Yes, Andrew, I'm using it to drive." Eve wanted to freak out, but she was too focused on the road.

"Right." Andrew leaned back in his seat.

They continued driving up California for almost six more hours before the box told them to take a strange off-road route. They drove through a forest; the bumpy roads shook and rattled the old car. As they neared the edge of the forest the car ran out of gas, and Andrew sighed.

"Are we gonna have to walk?"

"Come on, Andrew." Eve got out of the car and the box followed her. "Where do we go next?" she asked it.

"Keep to the path, you'll know when you find it."

"Find what?" Eve asked to no response. She and Andrew walked through the rest of the forest, not too far before coming to a stop at the end of a cliff, overlooking the ocean.

On the edge of the cliff stood a house that looked like it had been empty for quite some time. Eve and Andrew glanced at each other before walking forward. Eve knocked on the door and waited.

They stood in the relative silence of the ocean winds for a few moments before Eve asked the box, "Are we in the right place?"

Before the box could answer, the door swung inward, startling Eve and Andrew. Standing in the doorway was an old, disheveled man.

## ❖ CHAPTER 1 ❖

A messy gray beard hugged his face and his messy hair was white as paper. He wore an old and worn coat, as well as ripped jeans. A necklace, hidden under his dirty faded shirt, hung around his neck. He lifted his brow and eyeballed Eve. He tried his best to stand up as straight as he could.

"Evelyn Sanchez." The man smiled.

"You know me?" Eve asked.

Andrew looked up with excitement.

She and Andrew shared a glance.

"Come in! Come in!" The old man beckoned for them as he retreated into the old house. Eve hesitated to enter, but Andrew walked in without any reluctance. Eve only walked in to follow after Andrew, somewhat worried.

The old man whistled for the box and it came to him. He sat down in an old and torn couch and the box floated into his lap.

"Are you some sort of mad scientist?" Andrew questioned.

"Andrew!" Eve scolded.

"No, it's fine. Really," the old man insisted. "The name's Dapar, Tomas Dapar."

"Bond, James Bond." Andrew said, deepening his voice to mock the introduction.

"Honestly Andrew, shut it."

"You can call me Rex." Tomas insisted.

"Telling me your name is all well and good, but what good does that do me. Who are you?" Eve asked.

"You're here because the box chose you as a replacement Sentinel, correct?" Tomas looked up.

"Yes…" Eve squinted her eyes.

"I knew the Sentinel once. This used to be his home when he traveled around with his friends for five years. We were all scientists. Most of us. The lot of us, all on our own missions. And all on one. Having fun, time traveling. You know? But that was all over a while ago." Tomas continued trying to repair the box. "I can't tell you how long I've been waiting for you to show up. I can say I'm hopeful again!"

"So you're gonna be like Eve's old man mentor, right!?" Andrew asked, "Is that where this is going?" He couldn't seem to tone down his excitement if he tried, "You're Obi-Wan!"

"I sure hope not," Tomas chuckled. "Mentors always seem to suffer the same fate, don't they?"

"Andrew what is it with you and references?!" Eve questioned. "Calm down, this is real life!" She reminded him.

## ❖ CHAPTER 1 ❖

"Already feeling the sting of your responsibility," Tomas noticed. He stood up and pushed the box through the air over to Eve and it floated by her shoulder.

"Do you know why I was chosen?" Eve asked Tomas.

"I do," he answered.

Eve's eyes lit up as she asked, "Why?"

"Some things are better left unsaid." Tomas said with an intense and serious stare. "Until the time is right."

Eve shifted away slightly.

Tomas shook his head. "What matters is that you have a working time machine now." He gestured towards the box.

Eve stared at it with some disbelief but given the things she'd already seen she wasn't too skeptical of it.

"Don't use it to go on random adventures. Like you said, this is real life. Save the fun for later. Limit your risks. Stay as safe as you can while you can, because eventually you won't have the choice."

"Aw." Andrew groaned.

Tomas glanced at Andrew, and then down at himself, and his necklace. He stopped for a moment, pondering.

"Where do I go first?" Eve asked. "What's step one?"

"I can see you lack trust." Tomas eyeballed Eve and her overall stance. "Go somewhere quickly, wherever you need to so that you can prove to yourself, one hundred percent, that you've got a working time machine. Return here when you're done."

"How do I use this thing?" Eve asked.

"Hold it and think of a time and place. That's all there is to it." Tomas answered with his arms crossed. If Eve didn't know any better, she'd think he was about to cry. "It knows."

Andrew came in close to Eve and held his hand on her shoulder. They looked to each other nervously, before Eve reached for the box. She held it in her hands and stared at it for a bit.

"It isn't working," Andrew said.

"I haven't thought of a place yet…"

Just as Eve finished speaking, the two of them flashed away. They appeared in a desert lot, standing on the side of a road, across from which was what looked like their house, and suddenly Andrew seemed disappointed.

"Can't stop thinking of home?"

"We actually moved…" Eve looked around. "That's… insane."

"Have we moved in time?" Andrew looked around. "That's what's important."

## ❖ CHAPTER 1 ❖

An old moving truck drove up to the house. The side of the moving truck was painted with a faded logo of a moving company called 'Left Turn at Albuquerque Moving Co.'

Laura Sanchez stepped out of the truck. A little girl jumped out of the other side of the truck and ran to Laura.

They could hear them talking just barely. "Get Andrew out from the back, will you?" Laura asked of the little girl.

"Is that…" Andrew stared ahead. "Us moving in? After…"

"Your dad left, yeah." Eve nodded. "Say hello to California, us." Eve kept staring ahead. "We should go before mom sees us."

"Yeah, or we disappear or something." Andrew said, holding onto Eve's shoulder again as they flashed away.

They appeared back in the strange house in Monterey, standing right where they were before they left, though it was later in the day.

"Okay, great, you're back." Tomas jumped from a couch. "Took you awhile, got me worried there for a second. Word of advice, you've got a time machine, you should show up seconds after you left, it saves time."

"Sorry, how long has it been?" Eve asked.

"A couple hours, but it's alright." Tomas nodded.

"So, what am I supposed to do?" Eve asked. "About this whole... being a Sentinel thing?"

"Well, the Sentinel never really had any instructions but... I guess that's where it went wrong, huh? I'll tell you what you need to know at least for now, to get things started, until you get the hang of things yourself." Tomas wandered over to a computer station in the living room by a glass sliding door leading to the cliff backyard.

"So, for right now I've got this. Pretty soon all the planets in the solar system are going to align, and the effects of that aren't too desirable. I've been getting distress calls from the planet Modius. Their people are warning me about the planets aligning and I don't really understand what their problem with it is. Look, maybe it'll be an easy little thing for you to go off and practice your 'Sentinel skills', I don't know." Tomas looked toward a screen, blocking some of it from the view of Eve. "They're requesting help for... something." Tomas squinted. "I can't tell. Point is, you should head over there."

"To another planet? I don't even have a space suit! What if I can't breathe?" Eve was already thinking into the situation.

"People?!" Andrew asked excitedly, "Aliens?"

## ❖ CHAPTER 1 ❖

"Ah, the box has the whole breathing situation covered. Just don't stray too far away from it." Tomas approached Eve and Andrew. He picked the box from the air and shoved it into Eve's hands. He pushed Andrew closer to Eve so they were touching. "Alright, have fun." He grumbled.

"Wait, what do the people that need help look like?" Eve asked frantically.

"You aren't coming with us?" Andrew asked with a slight tremble and crack in his voice.

"Off you go." Tomas held his hand on the box and removed it quickly as Eve and Andrew flashed away.

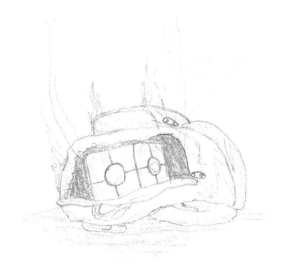

### ❖ Chapter 2 ❖
# The Last Quodstella

In a flash of light Eve and Andrew appeared on the surface of a strange planet. The ground was hard and rocky, but that didn't stop patches of grass from growing. They looked off into the distance at a vast field of bright green glistening grassy plains, littered with small clumps of glowing colorful phlasma crystals jutting from the ground, most of them purple.

They turned in awe to see an entire forest of crystals, tall and looming. The ground itself seemed to purr slightly, as if the planet was breathing. The chilly wind whistled down from above like a waterfall of air.

In the sky above them Eve could see a distant shining white planet, and behind it a dark black gas giant with a magnificent dark gray ring around it, and beyond that, a tiny orange planet, scarred with canyons.

Andrew tapped on Eve's shoulder to get her attention, but she wouldn't look away from the crystals or the distant planets. Andrew took it upon himself to physically turn Eve's body for her so that she could see what he was seeing.

Now in front of them they stared at the tallest and steepest mountains they had ever seen in their lives, not at all comparing to the distant purple mountains they had back home.

This mountain was so tall that it seemingly jutted straight past the atmosphere. The lack of clouds allowed them to follow the peak all the way into space. Staring at it aghast, they wondered how it could be possible. Beyond the grassy fields was a vast, flat and empty space of bluish rock. It seemed that maybe the massive mountains may be the only mountains the planet had to offer.

They would've been admiring the landscape of Modius all day had they not drifted their eyes down the mountain to see a cave at its base.

"*Come here,*" a voice called to them, swimming through their minds.

"What was that?!" Andrew looked around, startled at the voice. Eve squinted at the cave. They couldn't tell the direction the voice came from as it seemed to have been

## ❖ CHAPTER 2 ❖

projected into their minds, but they both assumed it was from the cave.

They shared a look with each other before cautiously approaching the cave and eventually they noticed a faint purple glow emanating from it.

"Do we go in?" Andrew asked.

"I don't know," Eve answered without looking away from the cave.

"*By all means.*"

The voice called to them again. Eve and Andrew's eyes widened and they stared at each other, fearful but curious as they were, they entered the cave without a second thought, but were met with nothing but darkness.

Andrew heard the pitter patter of many footsteps, and he began to shake nervously. "Eve, maybe we should get out of here."

"This planet needs our help," she insisted.

"Yeah, but what if we just walked into the thing they need help stopping? I don't know. I'm getting some scary vibes here."

"Shh," Eve shushed him, "Who's there? We're here to help."

"You got the distress call," the voice called to them. It seemed clearer and closer, and yet still they couldn't discern where it was coming from.

Andrew froze in his tracks as his eyes widened at the sight of the source of the footsteps. Eve stepped back a bit, but chose not to run.

Glowing purple creatures surrounded them slowly on all sides. They glowed with the power of phlasma, seemingly made of it. Their fur was phlasmatic and light, similar to flames, but it seemed held back by the hard, stone-like scales that covered the rest of the wolfish creatures' bodies.

The wolf-like creatures surrounded them, pacing around, their heads lowered as if judging the interlopers. Each wolf creature had a unique stone on its forehead, glowing brighter by comparison than the rest of their bodies. They seemed like small dragons, with the bodies of wolves, each individual varying by degrees of wolf or dragon.

One of the more wolf-like of the creatures, with a stone in its forehead shaped like a distant twinkling star, lifted his head.

"Travelers… Humans," he remarked, somewhat surprised that they were the beings that had come to help. "Don't be alarmed." He bowed his head in a way to convey

## ❖ CHAPTER 2 ❖

peace to Eve and Andrew, knowing they would naturally be wary of the beast.

It carried with it the same voice that had called to Eve and Andrew before, though the voice wasn't projected through its mouth, it seemed to be projected straight into their minds.

The wolf creature could tell that Eve and Andrew were confused, so it explained, "My friends and I are known as the Dragolupus. I am speaking with you telepathically, so that you may understand us. No language needed."

"Woah, that is awesome!" Andrew laughed.

Eve was still awestruck and a bit afraid, even if she wouldn't admit it. "What's your name?" Her voice wavered with nervousness, despite how hard she tried to hide it.

"Name?" The Dragolupus shifted an eyebrow on its expressive doglike face. "I don't often go by a name. Though, travelers such as yourself refer to me as Starlocke. And you are?" he asked.

"Eve Sanchez, from Earth." Eve nodded. "And this is my brother, Andrew."

"From Earth... you're in grave danger." Starlocke's ears perked up. The other Dragolupus around him retreated back further into the cave. "Our distress call was not to help us, but to aid in your survival."

"What?" Eve reacted quickly.

"Wait, what does he mean?" Andrew asked.

"Shut up." Eve demanded.

"The planets in your solar system are aligning. Modius will see that and be attracted to it. Your Earth may be destroyed."

"What do you mean Modius would see it?" Eve asked, "Isn't that the planet we're on right now? How can a planet see?"

"Modius is not a planet, though we do live on it. Modius is one of two of its kind that remain, a Quodstella. A planet-eater, in terms you can understand."

"A what?!" Eve shook her head in disbelief.

"That's awesome!" Andrew laughed, "Does it have a face?" He asked Starlocke.

"Yes." Starlocke nodded with a dog-like smile.

"Rad!" Andrew smiled.

"Andrew, please stop." Eve pressed her fingers against the bridge of her nose, "This is real life, not movies. Can you please just realize that!" Eve pressed.

"What's the fun in saving the world if you can't enjoy yourself doing it?" Andrew asked. "They could make a movie out of our story!" Andrew said, "If you don't make it fun who would watch it?"

"You aren't supposed to have fun saving the world!" Eve argued.

"I agree with the boy." Starlocke walked forward. "He brings up valid points."

"You've gotta be kidding me." Eve held her hands to her face. "Alright, then how do we stop Modius?"

"Blow it up!" Andrew suggested.

"First of all, no, Andrew, these…" Eve tried to remember.

"Dragolupus," Starlocke reminded her.

"Dragolupus live here! And second, how would we even blow it up to begin with? We're just kids!"

"I don't mean to sound indecisive, and I don't mean to pick sides, but this time I agree with the girl." Starlocke pointed his nose at Eve. "Explosions can be fun, but not when your target is an endangered species, and especially not when it's home to my kind.

"Though, we felt the need to warn you." Starlocke walked out of the cave, and Eve and Andrew followed. "You don't have to do anything right away. Modius doesn't travel that fast. It won't reach Earth for a while. We just thought you should know. We would appreciate it if Modius was not killed. It really doesn't have bad intentions, that's just how it lives, eating planets."

"Sounds evil to me." Andrew scoffed.

"Humans seem to be one of the unfortunate bunch of complex life forms that interpret evil in places where there is none." Starlocke growled.

A flash of light blasted in the cave, swiftly interrupting Andrew and Starlocke's conversation. Starlocke himself seemed to be startled by the unexpected flash of light and accompanying guest it brought with it.

Eve jumped back with a slight shriek and Andrew did the same, trying to hide the fact that he reacted the way he did.

"Dammit! What the—" a voice groaned as a small body fell into rocks and rolled down a pile of them until he fell out of the cave. The other Dragolupus from the cave ventured out to see the unexpected guest, staring quizzically at him.

"Ughh…" an Ilsian stood up, looking around confusedly, "This isn't Ilsose…" The Ilsian was Ganto, the pirate and bounty hunter from the Sentinel's Army, who had just fled the Extraverse in an attempt to return home, still wearing his custom-made tuxedo from the wedding. He dusted himself off.

## ❖ CHAPTER 2 ❖

He had shown up in the wrong place.

He glanced at Eve and noticed the box floating by her shoulder. He twitched his mandibles and stared. "Are you the Sentinel?" he asked.

"I think I'm supposed to be..." Eve answered hesitantly. Her eyes were wide and fearful as she examined the Ilsian's small frame and insect-like appearance. She wanted to scream, but the fact that she could understand the Ilsian and that it seemed to recognize the box, led her to believe it wasn't some creature to fear. She was stunned with confusion.

"*The Sentinel...*" Starlocke's ears perked up as he lifted his head. A tingling sensation ran through him. He twitched his nose.

"Eve, what is that thing?" Andrew pointed at Ganto.

"Why are you asking me? How am I supposed to know?" she said quickly.

"You're smart!" Andrew scoffed.

"It's an alien! What do you want me to say!?"

"Alien?" Ganto held his hands to his chest. "Rude."

The box began to glow as it answered for Eve, "The Sentinel died, Ganto. After you left the Extraverse. So did Vaxx. This is her replacement, Evelyn Sanchez."

"So, they didn't save the universe?" Ganto questioned. "Dammit, I was planning on living in it some more."

"Save the universe?" Starlocke asked. "The universe isn't in need of saving, is it? I think I would've noticed."

"Oh!" Andrew got an idea, "We should ask Tomas!" he suggested.

"I'm not sure I trust that guy yet." Eve pursed her lips, thinking.

"Welp." Ganto puffed out his chest and held five of his six arms to his side. He checked a band around one of his wrists as it dinged with a notification. "1982, huh? New time zone new job. I've got a bounty to collect. If I could just borrow your teleporter real quick and get out of here—"

"No," Eve refused. "You know about the Sentinel. You'll tell me more than this time machine and that Tomas guy; you've got nothing to hide. You're coming with me."

"When you realize I'm of no use to you will you let me use that time machine to get back home, at least?" Ganto asked.

"Maybe." Eve nodded. "Well, it was nice meeting you, Starlocke."

"We will meet again, Sentinel." Starlocke lowered his head.

❖ CHAPTER 2 ❖

"Don't call me that," Eve demanded. "Let's go, Andrew. And you…" Eve stared at Ganto.

"Ganto," he answered.

"Come on." Eve grabbed Andrew's hands and dragged him along as she approached Ganto and forcefully grabbed a hand of his.

"Oi! Watch it." Ganto tried to pull away but couldn't before the three of them flashed away and appeared just outside of the house in Monterey. Ganto pulled his hand away and slapped Eve's wrist.

"Ow!" Eve pulled her hand away.

"Look, lady, just because you don't know who I am doesn't mean you can go and boss me around!" Ganto yelled. "I could kill you right now and steal that time machine so fast you wouldn't even—"

Ganto was interrupted by the box firing a laser at his feet. Ganto jumped back and held up his hands in a sort of defensive battle stance.

"Don't," the box demanded.

Ganto calmed down.

Eve knocked on the door and waited for an answer. Tomas came quickly, like he was waiting for them. He looked down and saw Ganto. He smiled from ear to ear at the sight of him. "Ganto, good to see you."

"You know him?" Eve asked.

"I've never met this old man in my life," Ganto scoffed.

"I've known him for quite a bit now." Tomas explained. "Come in, come in." He gestured for the three of them to enter the home. Ganto came in with a confused look on his face. "So, what happened on Modius?" Tomas asked.

"We met a space dog," Andrew said with confidence and excitement.

"We met a Dragolupus named Starlocke," Eve clarified, "And this… thing."

"A proud Ilsian," Ganto grumbled.

"The planet Modius is alive, a Quodstella I think Starlocke called it, and it's going to eat Earth but it's going to take a while," Eve explained to Tomas.

Tomas held his hand to his chin and thought for a moment.

"Hey, Tomas." Eve thought of something. "If I'm the replacement Sentinel, does that mean I have to stop doing school?"

## ❖ CHAPTER 2 ❖

"If you can find time for it, go ahead." Tomas stopped thinking about whatever it was he was thinking about.

"How am I supposed to find time?" Eve asked.

Tomas lifted an eyebrow and stared at the box.

"Oh, right. But what do I do with this guy?" Eve gestured towards Ganto.

"Let me use the box and take me home so I can go back to being a bounty hunter." Ganto crossed his arms. "I didn't mean to show up where I did."

"Leave him with me." Tomas stood straighter. "You can leave and be back in an instant because of that machine. He won't be waiting long."

"Like hell you're keeping me here, you're taking me home!" Ganto protested. "Lousy desertion, this was…"

"Thank you." Eve nodded in almost a bow, ignoring Ganto. She shook her head, "I need some sleep."

"Mom's gonna wonder why we've been gone and where the car is." Andrew pointed out.

"Ugh, you're right." Eve thought for a moment.

"Hold on, are you two children?" Ganto laughed. He looked up at Tomas. "The Sentinel's replacement is a kid?"

"You didn't notice that before?" Eve looked to him.

"All humans look the same to me." Ganto's eyes narrowed. "Unless they're old." His eyes narrowed even further.

"You can teleport the car," Tomas told Eve. Eve was about to leave when Tomas had a thought. "Wait!"

"Yeah?" Eve turned around.

"When did you leave?" Tomas asked.

"Early morning." Eve answered.

"Sleep here tonight; you'll need it." Tomas insisted.

"Thanks." Eve smiled.

"Oh, so you trust him now?" Andrew snickered.

"Shut up." Eve smacked Andrew on the back of the head.

Tomas led them to a room down a hall as the box floated by him. Ganto, much shorter than Tomas, kept hopping up, trying to grab at it. The box floated out of the way with each attempt, as if part of a game of keep away.

Tomas opened the door to the room that Eve and Andrew would be staying in. The bed in the room was massive, taking up most of the room itself. "Shouldn't have too much trouble sharing the bed," Tomas said.

"Why is it so huge?" Andrew asked.

## ❖ CHAPTER 2 ❖

"It belonged to one of the Sentinel's friends back when they had this place. He was a Lorinian named Darru. Huge species, Lorinians."

"Pshft, yeah tell that to Terri. Lil' guy didn't get the memo!" Ganto chortled sarcastically as he continued to chase after the box. The box spun wildly down the hall. Ganto chased it into a room next door. Tomas snapped his fingers and the door closed. The box teleported to him and the door locked.

"Where's Ganto staying?" Andrew asked.

"I locked him up in the room next door. I can't keep him near me, I'm afraid he'd kill me or something." Tomas chuckled.

"Like hell I will!" The muffled voice of Ganto yelled from behind the walls of the room. It sounded like he hit the wall, but after the sound of furniture and lamps, pictures on the wall, and other miscellaneous items falling to the floor, it seemed from that point on Ganto would stop trying.

"He'll be fine," Tomas insisted. He turned around to leave, "Sleep tight, you two," he said as his goodbye.

"I like him," Andrew said.

Eve jumped into the bed and rolled over to face a wall. "Yeah."

Andrew laid down on the other side of the bed, looking up at the ceiling. "I'm kind of excited about all this."

"Easy for you to say, you're not the one with all the responsibility," Eve grumbled.

"Don't freak out about it, it'll be fun," Andrew assured her.

"Hey, can you two shut up!" Ganto yelled from the room next door. "I'm trying to escape."

"Goodnight, Eve." Andrew rolled over.

"Night." Eve kept staring at the wall, her teeth grinding, and brow shaking.

Eve and Andrew awoke the next day ready to leave.

"Come back when you can," Tomas called to Eve. "You need to be properly trained."

Eve stopped in her tracks and thought for a moment before saying, "What if I don't want to be a Sentinel? I don't think I'll be so good at it if I don't want to be doing it."

Tomas paused and Andrew waited for his answer anxiously. "I'm sorry, but you have to be."

"Says who?" Eve asked with sass in her voice.

## ❖ CHAPTER 2 ❖

"That's how it needs to happen. That's how it's always been. You won't understand until you're older but... I'm sorry, it needs to be that way." Tomas's face seemed to become clouded with what looked to Eve to be regret.

"Alright." Eve accepted her fate, "But I'm not calling myself the Sentinel. And I'm not gonna enjoy myself while I'm at it."

"Thank you for committing, either way." Tomas nodded. "Now go."

Eve led Andrew to the car. They got in and Eve rested the box against the steering wheel.

"Hey, Eve?" Andrew leaned forward in the back seat, resting his arms on the shoulders of the front seats. "Do you think this is dangerous? What you're doing?"

"I hope not." Eve tried not to think about it.

"I mean, I've been trying to see it as all fun and cool but... last night I was thinking, I was dreaming, you know? I mean, there's a planet out there that wants to eat the whole Earth... and the box said that the last Sentinel died, and someone else died, I'm just hearing a lot of death, and—"

"Hey, hey, hey, Andrew, calm down, it'll be fine-" Eve tried to comfort him.

"You don't know that! Eve, what if you die? What if I die?" Andrew cried into his arms.

"Andrew, Andrew... I won't let that happen..." Eve didn't know how to comfort her brother; she'd never seen him like this before.

"How?" Andrew sobbed into his arm. "Be careful." He looked up. The car teleported into the driveway of their home.

Eve looked straight out the back window and watched as the past versions of themselves drove off on their way to Monterey. "I will." Eve turned off the car and got out. "Now let's get back inside before Mom knows what happened."

"Evelyn Garcia Sanchez what in the world do you think you're doing!?" Laura yelled out from the entrance of the garage, in her nightgown.

"*Shit*," Eve sighed.

❖ Chapter 3 ❖
# Halloween Terrors

"No, mom, you don't get it! We weren't leaving, we just got back!" Andrew called out in a desperate attempt to defend his innocence, only realizing after he said it that it didn't help their case at all.

"What do you think you're doing? Eve, you don't even have a license, you could've gotten yourselves killed!"

"Mom, you don't understand!" Eve stammered to defend herself as she stepped from the car.

"What? *What* don't I understand? Get inside, you're grounded." Laura stood tall and held her hands to her hips, waiting for Eve to walk past her.

The box whirred quietly and hid behind Eve, following her. It cloaked itself in invisibility as Andrew watched, surprised. Andrew followed after Eve, holding his head low and shuffling his feet.

"And don't think you're off the hook, either," Laura scolded Andrew. "You too."

"For how long?" Andrew complained.

"A month." Laura crossed her arms.

"What?!" Eve turned around. "That's not fair!"

"What about Halloween!" Andrew whined.

Eve fumed, wanting nothing more than to tell her mother what was happening. Something inside her was holding her back.

"Room. Now." Laura pointed.

Eve and Andrew shuffled to their room, defeated and tired. They plopped into their beds and sighed. The box uncloaked itself.

"What now?" Eve asked.

The box whirred its gears and hesitated before speaking, "Tomas will contact you when you are needed. In the meantime, live life as normal."

Eve seethed at the idea, "*As normal?*" she questioned. "As normal?!" She stood up. Her hands flared with phlasma and the box backed up. "You did this to me! I'm not ready for this! Look at me! How can *I* save the universe? I'm nothing!

### ❖ CHAPTER 3 ❖

Everyone knows I'm nothing! When will you?" Eve screamed at the box and the flames crawled up her arms.

She saw Andrew out of the corner of her eye, cowering in the corner of his bed.

Eve didn't notice the passive flames spouting from her fingertips. She could barely feel it at all, but when she became aware of them, the phlasmatic flames vanished in an instant and she stepped back.

"You've got the wrong girl, box." She calmed down.

"I can assure you I haven't." The box was quick to respond. "You'll get used to it. Your job, that is."

"I hate the Sentinel." Eve sat down in her bed. "It's all her fault I'm like this."

"Hold no resentment for the person who helped save the citizens of the galactic cluster countless times. You will understand, eventually," the box assured her.

"Ugh." Eve dropped her upper body onto her bed. "I hate this."

The weekend passed by painfully slowly, and Laura begrudgingly agreed to temporarily lift the punishment for Halloween that Sunday, only because she had already helped

Eve and Andrew make their Luke and Leia costumes beforehand, and she didn't think anyone would still like *Star Wars* by next Halloween.

Eve finished doing her hair in two buns at the side of her head and was ready to go out.

She already felt that she was a little too old for trick or treating, but Andrew argued that 'You're never too old for free handouts.'

"Be back by nine," Laura reminded both of them as they approached the door.

Eve and Andrew set off for trick-or-treating, planning to wait outside their house for Eve's friend Melissa to show up.

Andrew didn't like any of Eve's friends, and Eve's friends didn't particular enjoy Andrew either, or his friends, specifically Kurt.

They stepped from the door, pillowcases for candy collection in hand, expecting to be met with no one just yet.

"Sup."

Andrew and Eve looked down and jumped back, startled at the appearance of the three-foot tall Ilsian.

## ❖ CHAPTER 3 ❖

"Ganto!?" Eve held her hand to her chest. *"Why are you here?"* She asked quietly, shutting the door so Laura wouldn't hear anything.

"Someone will see you!" Andrew warned, looking around.

Ganto shuffled in his spot. He wore a puffy, homemade pink sweater with six sleeves, accommodating all his arms. A bulge on his back stretched the sweater and hooked onto whatever it was under the sweater was a large Andromedan rifle.

"It's the ancient Earth holiday of Halloween, right?" Ganto asked, clicking his mandibles. "People will just assume I'm in costume." He shrugged. "I'm here because Tomas said that I'd be a big help to have around apparently. Plus," Ganto puffed out his chest and looked around, narrowing his eyes. *"I got a new bounty to hunt."*

"Here?" Andrew asked excitedly. "Who is it?"

"I can't say, it's secret." Ganto stood straighter and stopped looking around slyly. "Tomas gave the job to me and said if I can collect that bounty then he'll think about letting me go home. It's a win-win for me to be sure. On a side note, I sure am hungry, could go for some... what's it called..."

"Candy?" Andrew asked. "Come with us!"

"No." Eve denied it immediately. "Not with my friends." She crossed her arms.

"Oh, come on." Andrew rolled his eyes.

"He's an alien!" Eve squatted down and held out her arms straight toward Ganto. "I can't have him around my friends!"

"Why not?" Ganto asked.

"They'll hate you!" Eve argued.

"Then I'll kill them." Ganto crossed all his arms angrily, mad at the idea that anyone would hate him.

"HA!" Andrew leaned back and held his stomach, "Yes!" He smiled at the thought.

"No!" Eve punched Andrew in the shoulder, "That's exactly what I don't want!"

"Eve!" A voice called out.

"Oh no…" Eve puffed. She turned to face the road, and she watched as not only her friends, but Andrew's friends too crossed the street.

"Who's this?" Melissa was a tall brown-haired girl, not particularly dressed as anything as far as Eve could tell. She pointed towards Ganto.

"That's a rad costume." Kurt leaned out from behind the group of friends to comment to Ganto.

## ❖ CHAPTER 3 ❖

"Thanks." Ganto bowed. "See?" He smiled up at Eve.

Eve rolled her eyes, "This is Ganto, a uh..." She hesitated on how to introduce him.

"Our cousin." Andrew spewed quickly.

"Ok..." Melissa hesitated.

Kurt walked up to Andrew and excitedly began telling him his plans for the night, where they could go for the best candy output, and all the little details.

Melissa started gossiping to Eve, but she wasn't paying much attention, nervous about Ganto's presence.

Ganto checked a display around his wrist and looked around. "Hey, Andrew?" he tugged on Andrew's costume.

"What is it?" he asked.

"If I just, like... randomly disappear in the night, don't go looking for me."

"Why?" Andrew asked.

"My target," Ganto reminded him.

"Oh, alright." Andrew nodded.

"Hey, Ganto," Eve interrupted Melissa's gossiping and leaned over to the Ilsian, "No talking."

"But—" Ganto held up a hand.

"*No. Talking,*" Eve repeated.

Ganto nodded, accepting Eve's request, at least at first. Eve and Andrew's friends asked questions of Ganto's origins, suspicious of him.

Eve walked behind the crowd, anxious and ready to slap Ganto if he said anything wrong. But it seemed that Ganto had been experienced in hiding his identity before, and was doing well deflecting the questions, or answering with consistent lies.

Kurt began to question the methods behind the creation of Ganto's costume, but Ganto quickly brushed that off.

The group explored the neighborhood well into the night, soon getting bored of questioning Ganto. Eve's heart calmed significantly, and she allowed herself to enjoy the night, at least as much as she could.

Ganto didn't say much else, as his jokes flew over the heads of the group, but Andrew laughed along anyway.

Ganto should've known that old Earth humans wouldn't find the classic, 'Why did the Ilsian not pay the Lorinian? Because Sornopalis,' very funny.

Andrew and his friends laughed and annoyed Eve's friends for most of the night, trying their best to scare them around corners to no avail most times. Their haul of candy wasn't too bad, but Ganto had eaten so much of Eve's that she didn't feel like much was accomplished.

Throughout the night, they strayed further and further away from Eve's home. It was getting close to nine and Eve urged Melissa and her friends to start getting back.

"Gosh, Eve, we're just trying to have fun," Melissa responded, "Oh I know, we should explore the abandoned lots!" she said with a spooky undertone.

"Why?" Kurt teased. "What's the point, that doesn't make any sense."

"It's like our version of a scary forest, it's the best we got," one of Melissa's friends elaborated.

"I mean, I guess." Andrew shrugged.

"Guys, it's the opposite way from home and we need to get back. It doesn't even sound fun, it's just sand," Eve argued.

Ganto nervously checked a band around one of his wrists and put it away. "Yeah, you guys should be headed back. Sounds like a bad idea."

Eve looked at Ganto with a raised brow, confused as to why he was agreeing with her.

"You guys are just *scared*." Melissa smiled, slowly walking backwards across the street and towards the sandy desert lot.

"Am not!" Kurt argued, running ahead of Melissa. The group laughed and ran ahead. Eve, Ganto, and Andrew stood behind.

Andrew looked at Eve. "I'm gonna go with them."

"But, Andrew, we have to get home," Eve protested.

"Come on Eve, let yourself have fun." Andrew walked ahead.

Eve sighed and followed after him.

"Um... guys... Guys!" Ganto followed ahead, hurrying as they got ahead of him. "I don't think it's a good idea!" Ganto boosted himself with some sort of a jetpack hidden underneath his sweater.

The back of the sweater burned and fell off, revealing Ganto's exoskeleton body. The boost sent him forward just a bit as he skidded across the sand ahead of them. He held out his arms. "Stop!"

The group of friends looked at him in confusion, wondering not only how he got ahead, but why he was so against the idea.

"I'll stay here and explore the plot *for you* while you head home."

"Ganto... that doesn't make any sense." Andrew argued.

## ❖ CHAPTER 3 ❖

"Eve, get them out of here," Ganto demanded.

"Why?" Eve questioned.

"Okay, you know what? Don't listen to the Ilsian. I don't even know why I care, let yourselves die."

"Eve, what's this kid talking about?" Melissa asked her.

Before Eve could even guess at an answer, the sand beneath Ganto shot up into the air like a geyser. The group screamed and stepped back in fear as the sand continued to rise.

Andrew lifted his bootleg plastic laser-sword and turned it on. A tinny shriek puttered pathetically out of the blade as the light inside flickered.

He held it up in an attack-ready stance, adjusting his two hands around the handle, ready to strike.

The blanket of sand fell over them and revealed a massive worm-like creature screaming and wriggling around from a hole in the ground. Ganto was gone. It stared the group down with its toothy mouth-eye.

Everyone screamed and shrieked at its presence, and as they tried to escape, another one burst out of the sand on the other end of them, trapping their group.

The massive worms wriggled around and kept them from leaving.

A Terror drone lifted through the ground like a ghost, its tentacles sparking when its false eye met Eve. *"You."* The Terror's voice swam through the group's heads as it pointed a tentacle at Eve.

Andrew swung forward with his plastic laser-sword, which passed right through the Terror. The Terror turned its attention to Andrew.

"Eve, what's going on!?" Andrew asked nervously, looking desperately for an escape.

"I don't know! Do you think I know?" Eve blabbered.

The head of the worm that had swallowed up Ganto exploded. Ganto launched himself from the worm with his jetpack, shooting his way out with his Andromedan rifle. He landed on the ground near Eve, pushing up dust and sand.

He set his rifle to an electric stun mode. His back-holster jetpack sparked with blue flames and lifted him off the ground. From his elevated vantage point, he shot at the Terror, electrifying and killing it.

"What the hell!?" Melissa stumbled back, falling into the sand.

"This is my bounty!" Ganto informed Andrew and Eve.

## CHAPTER 3

Dozens of more ghostly Terrors lifted from the ground and surrounded the group.

"Oh." Ganto drifted away slightly, but a wriggling sand worm kept him in the ring.

"Eve, do something!" Andrew urged her. He looked around the ring of Terrors, holding his knock off toy sword out in front of him, as if it would do anything.

"But they'll see me do it!" Eve pointed out.

"It doesn't matter, Eve do something, we're going to die!" Andrew yelled.

"What's Eve gonna do? Nerd them to death?" Kurt asked with a shaking tremble. His voice cracked, breaking his faux confidence.

"Not now, Kurt!" Andrew scolded his friend.

"AGH!" Eve shouted as her hands burst into purple flames. She didn't know what she was doing, but a sudden adrenaline rush, the need to protect her friends, and the absolute fear pulsing through her seemed to guide the phlasma for her.

"What is happening!?" One of her friends yelled in confusion. Another one of her friends fainted on the spot.

Ganto stayed suspended in air, shooting at the Terrors as they rose. Eve blasted a flaming phlasma ball at one of the worms, and she turned around to do the same to the other.

The worms flinched and buried slightly deeper into the ground, but they kept wriggling and the Terrors kept coming.

Eve didn't know what she was doing, but she knew she needed to keep doing it to keep her friends alive. Like flamethrowers, the phlasma shot out with great power, burning the Terror worms with an intense inferno.

They dug underneath the ground entirely, presumably gone. Ganto continued firing at the Terror drones, taking them out one by one.

Eve jumped and blasted the Terrors with bright bursts of phlasma. From afar, the whole ordeal looked and sounded like a firework show gone awry.

Eve screamed, angry that the flames were doing nothing. She bolted forward at a Terror with a flaming fist, her whole body shot right through the creature, and she landed hard in the sand behind it.

The Terror turned around and opened its false eye and sparked violently.

"Ganto!" Eve held her arm across her face.

## ❖ CHAPTER 3 ❖

Ganto turned around and shot at the Terror, disintegrating it. "Only electricity kills the Terrors!" He shouted at Eve.

Eve jumped up at another Terror and tried to kill it. She saw the fear in her brother's eyes and wanted to keep up her promise. The Terror wrapped its tentacles around her and held her in the air. "I can't do electricity, just fire!" Eve yelled out to Ganto.

"Well just... do it better!" Ganto shouted over the screams of the Terrors.

Eve writhed around in the Terror's grasp, trying to break free, but any hit she sent its way passed right through it, while any hit it sent towards her made contact.

Its false eye opened and electricity started to spark, jolting Eve.

She screamed with all the power she could muster, and her eyes glowed. The sparks deflected to the Terror, not enough to kill it, but enough to scare it into dropping Eve into the sand below.

Eve held her hand to her head. "Agh." She looked up at the dozens of Terrors staring at her.

"Do something!" Andrew yelled. "Please!" He begged.

"No!" Eve braced for an attack, and her vision faded. She stood up quickly, like waking from a dream. She looked around her, and she stood in an empty space, a void of nothingness. "Where am I..." she asked.

"Your mind," the Terror's voice shook her skull. "It's boring in here."

"What do you want?" Eve quickly figured out she was hallucinating. "I'll give it to you!"

"Don't continue the legacy of the Sentinel," the Terror's voice grumbled, more calmly now.

"What?" Eve shook her head. "How did you..."

Eve's vision returned, and a flash of light blinded the group and pushed them away and into the sand. Eve shielded her eyes and sat up, trying her best to see what was happening.

All she could make out was a quick moving bolt, like purple lighting running and tackling the Terrors.

When the Terrors were gone, the lightning faded, and in its place stood Starlocke, the Dragolupus. His fur stood on end, and lingering sparks of electricity shone in it.

He shook himself like a wet dog and his fur drooped, his scales seemed to adjust themselves, and the electricity had entirely faded.

"Hey, it's Starlocke!" Andrew pointed happily.

## ❖ CHAPTER 3 ❖

Some of Eve and Andrew's friends had started to run off, but Eve stood up and yelled. "Hey! Get back here!"

Her and Andrew's friends stopped in their tracks, terrified. They stared at Eve like they didn't know her, they glanced at Starlocke and Ganto floating in the air above and were awestruck.

They couldn't even bring words to their mouths, until eventually Melissa was the first to speak up. "Eve... what's going on?"

Eve took a deep breath and prepared herself. "Say anything about this, to anyone, *especially* my Mom, and you'll regret it."

"What's going on?" Kurt asked fearfully.

"Eve's a superhero," Andrew bragged.

"Am not," Eve snapped. "I'm just... Cursed."

Starlocke growled at the group of friends, not trying to be menacing, but in a warning way.

"Use your words, furball." Ganto slowly descended back to the ground.

"I am here to protect you, if Eve fails." Starlocke lifted his head and ears.

"How did you get here?" Eve asked.

"I can run at near the speed of light, and I don't need a solid surface to run on. I ran here, from Modius, to save you."

"How did you know what was happening?" Eve asked.

Starlocke lowered his head and his ears perked up. He closed his eyes and the star-shaped stone on his forehead started to shine bright purple.

"Woah…" A chorus of voices rang within the group.

"The stone is an eye that can see through space and time." Starlocke opened his eyes again, and the glow faded. "Without strong detail, but it was enough to know that there were Terrors here," he explained.

"Hold on." Eve turned around. "Go home." She instructed of the friends around her. "Remember what I said. Tell no one," she reiterated.

The group nodded in fearful agreement and walked away with a purpose in their step, not saying a word between themselves.

"What are Terrors?" Eve asked Starlocke.

"Those floaty guys. Drones of the Krantharnic species, the worm things," Ganto answered first. "There's a bounty on Hive One's hivemind, 'Kranthar the Great', he calls himself."

"And he's here, on Earth. I can't understand why." Starlocke lifted his head. "Kranthar is the hivemind leader of

## ❖ CHAPTER 3 ❖

Hive One. They originate from the Black Star 7 District, Tornlozor, a gas planet orbiting Modius alongside Nidus and Illiosopherium. They migrated to Sol 1 District, to Titan, a moon of Saturn. These Terrors are a long way from home no matter which way you calculate it."

"Why would he be here?" Andrew asked.

"They wanted me…" Eve remembered what the Terror told her. "It pointed at me and it told me to not continue the Sentinel's legacy,'" she told Starlocke.

Starlocke looked down and away, thinking. "Interesting," he commented.

"Eve, it's 8:50." Andrew told Eve. "We're about half an hour away from home."

Eve's heart skipped a beat, but she quickly calmed when the box dropped from camouflage, revealing itself floating by her. She reached out for the box, knowing what it was telling her, and she held out her hand for Andrew. "Let's go home."

"What about Ganto?" Andrew asked.

"Tomas will pick me up," Ganto assured Andrew.

"And Starlocke?" Andrew asked.

Starlocke stared at Andrew passively.

A massive burst of electric light temporarily blinded them, and when it faded, Starlocke was gone.

"Oh, alright." Andrew drooped his shoulders.

"Come on." Eve took hold of Andrew's arm, and they were off in a flash. They appeared in front of their door, and walked in.

"Have fun?" Laura asked them.

Eve and Andrew groaned and went to their room, slamming the door.

"Alright," Laura said.

Eve and Andrew fell into their respective beds, and sighed. Andrew was the first to talk in the silence that followed. "That was crazy."

"*I did that.*" Eve gasped. "Those flames, that was me!" She seemed excited for the first time.

"And did Starlocke say that he *ran* here!?" Andrew smiled. "Through space? That's amazing!"

"I hope Melissa doesn't say anything about it." Eve quieted.

"Ah, she won't." Andrew scoffed.

A silence prevailed for a few moments.

Andrew broke it, "But if she does... cool points."

"Shut up."

❖ Chapter 4 ❖
# Terrors of the Tundra

Monday morning couldn't have come quicker. Eve had been awake since two in the morning, staring at her ceiling. When the alarm blared, she shot up. Though anxious to head back to school, she was on edge since her first real dangerous encounter.

As soon as she and Andrew arrived, they heard murmurs and rumors. People stared as they walked around, and soon the first bell rang.

Eve sat down in her class and it started as normal, but a few students had their eyes locked on her, and she sank into her seat, trying to hide herself.

She was livid at the idea that one of her, or Andrew's friends, must have said something. She couldn't understand how else people would be spreading rumors about her already.

Unusual for the desert, it began to rain. Eve didn't like how the last time it rained turned out, and she became even more nervous.

Lightning thundered in the nearby mountains, and the students ran to the windows to watch. The teacher tried to urge them not to, but they did anyway.

Again, already not a fan of lightning, and with previous not-so-preferable experiences with lightning, Eve was even more on edge.

In the confusion and distraction that was provided, the box, which was invisible above Eve's shoulder, said, "Eve, you need to get outside."

"Box? You followed me here?" Eve asked. "Quiet down," she whispered.

"You need to get outside," the box urged. The classroom had two doors. The students and teacher looked out of the window near one of them, and the door on the other side of the room was unguarded.

Eve snuck over to it and stepped outside as quietly as she could. The box instructed her to go to the courtyard.

Before she could ask the box what was happening, a bright and violent strike of thunderous purple lightning shone before her, striking the clock tower in the center of the

## ❖ CHAPTER 4 ❖

courtyard. Eve jumped back, startled. The lightning trailed down it, until finally, standing in the grass school courtyard, was Starlocke.

"What are you doing here?" Eve asked, looking around to make sure no one was watching, and catching her breath from the scare of the lightning. "You could be seen!"

"I found where the Terrors are hiding, I thought you would like to know so you can stop them." Starlocke's ears perked up.

"I don't know if I can." Eve doubted herself. "Will you help?" she asked.

"Sure." Starlocke bowed his head. "I would be delighted to."

"Where are they?" Eve asked.

"Kranthar is based in Russia, in the middle of a barren tundra." Starlocke paced around. "I don't know how I could get more specific for you, for teleportation convenience."

"I'll teleport to you. Go ahead of me," Eve insisted.

"Alright." Starlocke nodded. His paws sparked with short bursts of electricity before his entire body became like a lightning bolt, and he vanished quickly, zooming away.

Eve held out for the box but was quickly interrupted by a passerby.

"Eve? Where are you going?" Andrew called out.

"Andrew? Why are you out?" Eve looked around to make sure no one else was seeing her.

"I asked to go to the bathroom so I could see the rain," Andrew explained. "Did I see Starlocke just now?" Andrew asked excitedly.

"Ugh, come with me." Eve held out her hand, and she and Andrew flashed away.

Falling white snow blurred Eve's and Andrew's vision. The ground was covered in patchy white snow, and deep brown damp dirt. Trees were scattered around them, not very prevalent, but still filling in the shallow valley surrounded by rocky hills.

They appeared next to Starlocke, but also a surprise visitor, Tomas.

"Rex?" Andrew asked, "Why are you here." He shivered, "It's freezing."

"How are you here?" Eve asked Tomas.

"Why are *you* here?" Tomas snapped back, looking worried for Eve and Andrew. "And you?" he asked Eve. "Why'd you bring Andrew? And who's this?" Tomas looked to Starlocke.

## ❖ CHAPTER 4 ❖

Before much could be explained, the ground rumbled, a familiar sensation for Eve, fresh in her mind. This time around, the rumbling was much more intense.

Trees shook until the snow fell off its branches. Rocks lining the hills tumbled, and the damp dirt cracked, collapsing in on itself.

"Stand back." Tomas held out his arms.

The ground ahead of them burst up into a mound, pushing away the trees, before bursting at the seams and blowing dirt, snow, rocks, and trees into air.

A worm creature pushed itself out of the hole created in the ground ahead of them. As it rose with such blinding speeds, like the passing train, it kept rising and rising. The creature was massive in scale. Eve was quick to decipher that this Krantharnic was different.

The beast slowed to a stop, allowing its finer details to be studied. The beast was heavily armored. It lowered its face, armored with a natural chitin plating, shaped like a mighty battle axe.

Its five piercing eyes locked onto Eve, and the creature seemed to chuckle. Ghostly Terrors lifted from the ground and hovered around the beast-like phantoms.

The overbearing monster spoke with the same voice it used to project through the Terrors, "So this is the Sentinel? The one destined to defeat me?" Its voice rang in Eve's head, stinging with a sharp pain when it finished speaking.

"This is the hivemind," Starlocke explained.

"Kranthar," Eve and Tomas both said behind gritted teeth.

"What do you want!?" Eve questioned. She shook with the shivering cold and blood-boiling fear fighting for dominance in her veins.

Tomas was startled at her question and anger, especially because she said what he was going to say before he could.

"Why can't you just leave this world alone!? It's annoying!" Eve stomped forward, trying to be threatening. Kranthar did not move in the slightest.

"What do I want?" Kranthar hissed. His armored body wriggled and vibrated, and soon, the rib-cage-like armor extended like millipede legs, writhing around, and ticking at the worm's side.

"I want the best for the Krantharnics. I've seen through time." Kranthar twitched his head towards Starlocke and pointed at him with one of his massive insect-like arms. "Your

## ❖ CHAPTER 4 ❖

people showed me the future, the tragedy that befell the Terrors... Because of the Sentinel."

"What do you mean?" Eve stepped back, afraid at the massive creature but feeling an odd amount of sympathy.

"We were dragged into a war we didn't want to be a part of. We were seen as evil and killed by the billions because of him. I intend to stop that from ever happening."

"That's a paradox, Kranthar." Tomas yelled with his gravelly voice. "You know you can't do that."

"Can't I?" Kranthar scoffed. "In this broken universe we call home... *everything* is a paradox. I gather you would be familiar." The Terrors surrounding him stopped floating around him and floated idly in the air.

They opened their mouth-eyes and began humming at a low purr. "The Sentinel created impossible contradicting intercommunicating branched realities when he changed the course of the future with a simple decision. So why can't I?" Kranthar growled, lowering his head closer to the group. He breathed heavily on them.

Tomas stayed unnaturally calm. Starlocke didn't react at all.

Eve and Andrew's hearts pounded in their chests, begging to break free. Eve could hear Andrew's fear. She forced herself to calm down to assure him it would all be alright.

"And what happened!?" Eve stepped forward. Kranthar's eyes all met with Eve, and confusion seemed to blanket his face. His head jerked back slightly, wondering what Eve would say. "The Multiverse is ending," Eve growled. "Do you want your people to be safe, while endangering all the others?"

"I don't care for the others!" Kranthar bellowed. "Only the Originals are worthy of this realm. I will save them all!" Kranthar declared.

"Originals?" Eve looked to Tomas for answers, but instead Starlocke answered.

Starlocke beamed information psychically into Eve's head, filling her in, saying, "The Originals were created by Time in the Milky Way's own Black Star 7 District, on the planets Modius, Illiosopherium, Nidus, and Tornlozor. The Quodstella, Dragolupus, Gars, Deusaves, and the Krantharnics, or the Terrors as you know them by their drone names.

"They were first living things in the universe, the five original phlasmatic beings. Existing in a world before life and death, they were immortal, the only living things, in the

Multiverse ruled by Time, and created by her children." Starlocke lifted his head.

"The only beings that are worth preserving," Kranthar continued. "Then the two Deusaves from Nidus decided to mess everything up," Kranthar hissed. "Life and Death? No more immortality except for them?" Kranthar scoffed. "Who gives them the right?" He shook his head, "But no, that's beside the point. The first ever war was fought over that mess billions of years ago and that's behind us.

"But I will make sure that the Krantharnics as a species push on, despite the curse called death. And the end of the Multiverse is hardly an issue with me. I know of a way to escape the great dying."

"Why do you have to fight me then? Or attack my friends?" Eve snapped. "Get off this planet, leave me alone!"

Kranthar roared. "It wouldn't be enough! I need my kind to be left alone in the Galactic War. I can get my way because of my partnership with Time's more sensible child. But that can only happen if that war never happens! If the Sentinel is killed! Better yet, if he never exists."

"I- *AM NOT-* THE SENTINEL!" Eve yelled.

Tomas looked to her with some disappointment, but a hint of pride in his face. Andrew stepped back and hid behind Starlocke for safety.

"You don't know what you're for, do you?" Kranthar's armored plating curled into a smile as he laughed. "He didn't tell you?"

"What?" Eve looked to Tomas.

Tomas's eyes widened, he angrily turned his attention to Kranthar, "How do you know?"

"Like I said, old man, I've seen through time. I know who you are, Tomas," he snarled, "I know that Eve isn't here to save the universe, she's only a tool for you to use to ensure that the Sentinel can exist in the first place!

"You know that inexplicable coincidences and innumerable paradoxes muddy his existence, and that Eve is the answer to all of them!" Kranthar snapped his head toward Eve. Eve fell backwards into the snow, backing away from Kranthar. "You're a smart girl, you know what that means." Kranthar smiled.

"You're using me?" Eve asked Tomas. "If I'm dead the Sentinel won't exist." She looked towards Kranthar.

"Yes." He smiled slyly, "Now you're getting it."

"Don't listen to him!" Tomas urged.

## ❖ CHAPTER 4 ❖

"Well…" Eve stood up, gathering sudden bravery. She rolled up her sleeves despite the intense cold of the tundra. "I may be angry that I'm being used," she glared at Tomas, "But the fact that I have the powers I do means that the Sentinel *did* exist. That's all I need to know I'll survive *this*."

"Survive what?" Kranthar snaked his head back.

"Eve, no." Tomas stepped forward.

Eve's fist blasted into flames. She punched forward at one of Kranthar's eyes, and it easily impaled it, burying her fist into his pupil.

"AGH!" Kranthar flung his head upwards, taking Eve with him. She was flung far into the sky, screaming.

"Eve!" Tomas ran forward. "Close your eyes! Concentrate!" he yelled. "Fly!" he urged.

Eve closed her eyes hard, and soon her back flared into bright flames. Wings of phlasma burst from her back with a blasting sound that left a ringing in Tomas and Andrew's ears. She hovered above Kranthar, staring at her hands in wonderment. Her legs dangled beneath her, and she turned around, looking to Andrew. "Holy shit!" She smiled. "Are you seeing this!"

"Eve, watch out!" Andrew yelled.

Kranthar was rising from the ground even further, and soon he blasted completely from the ground, his whole body exposed as he flew through the air.

"Oh no." Eve backed away as Kranthar's shadow eclipsed her. "Andrew, get out of here!" She yelled.

Kranthar screamed with great intensity, four massive dragon-like wings unfolded from around his body and spread out wide, suspending him in air.

Droves of ghostly Terrors followed after him and his shadow. Kranthar righted himself, flapping his four wings hard trying to keep him afloat, his hundreds of legs dangling underneath him. His remaining four eyes glowed bright purple.

"Did he say that Terrors were phlasmatic?" Eve asked from her spot in the sky.

"Yes." Starlocke's voice bounced around in her head.

"Eve, get out of here, I'll deal with this!" Tomas insisted.

"What can you do?" Eve scoffed.

Tomas' hands burst into weak flickering flames.

Andrew stumbled back, startled.

Massive bolts of lightning shot from Kranthar's eyes. Eve turned her attention quickly, and her first instinct was to

## ❖ CHAPTER 4 ❖

fold her wings ahead of her. The box latched to her back and a lime green shield formed around her.

The electric bolts absorbed themselves into the shield and deflected off of it. The bright day sky went dark as the lightning cracked through the sky, burrowed into the ground, and burned trees.

Starlocke jumped in front of Andrew and absorbed the electricity bound to hit him. He howled in pain as the electricity coursed through his body. His image flickered and his fur stood on end.

Tomas held out his hands and a concentrated beam of phlasma burst towards Kranthar and knocked a chunk from his faceplate. The lightning vanished and Kranthar fell to the ground with a massive thud.

The shield around Eve vanished and she floated there in the air, watching. Eve looked forward and stared at the limp body of Kranthar. "Is he…" She floated forward slowly as her phlasmatic wings flapped.

"Eve, let me take care of this," Tomas insisted.

Piercing screams shook the air and vibrated the ground as Kranthar yelled into the sky, as did his Terror drones. His wings shot out and with a massive flap pushed him into the air. His body armor shook and glowed a deep purple. "Ha… *Not a*

*Sentinel.*" Kranthar chuckled. "You're more like him than anyone I've seen." Kranthar zoomed toward Eve.

"No!" Eve held her hands to her face and her arms burst into flames. They solidified into razor sharp crystals in an instant, surprising her. Kranthar headbutted her far far off. She rolled into the snow and kept going, creating a paved trail behind her as she rolled and rolled, her bones cracking as she launched through a tree.

"*Dammit,*" Tomas growled. He ran for Eve.

"EVE!" Andrew ran, following Tomas.

Tomas turned around and lifted his hand, clenching it into a fist. Roots of phlasma crawled up Andrew's legs, locking him in place. "Stay there," Tomas demanded. He continued running towards Eve.

Eve was limp on the ground, groaning and crying. She yelled, "HELP!" Her bones cracked as she strained her lungs to scream behind waves of tears, "HELP ME!" she cried out with broken breath.

Her life began flashing before her eyes. She saw her mother and Andrew, sitting alone without her. A Terror's image flashed across her eyes as light drained from them. Her lungs were filling with blood, and she couldn't breathe. It felt as though an immense weight had been dropped on her chest.

## ❖ CHAPTER 4 ❖

Starlocke followed, soon passing Tomas by.

Eve cried on the ground, most of her bones were broken, she was lying in a pool of blood, soaking into the snow, melting it with its warmth. She was dying, quickly.

"Stand back." Starlocke turned his head and lifted his tail, telling Tomas to stay where he was.

"No, no, no this isn't good." Tomas paced around not knowing what to do, "She's dying!"

"I said stand back!" Starlocke barked. He lowered his head and his third eye glowed. A beam of phlasma shot out and hit Eve.

Eve burst into phlasmatic flames and her wounds healed quickly.

"No! No, it's too soon! Dammit!" Tomas paced, clearly understanding what was happening.

"What's going on!" Andrew called out. "Is she alright!?"

"She's dead," Kranthar assumed.

"No!" Andrew fell forward while trying to break free from his restraints. "EVE!"

Eve's hair darkened and straightened. Her chest lifted from the ground as she floated up. She stretched taller and her face sharpened.

She opened her eyes, glowing bright purple as she rose. She looked down at her hands, watching as they changed. She opened her mouth to speak, but flames burst from her face the instant she did.

"What?" Kranthar straightened up and flapped his wings quicker. "What is this?! You foolish Dragolupus! You've abused Gar magic for the sake of a non-Original! That's blasphemous!"

"Eve?" Andrew said, confused and scared.

The flames vanished and Eve fell to the ground, landing on her knee. She looked up and around, studying her surroundings. "I'm alive." She stood up, breathing heavily. "I – My voice…" She confronted Starlocke. "What did you do to me?" She pointed at him forcefully.

"No!" Kranthar shook his head. "I will not stand for this!" he grumbled. "Agh!"

His Terror drones flew after Eve with great speeds. Starlocke jumped in front of her and shocked the Terrors into nothing. Several Krantharnics burst from the snow and screamed at the group as Andrew stood watching from afar, very confused.

## ❖ CHAPTER 4 ❖

Tomas ran up to Eve, she had phazed, and was renewed. They stood back-to-back, hands blazing. Starlocke paced around them, growling at the Terrors.

Tomas lifted his arms and massive spikes of phlasma jutted out of the ground and jabbed at Kranthar's wings. Eve couldn't manage much more than chucking fireballs at Kranthar. She blasted a few through his wings, causing him to flinch, and a few Terrors to drop from the sky.

Kranthar yelled in a deep growl, then eyeballed Eve. "Humans," he growled, and shook his head. "Phlasma doesn't belong to you." He flapped lopsidedly with his remaining healthy wings. "By the gods, you will be punished, Dragolupus. May Drakona have mercy on your soul." He looked to the sky and bolted into space, the Terrors following him.

Eve breathed out and tried to catch her breath. Tomas flicked his wrist and the restraints around Andrew dropped. Starlocke sat down in the snow as it melted around his warm fur.

"What happened to me?" Eve confronted Tomas. "Something's wrong, I don't feel right. I'm too pale."

"You've phazed." Tomas avoided contact with her new sharp ice-blue eyes. "When someone close to death is hit with just the right configuration of phlasma, their body is renewed to heal them."

"So, I healed?" Eve asked for clarification.

"Eve?" Andrew stared into Eve's face. He couldn't recognize his own sister. "Is that really you? I'm confused..."

"Andrew..." Eve was confused by his question.

"You're different..." Andrew stared at her. "You're not my sister."

"I had to do it." Starlocke looked away in shame. "To save your life." He seemed worried about what Kranthar had said.

"I've seen people phaze before," Tomas admitted. "You'll get used to it."

"No." Eve shook her head and stepped back. She laughed, and scoffed, "No I'm done with this bullshit. I'm done with *getting used to it*, alright? I'm not doing this anymore, find someone else."

"There is no one else," Tomas argued.

"I'm just a kid!" Eve screamed as her voice cracked. "Look at me, obviously I can't do all this crazy stuff, I almost just died, no- No!" Eve held her hands to her face and paced around in the snow. She wiped tears from her face. "No, this isn't real. Kranthar was talking about gods? The Originals?

## CHAPTER 4

No! None of this is real, it's one big dream." She talked mostly to herself. "I'm done," she asserted to Tomas.

"The world and the universe still need saving," Tomas reminded Eve. "It needs you."

"Why can't you do it, huh? You can control this stuff, why does it have to be me?" she yelled. "Huh?" She held out her arms. "Huh? Answer me!"

Andrew stared at her, trying to figure her out. She wasn't his sister, not anymore.

"I'm too old for this, I can barely—"

"And I'm not too young? Who are you? Who are you to decide who saves the universe on your command? Why me!? I want to go home!"

"I can't tell you, not now, it's not the right time." Tomas looked down at his feet, occasionally glancing at the puddle of blood in the snow behind Eve.

Starlocke's third eye stone began to glow as he lowered his head towards Tomas.

"Don't." Tomas held out his arm defensively. "Don't look for the answer yourself," he demanded.

"You have many secrets, old man." Starlocke lifted his head and the stone lost its glow. "Old, *old* man..." He shook his head.

"Take me home," Eve demanded.

"You have a time machine, you brought yourself here," Tomas reminded her.

"What about Mom?" Andrew spoke up from his relative, shocked silence. "Eve you've... you aren't *you* anymore, how... How are you supposed to tell Mom?" he asked.

Eve shook her head. "Andrew, I'm taking you home, and I'm leaving."

"What?" Andrew stepped back. "You can't just leave me!"

"And we both can't leave Mom!" Eve snapped back. "Look, one of us has to stay with her, and you haven't changed, and you need to stay safe. I'm not coming home."

"So, what are you going to do?" Andrew stepped back.

"Save the universe," Eve admitted without so much as thinking. She caught a glimpse of Tomas's smile and pointed at him aggressively. "*Not* because you said so! What else am I supposed to do?" she asked. "You ruined my life."

Eve sighed, and a long silence followed, nothing except the cold sharp winds of the tundra howling past them, and the subtle ambient sparking of Starlocke's fur remained.

"Come on Andrew, you're going home."

❖ Chapter 5 ❖
# Phlasma

Eve and Andrew appeared in front of their home, on the same day, after their classes had already ended for the day. Eve wanted to drop Andrew off without staying too long, so that she could avoid having to say goodbye, but Andrew had something else in mind.

"Don't leave me here, Eve, please," Andrew begged.

"Andrew, *please* don't make this harder than it needs to be."

"I wanna help save the universe with you! You're my sister! And you're cool now!" Andrew said, tearing up as he held onto Eve for dear life.

"Andrew don't make this harder," Eve wiped a tear away.

"You were always cool, okay?" Andrew cried.

"Andrew…"

"Don't go, don't go."

"Andrew, I can't stay home now that I've changed. I'm not about to try to explain this to Mom or drag her into all of this. I can't take you because I can't leave her alone. She needs you."

"I need you!" Andrew cried.

"One of us needs to stay," Eve said, choking on her words. Tears formed in her eyes, clouding her vision, but she tried her best to stay composed, and strong.

"And one of us needs to save the universe. You know you have to stay. That's how you help me save the universe, okay? You keep Mom happy."

Andrew nodded, wiping the tears from his eyes and hiding his face.

Eve continued, "The further I stay from you guys the less harm I put you in. This is my burden to carry, I don't want to put you two in any of my danger."

Andrew was slowly coming to terms with the change. "You'll visit me, right? And be safe?" he asked, hopeful, and holding back tears.

## ❖ CHAPTER 5 ❖

"I'll be safe," Eve assured him, not sure about being able to visit. She had no way to predict how busy she'd be. "And you'll be too, without me."

"What do I tell Mom? About where you are?"

Eve hesitated for a few moments, trying to come to a valid answer. "I ran away. Far away. That's all." She forced a smile.

Andrew jumped in for a hug, holding his sister in his arms, not planning to let go.

Eve closed her eyes and cried, *"I'm sorry."* She pried his arms off of her and stepped back. It was tough to see him through her still tears. She saw the pain in his eyes and knew that she had to leave eventually. Andrew needed to get inside, so she teleported away, leaving him behind.

She didn't know where to teleport, but something in her mind brought her to the Monterey cliff house. She dropped to her knees and cried into her hands, ignoring the sound of the front door opening.

"If it's any consolation, I wasn't planning on that happening, and if it didn't, you would've died," Tomas's old voice called out, calmly.

Eve looked up, expecting to be alone with him, but standing behind Tomas was Ganto the Ilsian and Starlocke the Dragolupus.

"Nice of you to join the party," Ganto greeted.

Eve stood up, wiped her sleeve on her face, and slowly made her way to the house. She stepped in with some sense of hesitation, unsure of herself and her new legs. She sat down on the nearest couch and was immediately taken over with a sense of awkward tension as Ganto, Starlocke, and Tomas stared at her.

"What now?" Eve sniffled. "What am I supposed to do?"

"So, you're willing to help?" Tomas smiled. He paced around and came to a decision. "If you really want to save the Multiverse, you need to be less passive about it and make your own decisions. Don't let the world happen to you, and instead have you happen to the world."

"How do I do that?" Eve questioned.

"By not asking so many questions," Starlocke concluded.

Eve stayed silent and stared back at them. There were so many things she wanted to ask, but not after what Starlocke said.

### ❖ CHAPTER 5 ❖

"Whenever something unknown to the Sentinel happened, he pretended like he knew things, and made his friends ask the questions for him, and when he was the only one around to answer, he made it up, and hoped he was right," Tomas explained.

"How do you know that?" Eve asked.

"Ah!" Ganto lifted a pointed finger, "That's a question!"

Eve was about to ask why Tomas referred to the Sentinel as a 'he', but then realized that was a question and determined for herself that the Sentinel probably phazed like her. Then she feared for a second the possibility of becoming a man, and the thought shivered her.

"There you go, thinking for yourself." Starlocke smiled and perked his ears up.

Eve was startled at his speaking; she could've sworn she was thinking to herself.

"I can read minds," Starlocke reminded her.

"Can you not?" Eve sassed Starlocke.

"That's a question!" Ganto laughed.

"Shut up!" Eve and Tomas scolded him in unison.

"Hey, Tomas?" Eve asked shortly after.

"This sounds like a question..." Ganto teased.

"I will not hesitate to end you." Starlocke growled at Ganto, his third eye glowing slightly.

Ganto shuffled nervously away from Starlocke, although his threat was empty.

"You know how this phlasma stuff works, and I don't particularly feel like almost dying again anytime soon... could you train me?"

Tomas's wrinkled face stretched into a beaming smile at the thought of it, and he cheerfully agreed, "Oh yes!" He rushed his way to the back door of the large home. Starlocke lifted from his sitting position and followed after Tomas like a large bumbling dog, wagging his tail, and Ganto trotted behind.

"So, you guys have made friends with each other, huh?" Eve asked as she followed behind them.

"Starlocke read our minds, he knows all about us, and I'm interested in his species and his planet so I'm keeping him around. As for Ganto, I'm keeping him here because..."

"I'll kill that pompous ancient worm monster in an instant for that bounty, lemme at him!"

"He needs to be contained. For his own good."

"Alright." Eve nodded as she made her way to the backyard on the cliff. She looked around at the large yard, torn

## ❖ CHAPTER 5 ❖

up with age. Phlasma crystals protruded from the ground, and patches of grass were burnt. Targets lay scattered across the ground and the weeds grew haphazardly.

"The First Sentinel and his friend, along with a Gar from Illiosopherium used to train here regularly," Tomas explained. He lifted his arms and a wall of crystal phlasma lifted itself from the ground. "I was trained by the same Gar that trained him. We all were."

"And Gars are one of the Originals, right?" Eve asked, remembering what Starlocke had said before. "And the Originals are…?"

"Exactly as I said before. The first living things, created by Time herself," Starlocke reminded her.

"But Kranthar said something about gods… how much is there out there that people don't know about? As far as I know there's only one God."

"Using the term 'god' to refer to the first of each species is a bit of an over exaggeration," Tomas elaborated. "He was talking about the first of each of the Originals, the original Originals, the Kings and Queens of their time, the forefront of the first ever war. Sogar, the king of the Gars, Kranica, the Queen of the Terrors, Modius, the king of the

Quodstella, Dile, the king of the Deusaves, and Drakona, the queen of the Dragolupus."

"So, they aren't gods?" Eve asked.

"Gods are a myth. All of this is painfully real," Tomas answered quickly.

"But time? You talk about it like it's a person."

"A Celestial Being, nothing more," Starlocke answered.

"Sounds like gods to me," Ganto scoffed.

"Now back to phlasma." Tomas tried to get the topic back to training.

"You mean the catalyst for this crazy religion that Kranthar is so bound to?" Ganto laughed. "Keep getting better at the stuff and you'll anger him more."

"He is right, you know," Starlocke reluctantly agreed, "The Krantharnics are among the most devoted to phlasma of the Originals, second only to the Gars."

"But what exactly is the stuff, because, I have this fire, and Ganto said there was lightning like you have," Eve gestured towards Starlocke, "But I thought that was just regular lightning."

## CHAPTER 5

"Regular lightning is the only place in the universe aside from black stars where phlasma can be found naturally," Starlocke explained. "Phlasma is very versatile."

"It can be anything imaginable."

Tomas lifted his hand and snapped his fingers. It was like the pop of a soap bubble when deep purple liquid burst from his fingertips and splashed to the floor. He twisted his arms around in a helix pattern and the liquid lifted from the ground in a dark black gaseous smoke, lifting to a cloud-like substance in front of his face.

He clapped his hands in the gaseous substance and it sparked with electricity like a small storm cloud. To show off further, he spread his arms wide, the phlasma traced his finger movements, and morphed into a near invisible beam of light between his hands. When he twisted his fingers in a certain way, sparks of dark lightning surrounded the beam as he shot it at Eve. She held her head.

Darkness swarmed Eve's vision. A flash of yellow jittered in front of her, chuckling, and vibrating with some essence of pure fear. She heard nothing but screams of the dead, and an image flashed in her mind.

"Sentinel, no!"

A man's voice echoed in Eve's mind, and the faint chuckling continued. Soon she saw herself standing in a dark place, watching clouded figures. She knew she was having some sort of vision again. The blackness faded and Eve's vision returned as Tomas pulled back on the invisible phlasma, concentrating it into a ball of purple flames in his hands.

Dark electricity lingered.

"What was that?" Eve asked, gasping for air.

"Emotional phlasma," Tomas explained. "A form of phlasma that can incite visions of the future and implant memories of others. It can be…" Tomas hesitated, "Deadly… in the wrong hands."

"Anything else, show-off?" Ganto teased.

Tomas continued to weave the phlasma between his fingers, waiting and thinking. He solidified the phlasma into a sharp-edged crystal ball. He tossed it around in his hands, and then threw the ball at the crystal wall in the yard. When the ball hit the wall, it shattered. Tomas clapped his hands together, and the phlasma stretched so wide that it formed a temporary wormhole before it quickly collapsed. Tomas evidently couldn't hold its form for long.

"Nice." Ganto nodded slowly.

## ❖ CHAPTER 5 ❖

Tomas turned around and focused on Eve again, "You're far, far off from any of this."

"So, I can only do fire?" Eve asked.

"You can do anything, it's just that it becomes way easier the longer you've been able to control and have been controlling the stuff, hence why I can make wormholes and give you visions."

"So, this stuff can be weaponized, then, right?" Eve stepped forward, preparing herself.

"You can use it as a tool, as a weapon, anything." Tomas paced around Eve.

"You can use it as a means of collecting information," Starlocke spoke up. "In fact, I'm not sure a human is best to teach you."

"I've been taught by a Gar," Tomas argued. "I'm more than qualified."

"Gars are great with the flame, but struggle with anything else." Starlocke stood up and walked peacefully over to Tomas and Eve. "Finding a Gar that can show you everything about phlasma is rare. He must've been educated."

"He was." Tomas wondered where Starlocke was going.

"Each of the Originals are masters of their craft, each being very well versed in a particular subset of phlasma. The Dragolupus are masters at lightning charged phlasma. The Krantharnics are best when they put their efforts into emotional phlasma, though they dabble in the electric variety, which can be their downfall if they aren't careful. The Gars, like I said, are experts with the flame. The Deusaves of Nidus want nothing more than to fly free through space with their space-time warping wormhole abilities, and the Quodstella form themselves with the power of solid and liquid forms of phlasma.

"You seem to be nothing more than a lackluster jack of all trades, master of none." Starlocke observed of Tomas. "Though, since you were taught by a Gar, you're well versed in the flame, I can see. And maybe you've just lost touch with phlasma as you've aged…" Starlocke stopped pacing and sat in the grass. "We will both teach you." He turned his head quickly to Eve.

"Alright." Eve tried to be optimistic.

"No," Tomas was quick to disagree after little thought. "I'm the one who's supposed to train her."

"I could be a significant help." Starlocke's ears drooped, as if he were disappointed.

## CHAPTER 5

"You know, there's all this talk about phlasma but you guys are both missing a big chunk of training." Ganto swung his rifle around. "In my experience with universe saving, having a bit of combat know-how instead of flailing phlasma around like a bumbling idiot seems to help."

"You know nothing of phlasma." Starlocke barked. "You are but an Ilsian."

"Oi!" Ganto stepped forward. "Ilsians are better than any of the stuck-up Originals by a longshot! Just because you've been around longer, and you've got magic tricks doesn't make you better!"

"You were thrown out of your own planet by the incompetent Lorinians," Starlocke growled. "I'd hardly call that great."

"Watch it!" Ganto's mandibles clicked violently.

"Hey!" Eve shouted. "All of you train me." She adjusted her stance. "Kinda want to get on with saving the universe so I can get back to living normal."

Tomas flinched at the mention of living normal, and he sighed. "Eve, you'll never get back to how you were. Especially not now."

"Not if I have anything to say about it." She stepped closer to Tomas. "I'm in charge here." She pressed her finger against his chest. "I take it the Sentinel was a take charge guy, and if I'm his replacement, I'm gonna call the shots."

Tomas smiled, pleasantly surprised at Eve's change in demeanor. "Alright, *Sentinel*." Tomas chuckled.

"Don't call me that," Eve growled. She stood in front of the wall and widened her stance. She held out her hands. "Ok... so what do I do?"

"Blast the wall with a quick burst of phlasma." Tomas stood by her side.

"How?" she asked.

Tomas was about to speak up, but Starlocke stepped in.

"Phlasma *knows* you. It knows what to do because you think it," he explained. "The better your imagination, the better control you can have over the phlasma, but there's a catch." Starlocke sat by Eve's other side, sandwiching her between him and Tomas. "If you think *really, really* hard about it, it won't work. You have to let it happen organically."

"That's why it's so easy for you to use the stuff in the heat of battle, because you aren't thinking, you're just doing," Tomas elaborated.

"Alright." Eve took a deep breath.

"Shoot it!" Ganto yelled.

## ❖ CHAPTER 5 ❖

Eve closed her eyes and quickly was shot back by a massive blast of searing phlasma that exploded from her palms. It shot forward so quickly that the shockwave caused Tomas to stumble, and Ganto to fall over on his backside. The flames engulfed the wall and shattered it easily. Eve snapped up from the ground and stared wide eyed at the no longer existing wall. "Woah!" she exclaimed.

"That was… impressive." Tomas smiled proudly.

Ganto squirmed around on the ground like an upside-down cockroach before righting himself again. He groaned as he pushed himself to a standing position again.

Starlocke, Tomas, and Ganto continued to train Eve throughout the day. The constant training kept Eve's mind off her family and her old life, she was distracted by the fantastic abilities she possessed.

The idea of using her powers to fight didn't really even cross her mind until Ganto was combat training her as the sun set. Something about the phlasma calmed her. It was peaceful, even if it was only for that day.

As training whittled down and was coming to an end that day, Starlocke ran home to Modius, and Ganto made his way to his own room in the old house. Eve was getting ready to call it quits, uncomfortable in her dirty clothes.

"Do you have any clothes? Mine are kind of bloody and a bit big," Eve complained to Tomas as they stood alone in the living room.

"Down the hall, to the left." Tomas stood around awkwardly, like he forgot what he was going to do.

Eve followed Tomas's instructions and came to a stop in front of a closet. She opened it up and was met with an entire rack of the same outfit. A blue flannel, purple t-shirt, jeans, and a pair of red sneakers.

"Great fashion sense," Eve said loud enough for Tomas to hear. "Such variety."

"That was the Sentinel's wardrobe, don't sass me about it," Tomas said back, still thinking.

Eve held out her hand for one of the flannels and stopped for a moment. She saw something in the closet out of the corner of her eye. It was a small phlasmatic stone, but it was dark, lifeless and cracked. She ignored it and took the clothes.

She came back out into the room wearing one of the first Sentinel's old outfits. The flannel was a bit big but everything else fit fine.

"Eve." Tomas called out from a hallway across the other side of the living room.

## ❖ CHAPTER 5 ❖

Eve squinted down the dimly lit hallway across the living room from Tomas and squinted her eyes at him as to ask '*what?*' without saying anything.

"Come here," Tomas beckoned.

Eve hesitated and followed after him.

"The Emissaries of the Extraverse," Tomas whispered as he led Eve to a room.

"What?" she asked, not sure what he was meaning.

"One of them had a huge collection of rêve stones, memories of the Sentinel, and essences of people all condensed into little phlasma stones."

"Alright..." Eve stopped in front of the door Tomas was reaching for.

"I have some." Tomas smiled.

Eve stayed silent and followed Tomas into the room. He flicked a light switch and lights flickered on, shining light on the massive pile of stones, glowing faintly, dimming and growing brighter like a beating heart.

Eve stared at them, wondering. Tomas stared ahead and sighed, he seemed frightened and Eve picked up on it.

"You look like you've seen a ghost," Eve teased.

"This room is cursed." Tomas's face grew pale.

"What?" Eve asked, becoming worried.

"Phlasma is a very... very interesting thing. You see, it's the first form of life ever present in the Multiverse, across all universes. When a human is infused with powers, the phlasma within them becomes like them, and when they die, and become a stone... there's a side effect."

"Ok..." Eve couldn't keep her eyes off the stones.

"Phlasma ghosts." Tomas swallowed a lump in his throat.

"What?" Eve stepped away, suddenly scared of the room. A slight cold breeze shook through her body.

A light, fading, image of a person floated from the pile of the rocks, it flew close to Eve, and stopped in front of her cold pale face.

"Who's this..." Eve stared into the eyes of the mostly invisible glowing ghost.

"That's the First Sentinel. When he phazed, a piece of him was left behind, and it was captured in a stone so it wouldn't roam around."

"I'm sorry..." The ghost spoke in a soft, quiet voice. "Matrona..."

"Who?" Eve questioned.

Tomas held out his hand. The ghost was pushed back into a stone. "These ghosts are just the subconscious. These stones are not of *dead* people per-say. Just shadows of a previous incarnation. It's the ghosts of the dead that are troubling. They exist forever... they never get rest.

"They can't interact with the world around them. Not in the traditional sense. They can interact with other ghosts, or things structurally similar to them, like the Celestial Beings that reside over the Extraverse... but they'll never be the same again. They can't feel the sand pushing through their toes when they walk across the beach... or taste a glass of OJ with breakfast... the simplest of life's niceties... gone..."

"Who are you?" Eve asked. "You're not just someone that *knew* the Sentinel. You've collected his soul!"

Tomas hesitated before answering. "Not souls, phlasmatic molds, shadows... It's too complicated to explain." He coughed.

"Alright..." Eve wasn't satisfied with his answer but knew he wouldn't budge. "And the Emissaries?" she asked, hoping it was something that he would feel comfortable elaborating on.

A stone on the floor glowed. From it, a phlasma ghost of the Fifth Sentinel floated out. Tomas seemed particularly afraid of it.

"Who's that?" Eve stepped back, fearing it because Tomas did.

"That's the Fifth Sentinel." Tomas clapped his hands together and forced the screaming ghost back into its stone.

"Okay…" Eve wondered why he feared him.

"Go to bed." Tomas grumbled.

"What?" Eve was confused at his sudden change of mood.

"We'll train in the morning."

They continued to train in the morning, Starlocke returned to help, and Ganto helped Eve understand strategy and stealth. Starlocke helped Tomas construct a device to track Modius's movements while Ganto trained Eve. When it was Starlocke's turn to train Eve, she achieved something that surprised Tomas.

Her fingers sparked with bright flashing lightning, as blue as her eyes. She formed a small, shaped ball of phlasmatic electricity in her palms, keeping it contained and controlled for a few seconds before it burst into a quick flash of light in her face. The sound it made when it burst sounded like shattering glass, and Eve shook her hands like they stung.

## ❖ CHAPTER 5 ❖

"What was that?" Tomas asked. "Electricity? That's way faster than the Sentinel was able to control it..." Tomas stared, confused.

"A testament to the teachings of a Dragolupus," Starlocke bragged.

"It was *really* cold." Eve complained as she shook her hands. They stung like they'd been burned with a strong flame, but when it happened it felt like the stinging cold of the tundra. Her hands jittered, and in them was a patterned scar of electric veins.

"What?" Starlocke trotted closer to Eve to observe her hands. "Cold lightning..." Starlocke admired her hands, sniffing them with his warm nose. "Very interesting."

"What is it?" Tomas asked.

"Mr. phlasma know-it-all doesn't know a form of phlasma?" Ganto teased.

"You don't know about it!" Tomas snapped.

"I have an excuse!" Ganto chuckled.

"It's electric ice." Starlocke locked his eyes on her hands. "A phlasma form I've only ever seen once before, in children of the original Originals." He tilted his head. "First generation grandchildren of Time..."

Eve stared at her own hands, and she had a thought. "I'm ready," she said.

"For?" Tomas asked.

"Kranthar must still be out there, right?" Eve asked. "If I can stop him, then all I have to do is deal with Modius and then boom, I can go back to living like normal."

"Way easier said than done," Tomas reminded her.

"Oh yeah? Well I have a plan." Eve stood as tall as she could, showing off her confidence.

❖ Chapter 6 ❖
# The Flying City

Eve began to pace around the room, thinking her plan over. Starlocke and Ganto watched her pace with curiosity, eagerly waiting to hear her plan.

"So, Kranthar said that he saw through time, and that he wants to stop the Sentinel from ever existing... I'm assuming Terrors have access to time travel?"

Tomas answered, "This hive does."

"Then maybe Kranthar's next move was to go even further back, maybe he went to stop something that would cause me to never exist, *or* maybe he went even further to stop an event that would prevent all his problems from existing."

"That's a possibility," Tomas agreed, lifting his fist to his chin as he too began to pace the room.

"But there's no way to tell where he went, though, if anywhere at all," Ganto argued. "It would be like looking for a needle in the infinite haystack that is time itself."

"Found him." Starlocke raised his head and his third eye lost its glow. "I can see through time, Ganto." Starlocke glanced at him.

"Right."

"Where is he?" Eve asked.

Instead of answering, Starlocke vanished in a puff of white smoke and a blast of electricity, whizzing past them and outside the open door leading to the backyard.

Eve shrugged and held her hands out for Tomas and Ganto. The two of them vanished and appeared near Starlocke.

"You didn't say you could run through time." Eve walked up to Starlocke.

"I can run at the speed of light, all I needed was a wormhole and some patience." Starlocke sniffed around, looking.

"When are we?" Tomas asked.

The box glowed passively, revving it's gears, and answered, "4000 BCE, Earth, Russia. About a thousand years before the first recorded human civilization."

111

## ❖ CHAPTER 6 ❖

"Why would Kranthar be here?" Ganto looked around, disinterested in their surroundings.

"He sure likes Russia…" Eve commented, looking around for anything unusual.

"First *recorded* civilization," the box repeated itself.

"Alright, so?" Ganto wondered what the significance of the statement was.

"That doesn't mean *the* first civilization," the box explained.

"*Evaki!*" A disgruntled voice yelled from afar.

Eve, Starlocke, Tomas, and Ganto turned around to face the direction of the voice and were met with a sight that none of them expected to be met with in 4000 BCE. A futuristic city built on a platform of metal, within a circle around a massive fire pit standing before them in the snow.

"This doesn't make any sense." Ganto stepped back.

"*Patro sare ino?*" The figure that spoke to them approached. He wore heavy fur and a mask. He lifted the mask off his face and revealed his pale white skin and red eyes.

"What doesn't make sense?" Eve asked.

"He's speaking Andromedan…" Ganto stepped back, confused. "But—"

"Based on my studies, the Andromedans were a highly intelligent group of humans from ancient Earth, experimented on secretly by Gars, and they left for the neighboring galaxy before any other civilization formed," Starlocke said, staring at the man. "Why would Kranthar be here?"

Eve looked at Starlocke. "How do you know that?"

"I'm an intergalactic historian," Starlocke said.

"*Cool...*" Eve muttered under her breath.

"Hm?"

Eve shook her head. "Did the Terrors ever have any run-ins with Andromedans in the war?" she asked.

"They were on the same side."

"He's trying to stop the Terror's involvement in the war by any way possible..."

"*Oh sare ino presn?*" the strange pale man asked the group.

"*Li sose ino,*" Ganto answered. "*Ino granti li evaki triz placi.*"

Eve stared at Ganto in awe, not understanding what he was saying. She looked to Tomas, but he just shrugged. Starlocke was staring at Ganto with deep concentration.

"*Onso sare trie initiato li evaki. Project Losaca so trie initiato.*" The man seemed to be disagreeing with Ganto.

## ❖ CHAPTER 6 ❖

"What's happening?" Eve asked.

"I told them to leave for their own safety." Ganto turned around. "But he said that 'Project Escape' isn't ready yet. Seems like they were already planning on leaving."

"Well tell him to make it ready!" Eve snapped.

Ganto turned around and snapped his mandibles at the man, "*Creati it initiato!*" he yelled.

"*Agin aht vistindilo?!*" the man shouted back.

"What did he say!?" Eve yelled at Ganto.

"For what reason!?" Ganto turned around.

The ground rumbled, and behind the group the ground burst. Kranthar blasted from the dirt and shot out into the air, rising and rising until he burst entirely from the ground, soon crashing down onto the floor, wrapping himself up like a snake, and flapping his wings to keep his head up. He stared at the group with his four remaining good eyes. Terrors lifted from the ground and floated around him, sparking their tentacles.

"Is that reason enough!?" Eve yelled at the man.

"*Monstro!*" The man stumbled back, pointing at Kranthar, "*Ino rhey emi! Ino did triz!*"

"What, no!?" Ganto laughed, "*We* didn't do this! We were warning you!"

"Agh!" the man yelled and swung at Ganto with his arm. Ganto snatched the man's arm and ripped it from his shoulder.

"Ganto, what the hell!" Eve stepped back.

"He was making me angry!" Ganto snapped back.

"AGH!" the man yelled and fell to the ground, holding his wound into the snow.

"Ganto, come on." Tomas sounded disappointed.

"Silence!" Kranthar yelled. "You dare try to stop me?" He seemed offended, directing his statement to Eve. "Little girl?"

Eve turned around and shouted, "Leave these people alone!"

"So, you care now?" Kranthar twitched his head. "Interesting. What do you have to gain?"

The man with the missing arm continued to scream in agonizing pain. Ganto twitched his eye, trying to ignore the man.

"I'm protecting this universe and if you mess with the timeline, you'll jeopardize it for yourself and your people, so why don't you do the smart thing and back down!"

Ganto snapped the screaming wounded man's neck to silence him. Starlocke growled at him.

## CHAPTER 6

"What? It was getting annoying."

"No more killing, Ganto." Tomas turned around.

"But that's what I do!" he protested, gesturing to himself, "It's my thing!"

Kranthar was about to say something, but an explosion burst near his face.

The group turned their attention back to the platform city and saw that they had set up several cannons and had begun firing them at Kranthar. The fire pit in the center of the small city flared intensely, and some sort of force field started to form around the platform, very slowly.

"Talk about advanced." Eve stumbled in the snow.

"Why do you want the Terrors to suffer?" Kranthar growled.

"I want the universe to not break any more than it already has! This isn't personal!" Eve yelled at Kranthar.

"I'll make it personal!" Kranthar threatened.

"They always do," Tomas scoffed.

"I *want* this universe to end! I want the Multiverse to be born anew! I will help reshape the Extraverse!" Kranthar yelled.

"Wait... what?" Tomas wasn't expecting this. "That goes against wanting to save the future of your kind. You can't have one and the other!"

"My boss assures me that I can!"

"That's not possible!"

"What do we do?" Eve asked.

"You're in charge." Tomas shrugged.

Eve glanced at Starlocke and Ganto. Starlocke stood at the ready, his hind legs pushed into the snow like he was ready to spring into action at any moment.

Ganto pointed the sights of his rifle at Kranthar, ready for a command.

Eve took a deep breath and told them, "Go for the kill."

"That's what I like to hear." Ganto kicked back his leg and his jetpack sparked, launching him into the air.

Starlocke howled and ran into Kranthar at an incredible speed, causing him to float off the ground to avoid any more headbutts.

Eve tried to her best to ignite her wings again, but she struggled.

"Don't think too hard," Starlocke's voice rang in her ears. "Don't concentrate. *Fight.*"

## ❖ CHAPTER 6 ❖

Eve closed her eyes and jumped up. A burst of snow exploded underneath her feet and a pillar of solid phlasma shot out from the ground, pushing underneath her feet and lifting her into the sky.

Ganto fired away at the Terror drones flying around Kranthar. Any worms that burst from the snow were quickly taken care of by the barrage of cannon fire from the nearby platform city.

The fire pit in the center of the small city rotated on a platform and flipped itself upside down, blasting more powerfully than before. Jarringly, the platform the city was built on began to rise from the ground, and it floated there idly.

"Woah!" Eve was distracted for a moment. She turned her head back toward the battle.

"Watch out!" Tomas's gravelly voice yelled.

Kranthar's tail swung Eve's way, and she instinctively held up her arms, fearing a repeat of last time. The box thought quickly and formed its protective shield around her, only moving slightly after being hit full force by the swing of Kranthar's tail.

The shield dropped and Eve held out her arms. The pillar of phlasma extended a platform for her to walk on, and as she stepped forward phlasma trailed underneath her, assuring her constant footing.

She approached Kranthar and held out her hands. With a quick shock of electric ice phlasma, Kranthar jittered and froze in place. The massive beast was immobilized by a quick shock, which even surprised Eve herself. She stood before him and held out her arms. "Don't mess with me," she growled. "Leave, or I will kill you."

"But I want that bounty!" Ganto shouted from afar.

"Shut up, Ganto!" Eve shouted back. She directed her attention back to Kranthar. "Do you understand?"

Tomas stood on the ground, watching, and waiting, just in case. He was fixed on Eve's every movement and word, surprised by every action she took, proud.

Kranthar's eyes widened as the electricity faded. The Terror drones regained their movement and stirred back to life. Kranthar blinked and shook his massive, armored head. "Do you take me for a fool?" He chuckled.

"Do you take me for a Sentinel?" Eve asked.

Kranthar stood still, just as if he were frozen, and he transfixed himself on those words, wondering what Eve would say next.

## CHAPTER 6

"The Sentinel is dead." Eve scowled. "Care to join her?" Her fist sparked violently with electricity.

"Eve." Tomas stepped forward, worried.

"DO YOU HAVE A DEATH WISH!?" she threatened.

"Eve, calm down…" Tomas held out his hand.

"DO YOU?" Her eyes glowed a cold blue, sparking with the electric phlasma. Her body flooded with electric phlasma, covering her in the stuff, and it soon formed around her. Eve shook with an ambient glow, creating a light buzz as the phlasma around her vibrated.

Kranthar snaked his head back slightly, but not before Eve charged forward and headbutted into his face, launching him back in a bright fiery explosion that sent a loud blasting sound flying through the entire tundra. A shockwave blasted Eve away, and she hit the dome shield of the floating city. She started falling to the ground, but Tomas held out his hands.

A blanket of glowing purple liquid phlasma quickly formed underneath Eve, and then wrapped her in a ball. Tomas lightly let the ball down into the snow, dropping the liquid and giving Eve a soft landing. The phlasma surrounding Eve faded and she gasped for air.

"What was that?!" Eve yelled at herself.

"You're getting a bit power hungry, I think." Tomas looked over her quickly, inspecting everything. He held up her arm and looked around for any injuries. "Are you okay?" he asked, worried.

"I'm fine." Eve pushed his hand away, and gave him a confused look. "I'm alright." She stood up, and watched Kranthar lift from the ground in the distance. "We aren't going to be able to kill Kranthar; not now anyway."

"Dammit!" Ganto groaned. "I just want that bounty so I can get home already."

"Ganto," Tomas pointed him down. "You're staying here to help. You were a part of the Sentinel's Army for a reason, you can't let them down now."

"Sure I can," Ganto said. "They'd never know."

"We have to get these guys away from here." Eve gestured toward the floating city.

"How?" Starlocke asked.

Eve held out her arm for the box floating by her, and she teleported into the city with Tomas. Starlocke met them there shortly after. Ganto floated by the dome shield and knocked on the shielding, asking to get in. The box teleported away, nudged itself against Ganto, and teleported him inside, quickly returning to its place by Eve's shoulder.

## ❖ CHAPTER 6 ❖

"Ganto, you speak their language…"

"Yeah," Ganto confirmed. "I do."

"Tell them it's time to leave."

"Don't appreciate being used around here, but whatever," Ganto said before informing the people to evacuate the planet as quickly as possible.

The city blasted into the sky quickly, breaking from its idle floating. The city slowly approached the clouds. Eve ran to the nearest tower, a white and chrome building. She ran up the stairs, followed by Ganto, Tomas, and Starlocke.

At the top of the tower, Eve could see over the edge of the dome, and out into the sky and the clouds. Clouds obscured her vision, swallowing up the dome. "I think we're fine," she said.

She had spoken too soon. Kranthar's face pushed itself through the clouds as the massive beast twirled over the dome, hugging his wings close to his body as he flew over. Droves of Terror drones flew by them, materializing themselves through the dome.

Eve stumbled back in fear as a group of Terrors approached her.

Ganto lifted his rifle and blasted stunning rounds at the ghostly figures, while Starlocke shocked them with tiny bolts of lightning and Tomas shot waves of shocking energy at them.

"We are *not* fine," Eve corrected herself. She stood up and turned around, watching as Kranthar flew back up to the dome, his eyes glowing with electricity.

"The city isn't flying fast enough to out-speed Kranthar," Starlocke pointed out. "It is in a very vulnerable position. One wrong move and the civilization could be knocked out of the sky."

"And the future with it..." Tomas commented. "Eve, think of something."

"I'll go out there and fight him," Eve decided.

Tomas looked at her, worry flashing in his eyes, though his face disguised it. "Think of something better," he said.

"I'll come with you." Ganto kicked his jetpack into gear. "Gonna collect my bounty and bounce. Spark those wings up Eve, we're going for a fly." He floated up and looked down at the crowds of early Andromedans below him. "*Sendi nescendi ra caps!*" he yelled.

Eve sparked her back aflame as she prepared to form wings at her shoulder blades. "Don't think too hard," she reminded herself. "You got this."

## ❖ CHAPTER 6 ❖

The dome around the city started to lower, per Ganto's request.

Tomas looked at Eve, worriedly. "It's gonna be hard to breathe out there without the box, the atmosphere is getting thin. Don't stray too far away from it."

"Got it." Eve nodded. She glanced at Ganto. "Let's go."

Ganto zoomed out of the dome, away from the small flying city.

Eve leapt from the city, diving down into a free fall. The box dove after her. The dome closed behind them as they both flew down toward Kranthar. The box spun quickly by Eve, trying to keep up.

"What's the plan?" Ganto asked.

Before Eve could answer, Kranthar sped past them, flying in front of them and circling both them and the city as it rose. Within the city boundaries, Terror drones bombarded the ancient Andromedans. Starlocke and Tomas both did their best to strike them from the sky.

"I don't have one, go crazy," Eve answered Ganto. She turned around clumsily, arms low by her side, aflame with phlasma. Phlasma spewed from her feet like rockets, keeping her ascending with the city.

Eve tried not to look down, as a sinking feeling in her stomach started to make her feel uneasy. She glanced down for a moment. She thought that the clouds obscuring the ground would ease her fear of heights. She was wrong.

She looked back up and shook her head. She opened and closed her eyes, trying to adjust herself. The box was giving her a breathable atmosphere, but she was still lightheaded.

The sky around them darkened as they had begun to leave the atmosphere of Earth. Kranthar was flying right at Eve, head on. Wings formed at her shoulders, and she gave herself a push.

"Eve, watch out," Ganto warned.

Those weren't words Eve wanted to hear this high up.

"Eve!" Ganto yelled.

Kranthar was getting too close.

Eve closed her eyes and held out her hands. Phlasma shot from them uncontrollably. The flames spread far, pushing against Kranthar's face, but he kept flying forward.

"Eve!" Ganto launched himself forward, pushing Eve out of the way, just as Kranthar passed them by. The flames from her hands subsided.

## ❖ CHAPTER 6 ❖

The box was caught in the crossfire, headbutted by Kranthar. It quickly lost its glow and began to plummet to the Earth's surface.

"Oh no." Ganto watched as the box fell. His ticket home was fading away.

Eve struggled for air. "I can't breathe…" she gasped.

"Well don't tell me that! Save your breath!" Ganto scolded her.

Eve's eyes rolled into the back of her head. The flames at her feet, keeping her afloat, burned out, and her wings vanished.

"Uh oh." Ganto watched as Eve too started to fall.

Kranthar had taken notice.

"*Losi gorsh,*" Ganto commented to himself as he curled his arms in and rolled forward, quickly shooting his arms out as he began to dive down. His jetpack propelled him down faster, quickly catching up with Eve.

Kranthar shook his head and flapped his wings, launching himself up before he turned his head down and swooped over the rising city, jumping over it like a whale over a boat as he too began to launch down, chasing after Ganto, Eve, and the box.

"Starlocke, what's happening out there?" Tomas asked.

"Uh," Starlocke hesitated as he looked over the edge while Tomas was busy fighting off Terror drones. "Should I sugar-coat it?"

Ganto turned his head and saw Kranthar quickly approaching him. "*Jith*," he whispered to himself. He held his arms to his side and began to speed up faster. He caught up to Eve and looked at her unconscious body falling through the sky. They were approaching the clouds. "Sorry, Eve," he said as he sped forward, past her, and to the box.

Atmosphere reentry began to burn away at Ganto as he sped ahead. His jetpack beeped, seemingly as a warning. "I know, I know!" he yelled.

As he approached the box, he held out his hand. He looked back, watching as Kranthar hugged his wings to the side of his body, making him more aerodynamic as he sped toward Eve with an open mouth. The burning atmosphere sparked flames at the side of Kranthar's hard exoskeleton, surrounding him in a bright orange flame.

Ganto grabbed ahold of the box, just as he passed through a cloud. The box was crushed on one side, shattered in the corners. "Ha ha!" Ganto exclaimed triumphantly. "Now to get back home…"

## ❖ CHAPTER 6 ❖

"Warning!" the box flashed its lights. "Damaged: one teleport available, atmosphere correction abilities destroyed. Warning!"

"Dammit." Ganto flipped his body up, holding onto the box. He didn't want to, but he changed his mind. His jetpack pushed himself up forward, but slowly. The rocket propelling him flickered, giving out. His jetpack continued to beep. It had been severely damaged. He continued to fly up toward Eve. Kranthar was drawing closer.

The box repeated itself, "Damaged: one teleport available—"

"I heard you the first time!" Ganto yelled. "Don't rub it in!" The beeping of his jetpack grew louder, and more prevalent. "Agh!" Ganto closed his eyes. He held his arms back and launched forward, throwing the box into the air. It hit Eve in the back, teleporting her away. She landed in the flying city, next to Tomas and Starlocke.

Ganto's jetpack turned off, and he started free falling. Kranthar's mouth opened wider as he came closer to Ganto, and where Eve once was. Ganto closed his eyes.

Eve shot up on the ground, gasping for air. "Ganto!" she yelled with a gasp.

Starlocke looked out over the dome, watching as Kranthar drew closer. The stone in his forehead glowed as he launched himself forward at the dome.

The structure of the dome warped in front of him, creating a sort of hole as he sped through, to Tomas and Eve like a lightning bolt, in split second, but to Starlocke, his time altered, it was nothing more than a jog. He spun and tucked his legs in, diving down like a dolphin as he approached Kranthar at the speed of lightning. He reached out his paws, making contact with the tip of Kranthar's tail. He ran forward, on the back of the massive beast, until he jumped over his head, leaving a streak of lightning behind him.

He curled forward, rolling and pushing himself forward with phlasma. He grabbed ahold of Ganto in his mouth and turned to Kranthar's underside, where he began to run up his belly, just as Kranthar's mouth shut, in slow motion. Starlocke ran up the beast and launched himself into the domed city, rolling on the ground and letting go of Ganto.

It all happened so fast. A flash of light, and a bolt of lightning struck down Kranthar's back and up his underside, wrapping around him and burning his exoskeleton and exposed underbelly.

Kranthar screamed in pain and fell through the clouds.

## ❖ CHAPTER 6 ❖

"What the hell just happened!?" Ganto yelled.

"That won't stop him for long," Starlocke determined. "We need to get out of here."

Eve looked up, admiring the stars. The city had made it into outer space. "Woah…"

"Enough staring, what do we do?" Ganto asked Eve. "I saved your life by the way," he told her. "I coulda went home but I didn't. Don't know if you noticed, you were sleeping on the job."

"And I saved yours," Starlocke barked at Ganto.

"Bad move, honestly," Ganto said as he stood up. "I wouldn't have."

Eve shook her head and reminded herself of the reality of the situation. She stood up and looked around at the people staring at her for help. She turned her attention to Tomas. "You can make wormholes." She pointed to him.

"Well…" he shrugged.

"Make one." Eve pointed above the city, into space.

Tomas took a deep breath, and concentrated. A faint purple glow shone through his shirt by his chest as he raised his arms. He spread his arms away, and a wormhole began to form in the space above them. The city kept rising and rising until it flew right through the portal. Tomas clapped his hands together, quickly shutting the wormhole and disallowing Kranthar's passage through it. Eve stared at the space above her and was dumbfounded at what she saw.

Ganto's eyes glowed with happiness as he was met with a familiar sight, and Starlocke admired it with him.

The flying city was quickly approaching a small terrestrial planet, but behind the planet, overwhelmingly massive in the sky, taking up most of the space ahead of them, was the magnificent, blue-green, double-crossed ringed gas planet, Ilsose.

"Home..." Ganto clicked his mandibles.

The city started to right itself in space and prepare for a landing on the terrestrial planet ahead.

"Where are we..." Eve asked, awestruck.

"The Andromeda Galaxy." Tomas stared ahead, mesmerized. "The Ilsose District. Home of the planets Parv, IS-200, Dile, Basid, Loron, and that planet right there..." He pointed ahead at the planet the city was approaching, "Is about to be known as Andrometron. And the de facto 'sun' of the system, the gas giant..." He pointed at Ilsose.

"The rightful home of the Ilsians. Ilsose," Ganto spoke up, staring at Ilsose. "And in this time, it still is..." He couldn't take his eyes off the planet. "Until the Andromedan humans

## ❖ CHAPTER 6 ❖

start moving in, and then the Lorinians come and kick all of us out." Ganto spat.

"So, this is the start of it, huh…" Eve looked around the city they were passengers of, watching the people admire the planet they'd begun landing on. "The Andromedan Empire."

"You could call it that." Tomas crossed his arms. "Yeah, this is it."

"Is this a good thing?" Eve asked.

"That depends on how you look at it." Tomas shrugged.

Starlocke closed his eyes and his third eye glowed. He shook his head and it stopped. "I'm getting conflicting information about the goodness of this thing."

Eve chuckled.

"On one hand, you have leaders like Miser from Andrometron, and clones like Foxtrot… but then you have figures like Canshla, and Rhey…" Starlocke looked down, and his ears drooped.

Tomas looked away at the mention of those names.

"Who?" Eve asked.

"Not important." Tomas stepped forward.

Eve watched as the shield around the city lowered and the city landed. The air on the planet was breathable, and the people instantly set out to explore.

"We should be heading back." Tomas looked around.

"There's a problem." Ganto raised his arm to get attention on him, then he pointed his arm down at the box. It had lost all of its glow. "Kranthar broke it."

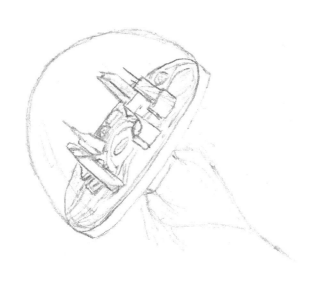

## ❖ Chapter 7 ❖
# A Savior

"You really did save me, huh?" Eve laughed.

"I did." Ganto nodded. "Don't take it personally, just for the universe."

"You sacrificed yourself for me, didn't you?" Eve smiled, she noticed Ganto's broken jetpack. "Thank you."

Ganto shrugged and wiped his face with his hand. He tilted his head and mumbled, "*Yeah, it's whatever...*"

Eve looked at Tomas. "How can we fix the box? You did it before, right?"

"I did." Tomas nodded. "But... I've lost my touch with... with everything. I'm not as great as I used to be at this sort of stuff, fixing things for the Sentinel and all. He was a great scientist, a genius, at his peak he could fix anything in a matter of minutes. This is more broken than when you brought it in to me before."

"Then how can I fix it? I'm not a genius." Eve leaned over to pick up the box, admiring it.

"I am." Starlocke pronounced, adjusting his stance to appear taller. "But I can't help much, I don't have… hands." He looked down, drooping his ears as he shuffled his paws in front of him.

Eve smiled.

"That's not cute, Eve, that's embarrassing," Starlocke growled.

"Hey, what did I say about reading my mind!" Eve chuckled.

"Hey, I'm a genius too, and I've got six hands," Ganto chimed in.

Eve, Starlocke, and Tomas all looked at Ganto.

Eve started to chuckle.

Tomas laughed too, lightly.

Starlocke stayed silent, but followed up with, "You can't tell, but I found that very amusing."

"Hey!" Ganto held his hands to his hips. "Ilsians are innovators! Scientists! Tinkerers! I can help out!"

## ❖ CHAPTER 7 ❖

"This is a time machine, not a spaceship," Tomas argued.

"Bet." Ganto snatched the box from Eve's hands and stormed into a nearby building in the small city. It seemed to be an armor or weaponsmith of some sorts.

An Andromedan gave him a weird look, but Ganto said something in Andromedan that pacified him.

Eve, Starlocke, and Tomas followed Ganto into the building.

Ganto slammed the box onto the table, and pried it open, taking off the panels and revealing the small core – a metal sphere with a slot for a single rêve stone, Matrona's.

A small yellow square of paper fell out.

"What's that?" Eve walked forward.

"Paper?" Ganto questioned. "That's a dumb component for a time machine. Maybe I don't know how to fix this thing, whoever made it was dumb."

Tomas looked at it, confused.

Ganto picked up the paper. "Oh wait... It's for you."

Ganto handed the paper to Eve.

It was a sticky note.

❖ A SAVIOR ❖

*For the new Sentinel:*

*Vaxx, if you're reading this, it means I'm gone.*

*But you knew this would happen. I knew this would happen.*

*When I'm gone, I need someone to finish what I started.*

*Don't do what I would've done. Do what you would do.*

*Refuse to live in my shadow. Make a name for yourself.*

*You aren't the Sentinel; you are better than that.*

*I was nothing more than the Sentinel.*

*You are our savior. Save the universe.*

*I believe in you, my love.*

*We will see each other again.*

*I promise.*

*Love, Your Sentinel*

"It wasn't for me..." Eve put the note down. She looked at Tomas. "Who's Vaxx?"

Tomas picked up the note and read it. "Things didn't go as planned for the Sentinel. Her wife was supposed to replace her. But they died together. The Sentinel didn't choose you as her replacement. The box did."

"Why?" Eve asked.

"Because it knew," Tomas said.

### ❖ CHAPTER 7 ❖

"Knew what?"

"What it needed to. Look, just because the note isn't for you, doesn't mean it doesn't carry with it the same sentiment. Live by those words, savior."

Eve turned away and looked at the pieces of the box that Ganto had dismantled. "What now?"

"All the parts are here that I need," Ganto said. "All it needs is a new shell and a reboot to the system. A quick shock should turn it back on.

"Where are we gonna get a new shell?" Eve asked.

Starlocke wandered outside. He approached the white and chrome tower, and headbutted a panel of the plating until it fell off.

He wandered back with the piece in his mouth, wagging his tail, then plopped it onto the table.

His forehead stone glowed as a small laser of phlasma shot from it, cutting the panel into six evenly sized squares. He then blasted the exact center of each face with a thicker laser blast, creating an evenly sized hole in the center of each.

Ganto took his sharpened hands and used them to scrape lines into the squares, making indents the same as the previous design, four lines around the circle, each drawn to the edge of the square.

He then pulled out a small tablet from his jetpack and plugged it into the core. Thousands of lines of code flashed onto his screen.

"Woah. Messy," he commented.

Eve grabbed a hammer from a tool rack on a wall and approached the six panels of the box.

She picked up parts of the previous box's design, the red outer shell, and began to heat up the edges with her flaming hands.

She placed small fragments of the shell onto the back of the panels, over the circle hole, and melded them to it, haphazardly hammering them in.

Eve then held up four of the panels around one, holding them in place as Starlocke blasted their edges with a small laser, melding the faces together.

Ganto unplugged the core of the box from his tablet. "The core should be rebooted; everything's intact." He placed it inside of the box, where it began to float in the center. "Not so bad if you ask me," Ganto bragged. "For an Ilsian."

Tomas placed the last face of the box on top, and Starlocke melded it on.

## ❖ CHAPTER 7 ❖

Eve hammered the edges of the box, smoothing them out into a flat face, giving the box flat edges, and a smooth look. She held up the box, her fingertips sparking.

Tomas helped, sparking electricity between his hands and the box. Starlocke did the same with his forehead stone.

The box glowed.

Light shone through the red in the circles of each face, and the box turned on, its core humming. "Hello," it spoke. It floated up, spinning around the three of them. It worked.

Eve smiled. "We did it."

The chrome and white box spun around, whirring its core.

Ganto stepped back, proud of himself. "Nice."

"Well…" Tomas stared at the box. "We should be headed back now. Let's take it for a test run, shall we?" He held out his hand.

Eve looked around at the city outside. "Will these people be fine?" she asked.

"The Andromedans? More than fine," Ganto grumbled. He held out his hand too.

Starlocke nodded, then ran, becoming a bolt of lightning as he vanished.

❖ A SAVIOR ❖

Eve smiled, and placed her hand on the box, holding out her other for Tomas and Ganto.

They flashed away.

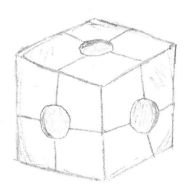

❖ Chapter 8 ❖
# The Sentinel's Sanctuary

Eve spent weeks living in the house in Monterey. She trained and she slept. The days would have been empty if not for Starlocke's company.

Ganto was there too, but he was Ganto, and his company wasn't nearly as enjoyable.

Tomas spent his days combing through files upon files of information on his computer. Eve couldn't figure out what it was he was doing.

One morning, Eve, Ganto, Tomas, and Starlocke were together in the living room, not unlike most days. Tomas stood idly at his computer.

Eve sat next to Ganto at the couch, and Starlocke had jumped up and curled himself next to her like a massive house dog. Eve waited for Tomas to say something.

While she waited, her mind drifted to her family. She hadn't been gone long, but she was already missing them. She shook her head, trying to drop the thought. Tomas still hadn't said anything, and she kept waiting. Tomas kept clicking through folders and folders of information, occasionally checking maps and strange consoles.

Ganto was impatiently tapping a beat against his legs with his six arms and clicking his mandibles together to supplement the beat.

Tomas turned to him and Ganto stopped tapping.

"Eve, there's something I have to tell you... I didn't want to have to tell you yet, but... I guess I'll only say what's important."

"Alright..." Eve wondered what Tomas was holding back.

"Kranthar won't be the only one after you. There's been a... galactic bounty... let's call it... set on you. It's actually carried over from the Sentinel and... how do I say this, time travel isn't very uncommon among the Sentinel's enemies, and they'll find you."

"How big of a bounty?" Ganto spoke up.

Eve and Starlocke both looked at him angrily.

"What?" he asked.

## ❖ CHAPTER 8 ❖

"And they're also targeting me." Tomas broke eye contact. "You and I shouldn't be in the same place all the time. They'll find us quicker. I need you to go off on your own way and be a Sentinel, save the Multiverse without me while I draw away any stray threats."

Eve flinched. Her face scrunched up in thought.

"That said," Tomas continued, "We're going to need to go one more place before I leave you alone."

"What? Where?" Eve stood up, ready to leave.

"A planet created by the Sentinel himself, and the safe haven for the humans of the future, Amalga-5." Tomas held out his hand for Eve. Ganto slid off the couch and ran up to her, holding one of his arms up to them. They flashed away.

When Eve appeared in a generic suburban neighborhood, she was shocked, expecting to be on a magnificent futuristic planet beyond her imagination.

Starlocke flashed into view.

"This…" Eve looked around. "Is disappointing."

"Look." Tomas tapped her shoulder and turned her around.

Standing before her was a statue of a man in a suit pointing towards the sky, unknown to Eve, it was Miser.

As a circular stone nestled within the base slowly rotated, it revealed the stone carved depictions of grand statues that baffled Eve, despite all she'd seen.

Vistor, Ganto, Terri, Vogar, the Sentinel and Vaxx embracing, Nick Tempus, Agro, Foxtrot, the Life and Death Masters themselves, Time and Celestae, and the Paradox Master flying with his phlasmatic wings behind them.

"Woah…" Eve couldn't keep her eyes off the grand statue. Starlocke walked up to Eve and sat down, also admiring the statue.

"Is that me?" Ganto looked at the immortalized version of himself carved in stone. "What is this…" A guilt brewed in his stomach. It was the team he had abandoned, and the statue included him.

"Amalga-5 was sent back in time by the Sentinel to act as a failsafe for the end of the universe. A member of her army, Miser, was put in charge of this planet and evidently, he told his people the story of the Sentinel's Army. He was a great leader," Tomas explained.

"How long has this planet been here?" Eve asked.

"A few hundred years. Miser became king of Canam. It's been so long. I'm sure he's dead by now… and he would have died never knowing if the Sentinel's Army actually did it,

## ❖ CHAPTER 8 ❖

if the universe was saved... if his work meant anything." Tomas looked away from the statue.

"Tomas..." Eve held out her arm.

"I'm fine." Tomas looked away from her. "Go around and explore, talk to people. Learn some things, use the information to the best of your ability and I'll be off."

"Why can't you just tell me things and make this easier?" Eve asked.

"You need to learn how to act on your own, Eve."

"Alright." Eve turned around and started walking down a hill.

"I know where we are." Ganto followed after her. Starlocke stayed behind with Tomas, walking and talking with him.

"How?"

"I've been here before, this town. It's where the Sentinel and I properly introduced ourselves. There should be a bar down there by the beach." Ganto started walking ahead.

"You heard Tomas, it's been a few hundred years, who knows if it's still there."

"Come on!" Ganto walked faster and Eve had to keep pace.

They eventually came across the very same bar that Ganto was talking about. A sign out front advertised, 'Great drinks, since 3057,' and they walked in. Ganto started talking with a few people, and Eve sat down.

A waiter came by and asked, "What brings you in today?"

"Um. Just visiting," Eve said.

"Oh, out of towner, huh?" The waiter smiled. "Where are you from?"

"Earth," Eve said, not expecting much a reaction.

The waiter jumped back, startled and completely taken aback by her statement.

Ganto turned around and chuckled at Eve. "Oh no, no. Why did you say that?"

"*Earth?*" the waiter asked quietly.

"Yes," Eve made clear.

"Nobody's come here from Earth for hundreds of years. Where you really from?"

"I'm from Palm Springs, California, 1982, the planet Earth."

"How?"

"Eve…" Ganto nudged her.

"I'm…" Eve hesitated. "The Sentinel."

## ❖ CHAPTER 8 ❖

Ganto slapped his face with all of his hands.

"Okay, nice trick. What'll it be today?" the waiter asked.

Eve's fists flared with bright purple flames and she showed them to the waiter.

"Ah, she's just a Gar!" someone in the bar yelled out.

"A what?" Eve looked to the man; her flames dimmed.

"You don't know what a Gar is?" a woman across the bar laughed, "So much for a Sentinel."

"What are you talking about?" Eve squinted in confusion.

The Lorinian bartender in the bar leaned over the counter. "A couple hundred years ago the surviving Gars moved into this planet after Vogar from the Sentinel's Army told 'em it was safe. They've been thriving here ever since. Even got a couple of their own countries now," he explained. "They think you're one of 'em on account of their shapeshifting abilities, and control over phlasma."

"Yeah! And if you were the Sentinel, you'd know that!" a woman across the bar yelled at Eve.

"Ok, look." Eve held out her hands to defend herself. "I'm not the Sentinel, I'm her replacement." She gestured toward the box floating by her shoulder. "The time machine chose me, and now I'm supposed to save the universe."

"Ah!" Ganto held up his arms, "Don't—"

"Save the universe?" the bartender asked.

"Eve..." Ganto approached her.

"You don't know..." Eve looked around at everyone. "You don't know why your planet was sent back in time..."

"What?" the waiter stepped back.

"Eve, come on, let's get out of here," Ganto pushed Eve towards the exit, looking around nervously.

"What do you mean by save the universe...?" the waiter asked, a hint of hesitant fear wavered in his voice.

"Are we in danger?" a woman looked around, afraid.

"Let's get out of here." Ganto made it to the exit with Eve when the door was blocked.

"Tomas," Eve greeted.

"Starlocke." Ganto nodded.

"Is everything alright here?" Tomas asked, looking around at the confused bar patrons.

"Yup." Eve nodded.

"Alright, well..." Tomas closed his eyes and stopped, like he didn't want to say what he was about to say. "I'll be going now."

## ❖ CHAPTER 8 ❖

"Right now?" Eve asked.

Without so much as an answer, Tomas vanished, startling Eve. "Okay…" she spoke softly.

"What now?" Ganto asked, turning around, "Because I don't particularly feel like answering to these guys."

"We have a problem." Starlocke looked to Eve. "Come to me." He vanished.

"You heard the dog." Ganto reached out for Eve's arm. "Let's go." The two of them flashed away, leaving behind the confused bar patrons, murmuring to themselves.

### ❖ Chapter 9 ❖
# Modius

Eve and Ganto appeared on the surface of Modius, next to Starlocke. Eve looked up into the night sky and saw the distant, dark, ringed planet Tornlozor, hiding behind Nidus, and eclipsing Illiosopherium.

"Home planet of the Terrors." Starlocke looked up at Tornlozor. "But apparently Kranthar doesn't like it enough to stay there."

"What do you mean?" Eve asked, uncomfortable at the mention of Kranthar.

"Well, first he stays in Russia, and now here?" Starlocke barked.

"He's here?" Ganto excitedly withdrew his rifle from his back and cocked it. The blue strips of light on the side

## ❖ CHAPTER 9 ❖

began to glow as it powered up. *"Alright alright alright..."* Ganto looked around.

"How do you know he's here?" Eve asked Starlocke.

"The Dragolupus have shared that information across our minds. He is digging through Modius and causing it pain."

"*MOGH*!!!" The ground grumbled and shook intensely. Rocks and boulders tumbled down the Crown Mountains behind them. The planet seemed to groan.

An explosion burst at the base of the impossibly tall mountain, and from it shot out Kranthar and a swarm of Terrors behind him. He had bored a tunnel through the entirety of Modius's Crown Mountain.

"Evelyn Sanchez!" Kranthar screeched.

Eve's fists flared with phlasma, and she stood at the ready, watching Kranthar's every move carefully.

"What a nuisance you are," Kranthar growled. "You share this quality with your entire planet..." Kranthar twitched his head towards Eve and snaked closer. "And Earth looks rather tasty to this beast." Kranthar looked down at the ground, gesturing towards Modius.

Starlocke growled.

Ganto lifted his rifle and was about to shoot, but Eve held out her arm at him, signaling him not to.

Kranthar lifted his head and floated softly onto the ground, curiously. The Terror drones floated around him slowly.

"You will not harm Earth. They did nothing to you." Eve tried to keep calm.

"Not yet they haven't." Kranthar clicked his jaw.

"How can we stop Modius?" Eve asked Starlocke.

"He's the last of the Quodstella, we can't kill him." Starlocke shook his head, thinking.

"Oh, so we agree on something then." Kranthar smiled at Starlocke. "Glad to see your allegiance to the Originals has not yet waned to oblivion. Come now, Starlocke, to salvation. Forget these pests."

"Your religious devotion to achieving an impossible reality is annoying, Kranthar," Starlocke barked.

Kranthar snaked his head back, offended.

Eve leaned over to Starlocke, quietly asking him, "Which side of the Crown Mountains are we on?"

"The North of Modius's head." Starlocke perked his ears up, he knew what Eve was planning. He barked at Kranthar, "You directed Modius' attention to Earth!"

"Indeed, I did." Kranthar smiled. "He was already headed for your solar system; all it took was distracting his

## ❖ CHAPTER 9 ❖

eyes toward Earth and causing him pain. His simple mind thinks that Earth hurt him. You can't turn him away from it now."

Eve turned her attention to Starlocke. "Starlocke, go!"

Starlocke ran through the tunnel in an electric flash. Eve held out for the box and Ganto and her flashed away, appearing far outside the other side of the tunnel just as Starlocke had finished running through.

Eve looked over the landscape, which was vastly different from the other side of Modius.

They were far from the mountains now. All around them, instead of bright green grass, the ground was nothing but a flat plain of purple-grayish stone, stretching to the horizon.

The rock was covered in craters, and scarred, it seemed. Eve assumed that eating planets could get dangerously messy.

She turned her head slightly and stared in awe at what lay ahead of her. A steep cliff dropped into a vast ocean of bubbling and constantly moving lava. "What's that..." She stared at it.

"Modius's Western sea," Starlocke answered. "His left eye..."

"How much time do we have before Kranthar gets through the tunnel?" Eve asked Starlocke. But before he could answer, Kranthar burst through the ground near them and began to approach Eve.

"*MOGH*!!" the planet groaned again, in more pain than before it seemed. The lava in the ocean splashed up slightly in waves, and the ground rumbled.

"Get on!" Starlocke gestured to his back with his head.

"What?" Eve was startled at the request.

Ganto jumped onto Starlocke's back without a second thought. Eve jumped on shortly after, and Starlocke's paws sparked with electricity. He ran, and Kranthar followed him, screeching.

Starlocke leapt from the cliff's edge of Modius's eye. Eve screamed as they approached the lava, though Ganto exclaimed, "Woohoo!"

Kranthar dove down the edge of the cliff and leveled out just before hitting the lava. Terror drones materialized through the walls of the cliff, following after Kranthar and speeding ahead.

Starlocke's forehead stone glowed as a solid chunk of phlasma formed in the lava ahead of him.

He landed on it, but didn't linger as he kept running forward, his sparking paws and speed keeping him from sinking into the lava.

## ❖ CHAPTER 9 ❖

Ganto stood up on Starlocke's back, and Eve held his feet in place as he began rapid-firing at the Terror swarm.

Eve reached her hand back and blind shot a fireball at Kranthar's faceplate, hitting him straight on, causing him to flinch.

The heat of the lava was getting to Eve. "Where are we going?" she asked Starlocke. Sweat beaded down her forehead, her hands grew slippery. She couldn't hold on with much grip.

"Regrettably, we must injure Modius quite significantly to save your planet," Starlocke answered. "We need to get to his pupil. It's rather large, we can't miss it."

"How big?" Eve asked.

"About the size of an average continent on your planet," Starlocke lowered his head, as if scanning the lava.

"What the hell, how big is Modius?" Eve yelled.

"Huge!" Ganto yelled as he kept firing away. He stopped as he noticed something concerning. "Uhhh, *guys...*"

Starlocke turned his head for a moment to see what Ganto was worried about.

Seemingly catching up to their speed, the cliff appeared to be chasing them.

"Hold on!" Starlocke yelled, "Prepare for a blink!"

"What!?" Eve turned around. The massive slab of land was fast approaching. Kranthar and his drones were not turning away, but as the land started sliding closer and closer, a wave of lava was being pushed up with it.

"Can't you go any faster?" Eve yelled.

"Much faster, yes!" Starlocke howled, "But do you *want* to fall off?"

"Good point." Eve looked away from the approaching eyelid landmass, and ahead she spotted a different, stationary landmass.

It was glowing purple, and evidently it was made entirely of phlasma crystal. "Is that the pupil!?" she asked.

"Hold on!" Starlocke yelled. He jumped, launching himself over the rocky beach of the pupil landmass.

Ganto jumped from Starlocke's back and began floating with his jetpack.

Eve jumped and kept herself afloat, propelling herself with a constant stream of phlasma. Starlocke kept afloat with some sort of electric power at his paws.

They floated just barely higher than the approaching land mass' edge.

❖ CHAPTER 9 ❖

Kranthar flew up and out of the reach of the eyelids just as the two massive land masses collided, smashing together and pushing up a huge wave of lava.

Kranthar stopped in his tracks as the lava wave approached him.

His swarm of Terror drones surrounded him, and the lava wave blanketed over him. Eve, Starlocke, and Ganto held their breath for a moment, wondering if he had survived.

The lava settled and the eyelids began to open once more, and there Kranthar was. His entire drone swarm had burnt away, but he was kept alive.

Starlocke fell and landed on the edge of the pupil landmass, and Eve and Ganto did the same.

"You won't accomplish anything from this!" Kranthar yelled. "Nothing!"

Eve glanced at Starlocke.

Starlocke had read Eve's mind. She knew what she was thinking and agreed with her plan. He nodded.

Eve knelt down and placed her hands against the burning hot crystal that made up Modius's pupil, and she concentrated.

She would have to drum up a significant amount of phlasmatic strength to blind a continent sized pupil, but Eve knew she could do it.

She closed her eyes hard, and just as she realized she was trying too hard, her shoulders loosened, and her eyes opened. They glowed a bright purple.

Her hands sparked, and the crystal underneath her cracked, ever so slightly. "Starlocke." She looked up, "Go to the other pupil."

Starlocke nodded and vanished.

"Ganto. Float," Eve instructed him.

Ganto kicked his jetpack back on and floated above the eye.

Kranthar laughed nervously, "What is this?" he questioned.

Eve concentrated harder and closed her eyes again. She thought of home, and Andrew. She thought of Tomas and Starlocke's training.

She thought of school and her friends, and longing for going back to it all. The crystal cracked more, and the electricity spread rapidly, consuming the entire pupil.

"What is this!?" Kranthar backed up.

## ❖ CHAPTER 9 ❖

Eve opened her eyes as they sparked with energy. "Leave me alone," she demanded. With a large shockwave of sound, the entirety of Modius' pupil cracked and shattered in an instant.

"*MOGH!!!*" the planet yelled in pain.

"Come on, come on," Eve mumbled to herself, waiting.

"*MOGH!!!*" the planet yelled again.

She knew that Starlocke had destroyed the other pupil too. She stood up and outstretched her arms victoriously, half bowing and smiling with the smuggest smirk she could manage.

"Modius is blind. He can't see the Earth, now he can't eat it."

"He's already headed for it, you've accomplished nothing!" Kranthar snapped.

When Starlocke appeared next to Eve on the floating chunk of pupil in the lava sea, she turned to him with a smile. Andrew had crossed her mind, and so too did his obsession with comics and movies.

"Do you know that one Superman movie?" Eve asked Starlocke.

"I'm a Dragolupus," Starlocke answered.

"There's this scene where he flies around the Earth so fast that he spun it the other direction. If we can get all the Dragolupus on Modius to run around the planet until they face him *away* from Earth... would that work?" she asked.

Starlocke lowered his head and thought for a moment. He looked up and nodded and vanished in a puff of electric smoke and a blast of wind. Eve looked down at Ganto.

"What do you want me to do?" he asked.

Eve gestured toward Kranthar. "Collect your bounty."

Ganto smiled and cocked the rifle. "About time."

Eve flashed away to the edge of Modius's eyelid and waited. In the far distance she watched as Ganto fought Kranthar.

The winds picked up. Electric sparks whizzed past Eve infrequently, but eventually a storm of rampaging bolts of phlasmatic lighting jet past her.

"Yes!" she yelled. She could tell that the Dragolupus had followed her plan.

She looked up at Tornlozor, Nidus, and Illiosopherium in the sky above, and watched as they started to slowly pass by in the sky.

The sky darkened as Black Star 7 fell below the horizon. It was working.

## ❖ CHAPTER 9 ❖

Kranthar's body crashed into the hard stone ground beside Eve, and she stumbled away. Ganto hit the ground with a resounding thud and rolled across the stone.

"Ganto!" Eve jumped up and ran after him.

He jumped up and stood quickly, teetering on his feet. "Did I kill the bastard? Is he dead? Where's my money…" Ganto looked around in a confused daze.

"Are you alright?" Eve asked.

"I'm fine, I'm fine. Got this bug armor to keep me going." Ganto patted on his chitin exoskeleton.

"Yeah, but so does he." Eve pointed at Kranthar, who slowly flew up again. His Terror drones helped lift him into the sky as he started to evacuate back into space.

"Coward!" Ganto shook his arms at him.

Just then, every running Dragolupus came to an abrupt stop. The ground shook underneath them and in an instant Ganto and Eve were surrounded on all sides by the majestic creatures.

Starlocke approached Eve and sat down.

A Dragolupus walked up to Eve, and with a soft voice it spoke, "We conversed with each other while we ran, and have made a decision on our future. We would all like your opinion on the matter."

"Oh… Sure…" Eve stuttered, confused as to why a being like a Dragolupus, let alone all of them, would be concerned with her opinion. She thought that maybe this was what being a Sentinel was like.

"We've determined that it is unsafe for us as a society to continue living like parasites on this Quodstella. We would like to know, in our effort to move away from this place, should we consider Amalga-5 an option? We wouldn't like to intrude, but if you would have us, we would be grateful for the support."

"Oh." Eve stepped back and thought about it. "Oh… I don't know, I mean, they'd probably be pretty accepting of it there… They've got Gars living there, I'm sure they'd be happy to accept another Original."

Eve felt confident in her reasoning, but it still felt strange to be making such large decisions for an entire planet without input from them.

"Thank you." The Dragolupus bowed, and they all turned their heads up.

"Wait!" Eve held out a hand and they stopped. "Maybe Starlocke and I should go there first and let them know… so they don't think it's an invasion."

## ❖ CHAPTER 9 ❖

"Excellent foresight." Starlocke nodded. He vanished in an instant afterward.

Eve held out her hand for Ganto's, and they flashed away.

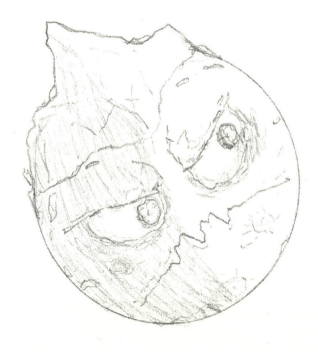

❖ Chapter 10 ❖
# The Raptor Cavalry

Eve, Ganto, and Starlocke appeared in front of the capital building of Canam on Amalga-5. The city was farther inland, and the buildings were built ornately, and in the style of ancient Earth empires. They approached a sort of castle-like building.

"What is this fancy place?" Ganto asked. "I don't like it... it's aura is smug and elitist."

Starlocke lowered his head as his forehead stone glowed. The three of them continued approaching the building.

Starlocke lifted his head.

"Hm. Interesting. This is the Castle of the Miser family. His family lineage has been ruling this country since the planet was sent back through time, seemingly to keep the Sentinel's request for Miser to keep her planet safe."

## CHAPTER 10

"We need to talk to the person in charge," Eve determined. They approached the building's entrance and knocked. The door opened to a Lorinian guard looking down on the trio with a judging eye.

"What do you want?" she asked.

"Take me to your leader," Eve said with a little smile. "I'm the Sentinel's replacement, this is Starlocke and Ganto."

"My heavens…" The Lorinian slugged back. "By all means." She gestured with her stubby arms for them to enter.

Eve, Starlocke, and Ganto wandered inside.

"Up the stairs, leads you straight to her," the Lorinian informed them.

When they made their way up the stairs, they approached an office marked by an important looking door, adorned with several decorations. Eve knocked once before the door swung open.

"Hello…" Eve looked in.

"I can't tell you how long I've been waiting for this moment." The woman sitting at a throne in the office smiled. "The Sentinel's replacement, huh?" She sat tall; her skin matched the tone of the light wooden throne she sat in. Her eyes were a deep velvet red, indicating a hint of Andromedan in her. Her hair was a deep dark brown.

"Eve Sanchez," Eve introduced herself.

"Queen Karina," Karina bowed in her seat. "Jane Miser Karina. Daughter of Miser and Gnatus, you may be familiar. Are you here about the, uh... *situation*?"

"So, you know about it?" Eve asked. Eve seemed relieved that at least someone had some idea of what was happening.

"How could I not?" Karina laughed.

"Hold on, *daughter?*" Ganto questioned.

"Well, adopted," Karina elaborated.

"No, I mean. Don't get me wrong, all humans look the same to me, but I can tell when they're super old. Hasn't Amalga-5 been chillin' here for more than a couple hundred years? How are you still alive? And not... old?"

Starlocke nudged Eve, reminding her of their reason for being there.

"Right," Eve acknowledged, and cleared her throat, "This is Starlocke," Eve gestured to him, "Do you have any open land for his species to move in? They're living situation is a bit tense, and they're looking for a safer place to stay."

"I believe we do have some a few colonies overseas open for such an occasion. We set them aside in the event that refugees would need a place to stay once we returned to the

### ❖ CHAPTER 10 ❖

Triplanetary Orbit, but, a home for the Dragolupus is as good a purpose as any, I suppose. And they don't up so much space with cities, so why not. If you don't mind me asking, why are they moving in?"

"Modius," Starlocke began.

"It's complicated," Ganto interrupted, "Can you please answer my question, I'm very confused."

"It's complicated," Karina brushed Ganto's question off with a hint of sarcasm. "Nothing dangerous is going on... Right?" Karina asked, leaning forward in her throne, curious. "You did say this didn't have to do with the end of the universe situation."

"Not really," Eve shook her head.

"But," Starlocke's ears drooped.

"Shh!" Eve hushed him.

"You guys are terrible at lying." Karina scoffed. "What's going on?"

"Do you want me to tell the Dragolupus that it's safe to move in or..." Eve shrugged.

"Already did." Starlocke looked to her. "They arrived the second it was approved."

"Oh... alright, wow." Eve shuffled her feet.

"So, do we tell her about Kranthar or…" Ganto tugged on Eve's flannel.

"Kranthar the Great?" Karina asked. "He was killed over… what a thousand years ago, now? Right? What about him? Or am I thinking about something else…"

"He's alive in our time," Eve said. "We've been fighting him. He's trying to change the future and that could break the universe even more, apparently."

"But you have it under control?" Karina asked.

Eve looked to Ganto and Starlocke. Their faces seemed confident, and it assured her in her thinking. "Yes. We have it under control, at least for now."

"That's good to hear." Karina smiled. "For a moment I thought I was the only one doing anything to help the universe out. Learning of your efforts calms me greatly, thank you."

"What exactly *are* you doing to help besides enforcing a monarchy?" Ganto asked in a sort of belittling tone. "And don't dodge the question this time."

"Our monarchy is mostly symbolic. We have a proper government. Otherwise, the people would riot. I'm in charge of protecting this world, just as the Sentinel had instructed my father to do, and just as my father instructed me to do.

## ❖ CHAPTER 10 ❖

"He retired in his old age. He spent his retirement training me and living in peace with my other father. Then Gnatus passed, and Miser followed shortly, leaving me here to finish creating the army he started; to help fight whatever threat it is that we're dealing with here.

"I'm trying my best to keep the promise of my family. I'm going to protect Amalga-5 under any circumstances necessary. I won't let the Sentinel down. I won't let my fathers down. Or my people."

"How have you managed to protect Amalga-5 for so long?" Eve asked. "You make it sound like your fathers passed recently... Shouldn't you be dead?"

Ganto waited for an answer.

"I live each year one day a month."

"What does that even mean?" Eve asked.

"We have access to Gar-tech time travel. Isn't very advanced, we can't go back, but I use it to go forward. I check in one day a month, then travel to the next, skipping the rest of it. It guarantees I'll be around longer. I've been living this way since I was ten. I'm twenty now."

"Oh, so you answer her?" Ganto scoffed. "Lady, what's an army gonna do? We're not even sure if the threat we're dealing with is a physical one! The universe is dying!"

"Ganto, come on," Eve nudged him.

"What!? It's true!"

"Whatever the threat may be," Karina said, "I can assure you my army is ready to fight it."

"Can you show us?" Eve asked.

"Follow me." Karina stood from her throne and beckoned for the trio to follow her.

They walked through an ornately decorated hallway. As they passed armed guards and torches, the hallway grew darker, and less elaborate. The lavish walls of oak and pillars of polished marble faded away as the hallway formed into a steel enforced corridor.

Karina turned into an offshoot of the hallway and lead the group to an outside courtyard, built like a massive colosseum, with cages built into the structure, lining the large circular wall.

Eve tried to peer into the cages from afar but couldn't quite discern what was in them.

Karina explained as she walked to the center of the colosseum, "As much as we like to praise the Sentinel around here, we can't ignore that, pardon my French, he did some weird shit back in the day."

"Like what?" Eve asked.

## ❖ CHAPTER 10 ❖

"Well for starters, Amalga-5 is a planet which has an ecosystem comprised of organisms plucked from Earth's prehistory."

Eve looked at Karina with a blank stare, confused.

"That is to say," Karina clarified, "Most of the animals here are dinosaurs."

Eve's eyes widened as she looked to Starlocke for confirmation.

Starlocke nodded.

"That isn't where the weirdness ends, either," Karina continued. "We aren't clear on the exact details, but according to a few scattered records, one time, when the Sentinel was drunk on some old 18$^{th}$ century wine he had lying around, or something, he came to Amalga-5 to check up on the wildlife and drunkenly infused some dinosaurs with *phlasma powers*?"

"What?" Eve shook her head, taken aback.

"Amalga-5's pre-history and history is a complicated mess," Starlocke commented.

Karina approached a cage and opened it.

"Wait a minute," Eve stepped back a bit.

"No way..." Ganto clicked his mandibles into a smile.

"*Ryah!*"

A large feathery beast burst from the cage, whizzing past Karina.

Eve stepped back, her hands flaring to life with phlasma.

"Woah woah woah!" Karina held her hands out in front of Eve. "Calm down there, miss." Karina smiled.

The large beast ran circles around the colosseum before returning to Karina's side. It cocked its head in strange angles like a chicken, peering its eyes at Eve. It towered above her, menacingly. The creature resembled a hawk. Its body feathered in mahogany brown plumage, its legs long and slender like a falcon, its claws large and deadly. Its arms were feathered like wings, although they were clawed and fierce.

The creature's fingers ticked at its sides. The beast's long fanned tail swung side to side behind it excitedly. It clicked its lizard-like mouth open and shut, waiting for a command.

"Woah..." Eve stepped back, admiring the animal. "This... thing... has phlasma powers?" Eve asked.

"This is one of them that does, yeah," Karina smiled. "This one's mine, Koda." Karina patted the dinosaur on the side. "We have an army of these majestic animals. Turns out however long ago the Sentinel gave some members of this

❖ CHAPTER 10 ❖

species, Krondicoraptor, phlasma powers, apparently some of them passed on the ability. Except, genetically, it isn't very straight forward to pass on phlasma powers.

"The genetic offspring of phlasma-powered raptors had to have their powers sort of... how would you put it... awakened? We had to spark it out of them with a phlasmatic shock to the heart. Turns out not all of them have phlasma powers, but at least the leaders of each pack do. We figure we can use them to fight off whatever threat is coming."

"Not to be a pessimist, but I feel like they don't stand a chance," Eve said. "You don't have like, planes, or... or tanks? Or something else?" she asked. "It's the future, I feel like we're well past animal warfare."

"The people of Canam thought the same," Karina explained, "But technology can be hacked. Learning from history, namely the Galactic War, the best way to win these sorts of things is to fight phlasma with phlasma."

"And these creatures are trained?" Ganto asked, admiring Koda.

"My family pioneered dinosaur domestication. We were one of the first families on the planet to own a pet dinosaur.

"I stop by one day a month to help our training program. Koda comes with me. We've imprinted on them at birth. They've been selectively bred over generations for tameness. They're trained as well as any old Earth horses, hawks, or dogs.

"That isn't to say they don't act out occasionally. They can be dangerous, though that sort of is the point. So far our efforts seem to have paid off in our own past wars."

Eve held her head and paced. "This is ridiculous. This isn't real."

"Oh, honey, it is." Karina chuckled. "Trust me, we still aren't used to dinosaurs, even the children born here aren't. There's a human instinct to fear them. But the phlasma burning in the hearts of these animals... it's all that we have left of the Sentinel, besides you. We think that the Sentinel used one of the phlasmatic stones in his possession at the time to give these animals their powers. It could've been some of his memories, or some of him. So... The Sentinel lives on in the wildlife of Amalga-5."

Eve looked up at the raptor, staring into its eyes. Her image stared back, reflected in the round eyes of the beast. A surge ran through her, and for a moment she felt a deep connection with the animal.

## ❖ CHAPTER 10 ❖

"The Multiverse is in bigger danger than you realize," Ganto added, interrupting Eve's trance-like stare. Ganto continued, "I don't think a few raptors are going to change that. As cool and as weird as it is."

Karina looked down and walked back into the metal corridor leading into her castle. Eve, Starlocke, and Ganto followed her. Koda trotted behind her.

"It's better than nothing, isn't it?" Karina asked. "I'm sorry that you didn't come back to an army of Sentinels or something like that. But we couldn't recreate whatever it was that gave these creatures their abilities. Now, granted, when the time comes, I'm not sure they'll be of much help.

"We have the Gars and now the Dragolupus here on this planet, and I'm sure they'll fight if they need to. They'll be a better help. But you shouldn't discount the efforts of a few. The Sentinel's Army knew that." Karina looked to Ganto, Starlocke, and Eve. "You three should understand that more than most, I'd assume."

The three of them looked between themselves, thinking. Karina continued, "The three of you versus the universe. Must feel pretty helpless. For the longest time it's been just me. You guys came to me today, and you brought me hope. I had hoped that my efforts would do the same."

"Thank you, Karina," Eve said. "Your efforts aren't in vain." Eve patted Karina on the shoulder as they entered her throne room. "If it comes down to us needing your raptors, we'll be grateful. Hopefully we won't have to."

"What a nice way of saying thanks but no thanks," Ganto scoffed.

Eve slapped the back of Ganto's head.

"Shut it, butthead," Eve broke her serious tone. For a second she was reminded of Andrew, and a deep home sickness brewed in her stomach. She shook her head to rid herself of unwanted thoughts. She looked up at Karina. "We really do appreciate it."

Karina smiled. "No, I get it. No hard feelings. It is weird, I know it is." Karina patted the top of her raptor's head and tossed it a treat. "But you're right. Hopefully we won't ever need to use them. Last resort, for the worst-case scenario.

"The day that dinosaurs fight on the battlefield is the day we are truly desperate. Because for now we're safe, right? I mean we were sent back in time specifically to keep us safe. So we're all good, right?" Karina asked.

"Yeah…" Eve nodded. She sighed and looked down at Starlocke and Ganto. "So where we do go now?"

"Back to Monterey?" Starlocke asked.

## ❖ CHAPTER 10 ❖

"Tomas left us on our own," Eve reminded him.

"We could stay in my cave," Starlocke suggested. "We could use some rest."

"Hang on, a cave?" Karina interjected. "No. Come on, follow me."

Eve, Ganto, and Starlocke followed Karina as she sent Koda back to her cage. Karina led them down through a hall into a courtyard.

"These are the guest quarters, like my own personal hotel." She walked across the courtyard to a lobby. She grabbed keys off a wall and tossed them to Eve. "Make yourself at home. It's the least I can do."

"Thank you," Eve said. "I think I'll be heading to bed now. I'm tired as hell. This means a lot."

"No problem." Karina turned to leave.

"Wait, Karina... um... If nothing comes up tomorrow, could we talk about the war, maybe you could fill me in on some things."

"I'm sorry, but I'll be leaving in the morning."

"To where?" Ganto asked.

"Next month," Karina smirked.

"Ah. Right. What an annoying way to live."

"See you around, Eve," Karina waved goodbye. "You've got this. I believe in you."

"Thanks for the land," Starlocke bowed.

"My pleasure."

Karina left through the hall.

Eve rushed to find her room, unlock the door, and fall into bed. Her body tensed with her sore muscles. Phlasma burned in her veins and her head pounded. She fell asleep instantly. Ganto plopped himself on the ground. Starlocke curled near him.

❖ Chapter 11 ❖
# Vacation on Amalga-5

As Eve awoke on a sunny day in Canam she walked out onto the balcony in her room. She looked over the inner city, to the rolling hills and scattered homes throughout the fern-laden wilderness interwoven through the streets.

Birds and small dinosaurs sang from the trees and bushes. Children ran through the sidewalk, playing with robots and their little pet dinosaurs.

Eve leaned her head on her arms and sighed. Andrew would love this place.

A knock tapped at her door.

Eve turned around.

The door opened, revealing Starlocke.

"I didn't say you could come in."

"You were about to," Starlocke said. Before Eve could respond he added, "And I know you asked for me to stop reading your mind but it's so hard not to. It's how I communicate. I'm sorry."

"I understand. What's up?" Eve leaned against the railing.

"You're sad. And exhausted," Starlocke noticed of Eve. "I want to thank you for welcoming my people onto this planet. We should spend today leisurely. Relax."

Eve's shoulders loosened as she stood up straighter and took a deep breath. "I would like that."

Ganto burst into the room, rolling onto the floor as a cloud of feathers and incessant squawking followed him. He fell and let go as a small dinosaur escaped his grasp and ran past Eve, onto the balcony.

"Ah!" Eve jumped out of the way.

"Get back here!" Ganto launched himself with his jetpack, pouncing on the creature.

The colorful creature glided away off the balcony, away from Ganto.

"*Dammit...*" Ganto sat down and caught his breath. "We were almost friends."

Starlocke and Eve stared at Ganto.

❖ CHAPTER 11 ❖

"What?"

"Off to a relaxing start," Starlocke said.

Eve, Starlocke, and Ganto ventured out of Karina's palace and into the wider world of Amalga-5. Eve wandered to the library, to research the Galactic War, and the Sentinel, though as the power of Rogar and Rhey were laid out before Eve in plain statistical detail, her anxiety climbed.

Starlocke led her away from research and instead to a park. Ganto led Eve back to a bar. Eve wandered to a beach where she watched Andromedan families splash in the water, Gars bathe in the sun, and the people of Canam relax.

Ganto wandered to a place as simple as a grocery store, amazed at the efficiency of mass produce, jealous that all his planet had to offer was shady street market vendors.

Between the leisure, when Eve would return to Karina's palace, she trained with Ganto and Starlocke.

The brief reprieve from responsibility turned into a week, the week turned into two, and soon, a month had passed.

Eve's hands flared with phlasma. She let them down as they dimmed, and the flames dissipated.

"What's wrong?" Ganto asked. "I said hit me! Come on! I can take it!"

"No, it's not that..." Eve walked away from the courtyard, back toward the lobby of the palace's living quarters. "Something's not right."

Starlocke followed. "Could it be that it's been a while since you've actively fought to protect the universe?"

"Well, we aren't wasting any time," Ganto said. "With a time machine, stalling has no consequences."

As Eve made her way into the lobby, Karina and Koda appeared through a portal.

"Eve?" Karina asked. "You're still here?" She checked a display around her wrist. "Oh. It has been a month, I thought maybe I'd miscalculated my portal. What's up?"

"Sorry, it's just..." Eve rubbed her neck.

"It's alright, it's no issue, really, I'm just surprised, is all." Karina patted Koda as she led the beast through the lobby, to the courtyard.

Eve stood beside Ganto and Starlocke, realizing what the problem was.

❖ CHAPTER 11 ❖

"I'm not so sure I can handle saving the universe on my own."

Karina stopped in her steps and turned around. "That's not the most reassuring thing to be hearing."

"Tomas always told me where to go, but since he left... What next? There's no instruction booklet on how to save reality."

Karina chuckled. "You're telling me. If there was, I'd be doing it wrong." She gestured to her pet dinosaur. "No way that's on the list."

"Can you come with me?" Eve asked. "I need someone by my side."

"Hey!" Ganto shouted. "I'm right here!"

"I'm offended," Starlocke said. "I know your words were not meant to be hurtful, but it is hard to read them any other way."

"I'm sorry, I didn't mean it like that, I meant..."

"Another human person," Karina clarified. "Look, Eve, I would love to travel the universe and save it more directly but, I have a responsibility to my planet and my country. I can't leave it."

"Then I don't know what to do."

"You wait," Karina said, "Until you're needed again. Not everything runs on a tight schedule."

"And we have time," Ganto reminded Eve. "This planet is a sanctuary in the past!" Ganto looked over at Karina. "When is this, actually?" Ganto asked.

"We've been keeping the calendar going since we teleported, to keep track, so for us it's 3345. Um, but as far as when we are in regard to Earth at this time… I think… 1982?" Karina clarified.

"It's the present?" Eve whispered to herself.

Ganto looked back up at Eve. "See? So unless Amalga-5 suddenly teleports back to from where it came, we've got nothing to—"

As Ganto was talking the ground shook violently. The sky shifted outside the windows.

"Uhh…" Karina stared outside. She rushed past Eve, back toward the entrance to the palace.

"Ok if we just teleported back to my present right as I was saying that, as bad as that is you have to admit that that timing was impeccable," Ganto said as he turned around slowly.

## ❖ CHAPTER 11 ❖

Eve, Ganto and Starlocke followed after Karina, rushing to the front of the Palace. They burst through the doors and stopped on the street, staring up at the sky.

The two halves of New Earth split far in the night sky. Janistar was visible just behind the ruins of the Galactic Jail super weapon.

The sky seemed to be melting and stars were dying. The universe was ending and they were indeed back in Ganto's present.

❖ Chapter 12 ❖
# The Flawed Prophecy

"You've gotta be shitting me…" Ganto stared ahead.

Starlocke's third eye glowed with burning intensity. "This planet is in extreme danger," he barked. "Leave."

"Wait! Starlocke!" Eve tried to stop him.

He turned around and stood his ground aggressively. "Something requires my attention." Starlocke glanced at the box floating by Eve. He turned his attention back to Eve. "I will return, I promise. You need only wait"

"Wait, Starlocke, I need you," Eve begged.

"I know. That's where I'm going. I'll see you soon." Starlocke charged forward and with a burst of electric wind, he was gone. The blast of wind seemed to jolt through Eve like a ghost.

## ❖ CHAPTER 12 ❖

"I need to ready my men." Karina said, running back into her palace.

Eve turned around to reach for the box floating by her shoulder, but a man ran into her. The box instantly camouflaged itself.

"Oh, sorry about that." Eve apologized for running into the man.

"You're in danger, you have to go," the man instructed her.

Before Eve could say anything to him, she looked away nervously, trying to figure out what to do. She caught a glimpse of Ganto, and an awestruck look spread over his face. "What?" she mouthed to him.

"Nice flannel," the man commented.

"Oh, it's actually—" Eve looked up and was struck with the same sense of awe and confusion that Ganto was in a near instant. "Who are you?"

"I'm the Sentinel, and you need to get out of here." He held out his hand. In his other arm he held onto a larger version of the box, orange and yellow with lines connecting the semicircles in each corner to the center circle. The First Sentinel held his hand out for a handshake.

"Wait!" Ganto reached out for Eve's flannel.

The Sentinel, Eve, and Ganto all flashed away in an instant. They appeared in a room with purple leaves draped across the walls. The floor of the room was a coarse dark green wood, and the table was absent of chairs.

"Where are we?" Eve looked around.

"See, you might not believe me… but we just *time traveled…*" The Sentinel held out his arms as a sort of way to show, *ta-da.*

"Wow…" Eve said with an obvious sarcastic undertone. "No way."

"It's hard to imagine, I know."

"Where'd you take us! Why'd you take us!? Who are you!?" Ganto approached the Sentinel angrily.

"I'm the Sentinel." He held out his arms to calm Ganto. "I just made this time machine recently and wanted to maybe try and use it to save a planet or whatever but turns out something crazy was going down on that planet that I really didn't want to deal with all that much. But hey, I saved you guys, so that's cool."

"Saved us?" Ganto scoffed. "Listen bucko, we were the ones doing the saving around there, alright? And if you think you're the Sentinel then you've got another thing coming, I'll tell you what—"

### ❖ CHAPTER 12 ❖

"Ganto," Eve interjected.

Ganto started to unclip the rifle from his back.

"Ganto!" Eve stepped forward. "Stop." She looked up at the Sentinel. "So, you're the first incarnation."

"You've heard of me?" he asked. "Who are you?"

"Answer Ganto first. Where'd you take us?"

"Only the safest place I know to be in the 1960's. The planet Illiosopherium of the Black Star 7 District."

A knock on the door of the room distracted the Sentinel.

"Hold on a moment." He approached the door and opened it.

As the door opened, it revealed that the room they were in was in the canopy of a high tree in a city forest of interconnected trees. A red Gar was let in, and Eve stumbled back. She hadn't seen a Gar before, but she didn't ask any questions. She already figured out what he was.

"This is a friend of mine, Kogar."

"Nice to meet you." Eve held out her hand to shake his scaly bird-like one.

"And you are?" Kogar asked.

"Eve Sanchez," she answered.

Kogar pulled his arm back and raised a fluffy brow curiously. He stared at Eve with some sort of shock in his face. "Hm." He stared.

Eve looked away.

"Hey, can we get back to saving Amalga-5 please, thanks." Ganto paced around.

"Since when do you want to save people?" Eve asked.

"Since I saw the universe ending—" Ganto covered his mouth and looked away. "Eve, let's go."

"Ganto, we're back in the 60's. We aren't wasting any time. Plus, it's the Sentinel."

"So, do you wanna go anywhere? I've got a time machine. The whole universe at your fingertips." The Sentinel smiled.

Kogar was staring at Eve the whole time, he held up a finger to stop the Sentinel. "Can I speak with you for a moment, Eve."

"Of course." Eve looked down and followed Kogar to another room in another tree canopy. Kogar closed the door. He lifted his arm up and a pillar of solid phlasma extended from the floor.

"Have a seat." He gestured for it.

"Thanks." Eve sat down on the stool.

❖ CHAPTER 12 ❖

"Has Tomas mentioned anything about the five years that the Sentinel traveled around with his friends?" Kogar looked around the room.

"Yeah, that's how I know who that Sentinel… You know Tomas?" Eve thought about it for a moment. "Wait, you were the Gar that trained him and Tomas!" Eve pointed at Kogar excitedly.

"You've shown up right at the beginning of his five years away." Kogar looked down. "There's a reason it was five years, and there's a reason it was in the mid 60's but… Tomas has told me about you. About the future."

"Tomas, from now or the future…" Eve tried to judge how much Tomas has always known.

"From now."

"How does he know about me?" Eve shuffled uncomfortably in her seat.

Kogar noticed how uncomfortable she was, and so he lifted his arms, extending the back of the phlasma crystal stool into a sort of backrest for her. She leaned back and Kogar explained, "These next five years, according to the Paradox Master, are absolutely necessary for a couple of things to happen in the future and the past…" Kogar hesitated, not knowing how much he should let Eve know, or how much he would be allowed to let her. "You are a product of these next five years."

"How so?" Eve leaned forward in her seat.

The door opened and the Sentinel peeked his head in, "So, are we going anywhere, or…?"

Kogar lowered his hand and the back of the phlasma seat pushed Eve up to a standing position before the chair vanished. "Where are we going?"

"Where does Eve wanna go?" The Sentinel opened the door all the way.

"Is Rex gonna let you go anywhere with Eve?" Kogar asked.

"Why wouldn't he?" The Sentinel leaned against the doorway.

"Let's just not go anywhere dangerous." Kogar shrugged.

"Ha!" Eve and the Sentinel laughed at the same time. "Anywhere I go is dangerous." They said simultaneously.

"Who are you?" The Sentinel asked Eve with a smile.

"Just Eve." She smiled, nodding.

"So… safest place to be, where's that?" The Sentinel asked Kogar.

## ❖ CHAPTER 12 ❖

"Right here in Japico city I'd say is pretty safe." He shrugged.

"Ha!" Ganto laughed. "Illiosopherium? Safe? Boy the 60's sure were different, huh?"

"What are you talking about?" Kogar asked.

"Ganto, shhh," Eve hushed him. "Japico it is."

"Follow me, I'll be your tour guide then." Kogar smiled and led Eve out of the room. When they came to the door of Kogar's home, they realized that getting down would be tricky. The Sentinel teleported Eve and Ganto down to the floor below, and Kogar followed. "What do you want to know?" Kogar asked Eve.

She heard him, but she wasn't listening. She stared up at the green night sky above. She saw Modius up in the sky, for the first time seeing his angry frowning face, and his glowing orange eyes. The massive crown mountains looked much smaller from the surface of Illiosopherium. Nidus was barely visible on the horizon, and Tornlozor didn't seem to be visible yet.

The canopy of trees they stood underneath didn't allow for the full sky to shine through the purple leaves atop the long red-brown barked trees. "

Hm?" Eve looked back at Kogar.

"Is there anything in particular you want to know?" he repeated.

"The Originals... is there anywhere I can learn more about them? I'm in sort of a position where any information could be helpful."

"Yes of course, the Temple of Sogar, just outside the city." Kogar led the way.

Gars ran food stands and shops in the bases of the tree houses. A bustling city ran under the treetops, and it was finally what Eve was expecting when hearing of alien civilizations. As they came closer to the gate, they spotted something.

"Who are they?" Eve asked, pointing at a group of Gars protesting. They chanted something in Garish that she couldn't understand.

"Oh, they're against the whole population living in this city alone. They want to expand past these walls and claim the rest of the planet for themselves. It's nothing much, just a new age hippie group. We get 'em every other decade."

"And who's that?" Eve pointed at a Gar standing in the center of the protesters. He wasn't holding a sign or chanting. He stared over the rest of the protesters with a stern and committed face, his bushy eyebrows twisted in an angry scorn.

## ❖ CHAPTER 12 ❖

"Oh, that's a the group's leader, actually. He gets a little crazy with the protests sometimes," the Sentinel answered. "We had to contain him the other day because things got so out of hand. He always talks about overthrowing the incompetent king, saying things like the prophecy will be fulfilled, war is imminent and so is our downfall, and out with Sogar in with Rogar, save the Gars, blah blah blah. That's his name by the way, Rogar. He thinks he's King material, or something."

"Prophecy?" Eve asked.

"The prophecy of the Originals, yeah." Kogar outstretched a hand for Eve. The Sentinel patted Kogar on the back as Eve took his hand and Ganto held onto Eve's flannel. The four of them flashed away. They appeared in front of a massive temple on a hill, standing just outside a gate. It looked old and rundown, ancient almost as if it had always been there. Something felt off to Eve about the temple's looming presence, like it was trying to tell her something.

"This place is old… how old?" Eve stared at the huge door entrance, where on either side sat a Scorlion, guarding its position, still as stone.

"Every planet in the Black Star 7 District has a temple built for each of the first leaders of the Originals, built by the opposite corresponding Originals. Sogar's temple was built by the leader of the Terrors billions of years ago, Kranica. Most of the leaders have died since."

"Most?" Eve questioned as they made their way through the gates.

"Sogar can phaze, just like the Sentinel and the Gars. He's in his third incarnation. He's used it as a way to cheat death. That, and Modius is still around. He's the first of his kind."

They passed by the Scorlions like they were nothing, and entered the temple. Eve looked around, and she spotted something carved into a stone near one of the towering walls, it was guarded by two Gars. She approached it slowly.

Kogar, the Sentinel and Ganto followed after her. The guards in front of the stone held out their hands, telling them to stop.

The carved stone tablet looked old and worn, and underneath it the words ⌐ − ⊤ − ⟨ ⌐ − Z − Z were inscribed. The stone was split into four sections with a figure in the middle. Eve recognized the central figure as Modius. In the four carved sections around it were the other Originals. A Gar, a Deusaves, a Terror, and a Dragolupus.

## ❖ CHAPTER 12 ❖

"Those are the Originals. Modius, Sogar, Dile, Kranica, and Drakona. Long ago, they ruled this part of the Galaxy with an iron fist. They were the only living things in a world without death. But they weren't the rulers of the universe, no… that was the three original Emissaries.

"Then one day, two Deusaves from Nidus became the Emissaries of Life and Death, and suddenly the immortal beings were made mortal. They fought a brutal war that lasted centuries, until Kranica, Dile, and Drakona were killed. The Gars won the war and were allowed to keep their ways of cheating death. After the war, the Dragolupus, who could see through time, wrote a prophecy out of resentment for the Gars."

"And what was the prophecy about?" Eve asked.

"The Sentinel and a Gar."

The Sentinel shifted in place and swallowed a lump in his throat.

Ganto gasped, and hopped a bit, "Oh, oh! I know this story! I was there for it!"

"Don't tell me what happens," Kogar scolded him.

"What? That's stupid, there's a prophecy, you already know," Ganto argued.

Kogar interrupted him, clearing his throat, "Along will come a mortal challenger with the combined power of a Dragolupus and a Gar, from outside of the Black Star's domain. A Guardian of their age, constantly thwarted by the disciples of a powerful banished god – one of which a power-hungry Gar, hailing from Illiosopherium, seeking more.

"Although the Guardian will appear to defend their cause, along the way the Guardian will lose themselves to their cause, and succumb to their true fate. The Gar that cheats death will fall on the winning side in the end."

"But…" Ganto lifted a finger to protest, and thought for a moment. "That can't be about the Sentinel…"

"Why not?" Kogar asked.

"Because it's wrong!" Ganto laughed.

The Sentinel's eyes lit up with a sense of hope.

"What do you mean it's wrong?" Kogar scoffed. "It's literally a prophecy told by beings that can *see through time*."

"Well, they're wrong! That Gar they're talking about is that crazy one we just saw outside, Rogar! And the Sentinel killed Rogar! He's dead! He never cheated death! The Sentinel won!"

### ❖ CHAPTER 12 ❖

"Hey! You can't say that in front of the Sentinel, he can't know his future!" Kogar flailed his arms angrily, "What do you think you're doing!?"

"The Sentinel loses his memory after those five years, right?" Eve asked. "It doesn't matter."

"The prophecy can *not* be wrong!" Kogar growled.

"Well I guess it is." The Sentinel patted Kogar on the back.

"The Paradox Master would know." Kogar looked away.

"Oh, come on! Don't bring him into this." The Sentinel laughed.

"Eve, I think it's time you go." Kogar floated for the exit of the temple.

"Don't do that, Kogar. She has nothing to do with this—"

"She has everything to do with this!" Kogar yelled. "She needs to leave, before she finds out too much."

"What's going on?" Eve asked.

"You have to go." Ganto tugged on her flannel. "Camo!" he yelled.

Eve's box lifted from camouflage floating above her shoulder. The Sentinel stumbled back in surprise, staring wide eyed at the box. "Is that…"

"Come on Eve." Ganto held on close as Eve reached for the box.

"Why me?" Eve whispered.

"What?" The Sentinel squinted at her, intensely confused. She couldn't elaborate before she flashed away.

## ❖ Chapter 13 ❖
# Suriv

Eve and Ganto appeared in a sandy desert lot. Eve collapsed to the floor, grasping the sand through her clenched fists, on the verge of tears.

Ganto looked around. "Oh no." He knelt down by Eve. "We really shouldn't be here, kiddo."

Eve looked up. She didn't mean to show up where she did, but it was on her mind.

Her house waited for her, just across the street. The old beaten-up car sat in the driveway.

Ganto looked quizzically at Eve's face. "Why are you crying? What happened?" he asked.

"I…" Eve sat up. She looked away, ashamed of herself. "I keep thinking about home. And Tomas is gone, Starlocke is gone… I… I want to go home."

"I'm here," Ganto said, gesturing to himself. "Is that not enough?"

"Ganto, I'm sorry, but it isn't the same. It's not that it's you it's that it's just you. It's just us now. I miss them so much."

"You can't see them," Ganto said, "How will your mother—"

"Evelyn?" Laura's voice called from across the street.

Eve's head shot up in surprise. Her heart skipped a beat as she heard her mother's voice. She opened her mouth to speak but words couldn't escape. "How…"

Laura ran across the street and hugged Eve as tightly as she could manage. Tears streamed down her face. Eve hadn't been gone long, but her absence had taken its toll on Laura. Andrew stepped from the door of the house and saw Eve and Ganto across the way.

"Eve!" he exclaimed. He ran across to hug her.

Ganto stepped back. "Huh?"

Laura leaned back and looked at Eve. She held her hand to her face and smiled. "My little girl… What's happened to you?"

"How'd you recognize me?" Eve asked.

## ❖ CHAPTER 13 ❖

"I told her everything," Andrew said. "She didn't believe me. But the longer that you were gone…"

Eve smiled and hugged Laura.

"Well now that you're back does that mean I can go with you again?" Andrew asked.

"Absolutely not." Eve stood up.

"*Man.*" Andrew crossed his arms in frustration.

"Eve, we just were setting lunch out, come in, please you have so much to explain. You too, Ganto." Laura looked down at the little Ilsian. She looked to Andrew. "It was Ganto, right? I'm not good with 'star war' names…"

"*Mom.*" Andrew looked away, embarrassed.

Eve smiled ear to ear, she missed this.

"Oo! What's for lunch? I could use some good eats!" Ganto rubbed his hands together as he crossed the street.

Later, Eve, Andrew, Laura, and Ganto sat around the table eating the lunch that Laura had prepared. Laura stared at Eve, trying to figure her out. She looked so different. She had to get used to it.

"You're staying, then?" Laura asked.

Eve flinched as she took a bite of her sandwich. She shook her head as she chewed. "I can't," she said. "The universe needs me."

"You'll stay at least for tonight though, right?" Andrew asked.

Eve looked down at Ganto to see if he'd be alright with it. He was busy chowing down on his sandwich. He looked up at Eve, crumbs falling from his mandibles.

"Hm?"

Eve chuckled, "Yeah." She looked up at Andrew. "Just for the night."

The group of them finished their lunches, and the day went on.

Later, Ganto was off with Andrew. Andrew showed him his games and comics, trying to get to know him better. Ganto asked Andrew if he was familiar with Ganto's favorite video game.

"Of course I wouldn't be," Andrew laughed. "You're an alien bug thing from the future!"

"My favorite game is an Earth game!" Ganto protested. "You should know it!"

"You're still from the future," Andrew laughed.

"It's from 1998!" Ganto turned around and yelled at Eve through the hall. "Eve! What year are you from again?"

"1982!" Eve responded.

## ❖ CHAPTER 13 ❖

"Oh dang." Ganto turned back to Andrew. The two of them laughed.

"Well write it down for me," Andrew said. "I'll make sure to check it out when it comes out in sixteen years."

"Okay well there's something else cool you should have but you can't wait too long for it." Ganto held out his hand and presented to Andrew an Andromedan pistol. "This is a top quality real-ass space gun. And it's for you."

"Woah! But, why?" Andrew asked.

Ganto scoffed, "Uh, because it's *cool*. When an alien gives you his gun you don't question it."

"Understandable." Andrew smiled as he looked as he took the gun. "Thanks, Ganto."

"No problem." Ganto clicked his mandibles and smiled.

Eve and Laura sat on the couch. Laura was looking through an old photo album, reminiscing.

"I thought I lost you," Laura said. "You could've been honest."

"I didn't want to endanger you," Eve said. "This new world I'm a part of is not forgiving. I didn't want to put targets on your heads just by association."

"I understand," Laura sighed. She looked up at Eve. "Be careful."

"I know, Mom." Eve smiled. As she turned her head, she thought she saw something out of the corner of her eye peeking through a window.

A small orange object ducked down, so as not to be seen. Eve looked up to where she thought she saw the movement, and she squinted.

"What is it?" Laura asked.

"Nothing..." Eve assured her. "I'm just paranoid."

"Mm."

Eve looked back down at the photo album, but not before she saw the movement again. She shot her head up. Metallic ticking clicked outside the walls of the house.

"You hear that too, right?" Laura looked around.

"Ganto! Get out here!" Eve called out.

Ganto skidded next to Eve, using his jetpack to get out to the living room as fast as possible. "What's up?" he asked.

Andrew ran out after him.

"Get your gun ready." Eve's hands flared to life with phlasma.

Laura jumped back, startled. She had only ever had it described to her by Andrew, never seen it in action. Eve slowly

❖ CHAPTER 13 ❖

moved toward the door of her house. Ganto followed her closely with his Andromedan rifle at the ready. Eve swung the door open. A small, yellow, elongated crystal-shaped robot with spider-like legs stood on the welcome mat. Its singular eye acted like the aperture of a camera and seemed to focus on Eve. It stopped in its tracks, like it had been caught spying.

"Hey little guy." Eve leaned in closer. "What are you?"

"Scanning," the robot spoke with a synthetic voice as its eye widened and narrowed.

"Um." Eve sat up and looked around. More of the robot creatures seemed to appear at the door. "Ganto..." Eve turned around. "You wouldn't happen to know what these are, would you?"

Ganto shook his head. "Never seen 'em in my life."

"Eve, what's going on?" Laura asked.

"Name confirmation." The robot chimed. Its eye glowed red as its body dimmed and blades extended from its legs. "Target acquired." Its voice deepened.

"What the hell?" Ganto stepped back. He noticed something about the glowing yellow material that made up the robot, and it tipped him off. "Calcurus..." he whispered. "Andrew! Get out of here!" he yelled behind him.

Eve reached for the box and instantly vanished, appearing quickly behind the swarm of robots, to draw them away from inside the house. Ganto turned around and instructed Laura not to leave the house. He kicked his jetpack into action and flew over the bots, landing by Eve. Laura shut the metal screen door, so she could still see outside.

"Eve, you better be careful. I'm pretty sure these nasty guys are made of Calcurus. The stuff's indestructible."

"Indestructible?"

"Mostly, lift your shield. Siege shield!" Ganto yelled as the robots closed in quicker.

"Siege shield!" Eve yelled and covered her face with her arms. The box fell to the ground and an electric blue shield formed around them.

As robots pounced on them, they hit the shield, turning it a dark red as they disintegrated on impact. The remaining robots stopped in their tracks. They slowly paced around the shield, not drawing their eyes off of Eve. The robots stopped pacing, and one of them stood taller in front of Eve. Its speaker blasted with static before it toned down. The sound of something hitting the mic blasted from the speakers before they heard a gravelly voice clearing its throat.

## ❖ CHAPTER 13 ❖

"Well would you look at that... I thought I could find you here, ya know these bots are better at tracking without the boss's help now, I'd say."

"Who are you?" Eve asked.

Laura held her hand over her heart. She feared for her daughter's life. She heard stories of her heroism from Andrew, but could never picture it, or believe it. But there was Eve, right in front of her.

"An associate of Kranthar's. The name's Suriv. Of course, this isn't me." The robot turned its head to gesture to the other bots. "These are just my little projects."

"Suriv!?" Ganto yelled. "I thought I recognized your voice, you *bastard*!"

"You know him?" Eve asked Ganto.

"Why did you have to make it so hard for us and Vistor! Huh? You could've backed off! I thought you died with Vel-Ant! You should be dead, dammit!"

"Chill out, Ganto." The robot stepped forward menacingly. "This isn't about our previous scuffle. I had nearly forgotten about you, puny cousin... No this is a much grander cause..."

"What do you want?" Eve asked.

"Like, in general, or my grand plan?" The voice boomed. "Should I do a cliché villain motivation speech or is that not what you're looking for? Should I tell you about my tragic past and how father said I would never sit on a throne of power? Oh, boo hoo. How about I make something up to make you feel better? Maybe I'm a disgraced knight who failed to kill a dragon? Is that what you want?"

"Make it quick, asshole," Ganto pressed.

"You see all my associates want something different, and I couldn't care less what they wanted."

"Then why are you working with them?" Eve asked.

"Hey, could you shut up? I'm monologuing here," Suriv coughed. "To make things simple I just want power, ya know? I mean I tried for the throne of Ilsose, but that didn't work, clearly."

"You *killed* Vistor's family! He did nothing to you!"

"Point is, Ganto, that I've set my eye on higher goals this time around, and I just need to work with whom I need to and *for* whom I need to to get there. And part of me getting what I want includes pleasing my boss. If he wants you dead, then I'll kill you. It's nothing personal… but then again, I'm an emotionless Ilsian, take that with what you will."

Laura stumbled back. "Did he say *dead*?" Laura asked.

## ❖ CHAPTER 13 ❖

Andrew stood by her side, comforting her. "Eve will be fine, Mom. She's a superhero."

"Who's your boss!? Where can I find him!?" Eve yelled.

"Ha! Find him?" Suriv chuckled. "He finds you."

Eve furrowed her brow and scowled at the robot. "Reverse the shield," she told the box.

"Wait what?" Ganto looked to her in confusion.

The shield opened up from behind them and started closing in on the robots like an inverted sphere, drawing them in like herding sheep into a circle until the shield encapsulated them outside the box and in front of Eve. Some of the robots tried to escape but burned up in the siege shield when they tried.

"Collapse the shield," Eve demanded. The dome closed in on the robots, disintegrating them as it grew smaller and smaller. "Stop!" Eve yelled, and the dome paused. "Drop it." The shield vanished and all that was left of the robots was half of a singular robot, allowing for Eve to see into the inner workings.

"Wow... impressive." Ganto stood up and approached the robot half. He picked it up. "Now what?"

"That material, where'd you say it was from?" Eve asked.

"In my time, Janistar's government mined it out of Janistar's Calcurus fields and Amalga-5's moon. But I knew this guy, a really bad guy, Rhey. He stole a ton of Calcurus-B, it's called, but I don't know how Suriv would be working with Rhey... Mostly because Rhey's dead but that's beside the point."

"Do you recognize this technology?" Eve pointed at the inside of the robot.

Ganto looked closer in the robot. "I think I do recognize it, well actually I don't recognize it, but that's the thing. It isn't Andromedan, it isn't Wayan, it isn't Garish, and it isn't Lorinian, it's more Ilsian looking than anything, but not entirely... I can't tell what it is..."

"Do you think that maybe if we tracked down its origins that we could find Suriv or who it is he's working for?"

"Maybe." Ganto stared at the robot piece intently. "Yeah, maybe."

Eve pried a panel off of the box, exposing its core with a singular rêve stone inside. She held out her hand for Ganto to give her the piece of the robot, which she put in the box, then

### ❖ CHAPTER 13 ❖

sealed it up again, locking the panel back into place. "Safe keeping," she commented. She looked up at her mom.

"Eve..." Laura called out behind the door. She opened it. "Eve, honey... are you going to be okay?"

"Mom..." Eve approached Laura. "I'm sorry, I can't stay the night. I really have to go."

Laura stepped forward and hugged Eve as tightly as she could manage. "*I know.*" She looked Eve in the eyes and said, "Go do what you need to do."

Eve nodded. "I love you, Mom."

"See ya, dork." Eve smiled at Andrew.

"Nerd," Andrew retorted.

Eve looked down at Ganto. "Where should we go next?"

"We need answers from Kranthar. And then we kill him."

"Let's go." Eve held out her hand and they flashed away.

❖ Chapter 14 ❖

# Home too Soon

Eve and Ganto appeared on what seemed to be a planet of molten lava and large ragged rocks. Eve was surprised at their new location, stumbling slightly.

Ganto held her in place.

"Where are we?" she asked.

"Looks like IS-372..." Ganto looked around, uneasy with his footing, his eyes darting around.

"It is," the box confirmed.

"Why would Kranthar be here..." Eve looked around.

"Rhey was here once... I don't know..." Ganto swallowed a lump in his throat as he began to walk around, checking the ground for safe footing. Eve followed after him. "Yo, cranberry! Get out here! We got some questions!" Ganto

## ❖ CHAPTER 14 ❖

yelled out into the vast and empty plains of lava and rock. "Come on!" He waited. "We don't got all day!"

The ground beneath them rumbled, and Eve flared her fists in preparation. Kranthar burst from a nearby cave in the ground and made his ascent.

His voice boomed in the air, "So you've met a colleague of mine!" He flapped his dragon-like wings to keep his body afloat, while the rest of his body remained buried. "Did you come here to give up and die?" Kranthar growled. Terror drones passed through the ground and floated around Eve and Ganto.

"Come on Kranthar, you know that every time you and I fight, I always win." Eve shrugged. "Don't put up a fight, we just have questions."

"And I have a boss to please and orders to kill," Kranthar growled.

"Who is your boss?" Eve asked.

Ganto withdrew his pistol and set it to stun.

"Even if I told you, you couldn't find him." Kranthar snaked his head lower to get a closer look at Eve. His eyes sparked with electricity as his gaping mouth pushed out hot air, breathing slowly on Eve. "Give up."

"Where's Suriv?" Eve asked.

"No more questions," Kranthar hissed. "You won't need them when you're dead." He jabbed an arm toward Eve, but she quickly dodged it. The Terrors closed in on them, and Ganto fired away, screaming as he did.

"Go away! Get out of here! Die!" he yelled as he fired, knocking down the drones in swaths.

Eve kept dodging jabs from Kranthar. When an arm came her way, she grabbed onto it. Kranthar pulled her up into the air. Eve flew through the air like a ragdoll, panicking and not knowing how to stop. Before hitting the ground, she pushed out her arms and burst phlasma from them to act as counter propulsion, which worked to slow her fall.

As she hit the ground she scraped against a hot jagged rock, tearing a gash in her leg and arm. She rolled over on her side and looked up to see Kranthar leaping into the air like a dolphin from the sea, planning to dive right on top of her.

"Ganto!" Eve yelled, holding up her arms.

"Eve!" Ganto dropped his pistol and ran after Eve. Before he could get to her, Kranthar slammed into her and had already begun digging into the ground. "No!" Ganto stopped at the end of the tunnel that Kranthar was burrowing deeply into. "NO!"

## ❖ CHAPTER 14 ❖

Unknown to Ganto, Eve had concealed herself in the safety of the box's spherical shield, which Kranthar was pushing deeper and deeper into the ground. She had thought about switching to siege shield to disintegrate Kranthar's face on the spot, but the risk of burning herself stopped her. Kranthar kept forcing the shield down, down, down, further into the rock.

"AH!" Eve yelled as the shield cracked and shattered. Her back hit the box and she teleported away, appearing next to Ganto and hitting the ground beside him.

"Eve! You're okay!" Ganto ran for her.

Kranthar burst from the ground underneath Eve, flying into the air. Eve was pressed up against his faceplate, screaming in shock and fear as she rose steadily into the air.

"EVE!"

She collected herself quickly, and with a flaming fist she punched Kranthar. Her fingers cracked and she screamed in pain.

Regardless, she punched again and again, and again once more before it happened. Almost a mile in the air, Kranthar dropped his head down. As Eve fell down the length of Kranthar's body, he slammed her in the side with his tail, pushing her back into the air, before he slammed down with his tail, launching her into the rock below.

Ganto ran to where she landed, she was unconscious and dying.

"No Dragolupus with you this time! No Gar magic! No tricks!" Kranthar yelled. "She's dead." He snapped his jaws and looked away from Ganto, flying off into space.

"Eve, come on…" Ganto shook her body. "Somebody help… HELP!" Ganto yelled out into the empty fields of lava. No one would be there to help him, he knew it.

A mechanical flash sounded behind Ganto. He turned around, extremely hopeful, then his eyes grew wide. "Paradox Master…" he gasped. "But…"

The Paradox Master didn't say a word. He withdrew his phaze gun, and shot Eve's body, initiating a phaze. Eve burst with phlasmatic energy, healing her. Her face rounded out, and she shortened a bit as she stood. Her skin darkened and her eyes lost their piercing blue hue in favor of a deep dark brown. Her hair curled and became frizzy and shorter. She gasped for air and adjusted her balance as she felt her body change. She had phazed once again.

## ❖ CHAPTER 14 ❖

"Who are you..." were the first words she could manage. She lifted a weak finger and pointed at the Paradox Master. "Who are you?"

"I'm the Paradox Master," he said, simply.

He holstered his phaze gun and stood, waiting for more questions. Ganto squinted as he had a sudden thought.

"Why are you here? Why'd you save me?" Eve asked, breathing heavily and looking around for any sign of Kranthar still around.

"Time sent me on this mission. She didn't give me any details. I don't even know why she wanted me here. Who are you?" he asked.

"Eve Sanchez," Eve answered, standing her ground and getting used to her new body. "Evelyn."

The Paradox Master stepped back on the rocky island and held his breath a moment as his eyes widened. He looked away from Eve, and his eye caught Ganto. He looked away from him, and then at his box, floating by his shoulder. "I... I have to go..."

"Wait!" Eve stepped forward. "You know who I am? Why don't I know you? Tell me."

The Paradox Master vanished.

"God dammit! What is up with all the secrecy!?" Eve complained. "I almost died, tell me something!" she yelled to no one. "It's like they don't want me to save the universe at all! Doesn't anybody realize that I need information!?"

"I mean, I think Suriv and Kranthar would rather you not save the universe… just a hunch."

"But what about the Paradox Master guy and Tomas!? And even that Kogar guy… and the box!" Eve pointed at the box floating by her shoulder. "What's going on?" she asked it.

The ground underneath them rumbled.

"You lost!" Eve yelled. "Leave me alone!" She screamed at the ground, scolding Kranthar, annoyed at the apparent signs of his return.

The ticking of small robotic feet signaled a different presence instead.

"They're back." Eve recognized the sound from Suriv's little robots.

"They've tracked the piece inside of me," the box explained. "He's here."

"Who's here?" Eve asked.

From the lava a large bright yellow and orange crystalline structure whirred its way out. Lava dripped off of the shell slowly, sizzling and popping as it did.

## ❖ CHAPTER 14 ❖

Massive robotic legs shot into the ground and anchored the machine as it turned to face Eve. Its aperture eye widened and narrowed, focusing on Eve. The giant thing resembled the little robots closely, but much larger. A mouth-like sliding door swung open and inside, behind a light Calcurus shielding, was a small being that looked remarkably similar to Ganto, but with a yellow exoskeletal skin.

His head wasn't decorated with nearly as many antlers. They were a light blueish color and seemed to have broken off. His eyes were sharp and calculated. Half of his face was severely burnt and scarred. On the same half of his body he was missing two of his arms, and on the other side, a third. His waist seemed to be tied into the robotic shell, as it seemed he only had one full leg. He grimaced and clicked his mandibles at Eve.

"Suriv." Eve stood tall.

"You look different from when we last met," Suriv commented.

"So do you." Eve stepped back as her hands sparked with electricity. She didn't think she was ready to fight again, especially not after just having phazed.

"Looks like I just missed my colleague by a hair…" Suriv closed his hatch, and the bot began circling Eve, its sharp blade like feet shaking the ground with every step. "But I can distract you on my own."

"AGH!" Eve shot her hands out and electricity burst from them, covering the robotic shell whole. She stopped when she noticed it did nothing as Suriv kept pacing around her menacingly. The sparks lingered over the looming beast as smaller robots crawled out of the ground.

"Eve, the box's shield," Ganto reminded her. "He's Calcurus, use it."

"Oh, that won't be necessary." Suriv glowed. A shield surrounded him, very similar to that of the box's. "You can't get past this; the shields will just collide."

"Is that true?" Eve asked the box. It didn't respond. "What do you want, Suriv?" Eve followed his pacing. He wasn't attacking yet, and that worried her, she just wanted to get the fight over with.

"Isn't it quite clear?" Suriv chuckled. "I already admitted that I'm distracting you."

Ganto kicked on his jetpack and pointed his pistol at Suriv. "Tread carefully, bud," he warned.

"What's a pistol gonna do?" Suriv questioned. "I've survived much worse, and all it did was make me stronger, I'd advise against trying to stop me from getting what I want, this time."

"What do you want?" Eve asked. "We can bargain as long as you let me live and let me keep the universe from dying."

"I want the Multiverse to die. The whole shebang. Boom! Gone."

"Well that's a bit of a conflict of interest, isn't it?" Ganto cocked the pistol.

"I want to rule over a new universe. I want to dethrone the Paradox Master and take his place among the new Emissaries."

"What's up with you and dethroning?" Ganto spat. "Accept your place as failure trash!"

"The *new* Emissaries?" Eve questioned. "What new Emissaries?"

Suriv squatted down as the gears in his legs seemed to rev up. "Okay I'm bored. I'm going to kill you now." The mechanisms in his kneecaps clicked and snapped as springs launched Suriv into the air toward Ganto. He tackled him into the rocks far ahead.

"Ganto!" Eve jumped and propelled herself with a burst of phlasma in his direction. She kicked her leg up and a phlasmatic crystal from the ground shot itself toward Suriv, disintegrating on impact with his shield. Eve noticed however that Ganto didn't disintegrate when he was hit with the shin of one of Suriv's legs. They weren't shielded.

She lifted her hands up, and roots of phlasma snaked their way from the ground up Suriv's legs. Eve clenched her hands into fists and the roots electrified with an icy edge. The metal in Suriv's legs was different, it wasn't Calcurus, and it began to crack as the electricity pierced through the metal with an ice-cold sting.

Ganto backed away as he watched Suriv struggle to stand, falling to the ground slowly, fighting against it as best he could. An aperture at the base of the cylinder of metal that acted as a waist for his four legs opened, and a burst of a blue fire rocket shot out from it, pushing him up and against the pull of the phlasmatic roots holding him down.

Eve struggled to pull her arms down, as if she were physically pulling a lasso around Suriv. Suriv himself tried his best to escape by propelling himself into the air.

"Eve! Watch out!" Ganto yelled.

Eve felt the touch of an electric tentacle at her neck, and she fell to the ground, her vision completely blurring into pure blackness.

## ❖ CHAPTER 14 ❖

A Terror slipped her into a trance-like state.

The darkness surrounded her. All sound had flushed away, except for her pounding heartbeat.

A tiny red flame ignited itself, burning like a candle, flickering in the void.

*"Fear..."*

The tiny red flame grew into a flash of red light that overcame her vision. She seemed to be standing in a black room, inside some sort of a projection of a quickly spinning, burning red galaxy.

Eve opened her eyes and took a sharp breath. She stood in the void, arms out at her side, knees bent and legs parted as if she were ready to attack.

*"It is the only way to rule a universe cursed with life. Shame..."* The voice continued to boom in Eve's head.

"Who are you?" Eve asked.

*"I am more than you can imagine. I am the creator, and will be the recreator, of this Multiverse. You will not stand in my way,"* the voice demanded.

"Why are you doing this?" Eve asked.

*"He ruined my creation! And they did not respect my authority."*

"Who's he? Who's they?" Eve looked around in her apparition. "You talk to me like I know these things, but I don't!"

"*You do not. You need not.*"

"Listen, guy." Eve looked around confusedly. "I'll do whatever you want so long as you let this universe live. Anything."

"*Anything?*" the voice asked in a deep rumble.

"Anything," Eve affirmed.

The galaxy shifted and pulsated as if it were thinking. The voice boomed again, "*Meet your maker.*"

Eve's vision quickly faded as she opened her eyes and the light of the bright lava overcame her. She screamed with burning intensity as her head throbbed. The box shone and pulsated purple from within, as if the rêve stone inside was reacting. Eve's eyes glowed red for a moment as her scream deepened.

"AGH!" She writhed around. The Terror that incited her vision had been killed by Ganto, but Suriv had already escaped the shackles of Eve's trap. He floated above her, watching curiously.

"*KILL HER!*" the voice boomed from Eve as her eyes deepened. It seemed directed at Suriv. "*DO NOT BE A*

## ❖ CHAPTER 14 ❖

*DISAPPOINTMENT LIKE THE KRANTHARNIC! KILL HER!"* Eve's body floated up as red phlasmatic flames consumed her.

"What the hell…" Ganto stumbled back.

"Sir—" Suriv's voice trembled.

*"WHAT IS YOUR HESITATION?"* the voice shouted from Eve.

"I've found another way to destroy her," Suriv answered. "I've told Kranthar of a way to stop her, she won't come back from it. We've seen the Sentinel recover from death, but Eve can't recover from this."

*"From what?"* the voice asked.

"Her family," Suriv answered.

The red drained from Eve's eyes and was overcome with a bright burning blue. The red phlasmatic flames vanished and were replaced with electric ice. She fell to the ground and gasped for air. "What did you say!?" she demanded an answer.

"How did you—" Suriv floated away.

*"What did you say?!"* Eve asked. She looked around frantically and reached for the box. "Ganto, come on." She held out her hand and they flashed away as quickly as she could manage, leaving Suriv behind.

Eve flashed back into her home, standing in the dark living room with Ganto. She heard screaming coming from a hallway. "Mom!" she yelled.

"This isn't good," Ganto whispered to himself before running after Eve.

"Eve!" Laura ran from the hallway and hugged Eve tightly in her arms.

"Mom…"

"You changed again…" Laura stepped back, tears in her eyes.

"Mom, watch out!" Andrew yelled from the hallway.

A ghostly tentacle wrapped around Laura, tearing her from Eve's grasp. A Terror drone held her into the air.

"Let go of her!" Eve yelled.

"AGH!" Andrew ran into the hallway with a shower curtain pole in his arms. He shoved the metal rod into a wall socket, breaking the socket and electrocuting the metal rod. The electricity sparked up his arm, shocking him, but he pushed through, stabbing the Terror with the pole, and killing it.

Andrew dropped the pole and fell to his knees. When the Terror vanished, Laura fell to the floor, gasping for air.

## ❖ CHAPTER 14 ❖

Eve ran up to her and hugged her, pushing her fingers through her hair. "Mom, I'm so sorry, I shouldn't've come home…"

"Don't blame yourself," Laura laughed with a short cry. "It's not your fault."

"Eve, I don't think it's safe here," Ganto said.

"Ganto!" Andrew stood up. He held the Andromedan pistol Ganto had given him in his hand.

"Hey, buddy." Ganto smiled. "Set that baby to stun, you're gonna need it."

"Mom, you need to get out of here," Eve said.

Eve smiled as she lifted her mother up from the floor. She had accepted that living a normal life was a goal she would never reach, but having her family back was the next best thing. She wanted nothing more than to be with them again, and she chuckled at the thought of it. "We'll get out of here, I promise. You'll be safe." Eve smiled and nodded with tears in her eyes.

"Eve!" Andrew yelled.

A ghostly tentacle shot up from the floor and through Laura's chest. The tentacle solidified and ripped through her almost instantly.

"NO!" Eve yelled, stumbling back. "NO!"

"MOM!" Andrew yelled, blasting the gun. The electric stunning blast killed the Terror, but it was too late. Laura fell to the floor, dying.

The Terror lifted from the ground and swung a tentacle at Andrew, grabbing the pole from his hands and hitting him across the head with it, knocking him to the floor.

Eve angrily blasted the Terror with a shock of electric ice, killing it. A Terror materialized through the wall behind Andrew.

"Step away from the boy!" Ganto yelled, lifting his pistol.

The Terror drone lifted a tentacle and blasted Ganto with an electric shock, sending him flying into a wall.

Andrew sat up, rubbing his head.

"Andrew!" Eve ran for the Terror, her hands burst into flames.

The Terror smacked a tentacle and flung Andrew into a wall.

Eve heard bone snap.

"Eve..." Her brother's voice beckoned lightly.

She blasted her flames at the Terror to get its attention.

It darted its mouth-eye to her and spoke with Kranthar's voice. "Now I win."

## ❖ CHAPTER 14 ❖

Eve lunged at the Terror, her whole body electrified. The Terror vanished in a near instant before she could touch it. She looked around in horror, before a tentacle burst from the wall behind Andrew. "No!"

Eve jumped for it, but it was too late as the tentacle pushed into Andrew's chest and solidified, just as it had with Laura.

Ganto stood paralyzed with shock, watching but not knowing what to do. He saw the Terror appear behind Eve and instinctively shot at it, killing it. He ran to Eve's side.

"Andrew, I'm sorry. No, this wasn't supposed to happen," Eve cried. "I left you so that you could be safe, don't go."

"Eve…" Andrew held out his hand and in his dying breaths he barely managed with a raspy voice, "Finish this…" His head drooped.

At that moment a Terror approached behind Eve and Ganto, pushing its ghostly tentacles through them, Andrew shot at it and killed it before it could solidify and kill the duo.

With the shot, Andrew again fell limp.

"Andrew." Eve held her arms to his shoulders. "Andrew!" Her eyes were completely blocked with tears, she shook her head in denial. "Andrew, it's me, I'm here. It's Eve.

Andrew, come on dork, wake up." She shook his shoulders. "*ANDREW!*" she yelled.

"Eve." Ganto held out a hand.

"NO!" Eve slammed her fists against the ground, devastated. "No… no no no…" She wiped her face of her tears.

Ganto didn't know how to console her, how to react, how to feel. He picked up the gun he had given Andrew and stared at it. A tear dripped down Ganto's face. That had never happened before.

Eve fell on her knees by her mother's body. She lowered her head by hers and cried. "*I'm so sorry.*"

## ❖ Chapter 15 ❖
# Tomas 'Rex' Dapar

The next morning Eve awoke holding Laura's hand tightly in hers. She stood up slowly, her clothes were drenched in blood. She kept her eyes off Andrew, and Laura, and walked away. The box followed her.

"Get away from me," she demanded with a tired voice. The box continued following her. "I said, get away from me."

"You aren't going to be a Sentinel anymore… are you?" the box asked.

Ganto leaned away from the couch he had spent the night on, watching Eve.

Eve stopped in her tracks in the hallway as she approached her shower. She took a deep breath, and turned around.

"All I wanted was to live a normal life. Kranthar and Suriv took that away from me to stop me from being a Sentinel… They took that away from my family. If I stop now, they died for nothing. I'm going to kill Kranthar and Suriv. I will save the universe if it kills me three times over. I will avenge my family, and nothing will stop me, box. I'm *not* the Sentinel. The Sentinel failed. I won't."

Eve got out of the shower and dressed herself in some of her mother's clothes. She slid on a pair of jeans, put a short jacket over her green top and was ready to go.

Ganto walked up to her and tugged on her jacket to get her attention. "You alright, Eve?" Ganto asked.

Eve looked away, holding back tears. She didn't say a word.

The box sat on the counter in her living room. Eve started walking toward it, but as she approached, she stopped in her tracks. A silhouette of a man stood in the corner of the dark living room.

## ❖ CHAPTER 15 ❖

"Who are you, what do you want?" Eve asked with a shaking voice, her hands clammy and shaking. "I'm warning you; I am *not* in a good mood."

Ganto whipped out his rifle and cocked it back. The charging sound of an impending blast heightened as the blue glow from the rifle lit the room slightly.

"Calm down," the gravelly voice of an old man spoke. "It's me."

"Tomas?" Eve's voice trailed off. She ran to him and quickly embraced him. "Where did you go? *I needed you.*"

"Tomas! What the hell!?" Ganto yelled. "Where were you?"

Tomas's eyes watered. He hugged Eve tightly. "Sit down." He led her to the couch and they both sat. He held her close as she cried. "I'm so sorry, Eve." Tomas tried to calm her, tried his best to make her feel better. "It's going to be okay."

"*How dare you!*" Eve cried. "I didn't want my family involved in this! I specifically avoided them to keep them as far away from harm as I could! It's not going to be okay... I can't bring them back... It'll never be okay..."

"I know, Eve. I know. I understand." Tomas looked away and sighed. "Eve… I feel like it's about time I'm honest with you… about time I explained myself."

Eve sniffled and looked up at Tomas, "What do you mean?" she asked.

"I think you've figured out by now that I was entrenched in the five years that the Sentinel traveled with his Gar friend. He traveled with the Paradox Master, a man that used to be the Sentinel."

"I met him," Eve interrupted Tomas.

Ganto stood back, listening from afar. His eyes lit up with understanding.

"A few things were meant to be accomplished during those five years. Toward the end of it all, the Paradox Master and the Sentinel went out on one last hurrah.

"They went to a drunken party on Janistar, late into the night. They didn't end the party on Janistar. The Paradox Master took the Sentinel with him back to the place they frequented on Earth back in the 60's, a bar in Albuquerque, New Mexico."

As Eve pulled away to look at Tomas, she noticed that he hid something in his jacket. A faint yellowish glow shone from within.

## ❖ CHAPTER 15 ❖

"The year was 1966. The Paradox Master was more sober than he made himself out to be. He knew," Tomas chuckled lightly, almost reminiscing, "Oh, he knew what he was doing. He directed the intoxicated Sentinel to the bartender... Laura Sanchez."

"What?" Eve drew her attention away from the object in Tomas's jacket and to him.

"They knew each other from the many times the Sentinel and his friends would visit the bar. So, it didn't take much work to get things going.

"The Paradox Master got them a hotel room. Then that was it. That was the last night of those five years. The Paradox Master wiped the Sentinel's mind of most of the five years the next morning, and sent him back home to New New York, 2072.

"Much later, much much later, the Sentinel would split the universe and continue on two separate paths. On one end, the Sentinel died, and on the other, he was granted the title of the Paradox Master, and was gifted with immortality. A curse, mind you. Five million years he ruled in the Extraverse before he retired.

"Now I'm not sure if you're putting together the details yet, but, Eve, the Sentinel was your father." Tomas lifted his jacket slowly. "Camo," he spoke softly.

The invisible object in his jacket showed itself. The box; small, orange and yellow, broken, cracked and old.

The light of the box shone on Tomas's faded red leather jacket, and a rêve stone glowed on an amulet around his neck.

His box flew up to Eve. An old, crumpled sticky note was stuck to the side of it. Eve took it off and looked at it.

Her face wrinkled in confusion as she read:

*A A A D E M O P R R S T X*

~~*T O M D A S P A R R A [E X]*~~

~~*T O M ? P A R R A ?*~~

~~*R E X*~~

*P´A´R´A´D´O´X´M´A´S´T´E´R´*

<u>T</u> <u>O</u> <u>M</u> <u>A</u> <u>S</u> <u>R</u> <u>E</u> <u>X</u> <u>D</u> <u>A</u> <u>P</u> <u>A</u> <u>R</u>

## ❖ CHAPTER 15 ❖

She looked up at Tomas. The box floated away and back to him. She blinked a tear out of her eye and wiped it away as she looked at Tomas with her mouth slightly agape, her head atilt with confusion.

"Eve... I used to be the Paradox Master... Before that I was the Sentinel..."

"You're... My..."

"Father," Tomas said.

"But—" Eve stepped back.

"Wait, what..." Ganto stumbled back.

"We're doing this together. No more secrets," Tomas assured her.

"I—" Eve didn't know what to say.

"You always wondered, why you?" Tomas smiled as he hugged Eve in his arms. "Why you're so powerful with phlasma..." he continued.

"The box never gave you the powers, it just shot you with enough of a spark to awaken them, hidden away in your genes. Like father like daughter."

Eve cried into his shoulder, "This isn't..." she choked on her words. "I don't know how to—"

"How to feel? Yeah, you get used to it." Tomas tightened his embrace. "I've been waiting for this moment ever since I remembered you five million years ago. I love you, and I'm sorry I ever left you... I'm sorry that this is your destiny... but I had to... there was no other way..."

"Dad." Eve squeezed tighter, sniffling. "I have a Dad."

"I have a daughter." Tomas closed his eyes.

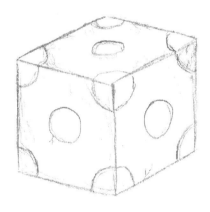

## ❖ Chapter 16 ❖
# Destined Departure

*This is the KESQ-TV news six-o-clock report. We have a development regarding the missing person's case that has stumped the Coachella Valley for months; where is Evelyn Sanchez?*

*Her mother, Laura Sanchez, and half-brother, Andrew Hall, were killed this weekend, and were found dead Saturday morning in their Palm Springs home.*

*Their untimely passing leads us to believe that Evelyn Sanchez, too, wherever she is, is no longer with us.*

*Authorities still have little to say on the circumstances of the horrific attack against the Sanchez family. No weapon has been found. No sign of break-in was detected. No motive is known, and there are still no prime suspects.*

*No other family members remain to be contacted.*

*As investigation continues, a public funeral and burial, funded by an anonymous donor, will be held at Desert Memorial Park for those who are affected by their loss—*

Tomas held his hand to Eve's shoulder as she cried. Ganto held his arm up to hold Eve's hand as he hid under a fuzzy blanket.

They watched from afar, under a tree which cast a weak shadow. Heat rose from the ground as a mirage.

Three headstones were placed next to each other. One of them was for Eve.

With a feeling of emptiness, Eve stared at it.

A small group of people from around the valley stood around the small public funeral ceremony for the Sanchez family.

Ganto recognized Kurt, there with his parents. Melissa was there too. One of Eve's teachers stood by as well.

A steady stream of tears dripped from Eve's cheek. She tried her best to not be loud about it, to not draw attention. Her head pounded with a sharp pain and an uncomfortable warmth as she held back her tears. No one recognized her or Tomas. It

## ❖ CHAPTER 16 ❖

would be strange to them if she were to cry. It was best not to draw attention to Ganto, either. But he insisted that he be there.

Ganto let go of Eve's hand and walked forward.

"*Ganto,*" Eve held out her hand to stop him.

The little lump of cloth that was Ganto waddled along through the short dry grass to the graves.

While people placed flowers on the graves, Ganto placed something else. A small gray battered and alien-tampered Game Boy, with Ganto's favorite video game from Andrew's future left inside it.

Ganto hurried back to Eve.

As he came to her, Eve dropped to her knees and hugged Ganto with an intense grip.

Ganto patted Eve's back.

Tomas swallowed a lump in his throat as Eve stood up again and looked at him.

"She didn't have to die... I really don't want to blame you... but you could've shown up sooner... you screwed up her life already the least you could have done was try to save her..."

"I'm sorry, Eve. As much as I do know... I didn't know about this. I didn't know what would happen. I couldn't've shown up any earlier without knowing. I'm so sorry. I really am."

Eve choked up, looking away for a second and holding her fist to her mouth. She closed her eyes, pushing out a tear. She looked back at Tomas. "Why did it have to be her?" She asked. "Why my Mom? She did nothing wrong. Why did it have to be her?"

Without much thinking, Tomas answered, "Because it had to be you." Tomas looked out over at the small group of people mourning. He sighed and said, "I really can't explain much more than that, but I mean it, I'm sorry. But it *had* to be you."

"What's so special about me besides what you made me?" Eve asked. "I was just a normal high school junior with like two friends. I had a brother and mother and I loved them and now they're gone because you're telling me it had to be me? They're gone because of the fight you said I had to fight. Why me? Why her?"

Tomas looked at Eve with tired, sorrowful eyes. "Eve... You are wholly unique. No one else could do what the Sentinel needed to be done. What the universe needs. What Time needs. No other person would have your same circumstances. Your location, your upbringing, your

### ❖ CHAPTER 16 ❖

surroundings, friends, loved ones. The classes you took, the mistakes you've made, the life you've lived, the lessons you've learned. Your personality... Your experience... Your mindset... Your mind, your genetics. Everything about you could not have been and will never be replicated.

"Everything about you. Everything that's happened to you. The way your life has shaped you. You are unique. Sure, everyone is. But you are the one the universe needed."

"How do you know?" Eve asked.

"You've made it this far," Tomas said. "You're beyond capable with your phlasma abilities. You're smart, and friendly. You befriended an intergalactic bounty hunter. You got the help of a Dragolupus on the side of the fight for the universe. When you go to the Sentinel's Army, the people that need you, you'll fit right in. They'll listen to you. Everything about your life has been leading up to saving the Multiverse, whether intentionally or not.

"I can't know for sure. None of us can until the Multiverse is saved. But I don't think anyone else would have made it as far as you have, Evelyn. It's you. It's always been you," Tomas said.

"I like you better than the Sentinel," Ganto chimed in. "If I'm being honest... The Sentinel didn't like me much..."

"Ganto would've run away if it weren't for you," Tomas said. "He did run away."

"Now I'm gonna help you save the hell out of the universe." Ganto nudged Eve. "It's what Andrew would have wanted."

Eve looked out at the graves. Chills ran through her body. Her hands covered her face as she stepped back and cried. Tomas hugged her to calm her.

Things were just now hitting her. This was it. There was no going back to a normal life, or any semblance of it. She knew, in some part, all along that she never could.

She lifted her face from her hands. Tiny cold sparks flickered at the tips of her fingers. She wiped away her tears and inhaled deeply, then let it out, closing her eyes and gathering her composure. She opened her eyes.

"I..." She looked at Tomas. "I have to do this. Or else it's all for nothing. For what future?"

"There's none without you," Tomas said.

"Yeah... And there's none with Suriv and Kranthar still around."

Tomas held out his hand. "Then we fight?" he asked.

Eve nodded and took his hand in hers.

## ❖ CHAPTER 16 ❖

Ganto dropped the blanket off of his head like a hoodie and held out his hand for them.

"I'm gonna help you kill Suriv so hard." Ganto cracked his hand joints in preparation. "I've got a lot of unfinished business with him, anyway."

Kurt, in the distance, turned and saw Ganto.

"Ganto...?" Kurt squinted.

Ganto saw him and saluted as the trio flashed away.

❖ Chapter 17 ❖
# Kranthar's Curse

Eve, Tomas, and Ganto appeared in a dark expanse of nothingness. Howling winds screamed in the inky black skies. Lightning struck around them, and it seemed to be raining some small solid material that clanked and clanged against sharp obsidian ground.

Neither of them could see far ahead of them. Tomas held out his box and pressed a button to let it glow brighter, causing orange light to flood the area. Eve did the same with hers, spreading red light over their surroundings.

"Where are we?!" Eve asked loudly to be heard over the screaming winds.

"Looks like Kranthar's finally decided going back to Tornlozor was a good idea!" Tomas trudged ahead through the blasting winds, followed by Eve.

## ❖ CHAPTER 17 ❖

"There!" Eve pointed ahead at a massive structure. That's a temple! Kranica's temple, probably!" She guessed. "He could be in there!"

"Good call!" Tomas followed her lead to the massive palace. It appeared to be built by the Gars, as the Krantharnics had built Sogar's temple on Illiosopherium. Above the massive door large enough for Kranthar to snake through was a large placard, identical to the stone carving of the Originals on Illiosopherium. Eve and Ganto walked in without hesitation, but Tomas shuddered slightly.

They walked around in the vast and empty palace. Eve yelled for Kranthar angrily, trying to get his attention. She was growing annoyed that he wasn't showing up. Tomas stopped in his tracks when his light shone over shelves. The top shelf shook him to his core.

A few Andromedan built, clone era, Clone Suppressor Helmets, identical to the one Rhey wore, sat on the shelf. How could they be there, in that time, if they were from the future? Below that shelf sat two glowing rêve stones. Tomas could tell just from glancing at them that they were extremely incomplete. "Whose are these?" he yelled into the vast room.

"What'd you find?" Eve asked.

"I need to know who these belong to."

"It's none of your business, *Paradox Master*," Suriv's voice echoed in the room. Tomas and Eve turned their heads to the massive glowing figure in the dark room. "Leave before you have to watch your little one die."

Tomas's fists flared, as did Eve's. The glow of Suriv's armor was barely enough to illuminate Kranthar's faceplate sneaking up behind Suriv. The beastly being's gravelly and garish breath echoed off the walls. "Killing your family wasn't enough to stop you?" Kranthar questioned.

"You made it worse for you," Eve threatened. "Now this is personal."

"Oh, is it?" Kranthar chuckled. "Should I kill your father too?" he asked.

Tomas groaned as he stretched his back, flaring his phlasmatic wings to life. "Good luck with that," he growled. "Whose rêve stones are those?" He pointed at the shelf. "Why do you have Clone Suppressor Helmets? What are you planning?"

"Multiversal domination," Kranthar answered succinctly.

"Out with the old, in with the new," Suriv added.

"I'll kill you both," Eve threatened, "Answer him."

## ❖ CHAPTER 17 ❖

"Hey Kranthar," Suriv turned to him. "Why not kill 'em both?" he suggested.

"That would be ideal." Kranthar nodded. He turned his head to them as his eyes sparked with electricity.

Suriv's eye aperture narrowed and a red light glowed behind it as a charging sound raised in pitch.

The trio were under fire. Laser blasts and strikes of electric phlasmatic energy bombarded them. Suriv and Kranthar were relentless in their attacks, not wanting any of them to escape with their lives.

As the smoke from the attack cleared, the lime green light of Tomas' box's shield shone through, protecting the three of them. The shield lowered and they stood before Kranthar and Suriv with confident stances.

Eve stared them down angrily. Tomas spread his wings. Ganto cocked his rifle.

Kranthar shook his head and a blast wave of electricity pushed Tomas and Eve back. Kranthar spread his wings, and Suriv stepped back. His voice bellowed and shook the walls. Terror drones poured into the room, their electric blue forms lighting up the area.

Tomas' smile quickly faded as the new light shone, allowing him to see more of the room. All around the walls stood empty men in suits. They were motionless, breathless, lifeless. All of them wore Clone Suppressor Helmets. All of their screens lit up one by one and a singular blue line bolted across each screen. It shook and jittered like an audio wave with their groaning voices.

"What the hell is this?" Tomas questioned Kranthar.

"My undead army of some of the clones that Canshla oh so foolishly wiped out in the future."

"Undead?" Eve asked Tomas. "He can do that?"

"You can't just bring people back to life..." Ganto scoffed.

"Phlasma ghosts," Tomas deduced. "Strong ones, all of them... And if they're being controlled by the helmets, nothing will stop them from killing themselves using dark phlasma. Ticking time bombs, each of them..."

"Kill," all of the clones' voices chimed. "Kill."

"You coward." Eve pointed down Kranthar. "You know you can't win on your own so you bring people from the dead just to do it for you!?"

Suriv ran up a wall with his insect-like legs and crawled across the ceiling. He let himself down and landed on his quadpodic legs behind Tomas, Eve, and Ganto. He closed them in from behind. Kranthar snaked closer from in front, and

## CHAPTER 17

the undead clones closed in on them from either side. Ganto stood short by Eve and Tomas' legs, his back against them. Eve and Tomas stood back-to-back, their hands flaring at the ready.

"What's our plan of action?" Tomas asked Eve.

"You're asking me?" She looked around nervously.

Ganto aimed his gun as he looked up as Terror drones circled them from above. "Think of something…"

Eve held her hands in the air and blasted the Terrors with a web of electricity. Ganto fired at the undead clones, who began returning fire.

Tomas lifted his arms and walls of phlasma burst from the ground, shielding them from the laser fire. He blasted fireballs at Suriv's legs, knocking him to the ground.

Eve pounced at Kranthar, hanging onto the edge of his faceplate. Kranthar tried to throw her off, but he smashed his head through the palace walls in the attempt. Eve swung herself around to the back of his faceplate, straddling his neck. She looked down at Tomas from above.

As clones approached him, emitting dark gaseous phlasma, a bi-product of their ghostly nature, Tomas erected phlasmatic spikes from his wrists and jabbed at them.

Eve emulated her father, phlasma crystal blades extended from her wrists, and she plunged them into Kranthar's neck. He screamed in pain, and the remaining Terror drones reacted similarly. Kranthar flew out of the palace and began flying circles around it, trying to get Eve off of his back. She was losing her grip, so she extended the same crystal blades from her feet and impaled them in between armor plating to keep herself anchored.

Ganto had been rapid firing away so much that the rifle needed to cool just as clones were closing in on him. He dropped the rifle and leapt at a clone. He grabbed onto its side with his two lowest arms and then jabbed at its chest with his remaining four spear tipped hands. Another clone tried to get the jump on him, but he evaded by turning quickly and impaling the clone with his antlers. He shook off the body, and his antlers cracked, breaking slightly.

Dark phlasma trailed from clones as they died, soon followed by apparitions of their form flying through the air. Their ghostly auras passed through Ganto, sending a shiver through his whole body each time.

"What the hell?" Ganto turned around to watch as the ghosts wandered away into the void.

## ❖ CHAPTER 17 ❖

"If the clones die while using all of their power then they vanish into total phlasma ghosts," Tomas told Ganto. "You don't have to worry about them, they can't hurt you. Unless you're also a ghost." Tomas lifted himself off the ground with his phlasmatic wings and flew after Eve and Kranthar. "Just keep fighting!" Tomas instructed Ganto as he flew off.

"Whatever you say, crazy guy." Ganto readied his sharp hands to continue tearing away at the clones.

Eve noticed that Tomas was coming to her aid. "Tomas, I'm fine, I got this!" Eve jabbed the blades into the back of Kranthar's neck even harder.

Tomas flew by one of Kranthar's wings as it passed over him. He lifted his hands and blasted the wings with multiple small phlasma crystals. They shot through the skin of the wing, ripping it. He flew underneath another wing, and did the same.

Eve electrified her blades as she continued to stab into Kranthar's neck, ripping at his flesh. Kranthar screamed as he flew. He swung his tail, trying to reach Eve, but he wasn't flexible enough. He couldn't reach her with anything. Terror drones swarmed Eve and blasted her with a collective bolt of lightning. She jumped out of the way and the blast struck Kranthar behind his neck, into the wounds Eve had left behind.

Kranthar fell back down to the palace with a wailing groan.

Eve jumped from Kranthar at the last minute and rolled across the ground as Kranthar's body slammed on top of several clones, smashing part of the palace.

Suriv glowed a bright white, seeming to disappear.

"We're not done with you!" Ganto yelled and ran after him. He jumped, intending to tackle the Calcurus beast, but he hit nothing and slammed onto the ground as Suriv vanished, teleporting away. Ganto cursed under his breath.

"If Suriv can tell that you've already lost," Eve began, "That's the moment when you should give up!" She yelled at Kranthar.

Kranthar was mumbling something in an alien language. Tomas stared at him curiously, trying to decipher it. Eve was getting nervous, and Ganto was on a rampage against the phlasma ghost clones.

Kranthar's head shot up, his eyes glowing bright green. Eve jumped back, startled, and instinctively held onto Tomas for security. She pushed away and stood her ground, deciding instead to appear powerful in the face of danger.

## ❖ CHAPTER 17 ❖

"By the power of Celestae!" Kranthar yelled. "With the sacrifice of my dying soul, and by the aura of Kranica's holy palace!"

"Tomas, what's he doing?"

"I don't know..." Tomas stepped back.

"I lay upon the three of you a curse of an inescapable death!"

Ganto turned his attention to Kranthar after hearing the inclusion of all three.

"Though I have failed my master, the Sentinel's successor will fall yet."

"Agh! Shut up!" Eve yelled. She pulled her arms up and massive crystal phlasma rocks shot through Kranthar from behind, smashing the rest of the palace to the ground and impaling Kranthar in the process. Kranthar's head fell limp, and the green glow in his eyes faded.

"Ha..." Eve caught her breath, "I did it!" She jumped excitedly. "Take that!" She spat in the direction of Kranthar's corpse. "You're dead!"

Ganto had finished killing all the clones, and what remained of the Terror drones began fleeing in a crazy daze, as they had just lost their hivemind and didn't know how to think. Lone wandering ghosts of the twice-dead clones wandered the palace mindlessly. Ganto finished killing off the few clones that remained.

"Tomas, we did it." Eve smiled. "We can save the universe now."

Tomas stared ahead, blank faced. "It's never that simple." He looked down at his hands. "Let me see your hands."

"What?" Eve asked. She coughed, and showed Tomas her hands. Ganto snapped the neck of one final clone, then walked up to them and outstretched his six arms, showing them his spike hands. On the palms of Tomas and Eve's hands, on the underside of Ganto's spikes, was an intricate symbol, seemingly burnt into them, blackening their skin and Ganto's exoskeleton. The symbol glowed a faint green, but soon faded as it burned its final mark into their hands.

"What is it…" Ganto asked with a cough.

"The curse of a Krantharnic," Tomas explained. "There's no escaping a death like this. It'll be slow, Eve you'll probably die at the normal human life expectancy, this curse is meant for Originals, but… This curse is more of a phlasmatic disease than anything… It's going to be painful… *Very* painful."

## ❖ CHAPTER 17 ❖

"I call bull," Ganto said. "This crazy religion the Originals all follow makes no sense. Phlasma? Sure, whatever. Ghosts? Alright, I can take it. But I draw the line at curses. This isn't real. We're totally fi— AGH!" Ganto held his arm and fell to his knees, wincing in pain. It felt as if an earthquake had shattered his exoskeleton, shaking him to his core. "Ah, shit..." Ganto stared at his hand.

"There's no way we can save the universe in the condition we're about to be in," Tomas said. "As much as you'd like to not believe it... We're cursed."

"But..." Eve looked up at Tomas, "We killed him... Kranthar's dead, it's over..."

"That doesn't matter. Suriv's still out there, he's still working for someone." Tomas cleared his throat, holding his hand to his heart as a stinging pain shot through him. "There's something else you need to do Eve."

"Wait," Ganto spoke up. The silence that followed was broken by the screaming winds of Tornlozor. The sky seemed to brighten just slightly as day approached, but the black gaseous skies remained. "Eve, let me borrow the box."

"Why?" she asked.

"I need to go back from where I fled. Back to the Sentinel's Army, so I can help save the universe. I've got no time to waste, not now."

"Do you really mean it?" Eve asked.

"I'll meet you there." He smiled.

Eve handed Ganto the box. He flashed away, and shortly after, the box returned. Eve looked up at Tomas.

"What now?" she asked.

❖ Chapter 18 ❖

# Adam Jaminski

Tomas and Eve appeared in front of an old and run-down building at the edge of a bustling city. No one was around, not at the edge. Eve could see the city in the distance, but her eyes were drawn back to the looming presence of the old decrepit building.

"Where are we?" she asked.

"New York, 2011," Tomas answered with a shiver. He approached the doors of the abandoned building. He held his hand to the door and closed his eyes.

"What is this place?" Eve asked of the building.

"There's something I need you to do before we both die. It's something especially important. I said no more secrets, remember. It's time to be completely honest. When Kranthar said, a while ago, that I was using you... he wasn't entirely wrong."

"What?" Eve asked. She wasn't surprised, but knowing now who Tomas was, it still hurt.

"Just like those five years with the Sentinel, sometimes certain things just... *need* to happen for timelines to work out the way they do. This time, it's your turn for five years gone. Except it's going to be much longer than that. And much less interesting. It's going to be torture for you."

"What are you saying?"

"This building, we're buying it," Tomas explained. "You're going to open an orphanage, and you're going to wait."

"An orphanage? What? Wait how long?" Eve's mind was overrun with questions, she was at a complete loss.

"Five years you have to wait for your true task. Until then the orphanage needs to be established and run normally. And after that your eighteen-year task begins. If it's any consolation, you always wanted to teach. You'll have some of that here. But when you're done, you have to skip forward in time, to 2052, you won't live long enough to wait—"

"What is this? What are you talking about? With this curse who knows how long I'll live."

## ❖ CHAPTER 18 ❖

"I do." Tomas held Eve's shoulders. "Listen, this task is beyond important."

January 20th, 2016, New York City.

How miserable could someone be? How hard of a fall from grace can someone take?

Eve had just begun to accept herself as a Sentinel when she was instructed with a task of waiting, and a task of torture. Fueled by revenge and anger, she was forced to mourn the loss of her family the same way everyone else would; with time. She was ready to fight, all of her previous reluctance had vanished, and yet she was forced to wait. Not to fight.

She had been running the orphanage for her first five years already, and every day she would countdown until it began.

With each day her pain grew. The mark on her hand lightened her skin to a dead gray, and it spread. The symbol carved deeper, nearing the bone. She was prone to coughing attacks and unwilling sleepless nights. She aged quicker because of the curse. She was twenty-two now, with the appearance of someone almost three times the age.

She tried her best to see the light of the situation but nothing kept her going. Nothing except her father's orders. Today she marked the calendar for the beginning of when the physical torture would mean nothing compared to what was coming.

It had been almost exactly a year since the anomaly of a child, Adam Jaminski, was found in a nearby hospital. Nearly a year since the nurse who took ownership of the child was attacked by Gars at that hospital, a year since she'd been targeted almost daily by bounty hunters and attempts at the child's life. She finally gave in.

A ringing bell sounded, signaling the opening of the front doors. A woman came in with the one-year-old in a stroller. She looked nervous, and beyond tired. She approached the lobby desk.

Eve coughed, "You must be Julie."

"How do you know my—" the woman spoke up in fear.

"You want to drop off the kid. Jaminski, right? No paperwork required."

"Thank you." Julie nodded, she seemed utterly relieved. "Thank you so much." She left the orphanage as fast as she could.

## CHAPTER 18

"No problem." Eve grumbled under her breath.

A mechanical flash burst behind her. She swiveled in her chair. "Nice of you to finally show up."

"Eve, I'm sorry, but this needs to be done." Tomas walked to the other side of the counter and rolled baby Adam in. Tomas hunched over and moved slowly. The curse had not been kind to him. As old as he already appeared, the curse exemplified it. He looked ancient, as if he would crumble to dust at any moment if you so much as sneezed in his direction. "Do you remember the rules I told you? Your instructions?" Tomas asked with a raspy voice.

"Yes," Eve said, disinterested, "You still haven't told me why."

"Do not show this child any love. Don't even be absent, show him hate. Drive him mad. Never, *never*, let him be adopted. He should resent you if you're successful. He should resent all mankind."

"I thought we were the good guys." Eve leaned back in her chair.

"Eve, you know it's not like that—"

"Then tell me. Why am I supposed to torture this kid for eighteen years, huh? Tell me."

Tomas kneeled down by Eve's chair and looked up at her. "This child, Adam Jaminski, he's going to become the Sentinel."

Eve's eyes widened.

"He's going to become your father one day, he's going to become me one day, and trust me, he's going to forget everything about his life before the Sentinel, but you *must* promise me that you'll do your best to drive him insane."

"I can't do that, he's you!" Eve protested.

"See that's, ha… yeah that's why I didn't want you to know who he was." Tomas looked into Adam's eyes. "He's the Sentinel. He has an inherent need to protect, a near unrelenting drive.

"That needs to be removed, and if it can't it needs to be shaken. He needs to go insane, so that he hates people. So that he plans for mass murder, and so that one day, he builds some tiny, super powerful, ultra-portable nuclear bombs.

"Because if he never builds those bombs, nothing like them will exist. His research lab wouldn't exist, and neither would his scientific prowess. By the time he's the Sentinel, there's no way the Galactic War could be won, and Amalga-5 would never exist. It's how it's always happened. It's how it needs to happen."

## ❖ CHAPTER 18 ❖

"Before you ruined my life all I wanted was to be a teacher to help raise a better tomorrow. This flies in the face of all that I wanted. You could be a least a little subtle with how you ruin my life. I don't see how this helps save the universe, being a bad babysitter—"

"If he doesn't turn out the way he needs to, Eve, then the universe will split into *another* alternate reality. Remember before this all started, I told you everything about the past, you know what happened when the universe broke. I don't want that again. You don't want that again."

"Right." Eve nodded begrudgingly.

"Take care of yourself." Tomas stood up. "Not him." He looked down at baby Adam one last time before he flashed away.

Eve stared at the child intently. He stared back, completely lost and with a blank stare, unknowing of anything. He smiled as spittle foamed at his mouth. "Mama," he spoke. "Ma… ma!"

Eve shook her head. "Dammit."

"Don't pretend like I don't know what you're up to!" the ten-year-old Adam Jaminski yelled at Eve. The orphans looked at him like he was crazy, but they were used to it, just another one of his fits. "Daniel got to have a family! Braedon got to be loved! Why can't I? I saw those people, they looked at *me* first! THEY ASKED ABOUT ME! WHY DIDN'T YOU LET THEM!"

"SHUT UP!" Eve yelled, coughing and holding her mouth. "They weren't considering adopting you," Eve lied. "They hated you. Everyone hates you."

"That's not true!" Adam snapped back.

Eve slapped him across the face. The sting of the slap shot through Eve's hand. The curse magnified her own pain.

Adam looked up at her with pure hatred and anger in his eyes. He stormed out into the backyard of the orphanage, angrily slamming the glass door, shattering it as he exited. He yelled to himself outside, "It's not fair!" He sat down in the grass aggressively. He tore at the lawn, tossing dirt and grass everywhere. He turned around to face Eve. "You're evil!" he screamed. "I hate you!"

"Hate you too, kid," Eve responded. She angrily stormed back to her desk. She sat down and took a deep breath. She dropped her head down on the desk and cried into her

## ❖ CHAPTER 18 ❖

arms. The only thing she hated was treating Adam the way that she truly needed to. She looked at her hands, mutilated by the curse. They were shattering and flaking, and the curse was spreading up her arms.

Tomas was right about how painful it would be. It was like her hands were constantly on fire. Like her lungs were filled with shattered glass. As if a knife had been lodged in her heart, and it twisted in her sleep.

She looked around to see if anyone was looking, and when she saw that the coast was clear, she reached for the box sitting on her desk, and flashed away.

She appeared by a throne made of rubble in the Sentinel's old, abandoned lab on the dead Earth. She approached Tomas, who was staring over the sea. "Have you found a cure yet?" she asked him.

"I haven't been looking," Tomas admitted. He stared at the distant ocean. His face was thin, malformed, skeletal. His body wasn't responding to the curse well. He didn't have much time left.

"How am I supposed to save the universe if—"

"You'll find a way," Tomas insisted.

"I want this to be over with." Eve sat down in the rubble throne. "I'm sick and tired of all this."

"I know you are." Tomas approached the rubble throne. He adjusted his jacket and leaned against the backrest of the throne. "If you want to look for the answer yourself, check this." Tomas handed Eve a book.

"What is this?" she asked.

"Gar history on phlasma and its uses among the Originals. There may be something about the curse in there. I don't know."

"I can't read Garish," Eve reminded Tomas.

Tomas flashed away and appeared quickly with another book. "English to Garish 101." He handed it to her.

"How did this book exist?" Eve asked.

"It didn't. I asked a friend of mine to write it."

"But you were barely—"

"Time travel."

"Right, have to sort of remind myself of that every once in a while." Eve shook her head. "I'll find a way."

"Good luck." Tomas nodded.

Eve stared at the book.

Tomas looked back up at her. She hadn't left yet. "What?" he asked. "Are you gonna stick around for training again?"

"I don't know," Eve said. "I want to, but…"

## ❖ CHAPTER 18 ❖

"But?" Tomas studied Eve's face for answers.

"It feels like my limbs are being ripped from my body. Like I'm being torn to shreds from the inside out."

"Yeah…" Tomas looked away, holding his wrist.

"I'll stick around to train," Eve decided.

"Are you sure?"

Eve flinched as she prepared herself. "Yeah. Still have a universe to save, after all."

❖ ❖ ❖

"What do you think you're doing!?" Eve scolded a fifteen-year-old Adam.

"Get away from me!" Adam yelled.

"You killed a frog, Jaminski, get in the corner!" Eve approached him in the yard.

"The corner's for babies!" Adam protested.

"The corner is for idiots and undesirables like you!" Eve grabbed him by his shirt collar. "Corner, now," she demanded.

Adam ran into the orphanage. Eve saw him run upstairs. "Adam!" She followed after him, coughing. Adam was packing stuff into a case, shoving everything he could into it. He stood up to leave, and when he turned around, he was met with Eve standing in the doorway. "What do you think you're doing, Jaminski?" Eve pressed.

"Let me go, Sanchez." He attempted to walk past her and through the doorway, but she grabbed him by the arm.

"No one will accept you out there, do you really think you could make it on your own?" Eve squinted in anger. "You're an idiot-child, you couldn't last a day."

"I'm smart!" Adam protested. "Smarter than you!"

Eve slapped him. "If you were smart people would want you!" she snapped.

"PEOPLE DO WANT ME*! YOU JUST WON'T LET THEM!*" Adam pushed Eve.

With the curse, Eve's pain receptors went haywire. Everything hurt, and the small shove felt like a thousand tiny knives being shot into her flesh and lodging themselves into her bones. She reacted in a way she told herself she would never do. She snapped her fingers and a spark of phlasma ignited at her fingertips.

Adam stumbled back and fell to the ground, dropping his case, his stuff fell out and he scooted himself away and into the wall where he kept trying to push himself away from Eve. "You're a monster!"

## ❖ CHAPTER 18 ❖

Eve's hand flared brighter. "You're the monster!" she yelled. The door slammed behind her. "You're insane!" she screamed. The flame vanished and she coughed into her arm. She kept coughing and coughing, and the pain in her chest grew.

"Die!" Adam yelled. "I hope you die!"

Eve swept her arm to the side and Adam was flung into the side of the bed nearest him. He hit its wooden base with his head and was knocked unconscious. Eve fell to her knees and held her chest. "I can't do this anymore. I can't do this." She breathed heavily, trying to take in as much air as possible, even if it felt like breathing a fiery poison that rotted her insides.

The box dropped from camo near her, and it spoke, "Just three more years of Adam. Just three more years."

"I can't... I really can't..." Eve sobbed behind coughing.

"I could bear it at first. I was able to find some semblance of happiness when I could teach and raise the other children but it's no secret how I treat Adam. They don't trust me. They don't like me. Everything hurts, I can't keep going! Why can't I just skip ahead?" Eve begged. "I don't want to do this anymore, I'm dying! Dad, you're dying!" Eve gestured toward Tomas's bony arms and blackened neck, dying and flaking.

"I know, but it's what needs to be done. Three more years and you can skip forward."

"I'm starting to actually hate the kid... but I don't want to because he's you, and—"

"Trust me. I'm not him. I haven't been for a long time. The Sentinels never remember, at least not as memories of their own." Tomas paced around in the broken-down lab. "Any luck on that cure?"

"No." Eve looked away.

"Hm." Tomas looked over the sea. "You'll find it," he assured her. "You'll find it..."

Eve checked a tally off on a sticky note, one of hundreds that covered the board behind her. She stood up and approached Adam's room. The orphanage had been empty besides him for that year and half, and today was the day. "Adam." Eve knocked on his open door. "Get out."

### ❖ CHAPTER 18 ❖

"No birthday cake?" Adam teased. "What a surprise," he mumbled.

"Yeah, congratulations, you're eighteen, which means no one wanted you all your life, and now you have to go learn to want yourself, but even you know that you're just too—"

"I got accepted," Adam boasted.

"What?" Eve asked, surprised.

"To that school. I'm not stupid. I told you." Adam stood from his bed.

"Must've been a mistake," Eve grumbled and coughed. "Like you."

"You'll regret those words. The world will feel my pain." Adam picked up his case. "They'll accept me. I'll make them accept me," he growled to her as he walked past her. "You don't own me anymore! This place is empty now, so go sit on your high and mighty throne and die in it why don't you!" Adam shouted down the hall as he left and slammed the door shut on his way out.

Eve took a deep breath. She walked to the lobby downstairs, and she locked the doors. The box uncloaked itself by her shoulder, and she flashed away for the year 2052.

She waited for months and months on end for her final task to show up, and one day it finally did, on October 15th of that year.

It was a gray day. Clouds in the sky blocked out the sun, and outside, the normally beautiful fall trees were empty, all their leaves were scattered on the wet ground, brown and soggy with recent rain. Very few cars, and few people walking about made the day exceptionally quiet, something that Eve had become extremely accustomed to.

The doors opened with a slight creak. A blond man in a duster, bandana, and jeans stepped in, the Fourth Sentinel. Behind him came in a young woman, Amara Tempus, and with them a small child, Matrona Tempus.

Eve's eyes grew wide, she knew immediately, despite not seeing them before, who they were. She adjusted her nametag on her desk and sat up straighter, holding back a cough.

"Ms. Sanchez." Four remembered her but he didn't expect her to know him.

"Is that the girl?" Eve gestured towards Matrona. "Matrona?"

"How did you—" the Sentinel began, confused.

## ❖ CHAPTER 18 ❖

"I got a tip recently, from a…" Eve adjusted her reading glasses and looked down at a blank note, "A *'Paradox Master'*?" she feigned reading.

Four, and Amara both shared an equally confused look with each other.

"He made it a very clear point to me that the girl not be adopted by just *anyone*." Eve stepped down from her seat and walked around the desk to get a better look at Matrona. "He said she needed to go to someone specific, no questions asked. He just didn't tell me who—"

"Adam Jaminski," Four spoke quickly, with purpose.

Eve froze in place, like she was in the Russian tundra all over again. Shivers ran up and down her spine at the mention of the name. She waited a few seconds, adjusted her glasses, and went back to her seat.

"I'll keep that name in mind." She coughed, holding her hand over her chest. The curse was spreading deeper, she could feel it. She wondered why Tomas wouldn't tell her that Adam was coming back to adopt a child. She knew how Adam worked, she didn't trust him with a child, but she trusted Tomas.

Four flashed Amara away, and remained. He looked down at Matrona with a reassuring look. Four said nothing, and walked outside. Matrona stood around, confused, and lost. She held onto a journal that the Sentinel gave her like her life depended on it. Eve stared at her curiously. She snapped back into focus when the doors of the orphanage burst open, she wasn't expecting Adam to come so quickly.

"Sanchez," the thirty-seven-year-old Adam greeted Eve sternly.

"Jaminski," Eve answered back, just as stern.

Adam turned his attention to Matrona and he walked up to the counter, and placed stacks of money in front of Eve.

"You'd make a terrible father." Eve pushed the money aside.

"Give me the girl." Adam stood forward, threateningly.

"If it weren't for my promise, I wouldn't normally allow this. Take her." Eve broke eye contact with Adam.

"No paperwork? What promise?" Adam questioned.

"Take her!" Eve yelled. She couldn't stand seeing Adam again. "Leave!" She slammed her desk. Matrona burst into tears. Adam said nothing, and grabbed her arm, pulling her from the orphanage. As the doors shut, Tomas flashed into view beside Eve.

"You did it."

"It's about time." Eve stood up, and coughed.

## ❖ CHAPTER 18 ❖

"Have you found the cure?" Tomas asked.

"I'm not sure," Eve answered.

Tomas hesitated for a few moments, both of them stared at the doors of the orphanage. "Come on." Tomas held out his hand. "There's something I need to show you."

Eve took his dying hand in hers. Just clasping their hands around one another's sent a spike of pain up their arms. They flinched, then flashed away.

❖ Chapter 19 ❖
# The Beginning

Eve and Tomas appeared on a rocky beach. Waves crashed against stones, and seagulls cawed. The two of them stared over the water's edge for some time before Tomas spoke up.

"Walk with me." Tomas turned and began walking. The two of them traveled down a narrow sandy strip up against a tall cliffside lit softly by the overcast sky. Tomas led Eve to a small cave opening in the wall of the cliff. Unknown to Eve, the cliffside cave was carved right beneath Adam Jaminski's lab in New York.

Tomas stood in front of the cave for a moment, staring in. Eve waited curiously. She scanned Tomas up and down. He cleared his throat and lowered his head as he stepped into the cave. A concerned look covered Eve's face before she decided to follow Tomas into the small cave.

## ❖ CHAPTER 19 ❖

Tomas sat down on the sandy floor of the cave. He grunted as he sat, his bones shattering and joints grinding with a sort of burning familiarity. He gestured for Eve to sit by him. She crossed her legs, groaning as she sat. Tomas leaned against a rock. He let out a drawn-out sigh as he looked over the ocean horizon ahead of him.

"Yeah." He nodded to himself. "Yeah, this is the place." He smiled as he calmly looked over the ocean.

Eve stared at him, her wrinkled face twisting, and her brow lifting.

Tomas grunted and turned around, pulling an object from around the rock behind him and placing it before him.

The object was a dark cube. Glowing strips of blue zigzagged around it. Right above the cube a phlasmatic ball of liquid floated, swishing around in place: a projector sphere.

Tomas held out his hand, and in it was a small stone, glowing light purple as hints of blue pulsated through it.

"What is that?" Eve asked.

"This is a stone extracted from the memory of Time."

Eve shook herself. As used to this strange world as she had become, it was strange how calmly Tomas told her that in his hands were memories from Time herself.

"She gave it to me when I retired, so that I could understand the full extent of the danger that I was running away from… the danger that you had to be prepared to face. It tells a story as old as Time herself. The story of her hidden past. This is vital information." Tomas presented the stone to Eve.

She stared at it. Her future was dictated by this tiny rock.

Tomas plopped the stone into the floating orb of liquid. He snapped his fingers, and a wall of phlasma stone closed the cave entrance, filling the cave with absolute darkness. He swished his hands in front of him and created a cloud of phlasma in front of them. Then, in an instant, the floating orb glowed and filled the cave with a brilliant light.

"This is Time's very first memory…" Tomas whispered. "Behold… *the beginning.*"

## · THE PARADOX MASTER ·

A blue ball of misty phlasma floated alone in an empty white void. A galactic shape spiraled at the center of the floating orb. Eve watched as merely a spectator alongside Tomas.

The orb seemed to look around, curious of itself, of its consciousness. The orb shifted, growing a body and a head to

## ❖ CHAPTER 19 ❖

contain the galactic spiral shape that seemed to both be the brain and heart of the being.

This was Time.

As she looked around, she seemed lost. She clenched her fists, and in an instant, a rectangular shape formed itself in front of her, then expanded inwards with a blast of light, pushing forward a hallway of darkness before expanding forever outward within the confines of the doorway that had been created in that split second.

Time stepped through the threshold and entered a vast black void, leaving the white behind her. She looked down at her hands, admiring the specks of glowing white that floated around in herself. As she closed her hands, the dark empty void she stood in became filled with the same specks of light, shimmering like distant stars.

Time lifted her arms, and a throne of ever shifting gold stood before her. She sat in it and sighed, as if lifting a weight off her shoulders, like she had been holding her breath. Having just been born, creating all that she had proved to be tiresome.

"Time knew nothing," Tomas explained. "Of course, this was the first ever anything. She was the first thing. She invented the concept and passage of time, accidentally, just by existing. She didn't know herself, or anything, because there was no knowledge. There was nothing to know."

"So she just sat there?" Eve asked as she watched Time sit in her throne, completely still.

"For millions of years," Tomas said. He coughed and held his wrist as it stung. He shook his head to clear his mind and continued, "Needless to say, she had a lot of time to think. She knew everything. Every bit of nothing. There wasn't much to learn. With the absence of things to learn about she decided to make things up, pretend like she knew stuff that wasn't real. Then she remembered who she was. She could make real what previously wasn't. So, birthed out of boredom..." Tomas flicked his hand and altered the composition of the cloud of phlasma in front of him. "She started to shape existence."

The memory projection faded and shifted like static. A new memory filled the cave.

Time sat in the same place, it seemed as though nothing had happened at all, when, in the blink of an eye, she stood.

She turned to her side, admiring her hands for a moment. Then she clenched her phlasmatic fists and created two more thrones beside her. A rocky throne of stone and purple phlasma crystals and fire formed itself at one side of the golden throne, and at the other, a throne of silver rose up like a small tower.

## ❖ CHAPTER 19 ❖

As Time's galactic brain spiraled quickly and pulsated with a burning white light, a figure formed in the seat of the phlasma throne.

This figure was a mirror image of Time. Though this figure was green, and his inner galaxy purple.

"Celestae, my son," were Time's first words. "Master of the master element, Phlasma," she declared.

Celestae bowed. Though he had just been created, he had been bestowed with all of Time's knowledge. He understood.

Time turned to her side and created another figure.

This figure was dark red, with a burning blue galaxy shifting vividly in his head. He sat as a looming presence in his silver throne. Already he seemed discontent with his being, not asking to have been born.

"*Ultimae...*" Time spoke, "my son. Master of that which keeps existence from crumbling. My *Paradox Master*."

Ultimae bowed.

"Woah, wait a minute..." Eve looked to Tomas. "He was the first Paradox Master? Who is that guy?"

"Time's secret. Her shame," Tomas said.

The memory shifted once more. Time watched over her sons and they stood in the white void lobby of the Extraverse.

❖ THE BEGINNING ❖

They each created their own rooms, much like their mother before them.

They were practicing their ability to create.

"What more could we make?" Celestae looked to his brother Ultimae.

Ultimae stared into his room and thought hard about his brother's question. He looked to Celestae and held out his hand. "Watch this, brother," Ultimae spread his fingers as a sphere glowed in his hands, soon becoming a tiny rocky planet. Perfectly round, uniform, gray and lifeless. Ultimae's galaxy pulsated with pride.

"What is it?" Celestae asked.

"A seed," Ultimae called it. "If we make enough of these they could grow indefinitely. It would be a sight to behold. The complexity it could create, patterns of floating seeds... forever expanding... could you imagine?"

"Would they be as big as the stars that mother created?" Celestae asked.

"They would grow much larger. They would house the stars and create more seeds within and surrounding themselves, in separate systems, themselves creating larger systems which spread in patterns of systems, those too also creating patterns, uniformly structured, forever and ever. Ongoing fractals of star patterns... Universes that contain stars

## CHAPTER 19

that bring structure and order to the smaller seeds, the planets. It would be magnificent."

Celestae rubbed his chin. "Interesting. Would we grow them in your room, or mine? Perhaps Mother's?"

"Think grander, brother!" Ultimae held out his arms. "A new dimension, outside the constraints of this Extraverse!"

"Would we need to ask Mother for permission?" Celestae asked.

Time watched over the brothers, eager to hear Ultimae's response.

Ultimae thought for a bit before saying, "This creation would be... Outside the constraints of Time's rule."

Time stepped away, taken aback.

"Uh oh," Eve mumbled. "Ultimae's a bad guy... isn't he?" she asked.

Tomas shifted his sitting position, taking in a deep breath. "Ultimae and Celestae went through with their plans."

The memory shifted, moving on to the next memory. Tomas shifted the composition of the cloud of phlasma in front of him, stretching it into a galactic shape and using it to demonstrate what he was explaining as the memories shifted.

Tomas continued, "They created what they called 'The Ultimate Creation.' At the time, absolutely nothing existed except the Extraverse and everything inside it. But with Ultimae and Celestae's new project, a new dimension was made. This was a massive plane of singularities, stretched across infinite nothingness. Ultimae had a plan, which was to watch the seeds that they planted grow. Nothing more, nothing less. It was merely a side project, something to keep them busy and pass the time. An experiment, an art project, whatever analogy you prefer.

"But these singularities did eventually grow into something more. Like seeds, they grew into their own things, separate but connected by a sort of... I don't know, dimensional roots, I guess. This created several offshoots of this plane... The Multiverse of universes."

The memory finished and shifted. It showed Time looking over a gaseous cloud that floated before her. She was alone in the Extraverse, and she seemed to be watching over the new Multiverse.

Through the shifting surveillance cloud, Time could see Celestae and Ultimae, standing in an empty field, on a planet in one of the universes of the Multiverse.

"Time admired her children, she always had. They were created in her image, just as powerful, and full of just as much potential as herself. She couldn't wait to see what the brothers would do with the existence she had birthed them into. Clearly, they had already begun tinkering with their ultimate creative and destructive power and unlimited freedom. This new creation, that Ultimae had planned to keep secret from Time, worried her, but also excited her. She had imagined her sons for the purpose of creating, after all. She had hoped that the three of them together would work to create beautiful things. She figured that watching her sons create would be fine for now."

Time pressed her face into the cloud and watched.

"Do you see this, brother?" Ultimae asked Celestae, from the surface of a random planet in one of the universes.

"What about it."

"These protuberances that jut up into the sky, they have disturbed the smooth nature of the rest of this planet." Ultimae pointed at distant mountains.

Eve frowned. The mountains were beautiful. They reminded her of home, as they seemed to be tinged with purple when obscured in the distance.

"Brother, is this not exactly what you wanted? To watch the seeds grow into that which you could not have imagined? We could not have created these protuberances ourselves. Our creation did it for us, and that is something we should embrace."

## THE BEGINNING

"Rah!" Ultimae flung out his arms. The ground rumbled, and the mountains smoothed themselves out. Just like that, the planet was smooth again.

Celestae's galactic brain pulsated, shrinking and shrouding itself in darkness.

Eve gasped.

Time appeared on the planet.

"Mother!" Ultimae jumped, startled by her sudden appearance in his secret project. Though, Time made no mention of its secrecy. She floated about, looking up at the sky, and admiring the clouds.

"I am proud of you, son," Time said.

Ultimae's galaxy pulsated.

"But you have ignored the inherent beauty of your creation." Time stared at a distant cloud. "How wonderful…" Her body shifted. She became a puffy white cloud, floating before Ultimae gracefully. "Did you make these?"

"No!" Ultimae roared. He clenched his fists, and every cloud in the sky was wiped away, and they disappeared.

Time shifted back into her normal form. "Son?"

"This is not my creation. Something is wrong with it, I cannot tell what."

"It is a complex system, brother, these things should be expected."

## CHAPTER 19

"Now that we know, I will not make the same mistake a second time." Ultimae vanished. Celestae followed.

The memory shifted once more, as Time sat back in her throne, staring through the surveillance cloud again. She was watching a clouded planet, one with beautiful mountain ranges and deep scarring canyons. Her galaxy beamed like a smile in her head.

"Time wanted to surprise her children with newcomers, ones that may show Ultimae the beauty that he was blind to in his creation. So she created *life* on that planet. New life, new siblings, to create with her existing children."

"The Originals," Eve said. She knew this part.

"*No...*"

"What?"

Time clenched her fist. Three new beings, identical to her in every aspect but color, appeared on the distant planet.

Time whispered, *"Cosmae, Nebulae, Solarae,* my children..."

Tomas whispered, "The Sarran, Time's new children, just as powerful..."

But, before Time could say much more to her new children, the cloud darkened, obscuring her vision. She stood from her throne and approached Ultimae's room. She flung open the door, met with a terrible sight.

A projection of the vast Multiverse filled the room, and Celestae stood before Ultimae with his arms out, trying to stop him. Ultimae's arms were stretched out at his sides, his galaxy glowing as he clenched his fist, and the projection of the Multiverse vanished.

Time fell to her knees and held her head.

"What did he do?" Eve asked.

"What have you done?" Time grimaced.

"There were too many issues with this attempt," Ultimae said. "We are starting over. This time, no mistakes. Just order."

"You... scrapped the Multiverse?" Time asked.

"Destroyed it," Ultimae said. "We have room to make another now."

Celestae held his head low.

"Come now brother, we must start again," Ultimae said.

Time scrambled to her throne and sat down. She opened the cloud again to find her new children.

"They were created in the Multiverse," Tomas explained. "As soon as they were born, they died. And no one knew but Time."

## ❖ CHAPTER 19 ❖

## • THE BROKEN UNIVERSE •

The memory shifted. "Ultimae and Celestae had created the new Multiverse, the second attempt. Millennia had passed since, and Time grew bored again," Tomas said. "She wasn't interested in the planets and stars that Ultimae and Celestae were so content with. She instead wanted to experiment with the very stuff that she was made of, in an effort to understand herself and her children. This stuff, the master element, she called it, was phlasma. Her lost children lingered in her mind every passing moment since they were snuffed out, and so, in her experiments, she used phlasma to create the first living things in the new Multiverse. She too, was trying again."

"The Originals..." Eve interjected.

"This time, yes," Tomas confirmed.

Time shook her head. She held her hand to the cloud and flicked through it, swiping her hand as images passed her by. She came upon an image of a burning purple phlasma star. Surrounding it were a few planets, namely: Nidus, Tornlozor, and Illiosopherium.

❖ THE BEGINNING ❖

Time clenched her fist, with a burst of light a large object appeared in the empty space. A large planet with a face. Its eyes opened and flared to life.

"Modius…" Eve recognized the Quodstella.

"The first Original," Tomas said. As Time created the rest of the Originals, Tomas explained, "The Originals regarded the three Celestial Beings as gods, and their praise gave Time and her children power. Just the mere mention of their names alone would make each of them stronger, more connected to their phlasmatic being. But that wasn't enough to make Time's children happy with her unwanted contributions to their side project."

The memory skipped forward a bit.

"What have you done!" Ultimae stormed into the Extraverse from the lobby with Celestae by his side.

Time turned slowly to face them.

"You ruined it," Celestae said. "You ruined our plan," Celestae begged with a glance. If Time interjected too much, this Multiverse could go the way of the first.

"You do not appreciate my contribution?" Time asked.

"It breaks the whole system!" Ultimae yelled. "How will we see the universes grow on their own if we are meddling with their growth? The presence of this pest, this- this Modius, ruins that system, and by proxy the rest! The patterns are broken! The fractal is shattered! We should not, no, cannot add stimulants or hindrances whenever we please! Undo this, I beg you!"

"I cannot," Time said. "It would be cruel to my children."

Ultimae's hands clenched into fists and they shook with red wisps of phlasma spewing from his fingertips. "*We are your children…*"

"These beings that I have brought into your domain are your blood, your cosmic equals," Time said. "You will treat them as such!"

"They are lesser than us!" Ultimae yelled. "You made them as such!"

"You should not have acted upon what is not yours," Celestae said calmly.

"You did the same," Time said. "And you are mine."

Celestae looked away. He understood. Ultimae wouldn't back down so easily. He clenched his fist, and a shockwave burst through the Extraverse.

Time looked around. "What have you done?" she asked.

"We can no longer act upon outside dimensions without being present within them," Ultimae said. "We are even, now. We created this Multiverse without consulting you, you created these pests without consulting us. No more. We will not create further. Stay out of our domain."

Time grumbled.

The beings sat in their thrones, silenced by an invisible crushing tension.

The memory shifted once more, revealing Ultimae sulking on his throne. He created a few small planets and tossed them into orbit around his throne, creating his own tiny personal universe to watch over.

"What's he doing?" Eve asked.

"Ultimae wasn't happy with his new restrictions alone. This is him trying to cope. He turned his throne into its own sort of self-sustaining, lifeless universe. A garden of planets, structured under the patterns he likes so much... but it wasn't the same. It wouldn't suffice."

The memory shifted again.

Vita and Morty appeared in the Extraverse, through the door from the lobby. They looked around, shrunken in their equal fear and admiration for the gods that sat before them.

"Now, eventually two Deusaves from Nidus of our universe came to the Extraverse, some say by chance, right at the cusp of a war brewing in the Black Star 7 district of their

### ❖ CHAPTER 19 ❖

universe. Time decided to make another executive decision, but as you would expect…"

Ultimae from the memory interrupted Tomas. "This is ridiculous!"

"How so?" Time asked.

"You cannot make these pests as Emissaries! They are not the same as us, they are vermin that you infested my project with!"

"They are just the same as you and I, child. They are your siblings in phlasmatic blood. When will you realize that you are not the most important being in existence?"

"I *was*."

Time paused.

Death covered his face with his wing.

"We were, mother," Ultimae corrected himself. "The three of us were gods. Now what, with this new *Life* idea you have…"

Life lowered in her throne, ashamed it seemed.

Ultimae continued, "Phlasmatic garbage like the creatures you have made will begin to spread across the Multiverse like a disease! And with Death, who knows what ramifications that could have for my creation."

"Balance," Time said. "Nothing more. It will provide balance. With life there must be death, or your creation would be overrun. You should be glad. Death is here for you, my son, a gift. I have put forward a peaceful compromise."

"My creation *was* balanced. You have introduced chaos. Mark my words, planets will crumble, and galaxies will shatter because of this new life you have allowed."

"You are being dramatic, my son."

"Nothing will come of this but chaos." Ultimae marched away, then shifted as the memory faded to the next.

"In a sense," Tomas said, "he was right."

Eve gave Tomas a strange look.

"Even though life technically existed in the form of the Originals, those beings were essentially just immortal sentient phlasma with different shapes and power. But now that Life and Death were Emissaries, life was indeed free to show up all across the universes, the same way that the universes themselves sprouted from their singularities, independent of a creator, of Time.

"Though this posed a problem. The Originals, which were previously immortal, were now mortal. They broke out into war over this change. Planets were destroyed, entire systems changed, universes began to differ from one another, no longer identical. The patterns were disrupted. This created

## ❖ CHAPTER 19 ❖

alternate universes. As life sprouted in universes all on its own, they too fought in wars and changed the very foundation of their space. This created, just as Ultimae predicted, chaos.

"Ultimae was mad about this, vengeful, even. He blamed Time. Not only that, but near none of the life outside of the Originals believed in the existence of the Celestial Beings, let alone knew about them. You didn't."

"No one on Earth did," Eve added. "Ultimae sure isn't the god I grew up hearing about…"

"Exactly. The existence of Humans and other life that sprouted in these universes all on their own, in the eyes of Ultimae, was meaningless if it didn't mean that they made him stronger in return. All they did was destroy what he had so carefully crafted. Pests, in his perfect celestial garden."

As the memory settled onto the next, Ultimae and Celestae both looked over a surveillance cloud, watching a particular subset of universes in the Multiverse.

"Much later," Tomas said, "Much, much later, Celestae and Ultimae were checking up on a paradoxical disturbance the likes of which they had never been seen. This paradox was so powerful that it sent ripple effects through the flow of time. It hadn't happened yet, but the effects had leaked into the past."

❖ THE BEGINNING ❖

"This…" Ultimae shook his head as he looked away from the cloud. He looked up at Time. His body pulsated a deep red, shivering with anger. "This is your doing. Your fault. What have I been warning you about all this time? Chaos?" Ultimae scoffed. "Inevitable. And now we can see it to be true."

"What is it, my sons?" Time walked over to Ultimae and Celestae to peer into the cloud.

"Three universes," Celestae began. "All of them have broken…"

"Your lesser children are *ruining* my domain!" Ultimae yelled.

"This was unforeseen," Time said. "I apologize."

"No," Ultimae said. "It has been foreseen." He pointed to the cloud. "This happens only five million years from now. We have ample time to prevent it, mother. You will fix this."

"I will not," Time said. "You of all beings should understand why, Paradox Master."

"We can stop it by resetting the Multiverse, starting fresh," Ultimae suggested.

"We will not purge the Multiverse of the life it has grown."

"The life it has grown is meaningless."

"To you," Time said. "To them, not so much."

## ❖ CHAPTER 19 ❖

"I do not care," Ultimae said.

Celestae spoke up, "Brother, the broken universes…"

"What about them?" Ultimae turned.

"They will be fixed."

"Thank you," Ultimae said. He turned back to Time. "At least someone is on my side."

"No," Celestae said.

Ultimae violently turned back around. "*What?*"

"They will be fixed… by the same being that caused the paradox… a human…"

"A *human?*" Ultimae grumbled. "I know nothing of such a creature. *Insulting.* No. No I will fix it."

"No." Celestae shook his head. "This… Adam Jaminski…"

Time's head perked up at the mention of that name.

"He will be the one who fixes it. He possesses no knowledge of you whatsoever, brother. And yet, with that in mind, he still calls himself… The Paradox Master."

Eve flinched. She stared at Tomas.

"A false prophet," Ultimae said.

"Well… he did fix the biggest paradox we have ever known. Well before you could get the chance." Celestae looked up to Ultimae. "And you had the benefit of foresight," he teased.

"RAH!" Ultimae swung forward and dissipated the surveillance cloud with his fist.

"Oh, Tomas…" Eve said as she watched the memory flicker to transition to the next. "You pissed off a god. Why would you do that?"

"As if it were on purpose," Tomas coughed. He held his wrist as a stinging pain shot through him. He was running out of time.

Tomas continued, "Ultimae lashed out against Time and Celestae, clearly. He had enough. In his eyes, his side project had gone terribly wrong. He wanted nothing more than to fix it, to prevent the breaking he had foreseen, and it's fixing. His side project was no longer entertaining to him, it was a frustrating chore. He wanted to start over, clean slate, reset the Multiverse and start again.

"But Time and Celestae were fond of the life that sprung from the Extraverse, they were impressed by the power of a human, and, I think needless to say, Life and Death both weren't too keen on the idea of their home universe being destroyed.

"Though Ultimae saw his vision as a vast improvement, a Multiverse 3.0, if you will… Iron out all the bugs, optimization, a bit of an update on the old model, more predictable, less chaotic... remove that oh so confusing and irritating variable that was sentient free-will wielding life... And that's when things get interesting."

## • THE EMPTY THRONE •

"You do not understand, Mother!" Ultimae shouted. "This new Multiverse will be without chaos. It will only have order, and strict structure. Every universe will be the same, with no room for change, no room for life, and thus no need for death. No room for paradox, or needless destruction. Uniformity. Growth. Peace."

Tomas whispered to Eve, "He hated change. All he wanted was a pest free garden full of the same flower. Time wanted a jungle."

"Ultimae..." Time spoke to him with a calm voice. She had tried many times before to speak to his senses, to calm him of his fears and irrationalities. But none of them worked. She had to try a different approach. Still carrying with her a motherly tone, she said, "If you do not accept that we will not go through with the mass genocide of your subjects... with your insane plan to rid this Multiverse of its complexity, life, and beauty... we will banish you. You leave us next to no other option. I am sorry, child."

"You cannot do that," Ultimae protested. "You created me to be the Paradox Master. No one can take my place."

"If we need to, we will find someone who appreciates the perfect complexity of your own creation."

Ultimae shook his head. "We have very different ideas on what is perfect," he said.

"We do," Time said.

"And you are wrong."

Time hesitated before responding, "If I make what is imperfect... then what are you?"

"Trying to be better," Ultimae responded. His arm quickly formed into a sharp tipped spear. He flung forward with his fist, trying to stab at Time's galactic spiral in her head.

Eve flinched, startled by the sudden attack.

Celestae tackled Ultimae down, rolling with him on the ground. Life and Death blasted at them to push them apart.

Ultimae stood up, his fists flaring. He held his arms out wide. A projection of the Multiverse appeared. He prepared to clench his fists.

"I tried to be reasonable, mother. But I am afraid I must enforce my will against your best wishes."

## CHAPTER 19

Time held out her hand. "You bring me no other option. I am sorry, my son." She looked away as a bright white beam of light shot from her palm and cast Ultimae out.

The memory flickered.

"He fought to reset the Multiverse one last time, but he lost. His own family turned against him. They banished him."

The memory showed the remaining two Celestial Beings sitting, thinking, contemplating their actions, and their next steps.

"The broken universes… This puts forward a dilemma…" Celestae paused, "You do understand what this means, Time… someone has been calling himself the Paradox Master without permission."

"I am aware," Time responded. She had been aware for quite some time. "I have been keeping watch on him, through the eyes of a human, with whom he travels alongside. Would you like to see the man?"

Celestae asked, "Do you think he could be a valid replacement for—?"

Time interrupted with a calm motherly tone, trying to assure her worried son that everything would be alright, "Celestae… He is the only replacement."

❖ THE BEGINNING ❖

Tomas whispered, "She refused to let Ultimae's name be uttered, to avoid giving him the strength he needed to return."

"Death," Celestae looked to Death. "Bring him in."

Soon, the Fifth Sentinel, plucked right out of five million years in the future, was ushered into the Extraverse by Death, and the title of Paradox Master was formally transferred to him. The empty throne was pushed away, and a new era of the Extraverse began.

The memory faded and the light from the cave vanished as the stone fell from the projector orb. The phlasma wall covering the entrance crumbled into dust and the light of the bright blue sky flooded the sandy-floored beach cave once more. Eve shielded her eyes.

Tomas kept talking. His voice was getting raspier, his arms shakier, his eyes more desperate. Telling the story was draining him. He seemed to be tearing up.

"Now there's something the Sentinel never knew, that I didn't know until before I retired as Paradox Master… Ultimae is still out there, regaining his strength. For millions of years he's been fighting those who oppose him from all over the universe they banished him to. And what do you know? The universe he was banished to was the very broken universe that pissed him off in the first place.

"He's been ruling over puppets of his for ages in order to claim the Extraverse as his own. In the beginning Sogar worked for him, then Kranthar worked for him, Suriv still works for him, Rogar worked for him, trying to get control over Time while she watched the Sentinel, and most recently Rhey worked for him. Ultimae possessed Rhey and helped him break into the Extraverse, and now that the shatter provides an easy way into the Extraverse, and the universe is ending, this is the prime time to strike. I need you, Eve. They need you."

Eve looked away. Her heart pounded, burning in her chest.

Tomas continued, "Kranthar is dead now, as are Rhey and Rogar. Ultimae's ran out of phlasmatic puppets, he only has Suriv, and Suriv is just a spoiled half dead Ilsian from a slum planet, he can't do much... Ultimae can be stopped but the Sentinel's Army needs you... the Multiverse needs you... Time was mistaken. She wouldn't let anyone know of Ultimae because she knew he would gain strength at the mention of his name.

"That was her mistake. She thought that ignoring the problem would make it go away. But every civilization that Ultimae has destroyed learned to scream his name. They learned to yell it out in fear as he slaughtered them and leveled their cities. He gains strength regardless of his banishment. You need to give in, and give him what he wants, lead him to attack before he's strong enough, overplay his confidence. That will lead to his failure."

"Ultimae spoke to me..." Eve remembered. "In a vision. He's too powerful already..."

"No. You can stop him." Tomas smiled. He coughed and fell onto the rock. The stars vanished. His throat stung. All this talking took a toll on his old body.

"So much for that cure, huh..." He chuckled. The curse was getting to him. He could feel the gray ash of the curse spread to his heart, burning his veins as it traversed through him like a forest fire. He knew these were his last breaths. His story was over, it was Eve's job to finish it. He turned his head to Eve, and held his hand to her face.

"Not now... Don't die," Eve begged, holding on. "I can try something that might work, it might be a cure, I'm not so sure... I- I can turn you into a rêve stone, and I can resurrect you from it, and then you turn me into one and resurrect me

## ❖ CHAPTER 19 ❖

from it too, it's like phazing but a total resurgence, it might work to get rid of the—"

"Shhh." Tomas extended a finger to hush Eve, "You misunderstand... this is my time. I've been waiting more than five million years for this."

"You can't die..."

"You know, I realized something."

Eve stared in silence at the life draining from Tomas's eyes, eager to hear what he would say.

"I had it all wrong. Embrace death, laugh in the face of it, or fear it. Code 5, Code 6, and me? No that's not how it is, or how it ever was. Code 5 kept the Sentinel in an everlasting loop, he lives forever, because *he* was the one that feared death. The sixth didn't laugh in the face of it for phazing himself for no reason, no he laughed in the face of it because he died in his seventh just to come back and brush it off like it was nothing in her Eighth. This is me, Eve... the immortal emissary, embracing death... It's been a long time coming." Tomas held out his hand and Eve started to be consumed by phlasmatic flames. He was going to attempt to cure her the way she thought would work.

"Dad, no!" she yelled in protest.

❖ THE BEGINNING ❖

"Go be the Sentinel I never was." Tomas smiled as Eve's entire figure was transformed in an instant into a rêve stone that fell into the sands of the cave floor with a soft thud. The box dropped into the sand next to the stone, then turned invisible. Tomas fell next to the stone, his fingers close to it, just barely moving. Phlasma lingered at his fingertips.

The phlasma trailed away and faded to nothing. His remaining strength left him. That was the last phlasma he would use. He stared at the stone and smiled. "Camo."

His time machine, old and worn, appeared before him.

A mechanical flash sounded before the cave.

Tomas was ready to die; he wasn't expecting company.

"Hey, long time no see." The Paradox Master, his younger self, knelt by his side. The first Sentinel stood with him, watching in confusion.

Tomas coughed, "Why are you here?" He smiled. "I don't have much more time. You're ruining my poetic ending."

"I don't want to die alone." The Paradox Master smiled. Tomas could see tears streaming down his face. "Come on." He groaned as he helped Tomas sit up. The Sentinel sat down on his other side. "Hang in there, five more minutes."

"Easy for you to say," Tomas smiled.

"I have something for you," the Paradox Master said.

❖ CHAPTER 19 ❖

Tomas looked into the eyes of his younger self in awe, wondering what he'd do, using all the strength he had left to stay alive, shaking like the old man he was.

The Sentinel held out his hand. Tomas' necklace snapped off his neck and flew into the Sentinel's palm.

Tomas looked at it, saying nothing.

"You and I really have a problem when it comes to remembering, don't we? Now I could put this in my mind right now," the Paradox Master gestured to his necklace. "But I know I'd forget it just as quickly." The Paradox Master nodded at the Sentinel.

The Sentinel held the necklace to Tomas's forehead, and the stone began to infuse itself into him.

Tomas' eyes rolled back into his head as a sudden burst of information exploded in his mind.

Everything about his past, every moment of laughter, his adventures with Amara and his time with Vaxx. The brief time spent with Matrona and Quinn, the Galactic War, the struggle in-between and after, his life as Adam Jaminski.

Kogar, Darru, and even all of his five years gone.

Every strange friend he met in every universe he had visited during his travels as the Paradox Master; wizards and dragons, space sharks, and Void Jumpers, cosmic paradoxes that confused even the master of paradoxes himself, books that held legends of the Sentinel, friends he had long forgotten, and wars he had helped end on worlds the likes of which no human has ever seen.

All the good and all the bad.

For a moment, every memory was back. Every single miniscule detail of his much too long life.

When the memories stopped playing back, Tomas gasped for air, his voice wavering he said, "Thank you."

Tomas clutched onto the amulet resting on his chest, his fingers shaking. He had let go of Amara long ago, releasing her from her immortal prison.

This stone held instead the parting words of an old friend – and every memory the Paradox Master had ever held.

For a moment, the pain was gone.

The shaking stopped. He felt alive again.

Tomas chuckled quietly, then, he whispered his last words, *"I'm free."*

The Sentinel watched Tomas's grip loosen, and he knew. He outstretched his hand and pressed his fingers against Tomas's eyelids, closing them.

The Paradox Master and the Sentinel shared a glance with each other.

"This is weird," the Sentinel said softly.

## ❖ CHAPTER 19 ❖

"A little bit, yeah." The Paradox Master stood up, not taking his eyes off of Tomas's body.

"Do we just leave him here?" the Sentinel asked. "Him? You... us?"

"Take his amulet, and his box, then yeah... I want this to be my final resting place."

"What do we do with his stuff?" The Sentinel stood up as he took the amulet off of Tomas.

"I don't know," the Paradox Master admitted.

The Sentinel had an idea. He picked up Tomas's box and opened a panel. He dropped the necklace in and closed it. "Go."

"Where?" The box chimed.

"Wherever it makes sense," the Sentinel said, and with that, the box disappeared.

The Paradox Master and the first Sentinel stood around in silence for a while. Ocean waves crashed nearby; seagulls cawed as the sun set. They stared at Tomas, and Eve's stone by him, which the Sentinel knew nothing about.

"We should go." The Paradox Master placed his hand on the Sentinel's shoulder and looked up at him.

The Sentinel couldn't break his stare away from Tomas' frail, lifeless body. "I hope I was happy."

❖ THE BEGINNING ❖

The Paradox Master flinched and wiped a tear off his face. "What?"

"When I died." The Sentinel gestured to Tomas. "When the version of us, that becomes him dies... I hope we were happy."

"We were." The Paradox Master sniffled as the two of them flashed away.

Tomas was left dead in the sand, and Kranthar's curse began to make quick work of his body as it shriveled and blackened slowly but surely over the next couple of months in that cave.

Eve's stone remained all that time, next to the corpse of the once great Paradox Master, until the day the stone's destined journey truly began.

Footsteps approached the cave entrance. A pale hand swooped down and snatched Eve's rêve stone.

❖ ❖ ❖
# PART TWO
## THE BANISHED GOD
❖ ❖ ❖

❖ Chapter 20 ❖
# The Last Sarran

War raged on a distant planet. Unfamiliar stars filled the night sky of a galaxy not touched by humans, of a galaxy unknowing of the Sentinel's plight or of the Originals. Beings much like a cross between a panther and a kangaroo rushed toward a dark armored humanoid figure.

Two of the creatures followed behind a leader whose eyes glowed with phlasma just beneath curled horns. The leading creature seemed special, it's phlasma powers seemingly unique to that specific individual.

A bright white owl-like Deusaves flew over the trio of creatures, ablaze with a ghostly white flame. It seemed to be aiding in their fight.

The creatures' spiked reptilian tails dragged behind them in the coarse dirt and gravel, ready to be used as weapons, wafting up dust as the creatures ran.

They ran from a once grand city, burned and scarred by war. Hundreds of dead troops surrounded them. This seemed to be the end of them. The leading creature stood on its hind legs as it drew nearer to the dark armored being and raised its arms and sharp claws to strike.

The dark humanoid figure glowed with deep red phlasma as it lifted an arm. His eyes were glowing behind his helmet which concealed his face. His cape flew up in the wind as a sword materialized from nothing in his hand.

The blade blocked the strike of the claws. The strange dark metal burst into flames that seemed to rip through time and space itself.

The attacking creature's unusual, seemingly both cat and dog-like face reacted in fear and tried to pull away.

The armored being withdrew his sword and held out his hand, a burst of red phlasmatic energy pushed the two creatures behind the leader into the ground.

The Deusaves flew down to help the downed duo of creatures. The leader of the pack rose to strike again as the sworded being rose his arm to wrap his fingers around the creature's neck.

"Fool!" the humanoid being yelled as he lifted the creature from the ground. "Have you not yet learned that facing me is futile? No creature has ever stopped a Celestial Being, let alone *me*."

"*Ultimae—*" the creature begged.

"*Say my name.*" Ultimae tightened his grip.

The creature choked.

"Sirr-*ia!*" one of the creatures that followed yelled from afar in fear and worry.

The Deusaves rose up and blasted a white phlasmatic flame at Ultimae, which Ultimae deflected with the flick of his sword.

"Every galactic cluster with the misfortune of holding life in it has had one of you inconveniences." Ultimae looked toward the hilt of his ghastly sword to admire the many rêve stones hanging from strings and chains dangling at the end of the sword, "Do you see those stars?" Ultimae looked up at the burning purple sky, still choking the creature.

"I made them. *They are mine.* Sarran like you always screw them up. You think space and time is your domain, you think it is yours to meddle with and travel through freely? To change and warp in your image? To break and conquer and create? A plaything? A hobby? A pastime? *Life was a mistake...* and death is too impermanent a fix." Ultimae pushed forward and dug the blade into the creature's chest, impaling it.

The creature screamed in agonizing pain as it seemed to be consumed by the space distorting flames. Another stone was added to the collection of seemingly hundreds at the sword's hilt as the creature disappeared.

"*Sirr-ia!*" one of the creature's friends cried in agonizing pain as the other stood up to run, charging at Ultimae, fueled by an unquenchable rage.

"Hold back!" the Deusaves screeched in warning.

Ultimae lifted his hand and electrocuted the two creatures with a burst of burning bright red lightning and thunder that roared through the night, tearing the sky.

The owl-like being's eyes widened with fear. He turned and launched himself from the ground, flying off and away into space, fleeing the battlefield.

Ultimae approached the burned corpses and stabbed each with the sword. As the bodies disappeared, stones formed on the handle and the blade itself, as if they were melded in as decoration.

## ❖ CHAPTER 20 ❖

"Their friends never learn to stay out of it. In every galaxy, can you imagine that?" Ultimae turned around, his cape flowing.

Before him flashed into view Suriv, armored in his robotic Calcurus shell. The cybernetic suit bowed before him with its insect like legs. "Sir. I commend you on your progress of threat termination, but you have to admit that eventually you'll have to confront her."

"I have many more threats to deal with now," Ultimae disagreed.

"According to my calculations, and need I remind you what I am, Ultimae, an Ilsian, you know, most analytical beings in the universe."

"I do not care." Ultimae shook his head and adjusted his helmet. He looked around at the corpses littering the battlefield. "I need a new host body, Suriv find me one or I will possess you."

"Ultimae for the love of- *Listen to me.*"

Ultimae's fist flared with red phlasma in anger.

Suriv stepped back, his aperture eye narrowed then widened, whirring mechanically as it did. "What I am saying, sir, is that Evelyn Sanchez, human from the Milky Way, is your single biggest threat currently. She's a descendant of that galaxy's Sentinel."

"Do you see this?" Ultimae lifted his sword, causing Suriv to step back in fear. Ultimae pointed to the stones dangling by the handle. "I have no trouble with the saviors, sirr-ias, sentinels, Sarran, whatever you want to call them, that Time throws at me. This Eve child is not even one to begin with, she is merely related to a Sarran that failed in his efforts. To somehow insinuate that that makes her stronger is laughable, Suriv."

"Even if you can't see that she's a threat can you at least see that she's your ticket to the Extraverse? You've possessed Rhey, you've gotten close, you saw how intertwined she and the Sentinel's Army are with the Emissaries. You can't keep putting off the inevitable. Not anymore. You have to keep climbing the ladder to the top. Everything's been leading up to this, you're almost at the top of the ladder and you refuse to step up."

"You are not the first to have told me this. For millennia disciples of mine before you have said the same thing. I have dealt with Sarran close to the Emissaries before, and every time *I strike them down*. And still, I am no closer to the Extraverse. More work needs to be done. I do not want to

## CHAPTER 20

fight off more than one Sarran at once, so taking them one by one is the plan, Suriv."

Ultimae paced and continued, "You can try to convince me, Suriv, but you are not special. Do you really think that Kranthar, Rogar, Rhey and you were my only help? I had Sogar helping me once. I thought he was the prophesied one, and he told me the same exact thing as you. He led me to destroy Kranica, Drakona, and Dile. He tricked me and betrayed me for his own benefit to end his war, let this be a reminder to you, should you ever bring up Ilsose again. I will not let my subordinates betray me again, though you may not be as slippery as a Gar."

Suriv's speakers warbled as he coughed.

Ultimae continued, "I was close to my goal, and Sogar said the same thing as you. Look where that got him. He was killed, and replaced in my ranks by Rogar, and even then, look what happened to him.

"The Milky Way and Andromeda are nowhere close to my priority, though they might be yours. I created the *Multiverse*. I live on a scale that your mind cannot even begin to fathom. Two galaxies amidst hundreds of billions?" Ultimae stepped forward with every word, pressing himself against

Suriv threateningly, pointing his blade at his robotic eye. "*Not my problem.*"

"I thought you knew…"

Ultimae stepped back. "What?"

"When did you leave Rhey's body?" Suriv asked.

Ultimae waited for elaboration.

"He did it," Suriv said, quietly but pointedly.

"Did *what?*" Ultimae stepped back.

"Exactly what he told you he would. Your temporary half-possession or whatever that was that I suggested before you got back to this. He's dead now, but the Extraverse is broken. You have an in. Are you gonna take my word for it now or are you gonna keep being a stubborn dumbass?"

Ultimae hesitated and lifted his blade. He noticed a stone form at the hilt, incomplete and ghostly in nature.

"So Rhey is dead," Ultimae thought to himself.

"Yes," Suriv answered.

Ultimae lowered his sword, stepping away from Suriv. "You are lucky that I need you or I would have killed you." In a flash of light, Ultimae disappeared.

"You're welcome," Suriv mumbled to himself as he stood alone in the battlefield. He flashed away.

❖ Chapter 21 ❖
# A Rêve Stone Through Time

A pale hand swooped down and snatched Eve's rêve stone from the sandy floor of the beach cave beneath the Sentinel's lab.

"Who would leave a perfectly good rêve stone just sitting here?" Canshla, the clone of the third Sentinel, asked. This Canshla had appeared on the beach, hailing from a time when the clone army still stood, when the Galactic War was well underway, and when Rogar was still alive and obeying the orders of his superior, Ultimae.

Canshla looked down at a machine, a sort of rêve stone tracker. His eyes wandered, stopping at the decomposing body of the Paradox Master. He wouldn't have known who the body was had he not seen the leather jacket that the mangled corpse wore.

"What are you going to use it for?" Agro asked, standing by Canshla's side, still a loyal subordinate of his at the time. "To give you phlasma powers? Or give some to a clone?"

"Don't get ahead of yourself... I have to keep this stone intact, for research... and for this." Canshla lifted an Andromedan rifle. On the side of the rifle was a slot, formed for a specific purpose by Canshla.

He attached the rêve stone to the side of his rifle and cocked it back. He pointed the rifle at the ocean and shot. A wormhole ripped through space and time in the waves.

"Woah..." Agro stared ahead.

"I've wanted to do research on these for a while. This will help with the Janistar problem. Come on, let's go. Time to make sure the Sentinel doesn't abuse the power of the rêve stones. He could have some that could be useful to us." Canshla and Agro vanished.

Canshla carried the rifle with the stone in his possession for a while, and so the essence of Eve traveled with him. It was not until Canshla's run-in with the Fifth incarnation of the Sentinel that the stone changed ownership.

## ❖ CHAPTER 21 ❖

Just after the death of Darru, the Sentinel was wondering if he had just had a planet given to him in the midst of the Battle of Janistar.

"They're headed to the cities. This was just their access point." Five noticed of the course of the battle.

"What do we do?" Amara asked him.

"Nothing until you hand me that stone," Canshla yelled out to them.

"Canshla." Five turned around, recognizing the voice. "What do you want?"

"Ever since I saw that stone I realized where Rogar was going wrong. He's after Time, but that..." Canshla pointed to Matrona's rêve stone around the Sentinel's neck. "That's priceless." Canshla readied his rifle. "And dangerous."

"You can't have it!" Amara yelled from the shield. "Lay a finger on it and I'll kill you!" She pointed the gun at Canshla.

"No one should have power over rêve stones. Especially you Sentinel."

"Oh and you should?" Five questioned Canshla.

"I know how to use it correctly, safely. You barely even understand how it works!" Canshla yelled.

"Oh and *you* do!?" Five stood defensively, Canshla raised his rifle.

Canshla gestured towards Eve's rêve stone, forged into the side of his rifle. "More than you could imagine." Canshla shot at the Sentinel, a wormhole opened up beneath him. Before the Sentinel fell in, he lassoed Canshla with him. The two of them traveled through wormhole after wormhole, fighting through space and time until they showed up on IS-53, the blue sand dune Quodstella.

The Fifth Sentinel finally got the upper hand, pinning Canshla to the ground and taking his rifle, snapping it in half and snatching the stone. "How did you get this. Whose is it?" Five asked.

"Give that back, you don't know what you're dealing with!"

"Only those who can control phlasma can make a rêve stone, whose is this?!" Five approached Canshla. He backed up in the strange sand. Five pushed Eve's stone into his pocket. "Not gonna answer, huh?" He pointed his arm out towards Canshla's face, his palm glowing. "Whose is it?"

"Found it in a cave. Next to a dead man." Canshla smiled and quickly snapped his arm up to his chest, like some

### ❖ CHAPTER 21 ❖

sort of salute, and pressed down on his cufflink. He teleported away.

The fifth Sentinel stood alone on IS-53. Eve's rêve stone was now in his possession, and the stone stayed with him until he went back to his destroyed lab to retrieve his old disintegration gun. He modified it a bit, and eventually attached Eve's rêve stone to it, allowing it to phaze things.

This was only temporary, until he donned his cloak, and returned to little five-year-old Matrona's room. He took the phaze gun from his pocket. He separated Eve's rêve stone from it. Five-year-old Matrona lay quietly in her sleep. She held onto her journal the Sentinel gave her like her life depended on it. Her first night with Adam, and the Sentinel was there. He carefully placed the rêve stone on her forehead, and it flared. The stone absorbed itself into Matrona, her hands now glowing. She woke and opened her eyes. The sight of the cloaked man startled her, but she stayed relatively calm.

"*Remember,*" the Sentinel whispered. "*Remember me.*" Unbeknownst to the Fifth Sentinel, he'd just infused the complete living essence of Eve into Matrona.

The Sentinel flashed away, thinking nothing of it, and he leaned up against a wall.

He took Matrona's rêve stone from his pocket, and fused it with the phaze gun, fixing the gun. He took Amara's stone from his pocket and made his amulet.

This was the night Matrona died.

Five soon appeared next to One's crippled and dying body, wearing his cloak, and wielding his phaze gun, which he pointed down at One. "Your job isn't done. I'll give you another chance... don't get used to it." He shot him and One began to phaze.

Amara was amazed at the power of the gun. Desperate, she asked the Fifth Sentinel for help. "Save her," she spoke softly, gesturing towards Matrona.

Five glanced at Four, pain and understanding in his eyes. He remembered what he tried with Amara, he tried to think of a way around it, but he knew that she was gone. "I can't do that." Five's cloak vanished in a puff of black gaseous phlasma. "There is something I can do though." He looked at Four. "Come here." He spoke with a hoarse, tired and defeated, voice. He kneeled by Matrona's body.

Five took Four's hand and placed it on Matrona's forehead. Four spread his fingers and lifted his hand, so that only his fingers touched her. Five stood back. "*Remember*," he spoke in a soft whisper.

## ❖ CHAPTER 21 ❖

Matrona's rêve stone slowly formed in Four's hand, the phlasma whispering with her memories as it solidified, and the last audible whisper spoke, '*I did too*'. Four stood up, holding out his hand, and the phlasma orb it in.

Five cupped his hands underneath it, and with a massive burst of bright purple flames, the orb condensed. He stepped away, and in Four's hands sat a bright, glowing rêve stone.

"What is it?" Amara questioned.

"A rêve stone."

The Fifth Sentinel didn't know the extent of what he just did. The complete, living and perfect essence of Eve was carried with Matrona. When she died, her rêve stone, dead and imperfect, still contained Eve. Part perfect rêve stone, part imperfect.

That rêve stone stayed with the Fourth Sentinel, and it stayed with him well into his Fifth incarnation, known only to him as Matrona's rêve stone. Near the end of Five's life, he prepared to draw up the instructions for the box and gather all the materials as well.

He wrote notes all across the paper in his rushed, nervous writing. A few hours passed, and the blueprints were finished.

He took out a plastic bag from his pocket, and dropped the rêve stones of Three, and Four's memories in, two of Two's memories, as well as Amara's and Matrona's essences. He placed the bag on the blueprints.

He wrote on the blueprints, and spoke aloud with his writing, "Enclosed are the more obscure elements needed for this build. I've included Bronze, Dark Matter, Amber, and a few assorted Crystalline Phlasma Shards. Whatever you do with this machine, no matter how many times its upgraded, or replaced, make sure to always include *these specific Crystalline Phlasma Shards*. If you do not, the outcome could be devastating. To use this machine, hold the machine, and think of a specific time, and specific place." Five dropped in the last few materials in the bag, and stood up. He took a deep breath, camouflaged his box, and flashed away.

The First Sentinel constructed the box with those materials. Matrona's rêve stone traveled, in the box, with the Sentinel throughout his First, Second, Third, Fourth, and Fifth incarnations. Soon the Fifth incarnation had to decide. "What kind of Sentinel am I?"

"You should know," the box responded.

"That's the problem... *I don't.*" He lowered his head onto the box. "What do I do?" He closed his eyes.

## ❖ CHAPTER 21 ❖

"What do you think is best to do? Do you embrace death, fear it, or laugh in the face of it?"

Five took a deep breath, chuckled, and muttered the words, "*Code 6.*"

Without hesitation, the box exploded violently, consuming Five in its flames. He began to phaze, the same way he did five times before.

The Sentinel fell to the floor, a different man again. The Sixth Sentinel stood up quickly, pushing his arms out for balance. "Ok…" He spoke to himself reassuringly. "Why did I do that?" He held his hands to his head and stared at the broken pieces of the box lying on the floor.

He knelt down by the destroyed pieces of the box, and admired them. His eye was drawn to what seemed to be the only surviving rêve stone from within the box. He picked it up and held it to his ear, listening to its faint whispers.

"Matrona's," he concluded of the stone's origins. Of course, unknown to Six, it was also Eve's rêve stone, the sole surviving stone of the blast of Code 6. Part imperfect, part perfect. The perfectness of a rêve stone containing the entire essence of a living person protected it from the explosion, preserving it.

Perfect rêve stones are near indestructible.

That stone would then be used in the construction of Six's new box, and the stone stayed with him throughout his Sixth incarnation. It continued with him in his Seventh, and then her Eighth. It wasn't until Eight was dying that the possession of the stone would change hands yet again.

"Come back. It's cold." Eight held Vaxx's limp body in her arms. Vaxx fell through her arms as Eight's body faded away.

"You used all your power," the Paradox Master informed her.

"No." Eight looked at her hands. "Not yet, I need more time." She looked around, unable to help herself, or Vaxx. She looked to the box, floating by her shoulder, containing Eve's rêve stone. "Box. Find a new Sentinel, ensure the Multiverse's safety. Give them time. I failed." She spoke with her final breaths as her phlasma ghost weakened.

"Affirmative." The box glowed, and it flashed away.

The box found its way into seventeen-year-old Eve Sanchez's backpack, and it shot her with a blast similar to the phaze gun, without changing her, awakening her hidden genetic phlasma powers that she inherited from the Sentinel, and strengthening them.

## ❖ CHAPTER 21 ❖

Eve would unknowingly travel with her own future rêve stone alongside her in the box for her First, Second, and Third incarnations. It wouldn't be until Tomas died in that cave and turned her into the very same rêve stone that sat contained in the box that the stone would meet its final destination.

The box watched as Eve became a rêve stone. It fell into the sand by the stone and turned invisible. It then waited, hidden in the cave, until Canshla snatched the stone from the sand.

The box knew now that the stone that Eve became would begin its journey, and eventually end up becoming the very stone that was inside the box at that moment.

The box was ready.

It waited for Canshla to leave, and when he did, the box uncloaked itself from invisibility. It spun to the old leather jacket, all that remained of Tomas. It slammed into it and flashed away with it. It was off to do what Tomas had intended the stone to do; to be resurrected.

The box appeared in a dense jungle. It floated around, aimlessly at first, until it started heading for a lone old structure in the jungle.

Eve, in her second incarnation, Ganto, and Starlocke were all standing before Queen Karina of Canam when it happened; when the box teleported Amalga-5 back to the present.

They ventured outside and stared up at the sky above.

The two halves of New Earth split far in the night sky, Janistar was eclipsed behind the ruins of the Galactic Jail planet. The sky seemed to be melting and stars were dying. The universe was ending and they were back.

Starlocke's third eye glowed with intensity. The box had sent him a message. "This planet is in extreme danger," Starlocke barked. "Leave."

"Wait! Starlocke!" Eve tried to stop him.

He turned around and stood his ground aggressively. "Something requires my attention." Starlocke glanced at the box floating by Eve. He turned his attention back to Eve. "I will return, I promise. You need only wait"

"Wait, Starlocke, I need you," Eve begged.

"I know. That's where I'm going. I'll see you soon." He charged forward and with a burst of electric wind he was gone.

Starlocke stopped in the middle of the jungle forest of Krondico on Amalga-5, standing before the lone building.

## ❖ CHAPTER 21 ❖

Vines grew around it and looked as if it had always been there. The box floated away from the slot where it sat. It had just finished teleporting the planet.

The jacket sat over it, almost like the box was wearing it.

"Why have you done this?" Starlocke asked. "Where's Eve?"

The box remained silent.

Starlocke looked around, twitching his ears and closing his eyes. His third eye stone glowed. "She's... gone..." He looked to the box for answers.

"She's here," the box answered. A circle on the underside of the box slid open and the stone fell out. It hit the ground with a soft thud, and Starlocke stared at it.

"Is that... Did she die?" Starlocke asked.

"She killed Kranthar, but not before he set a curse on her, Tomas, and Ganto." The box explained, "Tomas died while turning Eve into a rêve stone so that she could be resurrected without the curse. The stone has run into some problems along the way, and it has become partially mixed with the essence of someone else. Someone dead." The box explained. "Can you still resurrect it?"

"Potentially." Starlocke stepped back, using his hind legs as sort of an anchor. He lowered his head and chest, pushing his front legs out.

He closed his eyes and a beam of electric phlasma blasted from his third eye and into the rêve stone. He concentrated and the rêve stone glowed. It shifted and expanded. The box floated back.

From the stone a body formed. Her hair was long and curly, her eyes a deep golden brown, her skin just as dark as before, though her face was slimmer, and freckled. The stone remained in her chest when all was said and done, as if she had been resurrected as a strong phlasmatic ghost, though she was very much alive.

She fell to the floor and held her hand to her abdomen as a searing pain tingled at her core.

The box dropped the jacket onto her to cover her up. Starlocke had only resurrected a body, no phlasmatic clothing to match.

Eve's eyes stopped glowing and she gasped for air. Her hand found its way over the stone in her chest. She felt it.

Starlocke paused, looking up and standing normally. He tilted his head.

"*I did too…*" Eve let out, winded.

## ❖ CHAPTER 21 ❖

"What?" Starlocke asked.

"*I did too, and I always will.*" Eve stood up, pushing her arms through the sleeves of the jacket. She shook her head and held her hands to her temples. "Agh…" she groaned. "I'm alive…" She breathed deeply, painlessly. She smiled. "The curse is gone, it worked."

She clenched her fists and a dark purple phlasmatic dress formed itself over her, under the jacket, covering her up. She turned around, her eyes meeting Starlocke's, "Starlocke!" She lowered down to her knees and hugged around his neck, feeling his fur and scales. "I missed you!" She stopped, and backed away after a few seconds, a confused, blank expression fell over her face.

"What is it?" Starlocke asked.

"My chest is heavy… Something's not right… my mind is racing…" A dark and gaseous glow floated around the stone in Eve's chest.

"What is it?" Starlocke asked.

"*Where am I…*" Eve asked herself. "*Who am I?*" She paused. "Eve Sanchez," she answered herself, matter-of-factly. "*Matrona Tempus,*" she answered herself again, confused. She paused, thinking.

"Uh oh." Starlocke stared back at her. "You said there was an interference with the stone?" he asked the box.

"The Sentinel's adopted daughter, Matrona Tempus," the box answered.

"She's been resurrected as well… she's part of Eve."

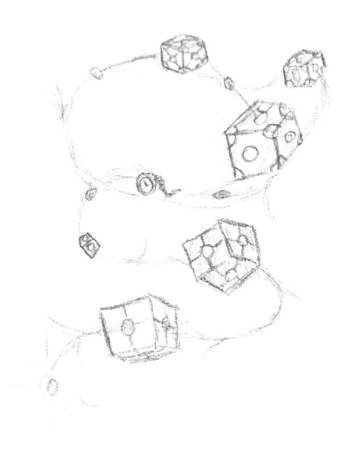

❖ Chapter 22 ❖

# Family of the Extraverse

"This can't be happening…" Eve looked down at herself, she walked around in the jungle, Starlocke followed after her. "*I was dead… I saw everything…* I saw everything, in that stone, I saw it all, the Sentinel's whole life… all in a split second. That is a *ton* of information to process all at once. My memories, they're… *they're my memories too.*" Eve turned to Starlocke, "What's happening?"

"Matrona Tempus and Eve Sanchez are now one in the same," the box explained, "But it seems that the perfect rêve stone has more control over the mind, you're mostly Eve."

Eve looked down at the glowing and swirling stone at her chest. "She's not me, she's talking through me. *I've escaped the stone and now I'm trapped in a body that isn't mine.*" Eve shook her head, "Sorry…" she said to the stone.

Her own voice responded, "*No, it's... it's way better, extremely preferable to reliving the moment of my death over and over and over again... thank you.*" Eve shook her head. "Wasn't me. Thank Tomas. Tomas is gone..." Eve remembered. "I have to save the universe!" she remembered again. "I saw it all! I know where I have to be!"

Eve reached out for the box and placed it down on the ground. She pressed the top panel and her vision shifted to a bright white nothingness that overcame her and Starlocke. They stood in the lobby of the Extraverse, and without hesitation Eve approached the door furthest left.

The Eighth Sentinel dropped herself to the floor and tried to hug Vaxx. Her body was almost nothing, and she was dying. "I just want to hold you." She cried with her final words as her body completely vanished.

The Sentinel's Army stood back, terrified and hopeless. "This is it," Nick uttered solemnly. "The universe is ending."

"What do we do?" Agro asked the Paradox Master as Foxtrot cried next to him.

"We wait for the Sentinel's replacement," he answered.

Eve burst through the Extraverse door. Starlocke bolted by and stopped near her in a flash. Eve's mind was swimming with thoughts and conflicting emotions. She'd seen all of this

### ❖ CHAPTER 22 ❖

before while in the stone traveling with the box, but it all felt like a dream. Details were fuzzy, but she was seeing it now and pieces were starting to align.

The Sentinel's Army all turned their attention away from the tragedy with a sense of hope shining behind their eyes. Eve's heart skipped a beat when the tragic scene registered in her mind. She worried for a moment, unsure of herself, and asked, "Am I too late?"

Without hesitation, Foxtrot, with teary eyes, snagged Agro's scythe and blasted a stream of phlasma from it at Eve, which she quickly deflected.

"Woah!" Eve jumped back.

Starlocke lowered his head and growled.

The Paradox Master's fists flared.

A mechanical flash sounded behind the door as it opened again. Ganto sauntered in with the box floating by his shoulder before it quickly vanished. He entered just as Foxtrot fired another blast from the tip of the scythe.

"Woah!" Ganto yelled.

"Ganto!?" Vistor, Terri, and Vogar, all exclaimed at once.

"Wait a minute…" The Paradox Master put his hands down.

"Who are you two?" Agro asked. "Ganto, do you know them?"

"Hold on a second, are you the Sentinel's replacement?" Nick asked.

"*Nick?*" Eve stared ahead.

Starlocke's third eye glowed, he understood. "Oh…"

"Guys, chillax." Ganto held out his arms to diffuse the situation.

"No, Ganto, I will not *chillax*!" Foxtrot yelled. "Arlo is dead! Vaxx is dead! The Sentinel is dead! You want me to *chillax*!?"

"Oh, right, timing…" Ganto stepped back, and away from Foxtrot's angry advances. "Listen, I can explain… I've been gone a long while."

"Do you know these two?" Vita asked him, gesturing to Eve and Starlocke with her head.

"I do. This is Starlocke, a Dragolupus and a new friend of mine."

"*Masi—*" Terri lifted an arm.

"I'm allowed to have more than one friend, Terri."

"What the *hell is happening!*" Nick pulled at his hair and paced around the Extraverse. He groaned as his stomach

## ❖ CHAPTER 22 ❖

twisted. *"What the hell is happening..."* he repeated, quietly to himself.

"And who are you, exactly?" the Paradox Master asked Eve.

"Evelyn Sanchez." Eve shuffled in place. It was strange to see the Paradox Master again, knowing who he was and who he would become. "I'm the Sentinel's replacement. You can just call me Eve," she elaborated.

"Eve?" The Paradox Master stepped back, staring at Eve and looking her over in an all-new light.

"What's happening here?" Eve looked around in confusion. The Eighth Sentinel's body had vanished, leaving Vaxx's body alone on the floor, with what was left of Rhey's in the distance.

The Sentinel's Army stared at Rhey's body near the tear in the Extraverse. Eve squinted as she could have sworn that phlasma was trailing from Rhey's body and into the tear as the Extraverse slowly repaired itself.

"If you had shown up any earlier you could've been a lifesaver," Foxtrot spoke up, calmer, though still shaking.

"The Sentinel just died," the Paradox Master added.

"Right, no..." Eve shook her head. "I saw it... I was here," she whispered.

"You were here?" Nick asked, stopping in his pacing tracks, "Then why didn't you—"

"She was inside the box." Time stood from her throne, her voice booming. "All along, she has seen everything. She is trying to process all of that information."

"You know who I am, then?" the Paradox Master asked Eve.

"Dad." Eve nodded.

"Woah, wait, what?" Nick stepped back in confusion. "What the hell is happening…" he said again.

"Something is strange about you…" Vita tilted her head. "You are more than Eve…"

"She was resurrected from a stone, more than a phlasma ghost because she was alive, but someone came with her," Starlocke spoke up.

"The consciousness of someone else lives inside me now…" Eve elaborated. She looked up at Nick. *"Nick, please tell me that's you…"* The part of her that was Matrona knew that it must be her brother.

Nick froze. He stuttered, *"Matrona?"*

Eve nodded with a smile, tears dripping down her face.

Nick's eyes widened as he ran after Eve and hugged her tight.

## ❖ CHAPTER 22 ❖

The Paradox Master flinched, "Wait, what's happening?"

"That's new," Life commented.

The Paradox Master shot a glance at her.

Eve looked up from Nick's embrace. "It's a long story. She's trapped in me, I'm suppressing her somehow, not on purpose, but sometimes, *I can break through and say what's on my mind. And It's a lot, so, so much.*"

Nick and Eve broke away from their hug.

"Hey, I know we've got a lot of stuff going on right now, but…" Agro stepped forward, shaking his head, still comforting a saddened Foxtrot, "Vaxx, the Sentinel, and Rhey just died, we've got a half child of the Paradox Master, half Nick's sister girl showing up, and the universe is still ending. What are we supposed to do next? We brought the Sentinel back before, what steps do we take to do it again."

"We can't," the Paradox Master said.

"What about Vaxx?" Foxtrot asked.

"We shouldn't," the Paradox Master added.

"Then what do we do?" Agro looked up to Time. "You should know," he said.

Eve turned her attention to Time, and her expression quickly morphed into one of pure anger and disgust. "You're Time."

"Indeed, I am," Time nodded.

Eve pointed a finger at her, "You've been hiding something from these people."

Celestae sat up straighter in his throne, excited that someone knew what he'd been trying to tell people this whole time.

"I know not of what you speak," Time protested.

"I know about *Ultimae*." Eve stepped forward, approaching Time.

Life's head shot up. The galactic shape in Celestae's head pulsated and brightened.

Someone finally said it.

Time's galactic spiral expanded quickly, startled. "Do *not* say his—"

"I know that Ultimae is out there, that he just helped Rhey break the Extraverse. That long ago he enlisted the help of Rogar to try to *hunt down my mother because you possessed her*." Matrona's conscience took over. "*What else are you hiding?*"

"Who's Ultimae?" the Paradox Master asked.

## ❖ CHAPTER 22 ❖

Time interrupted, "Stop saying—"

Eve looked to him and said, "The Paradox Master before you. The banished Celestial Being and the 'boss' of the Sentinel's enemies. Ultimae is the *real* reason the universe is ending."

Time stepped back and sat down in her throne again, falling into it with a winded thud. The Paradox Master stared at her in disgust, he knew she was hiding something. Life looked away nervously, knowing the time would come. Celestae looked to Time eagerly, he was waiting for the moment that she would be called out on her secrecy.

Time covered her face with her hand. The transparency in her head darkened so that the galaxy object shifting in her mind could not be seen. What seemed like a star dripped like a tear drop down Time's face.

Eve spoke up, "Why didn't you tell them about Ultimae? You could've prevented so much—"

"SILENCE!" Time looked up, tearing her hand away. She seemed to be crying. "Do not say his name!"

"*Ultimae!*" Eve yelled.

"STOP!" Time stood up, holding her arm out forward.

Eve pushed back, her hair flung out like a burst of wind had hit her in the face, and she froze in place, unable to move much more than her eyes.

"I did not talk about the banished one, because the spoken name of a Celestial Being gives them power. His name gives him the strength he needs to return... He cannot retaliate without power... without his relevance."

Celestae stood up. "Mother, he spreads his name like a disease. He gains strength himself, he tears down civilizations to a breaking point, only to plaster his name about, so that they might warn others of his power. You *know* this. We cannot stop him while we fear him."

Eve darted her eyes up to Time.

Time dropped her hand and fell back into her throne, defeated.

Eve fell forward. Nick ran to her and caught her, helping her stand. Eve nodded a quick thank you before she turned her attention back to Time. "Time, you can't ignore a problem and hope it goes away. Celestae's right. We need to give him what he wants."

The Paradox Master stumbled, wiping away his tears and holding his chest. "The fight isn't over... We could barely stop Rhey and he was just *working* for this... this *god.* And we

## ❖ CHAPTER 22 ❖

lost Vaxx and the Sentinel because of it. What does he want?" the Paradox Master asked.

"To reset the Multiverse and make the Extraverse his. And to do that he needs all the power he can get. So, we should give it to him," Eve answered.

"Why make him stronger?" Time disagreed.

Eve stood her ground, explaining, "The more power we give him, the more overconfident he becomes. He might make his move and attack before he's fully ready. His power will be his downfall. We draw him to us, then stop him."

Celestae shook his head, "You make it sound easy. You have no idea the extent of power a Celestial Being has, even if their name has not once been uttered. To feed him strength is to sharpen a blade that can cut diamonds."

*"But we have the sharper blade."* Eve looked up at Time. "Time's name is a word. A word spoken every day, in countless languages across the Multiverse. That's what makes her the strongest Celestial Being. Time is our key to winning. There's no way Ultimae can outpower her." Eve looked around at the Sentinel's Army. "Plus," she added. "There's only one of him. We have two Celestial Beings on our side."

Time and Celestae shared a look.

"Let me get this straight," the Paradox Master interrupted, "I didn't break the universe? The Sentinel didn't? All this chaos and torture we've had to go through... for nothing?"

"You did," Time said. "But you fixed it, for the most part. The banished is exploiting the weaknesses left behind to break his way out and get to here, where he can manipulate all universes, broken or otherwise." Time turned her head to the shatter. "And he has already begun to snake his way in."

"Then what do we do now?" Agro asked. "We can't just send Time in to kill him, that would be too risky, right?"

"You cannot kill a Celestial Being." Time looked down at Agro.

"Then he's going to win either way." Foxtrot looked away. "Unless Time and Celestae can fight this god for the rest of eternity... There's no hope."

"At least Amalga-5 is safe for now, right?" Nick asked.

"Amalga-5 has returned," Starlocke informed the Sentinel's Army.

"We just sent it away!" the Paradox Master argued behind confused tears.

"It's been gone for a couple hundred years," Ganto explained.

## ❖ CHAPTER 22 ❖

"Who sent it back?" Agro asked.

"I did," the box chimed.

"Since when did you start making decisions on your own?" the Paradox Master wondered aloud.

"I was instructed to do so," the box answered. "By you."

The Paradox Master tilted his head, confused.

"What's the next plan of action?" Foxtrot wiped tears from his face.

"I think we all need rest," Vistor suggested. "With Rhey gone, this banished guy's team must've taken a big hit. There's no way he'd attack now."

The Army looked to Vistor. He held his stubby arms close to himself, quietly pained inside. He sniffled. "We've lost a great deal in the last month. We've lost a great deal today. This was supposed to be a happy day. We need rest."

"Where do we rest?" Eve asked.

"We'll make room for you in the Pantheon." Agro nodded.

The Sentinel's Army lined up to leave the Extraverse. Vita and Vistor helped escort Vaxx's body from the Extraverse.

Time spoke up. "Paradox Master, stay, guard the shatter. Just in case."

"Oh, I'm gonna have a long talk with you." The Paradox Master shook his head at Time as he made his way back to his throne.

Everyone stepped from the door of the Extraverse that led them directly to the hangar of the Pantheon. Ganto excitedly ran back to his ship, the Freysent. Terri and Vogar followed after him. "It's good to be back, baby!" Ganto exclaimed.

Foxtrot and Agro made their way to the elevator. Agro consoled Foxtrot as they walked. Vistor ventured off to another ship. Eve sat down at the workstation by the elevator that the Sentinel used after her lab on Janistar was destroyed.

Nick approached the desk and stood around. "Hey, Matrona..." he said.

"Eve," she corrected him. "Your sister's in here but I'm not her." Eve gestured toward her head. "I'm sorry."

"Can I talk to her?" Nick asked.

Eve looked down at the table and sighed. *"This is all pretty crazy, huh?"*

"Yeah." Nick smiled. "It is. But hey, you're gonna save us. I know you are."

## ❖ CHAPTER 22 ❖

Eve smiled. "Yeah, I hope so."

"She's not really back, huh?"

"Not really." Eve shook her head.

Nick thought for a moment, and then he realized something. "Could she ever be?"

Eve looked up to him with sorry eyes.

"The Sentinel died. We resurrected her as a phlasma ghost, it's possible to bring someone back from the dead but do you think we could do it if they aren't in a stone and they're in another body? We could separate you two," Nick suggested.

"Nick," Eve looked down, holding her fingers to the bridge of her nose. "Look. Trust me. I know how it feels to lose a sibling, especially after not being with them for a while, but… I don't think it's realistic, or worth it."

"What does Matrona think?" Nick asked.

Eve sighed, "*I want to be free, trust me, but…*"

"But what?" Nick asked.

Eve shook her head as it stung. She pushed her fingers through her hair. "I can't think straight with someone else thinking in here… It might help to have a clear mind…"

"You'll separate her, then?" Nick asked.

"I'll talk to someone more qualified than me with phlasma ghosts about that, later. For now, I think I really need some rest. *The both of us.*"

"Good call." Nick waved goodbye and made his way to the elevator. Eve took some of the towels and paper from the desk and slid them onto the floor, making a makeshift mattress, and she quickly fell asleep in the hangar.

Eve's dreams took her to a strange place that she couldn't quite pinpoint. She stood on a cliff overlooking an ocean, with a lab behind her. Illiosopherium glowed orange in the night sky, and everything seemed deadly still, frozen in time. She turned around and was met with a person, blonde and short, with blue-green eyes.

"Hey, Eve." Matrona smiled.

"Matrona." Eve recognized her. "I guess we have time to talk, huh?" She chuckled. "Hey, we're technically sisters, right?"

"Yeah, I guess so." Matrona smiled. "Man…" Matrona looked down at herself. "Never put me in a stone again… no one should have to be trapped like that…"

"What do you mean?" Eve asked. "I was in a stone, everything just felt like a dream."

## ❖ CHAPTER 22 ❖

"Not for me, I was dead. I had to relive my dying moments forever, I thought I'd never escape. Yet here I am." Matrona looked at Eve. "I want to help save the universe with you, but it's going to be hard if I'm trapped in here."

"Why do you want to be back? After dying you really want to jump back in?"

"Of course I do," Matrona said, bluntly. "Your memories are mine, now, and you saw everything the box saw. Ultimae wanted the Sentinel dead and he got that. I can't let him get away with that. So, when I get my own body, I'm gonna fight until I die, and when I die again, don't let anyone turn me into a stone."

"Seems reckless," Eve commented.

"If I'm resurrected, I won't have much time, like the Sentinel. I'll go crazy doing what I can with what time I have and make the most of it without having to sacrifice you. You're cautious, I'm not. I don't think before I act and I'm afraid that with my mind in yours I might accidentally make you do something stupid, something you wouldn't do otherwise."

"I guess that makes sense..." Eve admitted.

Matrona looked down at her body as she faded away, becoming transparent. Eve's surroundings darkened.

"What's happening?" Eve asked.

"I don't know..." Matrona said before she vanished and the darkness had taken over completely.

"*Fear the empty throne...*" a voice whispered in her head. Eve shot up in a cold sweat, surrounded by darkness, and nothingness. A figure faded into view. He appeared tall and looming, much like Celestae and Time. He was glowing a deep translucent red, and the galactic shape in his head spun quickly and jittered like it was broken. "*Do not try to stop me. You would simply be wasting what little left you have of your life.*"

Eve remained speechless, aware that she was dreaming, she stood her ground.

"*You will regret ever having been born,*" Ultimae threatened. "*I may spare you if you let me make quick work of those who oppose me. You can lead the new Multiverse with me...*"

"No," Eve answered quickly and succinctly. "You just need more goons to work for you, I won't be like them, easily stopped by a Sentinel. Do you think I'm stupid?" Eve snapped. She somehow felt this was more real than a dream. It seemed as if Ultimae were in her head. She knew the feeling of someone else being in her head, and this was it. "Leave me alone." Eve approached him.

## ❖ CHAPTER 22 ❖

"*Or what?!*" Ultimae's voice reverberated through her mind.

"AGH!" Eve screeched as her eyes glowed a bright blue. Her fingers sparked with electricity, and her hair floated as if gravity had vanished. Her body surrounded with black gaseous phlasma, and soon her dream vanished. She was floating above her makeshift mattress, sparking with electricity and burning with dark phlasma. She took a deep breath and fell to her feet. Her eyes returned to normal and she caught herself on the desk. She caught a glimpse of a witness to her dreaming. "Starlocke," she greeted.

"I saw your dream," Starlocke admitted. "You seemed afraid, so I read your mind..." He walked forward comfortingly. He sat down next to Eve and rested his head on her leg, drooping his ears. Eve pet his head, pushing her fingers through his fur and feeling around the stone in his forehead. Starlocke closed his eyes and let out a drawn-out breath.

"What's wrong?" Eve asked Starlocke.

Starlocke pushed his head in closer, as if hugging Eve. "Before I met you, I was a time traveler myself. A traveling historian documenting the universe and meeting other travelers like yourself along the way. I met a human, on my first trip to

Earth, shortly before I met you. We became good friends for four years. I was going to visit him again."

"What was his name?" Eve asked.

Starlocke closed his eyes tighter. A glowing tear of sorts formed in his eye, dripping slowly down his fur.

"Starlocke?" Eve asked.

"I only just found out who he was. He called himself A.J.... I was just told the Sentinel's name by the Paradox Master. Adam Jaminski, though he went by A.J. a few times, the last time before she died."

"Oh…"

"All this time… I'll never see her again… I promised that I would visit again, and I missed my window…"

Eve caressed the side of Starlocke's face, trying to comfort him.

"I could've helped earlier. I could've stayed, I didn't have to leave. What if I was around for Rhey, what if I could've stopped him, what if I could've saved A.J.... If I had helped would the universe need you? Would your life had been left alone? Would you be happy?"

"Hey, hey, hey." Eve hugged Starlocke around the neck. "If you hadn't have left then you would've never met

### ❖ CHAPTER 22 ❖

me. And you know what? You saved my life. The first time I phazed. And now we're gonna save the Multiverse. Together."

Starlocke nodded. "Thank you," he said.

Eve smiled, still petting Starlocke.

"My people are grateful, too. For their new home."

"Amalga-5 welcomed them?" Eve asked.

Starlocke nodded as he closed his eyes to sleep, still projecting his thoughts into Eve's head. "They call it Starwynn. They named it after me, Starlocke, and you, Evelyn."

"Really?" Eve smiled.

"Yes…" Starlocke's projected voice softened. "I went there to meditate. The beaches are beautiful. I could run through the tall grass forever. It looks golden in the sunlight."

"Sounds beautiful."

"Yes… I hope I get to live there one day. Peacefully."

Eve paused, still petting Starlocke. She sighed. "We'll be fine, Starlocke. I promise."

Starlocke's mouth twitched into a smile in his sleep.

"We are gathered here today..." Vistor spoke atop a pedestal, standing in front of an altar outside the statue of the Sentinel's army on Amalga-5. Information that Tomas had neglected to share to Eve before, was that the statue had been built overtop what used to be the Sentinel and Vaxx's home.

The Sentinel's army and members of the public gathered around as Vistor led a funeral ceremony for the Sentinel and Vaxx. "Not to mourn the loss of fallen heroes, but to celebrate what they've done to help us. So much that you, the people of Amalga-5, are unaware of, and do not fully understand..."

Eve shook her head, part of Matrona was thinking something and wanting to speak up, but she resisted it.

"And so, we thank them. Without a physical body for the Sentinel, Vaxx will be buried here with the time machine the Sentinel gifted her long ago, a symbol of the Sentinel's presence. And now a moment of silence."

A whisper neared Eve's ear, "She was a lot like you, you know."

Eve turned to face the Paradox Master.

"She never asked for all of this. She was sucked into this world of war at a young age like you. There were a couple of times where she almost gave up. But later she knew... there

## CHAPTER 22

was no escaping a life touched by the Sentinel. And so she went with it, she embraced it."

Vistor lifted his head and adjusted his crown. He stretched a stubby arm to wipe away a tear under one of his bulbous red eyes. "Thank you." He called off the moment of silence and the public dispersed.

Eve nodded at the Paradox Master, letting him know that she understood.

Ganto approached Eve and stood short by her. He tugged at her dress to get her attention. "We're headed off to the bar, wanna come?" he asked. He gestured toward Terri and Vogar behind him. "Wouldn't hurt to relax."

"No, I'm okay." Eve remembered what the Matrona part of her was meaning to say. She turned back to the Paradox Master. "These people *really* don't know? Do they?"

"About what?" he asked.

"Oh come on, Tomas, I know you know what I mean. You aren't stupid. The universe... ending... the Multiverse... in danger? *Ringing any bells?*"

"No, they don't know."

"Why not? Did the Sentinel not think it was a good idea to let them know?"

"He didn't want to cause panic, I don't want to cause panic."

"You didn't ever think that any of them could help?" Eve asked.

"It's too dangerous," the Paradox Master argued.

"That didn't stop you from letting Vaxx tag along. *Or me. Or my Mom. Or Quinn,* or me, or my family and friends."

The Paradox Master remained silent. The crowds dispersed around them, leaving the statue and returning to their lives. The Sentinel's Army remained.

Eve shook her head at the Paradox Master as she left him to approach the statue. She sat down by where they buried Vaxx. A faint flash could be heard from under the ground, but Eve ignored it. Foxtrot approached her.

"You knew her?" he asked.

"I know of her," Eve answered quietly. "I saw everything the box saw, the Sentinel's entire life, her time with him... It's murky but I feel like I knew her. You know?"

"I know *exactly* what you mean." Foxtrot chuckled. "As a clone, I share memories from the Sentinel up to his third incarnation and it feels just like that, murky. Same with Agro." Foxtrot gestured toward Agro standing by Vistor and chatting with him. "And all the clones," he spoke softer.

## ❖ CHAPTER 22 ❖

"I'll make this right." Eve stood up. "All of this." She turned to face the civilians leaving. "They should know. I won't make the same mistakes the Sentinel did. I won't let anyone get close enough to me that they feel they're obligated to help."

"Aside from the Army." Foxtrot shrugged. "And your friend, Starlocke."

"Right." Eve looked down.

"Sometimes you can't help it, you know?" Foxtrot shuffled his feet. "I fought for the bad guys for a long time until they turned my friend into a monster and I ran away. That's when I met Vaxx. I guess you could say she was *my* Sentinel. She dragged me into all of this, and I wouldn't trade it for the world," Foxtrot explained.

"Starlocke seems happy that he's a part of this." He gestured toward Starlocke, who was talking with Agro. "From what I've heard, you helped the Dragolupus settle down here, given them a safer home. Point is, maybe don't try to isolate yourself."

"Yeah." Eve nodded. "I guess."

"Anyway." Foxtrot pursed his lips. He didn't know what else to say. "I'll be off then."

"Right." Eve nodded.

❖ Chapter 23 ❖
# Cosmic Brothers

Eve showed up in the Extraverse the next day to check up on the state of things. She noticed in the hub of thrones that Celestae was missing, and without a word she left the hub and returned to the white void lobby and approached a door. She extended her arm to open the door, but hesitated for a moment, deciding instead to knock.

With one knock the door swung open. She peered her head in and saw Celestae sitting on his own, lone throne of crystal and phlasmatic flames, watching over a cloud of stars sitting before him. Images flashed before him in the small cloud like a thunderstorm, but something about it reminded Eve of flickering film from a projector.

"May I?" Eve asked, gesturing for her to come in.

## ❖ CHAPTER 23 ❖

Celestae silently nodded. Eve walked in and approached Celestae, standing near the warmth of his throne. She glanced at his empty starry figure looming beside her before drawing her attention back to the flickering cloud of light. "What's this?" she asked.

"I am keeping an eye on my brother. But, alas, the information is… murky… to say the least."

"Cloudy works too," Eve said quietly.

"Ultimae has some sort of infatuation with a few planets in particular for hiding out in. Tornlozor in the Milky Way, and two planets on the edges of the universe, IS-372, and 247. Draw a line between each of these planets and you get a triangular plane with Amalga-5 right at its center," Celestae explained, "But I do not know what it means."

"What're you keeping watch on now?" Eve tried to make out anything from the cloud.

"I cannot see. I survey all four of the planets in question, and yet my brother is nowhere to be found. I can safely say the same for Suriv, his sole surviving disciple."

"So what? You're saying we lost him? He's gone?" Eve pressed.

"I am merely saying I know nothing of his whereabouts. I am not saying he is unfindable."

Eve thought for a moment and couldn't think of anything to say. Though, as if something in the back of her mind broke through, she said, "*If Ultimae's been around this whole time, from the beginning, and you were able to see him, always... why would it only change now? We don't need to find him; he's going to find us.*" Eve shook her head. "Yeah, actually I think I'm right." She held her head in her hands for a moment, a stinging pain shook her.

"Why would Ultimae be ready to attack now?" Celestae questioned. "He is low on men, and this is the weakest he has been. You have just inherited an army; this is the least opportune time for him to strike."

"*Desperation*," Eve suggested. "Or..." She thought, "This is just what he was waiting for? *This is what he wanted all along.*"

"What are you saying?" Celestae stiffened in his seat.

"*No more Sentinel...*" Eve suggested.

The cloud in front of Celestae grew dark red and shifted and jittered as if it were angry.

"What's happening?" Eve asked, worried.

"The phlasma is acting up." Celestae stared blankly, his body color darkened in fear. "I am afraid that maybe..."

## ❖ CHAPTER 23 ❖

"The human is correct," a voice boomed. The Extraverse shook violently, and the walls around Celestae's room faded away.

The Paradox Master's room leaked into his, and Life and Death's room did as well, it seemed as if all the rooms were fading together into one, combining with the hub. All of the rêve stones of the Paradox Master's collection fell to the floor as the walls holding up the shelves vanished. The Paradox Master scrambled to pick up a few he deemed important.

Soon all rooms became one, and the Emissaries stood around the thrones, staring at the tear in the space in front of them, left by Rhey. A deep red, pulsating light, emanated from the tear. "Though I am far from desperate."

"*Ultimae*," Celestae scowled.

The tear opened, and light poured in. A figure stepped from the crack and calmly entered the Extraverse. The caped figure donned in dark armor stood before them. His eyes glowed behind the helmet that concealed his face.

Time chuckled. "So you could not show up in your true form? You hide behind the shell of a Sarran so that you may fight your creator with what little strength you can muster?"

"Do not challenge me, mother," Ultimae limped into the Extraverse, small and insignificant compared to his celestial mother and brother.

"Why? Are you afraid, my child?" Time taunted Ultimae.

"Do not test him," Celestae whispered.

The Paradox Master, Life, Death, and Eve stood back and watched as the Celestial Beings paced around one another. A deep stressing tension filled the Extraverse like a suffocating gas.

Eve stared at Ultimae. With the knowledge she'd gained from traveling in the box as a stone, she knew that Ultimae was indeed possessing a body. But she knew from seeing Amara possessed by Time, that a body holding a Celestial Being was still nothing to scoff at. Her fists flared at the ready.

Ultimae could see the tense and aggressive nature behind the eyes of the Emissaries and Eve. He stopped pacing and looked up at Time.

"I am here to talk," Ultimae said.

"To bargain?" Time parried.

Ultimae hesitated, looking away. He twitched his head up and responded, "You may want to. I will not. I am here to state an inevitability. A fact." Ultimae's possessed shell jittered and glowed with red as he looked around, relishing his position. He was in the Extraverse, where he wanted to be, where he fought to be for millions of years. "The Extraverse is mine," he said. "Rightfully so. I will take my throne back, and then *crush it,* and sit in yours, where I belong." Ultimae pointed at Time.

A red glowing figure emerged from the armored body that he possessed. The true figure of Ultimae stood before Time, towering above the body he had possessed, and standing just taller than Time and Celestae, peering them down. His body was a deep red, scattered with stars and with a galaxy in his mind that shifted with a deep astral blue.

The body that he had possessed looked around fearfully, searching for escape. Ultimae grabbed the creature, wrapping his hand around its waist, and holding it hostage by his side.

The Paradox Master flared his wings to life. Slowly, Eve extended crystal phlasmatic blades from her wrists. Out of the corner of her eye, she spotted Life. Life shook her head. She projected a message into Eve's mind, a whisper, "Don't do it. You won't survive."

Ultimae's voice boomed through the Extraverse, "The Multiverse knows not of the child of Time that brought them their existence. You erased me. I do not exist. It is your fault that I must carry out my destiny."

"My creations need not know of you, child," Time said. "We are not gods. We are not meant to be known, or worshipped."

"They know you. When will I be recognized for what I have done? For creating the foul universes your puny creations call home. The Quodstella were a pitiful attempt at recreating the grandeur that Celestae and I birthed. Our planets and stars you so neglectfully ruined with your experiment called life. You will never be as great as I, mother."

Celestae stepped in, "We wanted to watch our Multiverse grow, brother. Have we not done that? It has gone beyond what we could have imagined. Your efforts are misguided. You could change your ways and rejoin us peacefully. We can create another Multiverse, in your vision. We need not rid this existence of the first to create another!"

"Existence has been ruined because of this stain on our legacy!" Ultimae yelled. "I cannot have what I want while a reminder of my failings lingers. I will purge my poisoned garden and replant the cosmic seeds." Ultimae looked to Time.

### ❖ CHAPTER 23 ❖

"You will not have the pleasure of sitting in that throne to see it through. By any means I will strike you down. You will regret having made me... *your* ultimate creation."

Ultimae's fists flared as his sword formed in his hands. He seemed ready to strike.

"Time! Watch out!" the Paradox Master yelled. His wings flared to life and he pounced at Ultimae, fists ablaze with a burning purple flame. Ultimae turned his head calmly and lifted his hand. In an instant, the Paradox Master froze in place.

Eve was planning to follow up the attack, but the Paradox Master freezing mid-air changed her plans. She looked to Life.

Life shook her head, her eyes wide with worry.

Ultimae approached the Paradox Master with calm calculated steps. Their faces met mere inches from one another. The galaxy in Ultimae's head pulsated.

"*Adam Jaminski...*" he groaned.

"I actually go by Tomas these days," the Paradox Master winced as he tried to free himself from the time freeze.

Ultimae paced around him. Though faceless, Eve could see the sinister smirk in Ultimae's galaxy.

Time clenched her fist. Celestae stood behind her and held her in place.

Ultimae stopped near the Paradox Master. "I could add you to my collection right now," he threatened.

"Then do it," the Paradox Master grimaced.

"I know how you meet your end." Ultimae chuckled. "From one Paradox Master to another, I respect this existence enough to not harm it with another paradox." Ultimae withdrew his sword. "Your being is a tricky one. If I break your timeline right now, the very ramifications could destroy this Extraverse… You being immortal does less to dissuade me from killing you than your mere existence does… Otherwise… I would find a way around it."

"What's this, then?" the Paradox Master asked.

Ultimae shook his head. "You tainted my creation." He clenched his fist.

Dark red flames trailed from his fist and surrounded the Paradox Master. The Paradox Master flinched as the red flames seeped through his skin. The red phlasma pulsed through his veins. He jittered and twitched. He clenched his teeth and closed his eyes, trying his best to hold back his pain. Sweat dripped down his forehead. He opened his eyes, bloodshot, as he darted them to Eve. He saw the fear in her

## ❖ CHAPTER 23 ❖

face, and he knew he had to hide the pain the best he could. But it was too much.

Ultimae pulled his fist down, and with that motion, the phlasma inside the Paradox Master burst.

"I will not kill you," Ultimae said with a calmness about him that sent shivers down Eve's spine. There was no effort in the pain he caused.

The Paradox Master screamed as the veins in him popped, as his arms popped out of their sockets, as his knees popped and his fingers stretched, pulling the bones from their joints. His arms stretched from his body, as did his legs, and his back.

Ultimae clenched his fists harder, and the flames consumed the Paradox Master.

"AHH! AGHHH! AHHHHH! KILL ME!" The Paradox Master shrieked in pain.

"You may be immortal, but you feel the curse of life. *Pain*." Ultimae clenched his fists harder.

The Paradox Master's knees bent backwards, his elbows snapped, his limbs were distorted into unrecognizable twigs and snapped sticks.

"Let him go!" Eve yelled. Life held her back. "Dad!" she called out.

"AHHH!" The Paradox Master screamed, his face red with both pain and the phlasma that burned like a forest fire underneath his skin.

"STOP THIS!" Time yelled.

Ultimae's fist unclenched. He turned around, leaving the crying and destroyed Paradox Master floating behind him.

"You dare replace me with such a frail excuse of a Sarran? This one is the weakest I have met." Ultimae continued holding onto the creature whose body he had possessed as he stepped forward toward Time. "You have too much faith in your lesser children."

The Paradox Master twitched his head up to look at Time, as painful as it was. He pleaded with his eyes. An important question entered his mind.

Time said nothing. So Ultimae continued, "You would not have to suffer such senseless deaths had you not introduced the concept yourself." He gestured toward Death. Death hid his face, and shivered. "Had you not meddled with what was already perfect. Had you not stepped outside of your job, your rule."

"You stepped outside of yours."

Ultimae looked away for a moment, thinking. Then he glanced back up at Time. "Because I am more than what you made me. I am more than you. You are as you say. You are not a god… But I am."

Ultimae held up the body that he had used as a shell for himself to possess. The last Sarran, and he ripped him in half.

"*Oh my god!*" Eve turned away, covering her eyes as Ultimae tossed the two halves of the corpse across the Extraverse.

The Paradox Master fell from his time freeze and hit the ground with a thud and a painful scream as his bones cracked upon impact. He cried out for help.

Time stepped back.

"This will be easy if you let it be," Ultimae said. "Your attempts at stopping me have all failed. Every last one of them. This means that I have beat your game. I won. I have a right to return, I earned it."

Time clenched her fists. "You have one right."

Ultimae waited.

"You are the banished. That is your rightful place." Time held out her hands and a beam of bright white light shot from them.

Ultimae quickly dodged. The beam of light scraped the side of his head, and the galaxy in it flickered. He had been weakened slightly.

Ultimae held his hand to his head. In the brief distraction, Time sent out the beam of light again, striking Ultimae in the chest, and casting him out of the shatter. He had been cast out again.

When Ultimae was gone, Eve stood up and ran to the Paradox Master's side. Time sat down and held her head. Her galaxy flickered. Celestae patted Time on the shoulders, trying to comfort her. He whispered something to her, then approached Eve and the Paradox Master.

His bones were broken, his insides burned and scarred. If he weren't immortal, he would have been dead twelve times over.

Celestae grabbed a handful of rêve stones that had fallen from the Paradox Master's room. He held one to the Paradox Master's chest and began to heal him.

The Paradox Master groaned in pain as he shared that pain with Celestae. The stinging horror of Ultimae's destruction coursed through Celestae and caused his galaxy to flicker. As one of the Paradox Master's arms healed, he held his hand to Celestae's wrist. He sputtered as blood dripped from his mouth, "Don't do this. Don't. It will weaken you…" he stuttered in pain.

❖ CHAPTER 23 ❖

Eve pushed Celestae's hand out of the way and took the stone from his palm. Celestae tilted his head in confusion.

"Eve…" the Paradox Master closed his eyes. "Don't."

Eve held the stone to the Paradox Master's chest and healed him. As she shared his pain, she closed her eyes, and flinched once.

Just once.

A tear streamed down her face, but aside from that hint of pain, her suffering was hidden.

The Paradox Master looked at her strangely as his legs snapped back into place.

Eve opened her teary eyes. "I dealt with Kranthar's curse for over twenty years. Pain is an old friend."

The Paradox Master held Eve's hands in his and stood up, using her as support. Celestae helped him up.

He hadn't fully healed. His back was still malformed, his legs wobbly. He pushed Eve's hands away, denying the healing power of the stone, to spare her the pain.

Life turned her head to speak to Death, but he was gone. Life's head shot up in surprise. She scanned over the Extraverse. "Morty?" she called out. "Where is Morty?"

The Paradox Master looked up at Time with tired eyes. Pain shot up his neck as he asked, "Ultimae said that I was a weak Sarran... and that you have too much faith in your lesser children... What did he mean?"

Time stared at the Paradox Master. Celestae looked over to her. Life looked away.

Time sighed, and said, "Sit down, my child. I have much to explain, though I hoped this day would come sooner."

The Paradox Master glanced strangely at Time before limping to his throne, groaning as he sat.

"I created the first life in the Multiverse. Across all universes. The Originals. The Children of Time, they liked to call themselves. Celestae and Ultimae both were the first. Then came the Quodstella, then the Dragolupus to reside upon the largest of them. Then came the Deusaves, and the Krantharnics, and lastly the Gars."

"I know this," the Paradox Master said. Eve watched in anticipation. "I thought I knew everything, but recently it seems you've hidden the world from me."

Time continued, "Though when Ultimae showed signs of aggression, I feared I would have to banish him. I knew it would take a whole universe to stop him if he tried anything. Thus, in secret, I created a sixth form of life. The sixth Original, a failsafe, a universe protector... the Sarran. These phlasmatic beings had no particular shape to them. In fact, they were each different. I scattered them across the universe, not confining them to the Black Star 7 district with the rest of their phlasmatic siblings.

"They took the form of the most prominent and successful sentient species of the part of the galaxy they were created in, indistinguishable from their own kind. The Sarran were hidden in plain sight. Phlasmatically gifted versions of existing species brought about by their own ways were scattered across the universe, their only distinguishing features being their control over phlasma, their durability, and their innate desire and need to protect.

"They were equally Sarran and the species they resembled. In fact, there was one case of a Sarran with the appearance of an Original. Though the Sarran seemingly came from nowhere, as I had brought them into existence. It was hard for them to blend in as normal cases of the kind they resembled. Most became suspicious of their origins and soon found out, using that to their advantage to protect their galaxies.

"You, Paradox Master… are as equally human… as you are Sarran. The Sentinel was a Sarran."

The Paradox Master shook his head, holding his crippled hand to his forehead. "I'm… an Original…"

Eve stared at the Paradox Master, stricken with disbelief. Her father was an Original, a child of Time.

"It's a lot to take in, brother, I know," Life spoke up.

"Why didn't you tell the Sentinel this?"

"As I had said, most Sarran were so curious of their origins that they sought out answers on their own. The beginnings of their lives made little sense.

"The first time the Sentinel phazed, he tried to ignore his past life, pushing it aside and becoming a new man. He was content not knowing his parentage. And by his sixth incarnation, after learning of the cycle, he brushed it off as his explanation for existing. He never went looking for an answer, and neither had you."

The Paradox Master shook his head and held his face in his hands.

Eve spoke up, asking, "If the Sarran were created to stop Ultimae, then why don't we ask for their help?"

Time stared at Eve. The spinning galaxy in her head slowed, pulsating. The stars in her body twinkled, growing dimmer as her color faded. "There are over one hundred billion galaxies in your universe."

"And more than one Sarran for each." The Paradox Master shook his head, pinching the bridge of his nose. "She has a good point."

Time stared ahead blankly. The Paradox Master lifted his face from his hands, looking up to her, wondering the same thing. "You can't mean to tell me that Ultimae killed hundreds of billions of them…"

Celestae held his hand on Time's shoulder, and answered for her, "We have been around for longer than the Multiverse has existed… Upon being banished, my brother had only one goal, to wipe out the Sarran created to stop him… He just killed the last Sarran. He has led to the cause of the death of every Sarran in one way or another, except one, who died at the hands of another, and except you, and like he said; he knows how you go out. Soon there will be no Sarran left to do their duty and stop Ultimae. And so the responsibility falls onto you, Eve. The daughter of a Sarran."

Eve stepped away. She held her head and almost collapsed.

The Paradox Master turned his attention to her.

"How are we supposed to stop Ultimae…?" Eve muttered.

"What?" the Paradox Master asked.

"I'm not even a Sarran... Now I know how much I'm not a Sentinel..."

"That might be a good thing," the Paradox Master said. He glared at Time. "Eve, think."

"Okay." She shook her head. "Alright, well he's obviously weak," she began thinking aloud. "He had to possess a body."

"It takes less effort to possess a shell than to fight as yourself," Celestae explained.

"I thought so." Eve nodded, "Alright, so he's definitely weak."

"But a weak Celestial Being like him is still stronger than a strong human like you," Vita spoke softly. "I'm afraid your replacement of the Sentinel was far little too late. There's nothing you can do."

"You're right," Eve conceded. She looked away briefly before following up, *"But all of us, that's a different story."*

"What are you saying?" Time asked.

"What's so different about Ultimae?" Eve asked. "Between him and the Sentinel's Army he's only got one Celestial Being on his side and we've got two." Eve pointed at Celestae and Time. "So why is it that he's got the advantage?"

## ❖ CHAPTER 23 ❖

"His willingness to break what was once his. His complete and utter ignorance of the rules we so carefully set in place," Celestae ranted. "His pure hatred for what used to be his family, and the unbridled rage that burns within him."

"That, and," Time interjected, "Our being is fundamentally connected to the Extraverse. As a side effect of Ultimae's banishment so long ago, he has been removed from those shackles. The Extraverse is weak, and by association, so are we."

"You've accidentally made him stronger," Eve tried to clarify.

"Precisely," Time said.

"He will stop at nothing to get what he wants," Celestae added.

"And what exactly is that?"

"A new tree of power. A new Extraverse, and with it a refreshed Multiverse to rule over. Out with the old, in with the new."

"All because he couldn't have full control over this one?" Eve asked.

"He is but a petty child," Time insisted. "But on a scale to you so large that he is an existential threat."

"Right. What now?" Eve asked, shuffling her feet.

The Paradox Master let out a long sigh, holding his head as he realized something.

"What is it?" Eve asked.

"This is it… It's all been leading to this, from the beginning… I… I need to die."

"Tomas…"

"Paradox Master?" Time tilted her head. "Now? As the last Sarran you choose to die?"

"I can't do this anymore. I'm not strong enough to fix the universe and everyone's expecting me to be strong enough to be a Sentinel again but I'm too drained to be either. I've lived for far too long.

"Ultimae knows this and will take every precaution to keep me from the fight. I was the last straw for Ultimae. He hates me. I can't fight while he causes me the pain that he has. I'm done. I've done all I can do. As paradoxical as it is, keeping me around is only a hinderance."

The Paradox Master paced around. "I know what I need to know now. Ultimae knows how I die… and it isn't here. I remember where it is. For once in my life, I remember something…" The Paradox Master chuckled. He stopped pacing.

❖ CHAPTER 23 ❖

"For once I remember something, and it's *this*. It's time to let go. A bit of the past is holding you back, Eve." He turned his attention to Eve. "You can do this. But first I need to leave. I retire. Officially, as Paradox Master. This is it." He stared into the galactic shape floating at the center of Time's head, and he waited for her response.

"If you do this, I will have to revoke you of your Emissarial duties, strengths, and your immortality."

"That's all I'm asking for." The Paradox Master outstretched an arm, holding his other over his abdomen and then half bowed in a mocking way toward Time. "Let me go."

"Tomas, you can't go, not again, I need you." Eve approached him.

"The result of which," Time continued, "Will lead to severe drop in strength, accelerated aging, followed by the return to a normal human lifespan."

The Paradox Master paused a moment, thinking. He shook his doubts and said, "Just get it over with."

"Tomas, think this through, please. You can stay a little longer. I need help."

"You know I have to go, because you saw me. You know it happened." The Paradox Master smiled as Life turned her attention to him. She flew up to the Paradox Master and spread her wings, which glowed a radiant white. The Paradox Master outstretched his arms and closed his eyes. Life slammed her wings together and a shockwave of light entered the Paradox Master's body, pushing him back like a strong gust of wind. He shook his head and coughed.

"From this point forward, you are no longer the Paradox Master," Time announced. "And before you go…" Time leaned forward on her knee and held her hand to her head. She extracted a stone of her memories and handed it to Tomas. "This is everything you need to know," she said. "Everything that Eve needs to know."

Tomas nodded. "Thank you."

"Tomas, wait—" Eve stepped forward.

"Camo." His box appeared near him and he reached out for it.

"Tomas." Eve stepped forward. "You're going to die." Her voice wavered.

"I know." He smiled. "We all are, in the end. But I know something happens first."

Eve stared at him blankly.

"I'm about to meet my daughter." He smiled before flashing away.

## ❖ CHAPTER 23 ❖

A tear dripped down Eve's cheek. She held her hand to her heart and said, "He didn't let me say goodbye." She chuckled lightly. "Twice."

Life quickly returned to her perch.

Time collapsed the rubble throne into a pile of rocks, now merely a shadow of what it once was.

"So now the Extraverse is missing both a Death Master and a Paradox Master?" Eve asked. "Ultimae must be pretty excited to see our numbers dwindling." She crossed her arms.

"We'll be on the lookout for Morty," Life said. "He'll be back. He can't've gone long."

"And as for the Sarran," Time spoke up.

"It was a matter of time before he left," Celestae finished.

"Right." Eve looked down at her feet. "I was just hoping he'd stay a little longer. It was like I lost him and suddenly he was back."

"Tell the others." Life reminded Eve.

"Right." She nodded, and promptly left the Extraverse.

Celestae looked up at Time. "She is right, you know."

"About?"

"We are down a Paradox Master. Has there been anyone else you had your eye on without me knowing this time?" Celestae asked.

Time thought about it for a moment, the galactic spiral in her head shifted like a gear as she thought. "No, but I think I may have an idea for a replacement that won't crumble under the weight of immortality."

❖ Chapter 24 ❖
# Power Shift

"This is my new place, huh?" Eve asked Agro as they stood in a room on the Pantheon.

"Honestly, it's the safest place to be. The whole Army's been moving into this space station recently because, frankly, making a home base on any of the planets just puts a big target on them, you know?"

"Yeah, I guess." Eve stared at her new room, bland and empty, almost like a prison cell.

"If it makes you feel any better, all our rooms are like this." Agro smiled. "As soon as all this universe ending stuff is figured out, things will get better."

Eve continued staring into her room. "Do the others think of me as a leader?" she asked. "As a proper replacement to the Sentinel?"

Agro didn't respond, not right away. "No." He broke the silence. "I think we're all still just a bit… I don't know, hopeful isn't the right word. In denial, I think. She's dead, but she usually seems to find a way out of that sort of thing, you know? I don't know. These are weird times we're living in."

"No, I get it." Eve nodded. She stared ahead, across the room and out the window into space. She sighed. "Is there a meeting room in this place?" she asked.

"There is," Agro answered. "Are you calling a meeting?" he asked.

"Gotta catch everyone up on what's happening. Regroup. Formulate a plan. Try to cheer everyone up." Eve looked at Agro. "Can you do that for me?"

Agro stood up straight and saluted. "I'll call a meeting right away."

"Don't… Don't do that…" Eve chuckled.

"What? Salute?"

"Yeah, feels weird." Eve smiled.

"Just messing with you." Agro lightly punched Eve in the shoulder and walked past her and to the elevator.

Eve shook her head, smiling.

Agro stood at the elevator, keeping the door open. "Going up?" he asked.

## ❖ CHAPTER 24 ❖

"Oh, right." Eve followed him and went into the elevator.

The Sentinel's Army, all except the Emissaries, met up in the glass pyramid meeting room at one of the tips of the Pantheon.

Outside the glass pyramid and in space, the halves of New Earth floated in the distance. The scarred Janistar wasn't too far, watching over them. And nearer to them was the newly returned Amalga-5. A clean-up crew surrounded the debris of the destroyed Galactic Jail nearby.

The Sentinel's Army sat around a meeting table and looked to Eve with tired faces.

Vistor seemed the cheeriest of the bunch, holding his stubby arms together and eagerly awaiting information and plans.

Vogar sat with a notepad and a pen, and Ganto and Terri sat on either side of him.

Foxtrot and Agro flanked Eve on either side, looking over the Sentinel's Army.

Starlocke sat between Agro and Nick, wagging his tail.

Nick sat by, attentive but nervous, his foot tapping loudly on the floor. "Where's the Paradox Master?" he asked.

Eve looked away. "That's one of the things I'm here to talk to you about…" she said. "The Paradox Master has retired."

"What!?" Vistor's mood completely shifted. His eyes glowed with anger.

"Woah there, calm down your highness." Agro stood up, ready to protect the Army from his king.

"He can't just *leave!*" Vistor yelled. "We've lost both of our Sentinels now! How could he abandon us!"

"He had to," Eve said. "Ultimae ambushed us…"

"What…" Ganto stood up. "Eve, you fought Ultimae?"

"It wasn't a fight," she said. "*It was a statement…*" Eve looked away. The Army saw the fear in her face and shuddered. "*He ripped the Paradox Master to shreds from the inside out…* I healed him but… Ultimae is… *power*. Time banished him again, but she knows that won't keep him away forever, he'll be back. And when he returns, we'll need to be ready to stop him."

Eve continued, "Ultimae's directed his attention away from ending our universe and is fully committing to strengthening himself and preparing for taking over the Extraverse in order to create his new Multiverse. *So the good news is that our universe is safe for now*, the bad news is,

### ❖ CHAPTER 24 ❖

Ultimae's coming for us, and every universe out there with an intense determination and immense power."

"If we had a Sentinel we'd be fine," Vistor said.

"Come on, Vistor," Agro said. "Don't do that…"

"The Paradox Master was our only hope!" Vistor said.

"The Sentinel passed on the mantle, we *knew* she was going to die," Foxtrot said.

"She was going to pass it onto Vaxx," Nick said. He leaned back in his chair and held his hand to his head. "God, *this is a mess*."

"We have Eve," Ganto reminded everyone.

"We don't even know who this woman is!" Vistor said.

"She's my friend!" Ganto yelled.

"She's the Sentinel's successor. The box chose her. She's the Sentinel's daughter," Starlocke said.

"*Mais weh lu nont ewk ewk elle,*" Vogar said while gesturing in front of him with his arms in a focused way. He seemed to be getting a point across.

"Vogar," Ganto looked up at him, "*I* know know her. You can trust me! Also, don't say it like that." Ganto looked to everyone else, "We can trust her."

"We need to find a way to bring the Sentinel back," Vistor said.

"She's gone," Agro said.

"I said that about Arlo. We said that about the Sentinel once before. Even if the Sentinel's gone, what about Vaxx?" Foxtrot said. "There could still be hope."

"There is hope!" Ganto yelled. "Our hope is right there!" he pointed at Eve.

"I see no need for stress during times like this," Starlocke sat calmly, trying his best to be a model of calmness, "If we could all simply calm down—"

"Easy for you to say, space dog!" Vistor yelled.

"Vistor come on," Ganto nudged him.

Vistor ignored him, yelling, "Who even are you? I don't know who you are! The Sentinel didn't know you!"

"We were good friends in the 1800's," Starlocke protested.

"Then why didn't you help us!?" Vistor yelled.

"I wish I had." Starlocke's ears drooped.

"We can trust him," Ganto said. "Timing just wasn't great."

"You ran away," Agro stood up. "How can we take your word at face value? Can we even trust you, bounty hunter?"

## CHAPTER 24

"I'd like to say I've changed," Ganto pointed Agro down. "And you're one to talk, Canshla's right-hand man!"

"That's different!" Agro yelled back.

"Oh, *that's different*," Ganto mocked.

"Guys..." Eve stood up. Her fists clenched. She didn't know what to do. The yelling was getting to her. Her head pounded as her eyes shot side to side. She was lost. "There's no need to argue, these are tough times, I know..."

The Sentinel's Army couldn't hear her. They erupted into confused chaotic arguing. No one person's voice could be picked out in the mass of volume for more than a few moments.

"Guys, please!" Eve yelled. Nothing.

Starlocke backed away, looking back and forth without an idea of what to do. He barked. No one listened.

"SHUT IT!" Foxtrot yelled from near Eve. A piercing ring shot through the air and stung at the ears of all the members of the arguing Army. They all turned their attention to Foxtrot as soon as he spoke. He shook his wrist as if something stung at it, and then cleared his throat. "Eve was saying something."

"Thank you," Eve stared at Foxtrot's wrist in confusion for a moment before recollecting herself. She cleared her throat, "There's no need to argue. What's happened has happened. I'm here now. The box chose me. You may not like me, you may not like that I'm replacing the Sentinel. Hell, I don't like that I'm replacing the Sentinel. I sure as hell wish the Paradox Master didn't have to leave, but trust me, he did. It is the way it is now."

Eve stood up and looked around the meeting room at the Army. "Assuming we've been bought time with the whole universe ending thing put on hold and Ultimae recollecting himself, we have the luxury of planning time. We have the luxury of recollecting ourselves. This is a stressful situation, but it could be a lot worse. The Sentinel and Vaxx are dead. The Paradox Master is gone. But at least the rest of us are still here."

The Army looked around at the other members. They looked away, embarrassed by their behavior and understanding the gravity of the situation. They turned their attention to Eve.

"So, if you don't mind me trying to do my job," Eve said, "We need to plan something. Together."

Ganto stood up.

"Ganto," Eve acknowledged.

"All we gotta do is catch him off guard and surprise him. And then, boom. We have the upper hand."

## ❖ CHAPTER 24 ❖

"You're thinking about this from a mortal perspective," Starlocke lowered his head as if signifying his entrance into the conversation. He waited for the Army to acknowledge him before he continued. "Ultimae is just like Time and Celestae, fundamentally. The day you show me that you can surprise one of them is the day I plan a surprise attack on Ultimae."

"*Lin gnaz a ponti...*" Terri mumbled.

"He has a point, my ass, Terri." Ganto mocked. "I can surprise anybody! Nyiegh!" Ganto threw a pen lying on the desk by Vogar at Starlocke, which Starlocke promptly shot out of the air with a concentrated beam of electric phlasma from his forehead stone.

"*Unt asono-aim favniso pen.*" Vogar frowned.

"Oh sure, like you had a favorite pen." Ganto crossed his arms, mad that Starlocke had proved him wrong. "I'll buy you a new pen," Ganto muttered under his breath.

Vogar smiled.

"Point is, I already know that Celestae has an eye out for Ultimae," Eve said, "And there's no more that Time would be hiding from us. So, they'll keep us up to speed. Meanwhile, I think we need to form a plan of attack and a plan of defense."

Ganto raised his hand.

"That *isn't* surprise related," Eve clarified.

Ganto lowered his hand.

"All of you… be thinking of something."

Everyone agreed, mumbling something or nodding.

"Alright." Eve stepped away from her chair. "I'll see you all again. Get some rest."

As Eve rested later that day, static buzzed through speakers in the corridor outside of Eve's room. Vistor's voice boomed over the speakers. "Attention Sentinel's Army. Time has left the Extraverse to give us all an announcement. Everyone meet in the hangar, ASAP."

Eve slipped out of bed, stretching and groaning. She rubbed her eyes and looked out to the nearby elevator. *"What?"* She walked over and descended to the hangar. When she arrived, she was met by Starlocke, sitting regally before Time. His head was lowered and his eyes closed as Time spoke to him. Eve approached with a questioning brow raised.

"The Extraverse needs another Emissary, one powerful enough to repair the state of this universe and protect it from here on out. A being who is not afraid of eternal life. A new Paradox Master." Time looked down at Starlocke. "Would you be willing?"

"It would be an honor." Starlocke closed his eyes. "For me and my people."

## ❖ CHAPTER 24 ❖

"Hey, that's my friend!" Ganto yelled behind the group of the Army, jumping up and down to see Starlocke. "I know him!"

Time held her hand to Starlocke's forehead, and her palm glowed. "Though our Death Master is not with us today to grant you true immortality, and our life Master too busy to absorb your outgoing mortality, I still declare you, Starlocke, the Dragolupus of Modius, the new Paradox Master." Time lifted her palm away.

Starlocke stood and shook his head and body, shuffling his fur and straightening his tail, while shaking his scales into place.

His eyes glowed a deep purple and he howled upwards like a grand wolf.

The Sentinel's army cheered him. Vistor and Terri tried their best to clap with their stubby arms, Vistor compensated by excitedly flapping his elegant butterfly wings. It was a pleasant change of pace for Eve to see smiles.

Starlocke seemed genuinely happy as well, proud even. An Original like him gaining a position with the beings that created his kind must be a huge honor, Eve thought. She smiled, knowing that it was partially because of her that Starlocke was in this position.

Eve looked around at the Army, and though she didn't know them personally, she was becoming excited by the prospect of a new life. A return to normalcy had far been out of the question in her mind. She had a long time to think in that stone and she knew there was no going back.

But she thought that with a group like this, she could see herself getting along. She was only now beginning to appreciate that despite her being in a world of war and conflict she never asked for, having made friends with Starlocke and Ganto were some of the best things that could've happened to her.

She could've been doing this all alone, after all.

Her mind drifted and she wondered how happy Andrew would be in a place like this. Matrona's mind to took over and she wondered how much happier she'd be if the Sentinel were around to see this.

"Eve." Nick touched her shoulder, shaking her from this trancelike state of wonderment. "Are you alright."

Eve noticed her hands were sparking with small static bolts of cold lightning, nothing much but enough to get Nick's attention. "Yeah, I'm fine," she asserted, "I'm fine."

"Have you asked?" Nick asked.

"Asked what?"

## ❖ CHAPTER 24 ❖

"If it's possible that you and Matrona could—"

"Oh!" Eve remembered. "I'll make sure to. Trust me. She's been pushing at my mind."

Nick smiled, "Thank you."

Time and Starlocke vanished for the Extraverse, presumably so that Starlocke could begin his duties and pick up where Tomas couldn't, in trying to repair the universe. The Army started to disperse when a flash of light shone in the hangar.

Vita, the Life Master herself, appeared in the hangar through some sort of bright wormhole that closed behind her as she slammed her wings together and landed on the floor. She shook her feathers back into position and craned her neck to look over the Army. "Hello," she bowed.

❖ Chapter 25 ❖

# The Gateway

"Keeping track of time is so tedious," Ultimae grumbled in the darkness of a ruined temple. The winds of Tornlozor howled around him as he struggled to walk around in the state he was in. Ultimae, no longer possessing a body, paced around in the center of what used to be Kranica's Grand Temple. Suriv stood idly by, listening to his master. "When I take over, my new Multiverse will be timeless, better organized. How does that sound?"

"Great," Suriv's speakers chimed as his robotic shell glowed softly. "Just great."

"Is that sarcasm?" Ultimae stopped pacing.

"Not at all."

"Hm." Ultimae continued pacing. "Always hard to tell with your kind."

"What exactly are you planning on doing next? I was sort of promised partial rule over the new Extraverse a while ago and was wondering when—"

"I am working on it," Ultimae cut off Suriv. "Kranthar's inevitable failure has proven inconvenient to me as was expected."

"Are you absolutely sure that we need all five Emissaries to make the Extraverse work? Why can't it just be us two?" Suriv asked.

"Ideally it would be just me." Ultimae raised his voice. "If I could find any way around the Emissary requirement, trust me, Suriv, I would."

"Harsh, but understandable." Suriv revved his knee gears and paced with Ultimae. He stopped in his tracks. His armor glowed and his aperture-like eye widened. "I have an idea."

"Humor me." Ultimae continued his pacing.

"What about them?" Suriv lifted one of his legs to point at a shelf structure built on one of the remaining walls of the temple. On the shelf sat two rêve stones alongside some Clone Suppressor Helmets. "I'm assuming you made rêve stones of them for a reason?" Suriv guessed. "Couldn't've been easy, long distance, without much of a body to work from."

"They were a contingency plan."

"Isn't now exactly the time to use a plan like that?"

"They failed me before, I see nothing indicating they will not do it again."

"Did they really, though?" Suriv pressed. "I mean *think* about it. Rhey created the shatter in the Extraverse you needed this whole time."

"And as for the other?" Ultimae needed more convincing.

"I don't know about you but had the Galactic War not played out the way it did, we wouldn't be so close. And it was because of him, wasn't it?" Suriv darted his robotic eye to the shelves. "Think about it."

"Life?" Eve asked, turning around. The rest of the Sentinel's Army turned back around and huddled up in a group again. Life had just appeared in the hangar, right after Starlocke and Time left.

## ❖ CHAPTER 25 ❖

"Please, Vita." Vita bowed. "Don't be alarmed, I'm not here to warn you of trouble. Merely, a request Time has given me that I believe you all would be brilliant helpers in."

"That being?" Foxtrot asked.

"Time wants to limit ways that Ultimae or Suriv could enter the Extraverse. You may have noticed that, aside from anyone that's been banished, it's fairly easy to enter the Extraverse from anywhere. I merely teleport in and out with my wormholes, and Morty does the same. Time and Celestae can do this too, it's as easy as regular teleporting for you as well." Life pointed at Eve. "As of right now, Time has closed all means of entrance into the Extraverse except for the shatter atop the peak. With only one entrance, it's far easier to guard."

"Sounds solid," Eve agreed.

"The shatter however has two sides to it, one in the Extraverse, and one at the site of which the crack was created," Life explained.

"What are we supposed to do? Guard it?" Ganto asked. "What good will the army do if we're all just standing around some space crack all day instead of fighting?"

"Time instructed that I build a gateway, one that guards itself and only requires minimal Army personnel guarding it. We can work in shifts, but the gateway needs to be built first."

"Oo!" Vistor exclaimed. "I love construction!"

"That explains your outlandish tower that doesn't do anything," Ganto mumbled.

"It's pretty!" Vistor whined.

"*Ui so ilso unti blub.*" Terri whispered.

"Ha, good one Terri." Ganto nudged Terri's side.

"Guys." Eve tapped her foot. "Come on."

"Sorry." Ganto lowered his head.

"When do we begin?" Eve asked Vita.

Without a word, Vita vanished. Eve shrugged and turned around. She outstretched both her arms. The box floated by her shoulder. "Group teleport, come on." She invited the Army to come with her, all at once. In a flash, they vanished from the hangar and swiftly appeared next to Vita, high up in snowy mountains.

The large group teleporting at once could've been dangerous had Vogar not been floating, as they teleported on a cliff's edge with very little room for all of them. They scooted in both for safety and warmth, not expecting the cold mountain peak.

"Where are we?" Eve asked.

"I could use a sweater right about now." Ganto shivered.

## ❖ CHAPTER 25 ❖

"The highest mountain in Doxland, Amalga-5," Life explained. "Weakest point in the universe and location of the shatter."

Eve looked around and admired her surroundings. Out of all the places on Amalga-5 she'd seen, it was strange how both alien and intrinsically Earth-like it seemed. The towns of Canam, the Jungles of Krondico, the grassy plains beaches of Starwynn, and now the highest mountain peak of Doxland. She had to remind herself that it was real for a moment.

"Beautiful, isn't it?" Vita asked Eve, noticing she was distracted, while everyone else was staring at the rip in time and space at the top of the mountain. "The Sentinel's greatest achievement in my mind. The celestial brothers may have crafted a vast Multiverse, but the Sentinel made this planet. One person, on accident. He cultivated it. His garden. He built it in his image and let it become what it has. He threw in a touch of himself. He was like all the Celestial Beings combined in that regard. Though this planet is a spit in the face to Ultimae. Must be why he hates it so much."

"What do you mean?" Eve asked.

"He wants a universe entirely ruled by him. Time creating the Originals and the Sentinel breaking the universe and making his own planet did much to anger him." Vita laughed. "He doesn't want anyone playing with his creation in ways he didn't plan."

"He just seems like a bratty kid," Eve said.

"A big, celestial, dangerous, universe destroying, bratty kid," Ganto chimed in, looking down and staring off over the edge of the towering mountain. "Terrifying."

"So about this rip in time and space…" Agro stared at the shatter above the mountain's exact highest point.

"And dimensions," Vistor added.

"Yeah." Agro continued staring.

"How are we supposed to build a gateway around that?" Nick asked. "There's hardly enough ground."

Eve was about to agree with Nick, but she quickly remembered who she was, and lifted her arms. Phlasma crystals extended from the mountain's top and spread like growing rocks. Eve flattened the rocks overhead like a disc to make a solid platform of crystalized phlasma. Vistor ducked his head and Terri guarded his crown for him. As the platform extending above slowed, Eve let down her hands. A staircase formed from the edge of the platform and to the edge of the mountain cliff where they were all standing.

## ❖ CHAPTER 25 ❖

Ganto leaned over the edge and stared at the staircase precariously placed over a steep cliff. He gave Eve a look, "Um."

Eve flicked her arms up quickly and guard rails formed from the side of the stairs.

Vistor hesitantly lifted an arm.

Eve rolled her eyes and she shot out her arms. The stairs split in half and pulled apart. She filled the gap with more phlasma, essentially making the staircase wider.

"Thank you." Vistor bowed.

"How much have you been practicing with phlasma?" Vita asked. "Seems you're a pro."

"You know when you've got twenty-three years to spare sitting around doing nothing in an orphanage you tend to make some things out of boredom," Eve explained. She was the first to make the ascent up the stairs.

"*Ai lu nont ewk ege-ai hugno-izz bipescends.*" Vogar stared at the stairs nervously.

"Well then fly if you don't trust the stairs! Come on, brains, man!" Ganto laughed and made his way up the stairs second. The rest of the army followed suit and soon they were standing comfortably on top of the massive platform in the mountains, all surrounding the tear in front of them.

"Now do we just let Eve build the gateway, then? She made the platform, so I don't see why not," Nick asked.

"No," Vita said. She approached the portal and stared at it. "No, it needs to be built a certain way. When this is built it will be considered a holy monument in the eyes of the Originals. It needs to be built by Originals. Preferably two of each kind, both for ceremonial and practical purposes."

"What practical purposes?" Ganto questioned. "If you want it to be secure just use Calcurus and make the humans build it."

"Garstone," Vita interjected, "A phlasma suppressing material only the Gars know how to make."

"The Andromedans stole the recipe during the first Galactic War," Agro interrupted Vita. "Wouldn't it be a waste of time to gather a bunch of Originals to build this thing that Eve can make in a matter of seconds?"

"It needs to be constructed properly," Vita argued.

"Shouldn't be too much of an issue," Eve said, siding with Vita. "Gars live here now; I know that much. The Dragolupus just moved in, Vita I'm sure you know where to contact more Deusaves."

Vita nodded.

"All we need are some Terrors."

## ❖ CHAPTER 25 ❖

"And Hive Two are our allies," Vistor reminded the Army. "Simple."

"Right." Ganto chuckled. "And that solves the issue of time needed for construction, how?" he asked. "I think efficiency is more important than legacy."

"Didn't Hive Two die?" Foxtrot asked.

"They crowned a new Hive Leader recently," Vita informed them.

"How are we supposed to get them all here then?" Nick asked.

"Do I have to do everything?" Eve rolled her eyes. She flashed away. She fell onto a massive round table, in a temple like room, surrounded by Gars, she seemed to be interrupting a meeting. At first she was afraid of the many reptilian beasts staring her down, but after studying their expression she noticed they were more confused than angry. She turned around on the table until she faced who she thought looked to be the most important Gar in the room. "Hello, I'm Eve. I'm the Sentinel's daughter, I'm here for a request by the Life Master."

The Gar in front her spoke in a calming voice, and eloquent dictation, "I don't believe we've met. Aragar." The Gar bowed. His shiny gray skin shifted with a royal purple as he raised his elegant white brows. "King of Woestyn, Amalga-5. What is Vita's request."

"You know her?" Eve stood up on the table. The rest of the Gars continued staring in confusion.

"The Emissaries are stuff of legend, of course I do." Aragar laughed jovially. He seemed old and wise among the Gars.

Eve shook her head, reminding herself of the scale of her place in legend. "Access to the Extraverse has been limited to one rift, portal-thing, on the top of the highest mountain in Doxland. We're supposed to build a gateway there, but Vita requested it be done by Originals. Would you be able to help?" Eve asked.

"Gladly. I would be honored." Aragar floated above the table and approached Eve, his royal purple cape fluttered behind him. "Take me to this place." He held out his scaly arm.

Eve hesitated before reaching out for his clawed hand. The two of them flashed away. She appeared at the mountain only moments after she had vanished. The Army was taken aback by the sudden appearance of a grand appearing Gar.

"King of Woestyn, the Sentinel's Army," Eve introduced him. "Sentinel's Army, Aragar," she finished her brief introduction and flashed away again. Quickly her surroundings were replaced with the stony grayish blue plains of Sanzi, one of the many moons of Ilsose. She looked around and yelled out, "Hive Two?"

With an unexpected blast of sound, a massive figure burst from the ground behind Eve. She turned around and instinctively flared her hands with bright flames, sparks of static shot between her fingers as she stumbled back. "Kranthar!?" she yelled in fear.

"No, child." The sweet voice of the massive creature laughed. When it slowed its ascent, the huge worm-like hivemind of Hive Two lowered her armored head to face Eve. "Kranthar died many cycles ago."

Eve dropped the flames from her hands and relaxed. She breathed heavily and smiled, "Sorry, just, not used to this." She stood straighter, "I am—"

"I know." The Krantharnic smiled. "I am Hive Two's new hivemind, Orso."

"Nice to meet you." Eve bowed. "Life requests—"

"I know." Orso smiled and shook her head calmly. "I will send my drones over at once to help."

"Thank you." Eve bowed again, unsure of how to act around this beast. She stood around, not knowing what to do next.

"You can go now." Orso laughed.

"Oh, right, sure, sorry." Eve laughed nervously and reached for the box, missing the first time, but as the box floated into her hand she flashed away and appeared on the golden-brown grassy beach of Starwynn.

She called out for any Dragolupus. "Hello!"

A blast of lightning whizzed by her, the wind pushing the tall grass in dramatic waves.

Eve turned around quickly, facing a Dragolupus that appeared more dragon-like that wolfish in nature.

"Hi, I'm Eve, and I need your help…"

The stone at the Dragolupus's forehead glowed.

"*Okay, you're reading my mind, cool cool, makes things easier,*" Eve laughed.

"Natri," the Dragolupus introduced itself. "I would be glad to help. You need two?" he asked.

"Yeah, but I mean, we do know a Dragolupus."

"Who is busy in the Extraverse?" Natri asked.

"I get that you can read my mind but—"

"Yes, I do have to show it off," Natri smiled.

## ❖ CHAPTER 25 ❖

"Okay, yeah if you have another Dragolupus friend that would be willing help that would be perfect," Eve said.

Another blast of electric energy whizzed past Eve as a wolf-like Dragolupus snapped into view next to Natri.

"Lino, at your service," the second Dragolupus said.

"Okay cool, follow me." Eve smiled, and flashed away, reappearing on the platform with the Army. She had showed up later than when she had left to give the Army time to catch up with Aragar. By the time she arrived, Orso's drones were already present.

Natri and Lino zoomed into view on the platform and they quickly exchanged pleasantries with the Army.

Vita appeared on the platform alongside a Deusaves with a similar appearance to that of a large owl. "Greetings, I have brought along the help of an old friend of mine, Strix."

"Hello," Strix introduced himself calmly. "I feel that I may be an immense help to you and your cause."

"You mean more than just this gateway?" Eve asked.

"Strix is a close friend of mine," Vita explained, "We fought together in the first ever war. He was trained personally by King Dile himself."

"You're a good fighter, then?" Eve asked, holding out her hand.

Strix lifted a leg to shake Eve's hand. "I don't mean to brag, but good may be an understatement."

"Eve, are you kidding me?" Ganto ran up to Eve's side. "This dude's a galactic legend!"

"And he didn't help out before?" Eve asked.

"I'm sorry about that," Strix bowed. "I was fighting a war halfway across the universe. I wasn't in contact with anyone, because…"

"He was fighting our war," Vita interrupted to provide clarification. "You were trying to fight alongside the remaining Sarran to stop Ultimae."

"You've had experience with Ultimae?" Eve asked.

Strix flinched, then nodded with a striking silence. He stood still, petrified. He opened his eyes. They were massive, and deep, seemingly filled with the stars themselves. He stared Eve down. It was only now that Eve noticed the scars that cut across his round face. He opened his beak, and spoke, "The Banished can't be stopped. This gateway of Garstone will keep him weak when he is near it, but I can't promise that you won't suffer the same fate as the Sarran I fought to protect."

Eve stepped back.

Ganto gulped. "That doesn't sound good…"

## ❖ CHAPTER 25 ❖

"The Sarran called me by a different name," Strix said, his voice cold and quiet. "They called me the Bird Before Death. An omen of the end times."

"Why?" Eve asked.

"The Sarran knew what they were fighting for. They knew he was coming. They sent for help, and they got me. None of the Sarran ever won their battles. They knew if I came to help, they were truly desperate, their fight would likely be their last."

"Um," Ganto shuffled forward, "Then can I kindly ask you to leave?"

Strix chuckled, turning his head to the side and covering his face with his wing. He turned back to face Ganto and said, "Ilsian, you have nothing to fear. This isn't a fight. I came to help with construction. Nothing more."

"Alright, bud, but if you get any of us killed by being here, I'll be pissed," Ganto warned.

A flash of lightning struck the platform, startling the group briefly before the light cleared to reveal a new sparking figure standing before them.

"Starlocke!" Eve exclaimed. "What are you doing here? Shouldn't you be keeping the universe alive, we have Dragolupus help."

"Woah, yeah, aren't you supposed to be off fixing the universe, or…" Nick worried.

"It's fine," Starlocke assured all of them. "I have time." His ears perked up. "I want to help. Let's get this built."

Over the course of the day and into the night, the Sentinel's Army helped the Originals: Aragar, Vogar, Vita, Strix, Orso via her drones, Natri, Lino and Starlocke, all build the gateway around the rift.

They lifted bricks of Garstone and carved away at it. They reinforced the disc stage of phlasma that functioned as the foundation for the gateway at the top of the mountain. They each worked together seamlessly to construct the monument with ease and efficiency.

It only dawned on Eve when they were wrapping up construction that Aragar didn't even know about the end of the universe, and the beginning of the end of the Multiverse. His people didn't know.

No one on Amalga-5 except the Dragolupus and the government of Canam knew. That didn't feel right to Eve. She thought about what Tomas had said, that he didn't want to cause panic, and that the Sentinel didn't either. She figured she'd respect that decision, but something dawned on her.

### ❖ CHAPTER 25 ❖

There was no Sentinel or Tomas to stop her from doing what she thought was the right thing.

"Aragar," she called out for him while everyone was putting the finishing touches on the gateway. "Can I speak with you a moment."

"Sure." Aragar pulled away from his work and floated over to Eve.

"You don't know why we're building this do you? Why the Extraverse is being restricted?"

"No," Aragar admitted, "Is it a defense measure?"

"Yes." Eve stared ahead over the mountainside, not wanting to make direct eye contact with Aragar's bright yellow eyes. "The Extraverse is in danger of being overthrown by someone who wants to start over, with a clean slate... on the entire Multiverse."

Aragar blinked in shock. Words couldn't make it to his mouth and he struggled with the concept. He nervously flapped his wings. "What?" he asked.

Eve pursed her lips and nodded.

"How long has this been happening? Who knows?"

"Not many do. It's been happening forever apparently, but the real danger hasn't been here since the end of the

Galactic War, but for you I assume that's been awhile. Amalga-5 was sent back in time to keep it safe, even."

"That's why?" Aragar asked in surprise. "You aren't kidding, huh?"

"No."

"And you're fighting this threat on your own?" he asked, with worry in his eyes.

"The Sentinel's Army is. Just them. The Sentinel never wanted to involve anyone, endanger anyone."

"All the countries of Amalga-5, though not all allies, I swear to you would stop at nothing to defend this and every universe. I'm sure Janistar's army would help as well. Or even the Deusaves, and Hive Two. You have the resources necessary to stop any threat."

"I guess my father just wanted to avoid unnecessary death."

"What's worse?" Aragar held his arms on Eve's shoulders and stared her down. "The loss of *some* lives in an effort to save the Multiverse, or the loss *all* life, across the entire universe, across every universe, *infinite* universes, *infinite loss of infinite life.* If nothing, I can assure you that the people of Woestyn are on your side." He spoke with elegance

## ❖ CHAPTER 25 ❖

and a certain wisdom about him. His old raspy voice carried the message clearly.

Eve looked away, crying. She smiled through the tears and held her hand to her mouth. She hadn't heard it said the way Aragar expressed it. She hadn't realized how much responsibility she had been carrying with her, and how much of it didn't need to be solely hers. "Thank you. So much."

Aragar smirked. "*Sarrinith.*"

Eve looked at Aragar, confused.

"It's Garish, for 'doing what's right.'"

Eve nodded. "Sarrinith."

"Alright." Vistor boomed with his annunciatory voice. "The Gateway is finished!"

Eve and Aragar turned around to look at the Gateway. It was built with what looked to be some sort of sandstone. Intricate carvings snaked their way up the pillars of the gazebo-like structure. The carvings seemed to move as if alive. The roof of the structure glowed with purity, phlasma crystals shone from underneath the roof tiles. On the faces of the slanted triangles that made up the roof, the depiction of the Originals from their temples was etched in.

In the center of the platform was the rift. The army ascended the few stairs into the platform itself. Two Scorlions, an addition provided by Aragar, guarded the rift. Their robotic exoskeleton shone in the yellow moonlight of Amalga-5. Their eyes glowed a peaceful green as they stood like statues, waiting.

The moonlight vanished as dark clouds covered the large moon in the starry sky. Snow fell on the mountaintop, and the Army felt accomplished. Lighting struck in the clouds overhead. The smiles of the Army faded when they heard a robotic chuckling. The Scorlion's eyes quickly shifted to red, and they stood alert like wary dogs. Their scorpion tails lifted, and their eyes darted around methodically as if smelling for danger.

"I can't believe that you would put everyone that Ultimae is targeting, all in one place like that. You stupid wannabe Sarran." Suriv crawled over the edge of the phlasma platform like an insect. His tall crystal-shaped glowing orange body rotated on an axel that functioned as his hip. He turned to face the Terror drones, who seemed ready to attack. He blasted each of them with a laser beam from his eye that disintegrated them instantaneously.

Eve flared her hands at the ready. Ganto withdrew his rifle from his back and sparked his jetpack. Foxtrot and Agro both unholstered pistols from their sides and turned them into

### ❖ CHAPTER 25 ❖

rifles, ready to fight back. Vistor and Terri slugged away, not wanting to fight. Nick took out his revolver with Calcurus bullets, recognizing that Suriv's shell was made of the stuff. Vita and Strix's feathers smoldered like a burning flame and their eyes glowed blue. Vogar and Aragar's nostrils burned with phlasma as they were ready to fight back. Starlocke, Natri, and Lino all lowered their heads and growled, their fur sparking.

Ganto leaned over to Strix and grumbled, "This is turning into a fight, you should leave."

"You need my help," Strix widened his stance and lifted his wings in front of him, ready to fight.

"And this Gateway of yours." Suriv turned his body to see it. "Pathetic."

With a strike of lightning above, a massive red object fell out of the sky and landed with a resounding thud on the phlasmatic platform, cracking it. The figure stood up. Ultimae, in his Celestial form, stood towering before them. "With the Extraverse leaking out and the universe leaking in. My power can be used to its full potential. The two are one in the same," he announced. "Bow to me."

"Never." Aragar floated forward.

"Very well." Ultimae scowled. His space ripping sword extended from his arm, larger than before. He dragged it across the platform as he approached the gateway, ignoring the Army.

Aragar blasted Ultimae with a pulse of phlasma. Suriv shot a laser at Aragar's wings, and he fell to the ground. Ultimae lifted his blade and impaled it into Aragar's heart, and in an instant the Gar vanished, being ripped to shreds as the starry flames of the blade consumed him, and his body was replaced with empty space until the flames vanished and were sucked back into the blade. The blade glowed, gaining strength, and another rêve stone was added dangling at its handle.

It all happened so fast. The Army couldn't react in time. The Army burst into action the moment the death registered in their minds. The moment the danger became clear. The moment they feared for their lives. Ultimae backhanded Vita off the mountain. Agro shot at Ultimae but the lasers simply passed through him.

Nick shot rapidly at Suriv, piercing his armor a few times. Suriv lifted an arm to slice at Nick, but Terri quickly barged in in his beastly form, headbutting Suriv to the ground. He fell like an unbalanced bottle and landed with a thud. Vistor came to Terri's aid and was about to stomp down on Suriv when he lifted a sharp metal leg into the air. Vistor dropped himself onto the outstretched leg, which impaled his entire body until he landed on top of Suriv.

"VISTOR!" Ganto yelled. He stopped attempting to fire at Ultimae and changed his jetpack course to Suriv.

Terri helplessly headbutted Suriv's downed body over and over with tears in his bulbous eyes. He had let his king down.

Natri and Lino both pounced at Ultimae simultaneously. Ultimae outstretched both his arms. His sword vanished as his hands twisted into pointed spikes. He pushed them out and stopped the two Dragolupus mid-air, impaling them both. Ultimae's arms solidified into crystal. He spun around and flung the two Originals off of the mountain peak, where their bodies tumbled down with the rocks.

As he tossed them over, he lifted his arms. The sword reappeared in his grasp and he sliced down. Strix flew through the air, twirling and dodging the sword just in time. He flew around Ultimae and blasted at his back with a burst of white flame. He spun and landed on the floor, skidding as he shot concentrated beams of white electricity from his eyes and into Ultimae's head. Ultimae flickered for a bit before he retaliated with an outburst of red energy blasted from his palm.

The red burst shot through Strix's right wing, disintegrating it.

"Agh!" Strix groaned as he was sent flying across the platform. He stumbled until he lay still on the floor.

Vita, injured on the floor, struggled to call out in pain for her friend.

Strix groaned. Ultimae lifted his sword to strike Strix down and turn him to a stone, but at the last second, Strix fell through a wormhole that Vita had created, sending him off to safety.

Ultimae turned and swung the blade at Vita, but his swing missed as his leg was headbutted by Starlocke. Ultimae kicked Starlocke away from him, as if he were a minor annoyance. Starlocke whimpered as he hit the floor.

Ultimae scoffed and turned away from the fighting, instead marching toward the Gateway.

"Ultimae, step away from the Gateway," Eve threatened. She stood by the Scorlions in front of the rift.

"Or what?" Ultimae chuckled.

Eve didn't respond.

"You do not know? Do you?" Ultimae stepped forward. He loomed over the newly built structure, and he

❖ CHAPTER 25 ❖

stood there, in front of the gazebo, waiting. "That is all you are, full of empty threats."

Eve knew he was right.

"I could stand here all day. It is no wasted time on my part, but look at them." He turned around. "Dying for you."

Suriv withdrew his leg from Vistor's body, letting the corpse slide to the floor. He used his rocket to propel himself up again. He kicked Vistor's body. It rolled off the platform, and fell down the cliff.

"*NON!*" Vogar exclaimed.

"You can't stop us," Suriv said matter-of-factly. "What are you doing?" He laughed.

Nick fired away at Suriv as fast as he could, reloading and reloading.

"*Nick!*" Eve yelled past Ultimae. "The body's behind the mouth! Shoot at the mouth!" she exclaimed.

Nick acknowledged and reloaded, firing at the mouth. He pierced a specific part of the armor and Suriv's mouthpiece dropped, exposing the Ilsian inside.

Unexpectedly, a wormhole opened up beneath Suriv, and he dropped from the scene. Vita landed where he once stood and slammed to the ground with a wounded wing.

"What are you doing! I could've killed him!" Nick yelled at Vita.

"I'm sorry." Vita shook her head. "I didn't know."

The Army turned their attention to Eve, standing in front of the rift, and Ultimae standing before her, holding the glowing sword. Ultimae crouched down to get to Eve's level. The galactic shape in his head pulsated with anger. "Why are you doing this? Why try to stop me? I am a god. You do not so much as hold the privilege to call yourself a Sarran."

"There are no gods..." Eve furrowed her brow as her fingers sparked with cold electricity.

"I created this world."

"No you didn't," Eve interrupted.

Ultimae was taken aback. His galaxy flickered. "You know your efforts are ill placed. You know you stand no chance. You can weaken me, but you cannot stop me. Why do you try?"

"*Sarrinith*," Eve growled. She shot her hands outward and with an intense strike of power, cold lightning blasted Ultimae in the chest. His phlasmatic body quivered and shook, and it pushed him back. But when Eve was well drained, she shook her hands, ready to blast again, but it seemed it had

## ❖ CHAPTER 25 ❖

accomplished nothing. Ultimae had only been pushed back slightly.

Vita created a wormhole underneath Ultimae in an attempt to push him away. Ultimae didn't fall underneath, instead he held out his arms and absorbed the wormhole. It ripped space around him, and loud winds bombarded the army. Starlocke anchored his feet and lowered his head, blasting Ultimae with a laser from his stone. Ultimae withdrew his sword, newly imbued with the power of the wormhole, and directed the flames from it like a counter beam at Starlocke.

The two lasers fought each other like reverse tug-of-war, while the rest of the Army watched. Eve blasted at Ultimae with another strike of lightning. With the brief distraction, Starlocke's laser took over and blasted away through Ultimae's chest. A hole formed in his chest and he stumbled back. "You do not understand what I am." Ultimae chuckled. "Do you?"

Ganto, Terri, and Vogar stood by the ledge where Vistor fell, hopeless. Foxtrot, Agro, and Nick stood around, lost and helpless. Their guns couldn't do anything now. Starlocke, Vita, and Eve were their only hope.

Ultimae groaned as his chest regrew. "I am not," His red phlasmatic body jittered and wavered as limbs burst from underneath his existing arms. "Bound to a mortal body," Another head sprouted next to the existing one, he wasn't doing any of this to gain an advantage, but merely to prove a point. "You cannot stop me!"

A dark blue-green force of energy shot out of the rift and into Eve's chest. She gasped for air as she stumbled forward and out of the Gateway. She looked up, her eyes glowing with the same dark blue-green color as the energy burst. When she spoke, her voice wasn't hers, "Back down, brother."

"Celestae?" Vita asked.

Eve's hands flared with blue-green phlasmatic flames. "This is your last warning."

Though Ultimae was faceless, the Army could sense his smug smile. "Try me," Ultimae threatened.

Eve screamed as she launched herself into the air. Electric wings of phlasma burst from her back and as she punched forward, Celestae's arm overtook hers, and she punched Ultimae in the face. Ultimae stumbled and fell to the ground, leaning over the edge of the platform. Eve floated above him.

"Celestae," Eve greeted her possessor. "Eve," Celestae greeted back. "Hope it's not too crowded in there for you

## ❖ CHAPTER 25 ❖

Matrona," Eve talked to herself. *"The more the merrier,"* she said sarcastically. She held out her hands and blasted a beam of phlasma at Ultimae's head. The beam consumed his head, and Ultimae struggled to fight back, flailing his arms. "Ganto!" Eve yelled. "The sword!"

Ganto quickly ran for the sword. He pried it from Ultimae's hands and stabbed it into his abdomen. In an instant, Ultimae, and the sword, vanished.

Eve floated to the ground, and Celestae remained in her head. Her sparking wings vanished as she turned her attention back to the Army.

"Is he gone?" Foxtrot asked, hopeful.

"No," said the Celestae part of Eve. "Celestial Beings are immortal; he will be back. He is very injured. Had Ganto stabbed the galaxy in his head we may have been in a better place, but regardless, this is not over."

"What do we do?" Agro sat down on the platform.

"He killed Aragar." Vita sat down as well. "And the Dragolupus. He obliterated my friend's wing; I fear the injury may be the death of him if he doesn't get it taken care of fast."

"He killed Vistor." Ganto looked out over the mountain's edge. "That *bastard*, Suriv…"

Agro whispered, choking up, "I don't see how we could possibly win this."

"You said he was immortal?" Nick asked Eve, the question directed to Celestae.

Eve nodded, her eyes still glowing.

"How can we stop him then?" Ganto paced around, angrily. "We're all gonna die!"

"Ganto!" Eve scolded.

"We are!" Ganto flailed his arms. "Look at us!" He flung his arms around. Tears formed in his buggy eyes. "LOOK AT US!" he repeated.

Eve hadn't seen Ganto this way before. It worried her. Ganto always seemed so care-free.

Terri and Vogar both cried at the side of the phlasma platform.

Ganto shook his head, crying. "Dammit!" he yelled. "Eve, we're all going to die! The only way to stop Ultimae is to kill him, and he *can't be killed!*"

"Ganto," Eve approached her friend.

"NO!" Ganto stepped away. "*My King is dead.* My *friend* is dead. Too many of us are *dead.* We're dead. We're all dead."

## ❖ CHAPTER 25 ❖

"We could give him mortality," Vita said. She stretched her neck and tried to appear taller. The Sentinel's Army turned their attention to her. "We could give him mortality the same way we did to the Originals."

"Would that work?" Nick asked.

"I don't know," Vita answered.

"Is it worth a try?" Agro asked, desperate for anything.

"Anything is," Eve said.

"But how?" Foxtrot asked.

Vita took in a deep breath, then looked off out to the horizon. She closed her eyes, and with a soft voice she said, "We need to find Death."

❖ Chapter 26 ❖

# The Ilsian Kings

Ganto, Terri, and Vogar set out to find Vistor's body and lay him to rest. Surveying the base of the mountain, they found his crown before they found his body. Ganto knelt by it, holding it in his hands.

"Sad?" Vogar grumbled softly.

Ganto wiped a tear and turned around, grasping the crown. He sniffled. "*Pissed.*"

Terri nodded.

The news of Vistor's passing was relayed to Ilsose by Terri and Vogar.

Ilsose had been without a king before, it was used to the old brutal system, a system where whoever killed the king got to take over, and rule was never really established; this was how things went. But in Vistor's era, after he'd taken over, he

### ❖ CHAPTER 26 ❖

tried his best to better the planet. And he did, so his death shook the planet to its core.

Eve told Woestyn's people what happened to their king, Aragar, and what he said. She told them about Ultimae, and the impending end of the Multiverse. She told Terri and Vogar to tell Ilsose the same. Foxtrot relayed the same sentiment to the rest of Amalga-5. Agro informed the people of Janistar.

Never had there been a day so hopeless. Not since Earth's evacuation in 3047. Not since the twice death of the Sentinel. Everyone felt the sting of this pain, the sting of the beginning of the end.

"Ganto..." Terri peered his head into the door of the Freysent in the hangar of the Pantheon. Ganto sat at the pilot seat, his head leaning on the dash, crying. Vistor's crown sat on the dash.

Ganto looked up. "Terri, now's not the time."

Terri gestured behind him.

A small green Ilsian stood there beside him. Ganto recognized him.

"Lefnis?" Ganto lifted his head a bit higher. He sniffled and wiped his face.

"Long time no see, Ganto."

Lefnis was an employee of Vistor's. He helped him run a smooth government and keep steady rule over Ilsose during his rule.

Ganto looked him over.

"This isn't how I imagined we'd be meeting again."

Vogar floated behind him.

"What is that?" Ganto asked, pointing to a small folder Lefnis held.

"Vistor's dying will."

Ganto stood up.

Lefnis opened the folder and pointed at a paper inside. "Vistor gave his whole back storage of royal food to Terri. Said he needs to bulk up. He also left his cloud estate in the upper layers of Ilsose to Vogar."

"Why are you telling me this?" Ganto stepped out of the Freysent.

"He left you the biggest asset of his, I'm here to ask if you're willing."

"His biggest asset?" Ganto asked. "He gave the cloud estate to Vogar, what do you mean?"

## CHAPTER 26

Vogar and Terri looked to Ganto with an air of seriousness that Ganto was unfamiliar seeing them in. A sinking feeling pulled Ganto down, he stepped down the ramp from his ship to balance himself.

Lefnis dropped to one knee and bowed.

Ganto tilted his head confusedly.

"Vistor the Great had one heir to his throne. It was you, Ganto. Ganto the Great."

Ganto stood up straight. A chill tingled up his spine. A tear fell down his hard exoskeleton. His antlers twitched, and he looked behind him into the Freysent, at the crown on the dash.

"For the first time in decades... Ilsose is back in the rule of an Ilsian. Vistor said it was the least he could give you, for helping him stop Suriv all those years ago. And for avenging his family and killing Vel-Ant. For sacrificing an Ilsian ruled government for one ruled by a Lorinian. He said he never understood why you helped him... just that he was grateful."

Ganto wiped his tears.

Terri and Vogar bowed.

"Don't do that." Ganto shook his head and clicked his mandibles as he cried. "Stand up, dummies."

"King Ganto the Great," Lefnis bowed. "Fight for us."

Ganto looked out over the hangar, and into space. He stood tall and closed his eyes. *"Thank you, Vistor…"*

Ganto flew the Freysent to Vistor's palace down on the surface of Ilsose. No one paid him much attention. They were either mourning, or too busy not caring.

Ilsose was strange like that. The Ilsians were happy that Vistor was gone, however bittersweet it was, and the Lorinians were distraught, for the most part. The rest of the species on the planet shared a variety of opinions of the monarchy of the planet, not all of them favorable.

No one knew nor cared about who Ganto was; they didn't know what to expect from this new era of rule.

Ganto walked the length of the palace, alone, quiet.

It was true that Ganto was a relative of Ilsose's long reigning tyrant before Vistor, the despicable Vel-Ant. The throne was back on track with its proper blood line.

That was the biggest worry of Ilsose. They fought to dethrone Vel-Ant. And Vel-Ant's sons, daughters, nephews,

## ❖ CHAPTER 26 ❖

and nieces fought for him to keep it. Suriv, Ganto's cousin, was one of the fighters for his cause.

Though some of the planet knew that Ganto fought against his family, alongside Vistor, Vogar, and Terri, they still held a cautious attitude toward anyone affiliated with Vel-Ant, regardless if they were with or against him.

Ganto sat in the throne. Back then, he hated Lorinians. But he saw in Vistor something that could change Ilsose for the better. He knew of his tragic past, his background. He knew what drove him. Though his hopes were high, nothing could ever fix Ilsose, not really.

Ganto closed his eyes and leaned his head back in the throne. Vistor was always too big for the throne of Ilsose. Terri and Vogar would always insist that it wasn't a weight issue. Ganto knew it was. But really, it was because the throne was meant for an Ilsian.

Ganto sighed. He didn't like the amount and variety of emotions that he felt. He shook himself.

"Aw, look at you. Playing King," a tinny voice projected through a speaker.

Ganto opened his eyes and looked down at the base of the staircase leading to the throne.

A scrappy looking gray Suriv robot stood there, a projection blasted from its aperture eye. A flickering static image of Suriv projected itself before Ganto. He clicked the mandibles of his mangled face together and twitched his head. His sharp eyes glared at Ganto.

"Why are you here?" Ganto asked calmly.

"To congratulate you, cousin. Of course!" Suriv smiled. "The throne of Ilsose! Back in the Vel-Ant royal family. A momentous occasion!"

"You better leave before I shred your stupid robot to pieces."

Suriv nodded. "Already more assertive than the pathetic Lorinian…"

"You have no right to call him pathetic," Ganto snarled.

"Well, I killed him, so."

Ganto shot up out of the throne and withdrew an Andromedan rifle. He blasted the robot in the eye and shut off the hologram.

Suriv's voice chuckled through the speakers. "Hold your felipods, pal. No need to lose your cool."

"Get out of my palace," Ganto growled.

## ❖ CHAPTER 26 ❖

"I'm sorry, but is it yours?" Suriv asked. The robot looked around. "If I remember how our old pal Vistor got the throne in the first place it was because he took advantage of Ilsose custom, right? He killed Vel-Ant. I killed Vistor. Technically, I should be king."

Ganto stepped back, his mandibles clicked nervously. "I killed Vel-Ant. Technically I should have always been king."

"Ah, but..." Suriv hesitated. "Whatever. I don't want the throne anymore. You can have it. I'll give you that. Take what little victories you can get."

"You haven't given me *jack shit,* Suriv you *dickless* piece of *scrap metal!*" Ganto marched down the steps and to the robot that Suriv's voice projected from.

"Vel-Ant would be so proud of us," Suriv said calmy, ignoring Ganto's anger, "Mostly of me. I'm going much higher places than the throne of this trash heap. No offense. I'm sure you'll do great... For the time you have left anyway."

Ganto held up the rifle and blasted at the robot from close range. The burst melted at the metal of the bot, exposing some of its mechanical insides. Ganto cocked the weapon and pointed again as he walked closer.

Suriv ignored him, and kept talking, his voice from the speaker growing more distorted as the metal melted, "Your friends can't save you now. No matter how many powerful people you surround yourself with, no matter how many things are handed to you on a silver platter, I'll always be right there to stop you. You're welcome by the way."

Ganto shot the robot again. The robot fell over on a melted and mangled spider-like leg.

"The throne was a parting gift from me to you."

Ganto screamed and kicked the robot while it was down.

"Vistor was a great King!" Ganto yelled. "You'll never be as great as him!"

"There wasn't a throne he could ever fit in, Ganto. Vistor is king of the dead now. And just as you've taken his place, soon you will be too."

Ganto blasted at the robot. The speaker melted and the tinny voice of Suriv came out distorted and warbled as he laughed at Ganto's anger.

"We stopped you once! We can do it again!" Ganto roared.

"Oh, it isn't me you have to worry about. You big dummy," Suriv's voice crawled out of the speakers. "This isn't

## ❖ CHAPTER 26 ❖

about petty family and political squabbles anymore. Nah, I'm just sitting back and enjoying the ride, killing Vistor was a happy little accident. No effort whatsoever, done and dusted."

Ganto stumbled back and wiped away a tear with one of his arms. His shoulders slouched as he held the rifle. He breathed heavily.

"I don't need to do a thing but make some Calcurus shit here and there. Ultimae's your real worry. And what in the hell are you gonna do to him, huh? You're all gonna die... that's what. I'll kill you just as easily."

Ganto wiped away a tear. "It isn't me you have to worry about..." Ganto breathed heavily. He sniffled. "You surround yourself with powerful people all you want... Things handed to you on a platter... I'll always be right here to stop you..."

The Suriv bot scooted back as the metal around it melted. A static silence breathed from the speaker.

"It isn't me you have to worry about... and you're right." Ganto wiped a tear away as he slowly lifted the rifle. "This isn't about petty family and political squabbles anymore. I killed Vel-Ant long ago. I'm not who you have to stop. Eve is your real worry. And what in the hell are you gonna do to her, huh?"

Ganto lifted the rifle and screamed as he bombarded the robot with laser fire.

The pathetic scrappy throw-away bot exploded in a pitiful flame and died out as the speaker cut away.

Ganto fell to his knees and slammed the floor.

As his pointed hand hit the tile he flinched and held his wrist. A quick pain pulsed through his body. He glanced at his hand. A gray sickness spread across his arm, burning like a fire under his exoskeleton. He shook his hand, and stood up, heading for the Freysent.

❖ Chapter 27 ❖

# Death

"Communication? You think *that's* the thing to focus on right now?" Ganto questioned Eve. Vistor's crown sat firmly on his head between his antlers.

"We need to have a plan, yes," Eve insisted. "The Army needs to be able to work together. If we could've planned, we could've avoided what happened to Vistor, and the rest of them."

"So what? You want me to teach Terri and Vogar some English? Is that it?" Ganto asked sarcastically.

"Yes," Eve admitted, she hadn't thought of that before, "It would be helpful."

"How about you learn some Andromedan or Garish?" Ganto pressed.

"Look—"

"Ha! Doesn't seem so easy anymore, does it?" Ganto chuckled. "There's bigger problems at stake here-"

"We could at least plan!" Eve retorted.

"We didn't plan for that! Strix even said, *this isn't a fight,*" Ganto pressed forward at Eve. "We can't possibly plan for things like this."

"We could at least be prepared," Eve argued.

A door opened in the corridor in the Pantheon where Eve and Ganto were waiting. Vita stepped from the door. The long feathers trailing from her head floated up to the handle to close the door behind her as she waddled up to Eve and Ganto. "Are you two ready?" she asked. She glanced at Ganto. "Congratulations, by the way, Ganto the Great. It must be an honor."

Eve and Ganto stepped away, collecting themselves.

Ganto straightened his crown.

Eve asked, "Where are we going again?"

"A very simple place I should've known Morty would run off to that I hadn't checked yet."

"Where's that?" Eve asked.

"Home." Vita extended her wing to Eve. The box floated to Eve's shoulder and rested on it. Eve took Ganto's hand and the three of them flashed away.

## ❖ CHAPTER 27 ❖

They appeared on a plateau. In the sky above, Eve could identify Tornlozor in the distance. The ground was a shining white, almost blinding with the sun's reflection. Quartz crystal extended as far as the eye could see. The vast, grandiose array of canyons and steep mountains, all shining pure white stretched to the horizon and beyond. Eve stared over the cliff edge and was taken aback when burning white birds swooped up from the canyon below and flew overhead, cawing and screeching regally.

"Welcome to Nidus, home of the Deusaves," Vita announced.

"Out of all the places in the universe I've been, this one's my favorite." Ganto stared over the landscape. "I've been here more times than I can count."

"Really?" Vita asked.

"Oh yeah. This is home number two for me, right here." Ganto smiled. "Riding on the backs of Deusaves through the canyons. It's a feeling you can never forget."

"Interesting." Vita smiled.

"Alright, now let's find this Death guy."

"Where do we look?" Eve asked. "There's so many places he could be."

"Like I said." Vita spread her wings. "Home." She jumped over the cliff's edge and swooped underneath. Eve looked over the edge and saw a cave underneath them. She sprouted her electric wings and floated down to the cave cautiously. Ganto sparked his jetpack and followed. The two of them stood on the cave's edge, not wanting to advance as they saw Vita staring across at Morty, huddled in the back of the dark cave.

"Why'd you run off?" Vita asked.

"I can't do this anymore," he answered after some hesitation.

"Do what?" Eve asked.

"Be Death. It's too much."

"No, come on." Eve sighed, "We need you now more than ever."

"Precisely why I can't do this." Death chuckled. "Because of my introduction to the Extraverse, things can die. Every death that has been suffered I have felt. My body and mind have been strained tremendously. I have suffered infinite deaths, and I am not prepared for what is coming. I can't sit in my throne while the Multiverse goes the way of the Sarran."

"That's why we need you," Eve said. "To help us stop that from happening."

## ❖ CHAPTER 27 ❖

"As if it could be stopped," Morty snarled. "Your hope is sorely misplaced. I'm sorry to say. I'm not the type to fight for something I don't believe is achievable. There was a time when I had hope. But the Sarran are gone. The Sentinel is gone. When I was simply pushed aside by Ultimae half-heartedly possessing Rhey. No effort, whatsoever. Ultimae broke through the Extraverse without even thinking that he could. And then he just left Rhey to clean up his mess, thinking nothing of his death. He stopped me *with just the flick of his hand.* No thought. No effort. I can't fight that. No one can."

Vita cooed. "Together we can."

"Vita, when I became an Emissary alongside you, I did it for *you.* You were so excited, but *me...*" Death paused. He hid his face behind his wing feathers. "I was just fine in my cave."

"You did it for me?" Vita asked.

"Of course I did." Death peeked over his feathers. "Did you really think I wanted to? You were so excited to meet Time, Celestae and Ultimae, the stuff of legend. And I was so afraid. Rightfully so, it seems. So frightened of their power, I didn't want to be like them. And look at what's come of it now. I was right to be terrified. *I* let this happen."

"How? How could you ever put the blame on yourself?" Eve questioned.

Vita stood frozen in shock.

"When I became the Emissary of Death, the Originals were no longer immortal. Life could pop up anywhere in the universe at its own pace and will. The humans showed up and in came Adam Jaminski, breaking the universe and muddling it all up so that Ultimae got angry. So that Ultimae got banished and vowed to come back and make the Multiverse *his* again. I *encouraged* Time to instate us as Life and Death because I knew it would make you happy. I *encouraged* Ultimae's anger."

"You couldn't have known," Vita argued.

"I should have known." Death stared Vita down. "I'm responsible for all of this. I quit. The death that will come, I will not be responsible for."

"By leaving you're responsible for the deaths," Eve said. "Without your help more will die."

"And I won't feel it..." Morty looked away. "Not anymore. That's all I want, to rid myself of the constant reminder of mortality."

"You can't just quit being an Emissary!" Vita pressed.

## ❖ CHAPTER 27 ❖

"I heard there was another new Paradox Master," Death mumbled.

Vita remained silent. Eve didn't know how to respond, and Ganto kept quiet.

"Look," Death uncovered his face. "I quit, alright. No more Death Master."

"You can't do this," Vita begged. "For the Multiverse."

"It was a doomed project from the start," Death argued.

"For me." Vita stepped forward.

Death looked away. "I'm sorry, Vita. I can't do that again. Not after the horrors that followed last time."

"You blame me, then," Vita said. "My hope and aspirations are to blame for the extinction of the Sarran and the decimation of the Multiverse? Is that it?"

"Yes."

Vita recoiled.

"Bastard!" Ganto spat at Morty. "How could you?" Ganto held his hand to Vita's back to comfort her in her dismay.

Eve shook her head. This was her last hope and he wasn't willing to help. She couldn't fathom a being that didn't care about existence.

"It isn't that dire, Morty," Eve argued, "All we need you to do is make Ultimae mortal so we can kill him, and—"

"Ha!" Death laughed.

"What?" Ganto shook his head. "Don't laugh, this isn't the time for that!"

"Did you really think that would work?" Death clicked his beak. "You didn't think Time, as selfish as she is, would make that very thing impossible? When we were introduced as emissaries, she made it a point to exclude her and her children from the effects we have. Your hope is misplaced. I'm useless now. I'm sorry." Death shook his head. "I really am. Go. I'm sure you can find someone else to do my dirty work while the Multiverse is still around."

"I believed in you." Vita's feathers stood up on end. "When we first met. I knew you could be something more. But I was wrong. You're nothing but a cavespawn. You aren't like the rest of us. You don't have hope."

"I said I was sorry."

"Sorry doesn't save the Multiverse, Morty." Life raised her head, her tail feathers flared. "I thought I knew you." She flew out of the cave in a blur. The sound of a wormhole opening and closing blasted outside.

## ❖ CHAPTER 27 ❖

Ganto tapped his foot. "You've made a mistake bird boy." Ganto held out his hand for Eve. Eve stared at Morty. She saw pain in his eyes. "Come on." Ganto waved his hand. "Let's go, chop chop. We've got no time to waste."

Eve held out her hand, still staring.

They flashed away.

❖ Chapter 28 ❖

# Cosmic Sisters

Eve and Ganto both appeared in front of the Gateway, where they promptly walked into the Extraverse, appearing next to Vita. Time and Celestae were talking with one another, and Starlocke sat near them, eyes closed and stone glowing. Vita turned around and looked at them. "You followed me?" she asked.

"Why are we here?" Ganto asked.

"*Ganto, could you get Nick for me please?*" Eve asked.

Ganto nodded and left through the shatter.

"You want something?" Vita noticed.

"*I've been meaning to ask for a while now. I don't know if now is a good time, but time doesn't seem to be something we have to spare at the moment.*"

## ❖ CHAPTER 28 ❖

"Is this a question of mortality?"

"*It's a question I could only think to ask you. Eve was sort of hesitant with it because,* because I doubted it would work. Is it possible to resurrect someone not from a stone but from a person?" Eve asked.

Vita hesitated. "Resurrection isn't something to toy with lightly."

"*I know. I don't mean to be alive forever, just for the fight.*"

"Why?"

"Matrona is clouding my mind. She's begging to be set free and I can't do my best when I'm thinking twice."

Vita waddled up to Eve and pointed with her beak at the stone in Eve's chest. "Matrona is still in the stone. I can remove her."

Eve's eyes lit up with excitement. A combination of her excitement for a free mind again, and Matrona's desire for a free body again made her ecstatic.

Nick entered the Extraverse through the shatter. "What's this about?" he asked.

"*Nick, I'm coming back.*" Eve smiled.

"Matrona?" Nick asked.

Vita nodded behind Eve.

"Wait..." Nick thought about it a moment. "She'll be like how the Sentinel was, won't she?"

"Yes." Vita nodded.

"*I'll make the most of it, I promise.*" Eve turned around. "We're ready."

Vita closed her eyes and lifted her wings.

Eve was pushed back as a trailing white light blasted from the stone in her chest. The stone lifted from her chest, and hole left behind was filled with new flesh.

The stone floated away and hovered before Eve. The white smoke phlasma surrounding the stone became cloudy and darker, shifting into the vague shape of a person before condensing quickly, remaining in the chest. A phlasmatic robe-like dress fell over the new body of Matrona. Her long, straight, now light brown hair, dropped over her shoulders. She was finally as tall as she felt. Her new face was long, her a shade tanner than when she was alive. Her deep brown eyes blinked with new life as she gasped for air.

Eve sighed in relief; her mind was free again.

Matrona's eyes met Eve's. "Thank you," she said quietly, her eyes watering. She leapt into a hug.

"Matrona," Nick spoke up.

## ❖ CHAPTER 28 ❖

Matrona turned her attention to Nick and ran up to him. They hugged and twirled around. "Man, if Mom could see us now." Nick chuckled.

Eve looked to Vita. "Thank you, so much."

Vita looked Eve down, staring piercingly into her eyes. "She doesn't have long."

Matrona looked down at her hands, they flared with dark phlasma, stinging her fingers. "I can use this to help the fight."

"Yes, but be careful," Vita warned. "Use too much and you'll vanish into a permanent phlasma ghost. Forever. A fate worse than death."

"Then I just need to die regularly again before I run out, right?" Matrona asked. "Then I'll be fine."

Vita shrugged. "You'll be dead."

"Better than whatever happens if I don't."

"That isn't your plan, is it?" Nick asked.

"Well, I mean," Matrona looked away.

"Hold on, is it?" Eve asked. "You didn't want to be free from me so that you could be free, you did it so that—"

"So that I could fight without sacrificing you." Matrona nodded.

"Don't be reckless," Eve warned.

"I have to be. Being in the stone was torture, and I shouldn't be alive. I'm back on accident. I'll make the most of it while it lasts but I need to die, for real this time."

"You can't do that..." Nick held Matrona's shoulders.

Ganto poked his head through the shatter and into the Extraverse. "Hey, I don't know if-" his eyes met Matrona's. "Oh, you're new..."

"Hi." Matrona waved.

"Anyway, Eve, the Army needs you. We have an idea."

"Sure." Eve approached the shatter, gesturing for Nick and Matrona to follow her. Come on."

"I'll follow." Vita ducked her head down and walked after them.

Starlocke caught a glimpse of them leaving. He opened an eye and looked up at Time, who sat still. He closed his eye.

"You may leave. For now," Time said.

Starlocke shot up and smiled, panting like a dog as he trotted over to the shatter and hopped out of the Extraverse.

❖ Chapter 29 ❖
# Camp Vistor

On the other side of the shatter, atop the platform on the mountain, the rest of the Army: Agro, Foxtrot, Terri, and Vogar sat waiting.

They all stared in confusion at Matrona.

"Who's this?" Agro asked.

"Matrona Tempus." Matrona did a sort of bow to introduce herself. "Alive and separate from Eve."

"Can you fight?" Foxtrot asked.

Matrona snapped her fingers, sparking a black stinging flame at her fingertips.

"Ah!" Nick held her hands shut and put them down. "No," he answered for her.

"Yes," Matrona answered for herself.

Nick and Matrona shared a look with one another. Nick's of concern, Matrona's of confidence.

"Good enough for me." Ganto shrugged.

"What was your idea, then?" Eve asked.

"Well," Ganto explained, "The Pantheon is a safe base of operations, away from endangering life on other planets, stuff like that, but… that leaves the Gateway unprotected."

"Good point." Starlocke nodded.

Ganto continued, "We think we should set up shop here, on the platform up in the mountains. Terri and Vogar drew up some plans for a log cabin idea…"

Terri held up a small piece of paper, showing off a basic drawing of a house on top of the mountain in pen. Vogar waved his shiny new pen proudly.

"They want to call it Camp Vistor, and I feel like, though it isn't very protective or anything, it's something, right? And…"

"We could build a bunker, something more solid," Foxtrot suggested.

Terri and Vogar shot their heads at him, their faces shifting to worry.

"No," Ganto shook his head, "This means a lot to them, I…"

### ❖ CHAPTER 29 ❖

"I like the idea, Ganto." Eve smiled.

Terri and Vogar shared a smile with each other.

"We don't need protection from a being that could just as easily smash a log cabin as a reinforced bunker... probably," Eve told Foxtrot.

"Definitely," Vita followed up.

"I guess," Foxtrot shrugged.

"We'll start on the building immediately." Eve smiled. "Who knows. Could be a good team building exercise." Eve smiled.

Ganto crossed his arms. "Okay, now it sounds lame."

Eve raised a brow at him and dropped her head in a questioning way.

"Kidding," Ganto laughed.

With the loose plans set, the construction effort was underway. The Army split into groups to help gather supplies and build the camp.

Matrona and Nick talked with each other for hours as they collected supplies for the log cabin.

Eve rode atop Starlocke as they trotted down the mountain in search of wood, the two of them knocking down trees where they could.

Ganto and Vita wandered off down a separate side of the mountain, they too gathered wood, as did Terri and Vogar separately.

Agro and Foxtrot picked up stones and placed down a foundation for the cabin atop the platform.

Foxtrot struck up a conversation with Agro. "Why are you still here?" he asked.

"Hm?"

"With the Army, I mean. Helping."

"That's a weird question." Agro chuckled with a smile as he placed down a stone. "I could ask you the same thing. Why are you still helping?"

"Well, I mean... at first I wanted revenge on Canshla..."

"Uh huh." Agro nodded.

"Then when I found out that Arlo was alive, I wanted to bring him back maybe... still get revenge. Well, then you killed Canshla, so Arlo became my priority and now he's really gone... So why are you helping?"

Agro scoffed, dusting his hands together as he prepared to pick up another rock. "I'm here for the same reason the rest of us are," he said with a confidence that made the answer seem obvious.

## CHAPTER 29

"And what's that?" Foxtrot asked.

"To save the Multiverse. I mean sure, what got me into this was the high of killing Canshla and the sudden understanding that I was fighting for the wrong side all along, but what kept me fighting was knowing that I could right my wrongs ten-fold and do the universe a solid. So you're just... here, then?"

"I mean, don't get me wrong, I wanna save the universe," Foxtrot argued.

"Uh huh." Agro laughed with a smug look on his face as he tossed a rock onto the foundation. "Why are you really here?"

Foxtrot picked up a stone and stood, staring at the shatter not too far away. "I mean... Arlo could still be savable... right?"

"Dude..." Agro stood up straighter.

"I know, I know." Foxtrot rolled his eyes sarcastically as he placed down a stone. "Wishful thinking."

"Stupid thinking, more like it." Agro shook his head. "More than a friend, huh?"

"Oh yeah." Foxtrot chuckled. "It's crazy, I lost him twice."

"I guess that's how it goes nowadays." Agro groaned as he lifted a particularly heavy stone. "If you're dead you're probably not really dead until you've died again, and even then…"

"Ha, yeah." Foxtrot stepped back to admire their progress. "Kinda makes you wonder, huh?"

"Wonder what?"

"If something's ever really too far gone."

"I'm sure that's not the normal, Foxtrot. I think it just has to do with the fact that we've got gods and phlasma freaks as friends and enemies. You're going down a path of dangerous thinking, man. I know your mind, it's the same as mine. You gotta move on, pal."

"I can't just move on," Foxtrot shook his head as he lifted another stone.

"Of course you can! Your mind is a carbon copy of the Sentinel's in his third incarnation. Just look to her for proof! With time she moved on from Amara and married Vaxx. She was happy, for what little time she had. You can move on too."

"The Paradox Master didn't," Foxtrot argued.

"That didn't do him much good, did it?" Agro asked. "Come on man, you aren't seriously still holding out hope for Arlo to come back, are you?"

❖ CHAPTER 29 ❖

Foxtrot didn't answer.

Agro lifted a stone and placed it into the foundation, staring at Foxtrot, waiting for an answer. "Foxtrot."

"I heard you."

"Come on, man."

"No. It's," Foxtrot shook his head. "Nothing." He moved a stone into the platform.

"Whatever's left of the man you knew is beyond gone. There's no getting that back." Agro shook his head and continued on with his work. "I'm sorry, but that's just how it is."

"Sometimes I wish things could just be normal," Foxtrot said.

"I wish I knew what normal was." Agro laughed.

"But sometimes… sometimes I think I could use the abnormal to my advantage…"

Agro gave Foxtrot a strange look. "What do you mean?"

"To us… death isn't the end."

The two clones were interrupted when a wormhole opened beside them.

"What the…" Agro stood back.

A tree fell from the wormhole and slammed into the platform. A voice spoke in the distance, seemingly from the wormhole, saying, "Wormholes make you lazy." The wormhole closed.

"Interesting…" Foxtrot stared at the tree.

"Man was he was a jerk, but then when that day came it was like I was kid again. I remembered all of Mom's stories and boom I was like… I need one of my own, ya know? And I got one, ya know with the T-Rex… but… It's like… Mom never said anything about war."

"We were kids. We wouldn't understand even if she did," Nick responded to Matrona's story as they trudged up the mountain, dragging a sled full of wood.

"Man, there's a lot we need to catch up on. I gotta tell you about Quinn."

"Quinn Carter?" Matrona asked.

"Yeah, you know her?" Nick asked.

"How do you know her?"

"Well, Auntie Aella sent me off to Grandad's house and I got an internship at the White House, and I met her. She

## ❖ CHAPTER 29 ❖

was their Sentinel Expert, and I was like, oh I know about the Sentinel."

"And then what?"

"They hired me as her assistant."

"What? How old were you?" Matrona laughed.

"Like, seventeen?" Nick chuckled. "Yeah, pretty crazy in retrospect but man that was... not a fun time..."

"Why?"

"Rhey tortured the two of us... For years. I didn't know why... if it was for kicks or just... I don't know..."

"Oh." Matrona looked down as she trudged forward. "Hey, you know what?" Matrona looked to Nick.

"Hm?"

"We've got plenty of time for our own stories. Stories to rival Mom's. When this is done, we can explore the universe, and—"

"Hey, Matrona I don't mean to disappoint but... I know you're excited to be back, and believe me I'm excited you're back but... I feel like when this is all done, we should head back to Tereglion. I've had my fair share of Sentinel related fun."

"I died at the height of it..."

"Exactly." Nick looked into Matrona's eyes. "I can't be a bystander to that again."

Matrona looked away, thinking to herself.

The two of them continued to trudge up the snowy path to the mountain's peak.

"Wow this is great," Eve whispered to herself.

"What is?" Starlocke asked. He held a rope in his mouth, using it to pull a plank of wood full of logs behind him.

"Having a clear mind again." Eve looked around at the snow and the distant horizon of plains and forest. "Also seeing Matrona and Nick reunite is just…"

"Andrew?" Starlocke asked.

"Yeah." Eve nodded.

"I'm sorry, I didn't know." Starlocke looked down. "I read your mind." He continued staring off as he walked forward. Eve swayed atop his back, calmy side to side.

"It's okay, it was a long time ago." Eve closed her eyes.

"Time doesn't make it okay." Starlocke shook his head.

"Well, what am I supposed to do, not move on?"

## CHAPTER 29

"I didn't say that," Starlocke disagreed. "I mean that time should not take away from the importance of his loss. You got revenge. You killed Kranthar. But that should not take away from it either."

"You're right, I still gotta get through Suriv and Ultimae."

"No." Starlocke chuckled. "I mean, yes. You do, but revenge is not the answer either."

"What is?"

"Not forgetting."

"You just want me to be sad all the time?" Eve asked.

"No, I want you to be able to remember when things were happy. Do not think of the death of the person think only of the person. When they die, they are not gone. How I understand it, when death was implemented into this universe it was meant to keep it stable and allow it to flourish.

"Death is natural. By no means am I saying that the means by which he left the living plane was not perverse, or avoidable or an evil act. I am only saying that maybe his life will have provided something to this universe that will allow it to flourish."

"Like what?" Eve asked.

"Why do you want to save the Multiverse? Besides the obvious? Why must you, personally, do the most to stop Ultimae, instead of letting us do the work for you?"

Eve thought for a moment. "For Andrew?" Eve said, almost questioning herself. "And Mom."

"Therein lies their contribution. They are not gone. They are helping just as much as the Sentinel's Army in the saving of the universe."

"But did they have to die?" Eve asked.

"Nothing happens for a reason. Not unless you apply one after the fact. Did they have to die? No. But because they did... Ultimae will be stopped."

Eve nodded. "Thank you, Starlocke."

"Anything, for a friend."

Eve patted Starlocke's fluffy neck.

"Wood. Wood. Wood wood wood. Gotta get some wood so I can... uh... wood up... the wood."

"Ganto, what are you doing?" Vita asked, slightly annoyed by Ganto's constant need to be saying something.

"Just, uhhh, getting some wood. Wood for the cabin."

## ❖ CHAPTER 29 ❖

"Yes, I know, I am too. You don't need to keep saying it, I understand." Vita chuckled as she blasted a tree with a thin wave of bright white phlasma, swiftly knocking it down. She opened a wormhole, allowing the tree to fall through.

"Wormholes make you lazy. Do you ever use it to steal food from someone when they aren't looking? That'd be funny."

The wormhole closed as Ganto spoke.

"Ganto." Vita turned her head slowly. "Please enlighten me. Why do you talk so much?"

Ganto looked around, then walked up close to Vita. Vita snaked her neck back, staring at Ganto with one of her eyes pointed at him, curious.

"Promise not to tell anyone else?" Ganto whispered.

Vita hesitated. "Sure?"

"I'm scared," Ganto admitted. "If I can preoccupy my mind with something it distracts me."

"Scared of what?" Vita asked.

"That's the stupidest question I've ever heard. Coming from you, that's a surprise."

"What?" Vita seemed offended.

"What do you think I'm scared of, huh? Fricken heights or something? I'm afraid of Ultimae, and the whole universe ending, like any sane person would be."

"But why are you afraid?" Vita asked.

"And to think, your questions couldn't get any stupider, and yet—"

"Ganto." Vita leaned forward, looking over Ganto. Ganto turned slightly. "Not all Ilsians are emotionless. Just Ilsians raised around Ilsians. But you weren't raised around Ilsians. Why are you afraid?"

Ganto sighed. "I don't want to lose any more of my friends."

Vita closed her eyes and nodded knowingly.

"Vistor was basically my dad or something. I had already lost friends before. If I let anything happen to Vogar or Terri I don't know what I'd do with myself, they're like family to me. And Eve and Starlocke, *man*. But if the universe ends and all of them go with it…"

"You'd go with it too," Vita reminded Ganto.

"I don't care about that, what kind of idiot would?"

Vita cocked her head sideways.

"Let's slice more trees up. Gotta get more wood. Wood wood wood."

## ❖ CHAPTER 29 ❖

Vogar and Terri were the first to make it back up the mountain with their load of wood. They had been talking about snow the whole way up. Vogar liked it, Terri didn't. It was a very heated argument. Neither had been convinced of the other's opinion.

Vogar had been shapeshifted as a mammoth the whole time, so he could carry as many logs as he could in his tusks. When they reached the top, he returned to his normal form and let the logs drop to the platform.

The snow stopped the logs from rolling away as they plopped into the fluffy white covering over the platform.

Vogar gestured to the snow as if to say, "*See!*" Terri had carried some logs up in his beast form, and as he regressed into his sluggish body, he too dropped his logs into the pile.

He frowned at Vogar. Maybe he had a point.

"Thanks guys." Agro nodded.

Another wormhole opened above the log pile, and a couple more whole trees dropped through, this time Ganto and Vita came with it.

Ganto landed with a thud into the logs while Vita glided gracefully down to the floor.

Matrona and Nick appeared onto the platform from one side of the mountain at the same time that Eve and Starlocke appeared from the other. They too dropped off their logs.

The Army stared at the massive pile of wood, then glanced at the rather sizeable stone foundation that Agro and Foxtrot had set in place.

"Welp." Ganto held his hands to his hips. "It's getting pretty cold, let's burn it. Big ol' bonfire, this was fun we could do it again."

The Army all gave him a similar look.

"Joking, joking." Ganto looked around. "Though it is getting dark."

"We need to be wary of night," Starlocke warned. "I hear that a dinosaur known as Yutyrannus hunts in the mountains of Doxland."

"Ha *ha*," Ganto mocked.

Starlocke gave him a rather serious look.

"Okay, so plan of action, anyone?" Ganto shook himself.

Eve concentrated hard as she formed a rather large square of soft, cloth-like phlasma in front of her.

"We'll sleep in shifts. Phlasma heated mattress."

### ❖ CHAPTER 29 ❖

"Oo." Matrona smiled as she hopped onto the mattress. "Very comfortable."

"Thank you." Eve smiled. She looked back to the rest of the Army. "Those of us awake will build the cabin."

"Alright, good plan." Agro nodded.

As most of the Army went to sleep on the phlasmatic mattress, some stayed up, standing in a circle around the supplies.

Eve, Ganto, Starlocke, and Vita all stood around, looking at each other.

"You guys aren't sleeping at all tonight, are you?" Eve asked.

"Nope." Ganto shook his head.

"Don't need it," Starlocke said.

"Need to be awake, in case Morty changes his mind."

"Alright." Eve looked at all the supplies at their disposal. "Let's get to work."

Morning quickly arose upon the final placement of the last stone needed to complete the fireplace indoors.

The orange-yellow glow of sunlight shone on the ramshackle construction of Camp Vistor.

The door was borrowed, Starlocke said, from the Sentinel's shack in London.

He had time traveled to retrieve it.

Many decorations inside were borrowed as well, whether from Vistor's palace, the Pantheon, Eve's house, Tomas's house in Monterey, or other familiar places.

Sunlight crept over the sleeping Army, as they slowly awoke.

❖ Chapter 30 ❖

# Life

Camp Vistor wasn't anything compared to other bases the Sentinel's Army or affiliates have had. It was merely a log cabin, big enough to snugly fit the entire Army, and keep them safe from the cold snowy winds of the mountain peak.

In the week that followed the construction of the camp, Eve would check in with Celestae, as he searched for Ultimae. Not a sign of Ultimae showed itself in that surveillance cloud, day after day. Eve had even sent the box out to look for Ultimae. It didn't know where to look for certain, only where to look based on patterns. They figured it may be their quickest way of locating the elusive being. The box still had yet to return from its search.

Ganto sat comfortably leaning against a pile of firewood in front of the peacefully crackling fireplace. He held a playing card in each of his six-pointed hands, combing over them carefully.

He wore a self-made pink knitted sweater with renderings of Terri and Vogar knitted on the front enclosed in a heart with the word 'friends' underneath. Vogar sat with him playing cards with Foxtrot and Agro. Nick was heating up some tea in the kitchen nearby for all of them, and Matrona sat at a table near him, talking with him.

Terri was also in the kitchen, staring intently at the oven with his bulbous blue eyes. He tapped his stubby arms on his belly and waited with a content smile.

Vita was growing anxious atop her perch by the stairs, and though everyone else was perfectly comfortable playing card games in front of the fireplace, she couldn't relax.

"Come on!" Ganto slammed down his cards in his bitter loss to Agro, and not his first one either. Ganto leaned back on the pile of firewood and looked over at Vita, who was nervously picking at her feathers. "What's up with you?" he asked.

"Haven't been out of the Extraverse for this long in a while, huh?" Agro teased. "Come on, relax."

Vita snapped her head up quickly. She shuffled her wings disgruntledly. "I am perfectly fine here."

## ❖ CHAPTER 30 ❖

Vogar cracked a joke to the Army along the lines of, 'You'd think an Emissary of life would be living life more.'

They all laughed. Vita was not amused. She shook her head, "No that's not it. I just think we should be out looking for Ultimae."

"And what?" Ganto laughed. "Fight him on his grounds, with his rules, and where he's comfortable? No, let him come to us when he needs to, we'll be ready, we're here," Ganto assured her.

"How can all of you be so relaxed about a situation like this? Your king died," Vita reminded them.

"Suppressed emotion." Ganto answered quickly. Vogar glanced at him. "At least for them, I'm just emotionless, so…"

"Right," Foxtrot mumbled sarcastically.

"Hey!" Ganto sat up straighter.

"*Ritiini*," Terri called attention to himself as he exited the kitchen holding a couple trays. He smiled excitedly and said, "Cookies!"

"Oo!" Ganto stood up and ran to Terri. He grabbed a cookie. "Thanks, pal." He patted Terri.

"What kind?" Foxtrot stood up to get some.

"Thank you!" Matrona said as she grabbed one.

"Eh…" Terri thought. "Cookie…"

Nick laughed, "Good enough for me," he said as he bit into one.

The smell filled the cozy cabin with a comforting warmth of home. Terri smiled. He liked making everyone happy.

"Terri, I don't get you," Agro laughed. "How were you ever a space pirate bounty hunter?"

Ganto waddled up to Vita with a handful of cookies. He held one out for her.

Vita pecked at the cookie.

"Eh," Terri thought. "Ganto... *Terno. Ets* Vistor *gifni imi Sornos, ui...*"

"Wow, didn't really take you for a money guy," Agro said.

"Lorinian." Terri smiled and gestured to himself with his stubby arms.

Agro chuckled.

The door to the log cabin opened to howling winds, sucking out the smell and warmth of the cookies. The door quickly closed as Eve and Starlocke entered together. She lowered her scarf and rubbed her hands together.

"Any news?" Foxtrot asked.

"No. As usual," Eve answered.

## ❖ CHAPTER 30 ❖

Terri slugged up to her and gave her a cookie.

"Aw, thanks," she said. She patted Terri on the head, then plopped herself down on the ramshackle couch.

"Hey Eve, before you sit," Ganto called out to her as he put his cards back into a deck.

Eve groaned. She sat up and took a bite of her cookie.

"Can I talk to you for a second?" Ganto stood and wiped wood shavings off the back of his knitted sweater.

"Sure." Eve followed Ganto as he led her to one of the cabin's rooms, which belonged to him, Terri, and Vogar. "What is it?" Eve asked as they passed Nick and Matrona.

Ganto reached out and stole a cup of tea that Nick was preparing.

"Hey!" Nick whined.

Ganto ignored him and turned his attention to Eve, "Are you still cursed?" He coughed before sipping the tea and biting his cookie.

"What?" Eve didn't understand what he meant.

"Cursed? Kranthar's Curse? How much more time do we have?" Ganto nervously ate another cookie. He made it to the room and closed the door behind him when Eve came in.

"Oh!" Eve realized. "No, I'm fine, why?"

Ganto turned one of his palms up. What used to be bright red chitin on his forearm had been reduced to decaying and chipped brown. "It hurts, Eve. I don't think I have much longer."

Eve flinched. For a moment she felt the pain in her own arm, stinging her. She shook her hand. "Oh god, I'm so sorry." Eve combed through thoughts in her mind, considering her options. She knew that there was a way to circumvent the curse, but she wasn't sure it would necessarily work on an Ilsian like Ganto. She decided against letting him know, to avoid giving him false hope. "What do you want me to do?" she asked.

Ganto thought about it. He sipped his tea before he spoke again, "I know we're supposed to be guarding this Gateway and all, but I feel like we should take a break, you know? Live life, have fun. If not just for one last time." Ganto proposed the idea. He could see the hesitation in Eve's face, "Some of us would stay behind to guard still, of course. It's just a thought."

"No, you're right." Eve smiled. "That would be nice."

"Cool." Ganto smiled. He shoved his last cookie into his mouth then kicked the door out and ran through the hallway with his arms swinging behind him. He stopped and

## ❖ CHAPTER 30 ❖

skidded on the carpet in the living room, ruining the cards Starlocke had just started setting up. Starlocke growled at him. "Everyone pack up! We're getting on the Freysent!"

"Why?" Agro cleaned up his cards.

"We're going to a bar!" Ganto smashed his teacup on the ground.

"Are you kidding me?" Nick put his hands on his hips.

Vogar complained that it was barely noon.

"It's gotta be party time somewhere on Janistar," Ganto argued.

Eve walked out and stood by Ganto, her arms crossed, waiting.

"Eve, are you hearing this?" Foxtrot asked.

"Yeah. Come on, get up, let's go."

The Army sat in silence staring at Eve.

"What?" Nick laughed.

"No, I'm serious, come on."

"But the Gateway," Vita argued. "Someone has to stay back and protect it."

"We'll stay back," Nick volunteered, gesturing to himself and Matrona. "We'll let you know if anything goes wrong and I'm sure the box will go get you and teleport you back like you were never gone."

"And I'll stay as well." Vita craned her neck.

Terri shook his head and smiled. "*Jon jon jon.*" He swayed back and forth in a dance like way. He reminded Vita about what Vogar said regarding the Life Master living life.

"Yeah, Vita, come with us," Ganto agreed.

"*Rer!*" Vogar clasped his hands together happily.

"Come on," Foxtrot teased, "It could be fun."

"Weren't you just against it?" Vita flapped her wings.

"Ah, doesn't take much to change my mind." Foxtrot smiled.

"Come on Vita." Eve held out her hand. "Before it's too late."

In the silence that followed, the Army waited for Vita's decision. She eventually flew from her perch and landed on Eve's arm. She shifted to her shoulder and sat, waiting. "What are we waiting for?"

"Ay!" the Army exclaimed simultaneously. Eve led the way out of the Cabin. Nick and Matrona stayed back.

Nick waved with a small towel he had resting on his shoulder, "Stay safe!"

"Have fun!" Matrona waved.

The Army trudged through the snow on the phlasma platform atop the mountain. They passed the Gateway and

## CHAPTER 30

approached the parked ship. Ganto pushed his way to the front of the group so that he could get to the pilot seat as soon as possible. Terri slugged in, keeping his cookies with him. Once everyone had entered, the door closed, and the ship took off. The Freysent sped its way into space, leaving Doxland and Amalga-5 behind.

Eve was sitting in the co-pilot seat with Ganto, infatuated with the view. No matter how many times she'd seen space in all her life, it always left her awestruck, even if it was the same old tired view. For Ganto it was probably as boring as a road trip from Albuquerque to Palm Springs was for Eve.

She stared across at the two halves of New Earth, which the ship was heading toward. Ganto planned on taking a shortcut through the split planet because Janistar was on the other side.

It baffled Eve to see Earth in this state. Though she knew that it happened far in the future from her native time, it still scared her. She knew from her time in the stone that it was Rhey who managed it.

She knew that Rhey was a human, a clone of the Sentinel, but still human. If he could so easily destroy her home planet, Eve imagined what horrors Ultimae could accomplish at full power.

She shook her head of these thoughts when they'd passed through Earth and Janistar snapped into view. Half of the planet appeared lifeless. That part of the surface had been scarred by the same space laser that destroyed New Earth. The scar cut deep, and anything in the vicinity had been destroyed and abandoned.

The other side of the planet however, that was party central. They zoomed into the night side of the planet, and into the heart of a booming city. Vogar commented on it looking like 'Ilsose on steroids', while Eve commented on it looking like 'super Vegas'.

Ganto hurriedly landed the Freysent in a spaceship parking lot, taking up two spaces with his oddly shaped vessel. They all poured out of the ship and into the parking lot, staring at the city.

"Where are we?" Eve asked.

"Darru Square, in the capital city. Party central of the Milky Way." Ganto danced softly to the music booming in the streets ahead.

"Man, this is my favorite step in saving the Multiverse from imminent doom," Agro commented.

## CHAPTER 30

"I agree with the sarcastic one," Vita complained.

"Come on, you'll have fun." Eve turned around.

"Oh, I know I will." Agro shoved his hands in his pockets. "I'll just ignore all the crushing guilt of *not* doing anything productive."

"Or drink it away, ayo!" Ganto started off for the city. The Army followed after.

Vita couldn't keep up with her steps, and if she flew, she'd fly ahead. She flew onto Starlocke's back. "Is this alright?" she asked.

"Of course." Starlocke continued walking forward.

Eve reminded the Army of something, "Remember, if it weren't for this, we'd still just be waiting at camp. The box is still out there looking, Nick and Matrona are guarding, and Celestae is also on the lookout. All we're doing is passing the time, same as always."

"Sounds like you're trying to justify this to yourself," Agro teased.

"Well, that and…" Eve hesitated.

Ganto looked back at her and nodded.

"Ganto's dying of a curse set on him by Kranthar. So, this is sort of a… last hurrah, I guess."

"Ganto!" Vogar and Terri exclaimed simultaneously in worry.

"It's fine." Ganto coughed.

"Clearly it isn't," Vita said worriedly. "A life lost isn't something to be relaxed over."

"I'm chillin'." Ganto laughed it off. "As long as I go out having fun."

Eve frowned, thinking. She glanced at Starlocke. They approached a small bar and entered. The place was mostly empty, besides the lone Ilsian bartender. There were enough seats for all of them in the dimly lit, red-hued bar. The short bartender's feet clicked against the tile ground as he efficiently took everyone's order.

Foxtrot and Eve sat across from each other at a raised two-seater table. The table had a built-in holographic chess game, which Foxtrot initiated.

Terri, Vogar, Agro, and Starlocke sat at a booth with Vita, watching as Ganto clambered to a small stage to sing his heart out.

As Foxtrot and Eve played chess, they talked.

"You've been seeming a bit down lately," Eve commented to Foxtrot as she moved a piece. "I don't know you well, just let me know if it's a normal thing."

### ❖ CHAPTER 30 ❖

"No, you're right to assume it." Foxtrot took over one of Eve's pieces. "Just, you know, ever since the Sentinel died..."

"You were close with her?" Eve asked.

"Not really."

"Vaxx?" Eve asked.

Foxtrot hesitated. His hesitation sort of confirmed Eve's suspicions, but they were quickly broken when he responded, "No actually... Rhey."

Eve looked up from the chess board as she moved a piece. "Rhey?"

"More of what Rhey used to be. Arlo."

"Right." Eve made a move. She'd been clued in about all of the mess with Rhey, and the Chosen Three.

"He and I were really close." Foxtrot pondered his next move, hovering the holographic chess piece over the board. "I tried to save him, at least keep him alive." He placed down his piece over one of Eve's, knocking it down.

"Sounds like you guys were pretty good friends." Eve made her next move quickly.

"I guess you could say that." Foxtrot stared blankly at the board. "I'd do anything to bring him back."

Eve looked up at Foxtrot with concern chiseled into her face. Foxtrot could feel the sting of her stare and looked up from the board.

"To bring Arlo back," he clarified. "Not that monster."

"Mhm." Eve waited for Foxtrot to make a move. When he did, Eve swooped in quickly, knocking down a pawn of his. "Checkmate," she declared.

"So it is." Foxtrot leaned back in his seat. Their drinks were brought to them. Foxtrot raised his glass. The rest of the Army sitting near them turned their attention to them. They all lifted their glasses as well, except Starlocke and Vita, who didn't have hands. "To Eve," Foxtrot declared. "Our Sentinel."

"To Eve!" The rest of the Army chanted, clinking their drinks together.

"Oh! Oh! Do the- uh- do the one!" Ganto cheered on Vogar as he stood before the whole Army. They'd been at the bar for quite some time, and most of them had their fair share of drinks.

Vogar was doing impersonations for them. He shapeshifted into a woman wearing a stark black suit, her hair done up in a bun. "Heylo..." Vogar spoke with a thick Garish accent, "Am magic gorl, do what say so Vistor can hayfe throne- listen to me! I hayfe card!" Vogar spoke with poor English, and he seemed to be impersonating someone he and his friends knew, because the impersonation got a laugh out of Ganto and Terri.

"I don't get it." Eve laughed, sitting next to Starlocke.

"Ok, ok," Ganto was laughing uncontrollably, holding his stomach, "Do someone she'd get!" He wheezed, trying to catch his breath.

Vogar shrugged and admitted in his language to Ganto that he had nothing.

"Alright enough of the charades." Starlocke jumped down from the booth and walked around. "You are all very intoxicated, I say it's about time we head back to the Gateway."

Vogar shapeshifted into Starlocke. "I say it is Gatehway tyme. Look me, am Starlook."

"HA!" Ganto reeled over on his seat and fell to the floor.

"It's not that funny, he just repeated what he said." Vita couldn't understand why Ganto was laughing so hard.

"Come on!" Eve teased, poking at Vita. "It's only funny if you're trying to have fun."

"That makes... no sense," Vita denied Eve's broken logic.

"Stop that." Starlocke paced around Vogar.

"Styop thaht." Vogar barked back. The two splitting images of Starlocke paced around each other, staring each other down in a circle.

"I'm serious." Starlocke lowered his head.

"Am seeryoos." Vogar snapped his mouth and smiled. He panted like a dog and wagged his tail. He barked at Starlocke.

"I'm not a dog." Starlocke drooped his ears.

Vogar shapeshifted into a Labrador and ran around the bar, barking and howling.

Eve smiled; she was enjoying herself.

"Hey, cut it out!" the bartender yelled from behind the counter. "Damn Gars," he muttered to himself.

"Alright, alright." Eve laughed. She waved her hands signaling for everyone to calm down. "That's enough."

"You guys really know how to make a dying Ilsian's night." Ganto smiled as he crawled his way back up to his seat. "Thank you all."

### ❖ CHAPTER 30 ❖

"No problem, bud." Agro gave Ganto a smile. "Man, you guys are like a family to me, you know that?"

Terri teased in his language, 'Well that's coming out of nowhere.'

"No, I'm serious, I'm serious." Agro giggled. "I love you guys. Thank you."

Eve smiled. She remembered something she had thought earlier. "Hey," she hiccupped, "Starlocke, can I talk with you for a second?"

"Sure." Starlocke bowed his head.

Eve led Starlocke outside and away from laughter. They stood out on the sidewalk. "So, phazing," Eve began.

"Yes." Starlocke raised his ears with curiosity.

"Does it work on any living thing?" She asked.

"It comes to the Gars naturally, but all it takes is a specialized burst of phlasma at any living thing and then, boom," Starlocke explained.

This was all Eve needed to confirm her thoughts, and she barged back into the bar.

"Wait, why?" Starlocke asked. His forehead stone glowed as he sat on the sidewalk. "Eve!" he barked. He ran back into the bar.

"Ganto! Ganto! Ganto!" Eve approached him.

"Hey." Ganto turned around dizzily. "What's up."

Eve slapped her palm onto Ganto's forehead.

"Oh, okay." He stumbled back. The Army stared in confusion.

Eve's hand burst into flames and almost immediately Ganto was reduced to nothing more than a rêve stone that dropped to the ground. She swooped her hands down to pick up the stone.

"Woah, what the hell!?" Agro screamed.

"What!?" Foxtrot stumbled out of his seat.

"Eve!" Starlocke scolded her from the door.

Vita stared at the stone wide-eyed and confused.

Vogar shifted back into his normal Garish form and asked what Eve had done.

"See for yourself!" Eve tossed the stone at Vogar excitedly.

Vogar caught it and stared at it. "Ganto?" he asked.

"Yeah, that's him." Eve nodded, she put her hands on her hips and held her chin up high. "I'm curing his disease."

"He's gonna be fine?" Agro asked. Terri asked the same in Andromedan.

"Yup." Eve smiled.

## ❖ CHAPTER 30 ❖

"Ayy!" The Army cheered. They tossed his stone around in celebration. Starlocke and Vita looked at each other with confused looks.

Eventually the stone made its way around and back to Eve. She upturned her palm with the stone lying on it and faced it toward Starlocke. "Let's bring him back." Eve smiled.

Starlocke smirked, knowing now what Eve had done. He stepped back, using his hind legs as sort of an anchor. He lowered his head and chest, pushing his front legs out. He closed his eyes and a beam of electric phlasma blasted from his third eye and into the rêve stone. He concentrated and the rêve stone glowed, shifting and expanding.

In Eve's arms a body formed, almost three feet tall, just as before. The chitin exoskeleton was a deep purple this time, and his new, intricate antlers were an intensely deep black. As the new Ganto formed in Eve's arms, he regained consciousness. His eyes met Eve's. "Hey, how's it goin?" he asked.

"Ganto, I cured you." Eve smiled.

Ganto let out a short breath that seemed to be the beginning of a laugh. He looked at his new, sharp, hands. He rolled out of Eve's arms and landed on the floor. "Woo!" He let out excitedly. "Yeah-ha!" He ran around. "I'm alive!" He raised his hands up in the air. Without warning, his six spear tipped hands burst into bright phlasmatic flames. The Army stared at him in shock. Eve's smile faded; she hadn't thought about this.

With Ganto's minor shock passing, he screamed, "HOLY SHIT!" He ran around the bar screaming and hollering, shaking his hands to try to get the phlasma off. The flames grew stronger and fired out more rapidly.

"Ganto calm down!" Eve instructed.

"Concentrate!" Starlocke yelled.

"Just think!" Vita insisted.

"Idiot." Vogar laughed.

Ganto approached the Army's booth and stuck each of his hands in their drinks. He calmed down, and though the flames hadn't hurt him, he turned his head quickly to Eve, looking up at her. "What did you do me?" he asked.

"You phazed, you're cured. I'm sorry about the side effects, I completely forgot."

"Sorry?" Ganto laughed. "*Sorry?*" he repeated. There was a pause where the Army waited for what he'd say next. He took his hands out of the drinks and wiped them on himself. "This is the best thing that's ever happened to me!"

## ❖ CHAPTER 30 ❖

The Army cheered and hurrahed. The bartender stood on a table and yelled. "Get out of my bar!" The cheering stopped. "Crazy loons!"

"Yeah, it's about time we get back." Vita chuckled.

The Army mumbled to themselves and left the bar. Ganto went on a whole spiel about his new powers, going on and on about how much more helpful he could be. Starlocke reminded him that he'd need training, to which Ganto replied that he wasn't 'gonna take any advice from a stuck up Original', which offended Vita, Starlocke, and Vogar alike. They all entered the Freysent, which Foxtrot offered to fly home, seeing as Ganto was still a little tipsy. By the time they had returned to Camp Vistor night had fallen on Doxland.

"Did you guys have fun?" Nick asked as they returned, entering the cabin.

"Surprisingly, yes," Vita admitted.

"You won't believe it!" Ganto yelled.

"Woah, you look different." Nick stared at Ganto.

"Check it out!" Ganto raised his arms.

"Not in the house." Eve was quick to stop Ganto from burning the log cabin to the ground, by pushing his arms away.

The Army went off to sleep fairly quickly. Ganto jumped up and down on the bed downstairs in the room he shared with Vogar and Terri, which kept them up, but that was their problem.

Agro and Foxtrot slept in the living room, on the floor and couch respectively. Upstairs was fairly open, like one big room with a loft. Eve slept in a bed across the room from Nick on the floor next to a couch where Matrona slept.

Eve lied awake, staring at the rafters in the ceiling, her eyes barely staying open with the sound of wind outside lulling her to sleep.

She thought of the Army and smiled.

❖ Chapter 31 ❖
# The Fall of Nidus

A loud crash of glass exploded in the night. The snowstorm atop the mountain rushed into the log cabin. Eve quickly awoke and jumped from her bed. She ran to the end of the loft and sealed the broken window shut with phlasma.

"What's going on?" Nick groaned.

"AH!" Agro screamed from below. "Get away!" he yelled.

"Agro calm down!" Foxtrot tried to calm him.

Eve peered over the loft. "Vita?" she asked.

Eve had expected that Vita returned to the Extraverse and was surprised when she saw her perched on the loft next to her. The Deusaves that had crashed through the window and was now writhing and injured on the floor wasn't Vita.

Eve hopped over the railing of the loft and landed on the ground with a thud, using phlasma to soften her fall. Vita flew down and landed next to her. Nick and Matrona peered over the loft's railing.

A regal Deusaves that resembled a hawk sat in front of them, injured and in pain. It's smoldering white feathers pulsated, and it cawed and groaned.

"Why are you here?" Eve asked.

The box flashed into view next to Eve, floating by her shoulder. "Celestae and I have located Ultimae," the box informed her.

"Where is he?" she asked.

"Nidus," the injured Deusaves groaned. "Save us." he pled. "Sentinel…" The Deusaves held out a wing before it died on the floor. The flames drained from the creature's plumage, and the light left its eyes.

Eve stood up and reached out for the box.

"You aren't going alone," Vita protested.

The rest of the Army had already made it out to the living room to see what the noise was about, and they stared at her, standing ready to go. "I know." Eve responded. "I'm not the Sentinel." She held out her hand for the rest of the Army. Foxtrot, Agro, Starlocke, and Vita took her hand. Terri, Vogar,

## ❖ CHAPTER 31 ❖

Ganto, Nick and Matrona were prepared to go when Eve stopped them. "Someone needs to stay back. This may be a distraction."

"I can help!" Ganto argued.

"You need training," Eve scolded him. "Stay here where it's safer." She flashed away with Foxtrot, Agro, Starlocke, and Vita.

They appeared in the blinding daylight of Nidus. The usual shining white of the quartz landscape was burning orange and red with the sunset and burned landscape. Fire roared over the cliffs of the wide canyon they stood in. Plateaus crumbled and caves collapsed in on themselves as the planet fell apart.

"No!" Vita yelled in protest. "No no no!" She flew into the air and down the canyon. Screeching Deusaves swooped around and fled in fear.

Wormholes blasted signaling their escape. Dark clouds of phlasma consumed Deusaves and killed them left and right. Eve stumbled back.

"Where is he?" Foxtrot asked.

"I don't know."

Starlocke lowered his head and concentrated. "Vita has found him."

"Let's go!" Eve flashed all of them away again, and they appeared at the mouth of a familiar cave.

"Morty…" Vita stepped forward.

Morty curled himself in a ball at the end of the cave, hiding his face.

"It's dangerous, let's leave," Vita called out.

"Starlocke…" Eve hesitated. "You said Vita found Ultimae…"

"She has." Starlocke nodded.

"Vita, careful." Eve held out her hand. "That's not him."

Morty craned his head around and showed his face. His eyes burned with a deep red. From the shadows Suriv appeared. His armor glowed to life.

"Morty!" Vita yelled.

"He makes a good host," Ultimae mocked. "An immortal one at that," he boasted. "You cannot stop me, not now."

Vita screeched in anger. She flapped her wings together and an instant pulse of light shot itself into Morty. Ultimae stumbled back, possessing the body that Vita had just imbued with mortality.

"What have you done?" Ultimae scowled.

## ❖ CHAPTER 31 ❖

"Careful, Vita," Eve warned.

With a quick and unexpected fit of rage, Vita launched herself at Ultimae. The two birds interlocked in combat.

"Alright." Eve cracked her knuckles.

Starlocke joined in the fight against Ultimae, while Eve, Agro, and Foxtrot focused on Suriv.

Suriv swiveled on his axel hips and spun around like a drill, shooting the laser from his aperture eye, breaking the rock in the cave, and compromising its structure.

Foxtrot and Agro fired at Suriv relentlessly, while Eve noticed that the cave was about to fall on itself. She threw the box to the ground. "Siege shield!" she instructed. The cave collapsed on top of the shield and the rocks disintegrated on impact.

Foxtrot, Agro, and Eve were saved from the collapse. The shield dropped and seemingly without any time passing, Vita, Suriv, and Ultimae possessing Morty, burst from the rubble.

One of Suriv's legs was damaged, and he struggled to move.

"Attack the legs!" Foxtrot instructed Agro. They began firing rapidly at Suriv's legs.

Vita pinned Ultimae down. Ultimae lifted a leg and crushed his talons around Vita's neck. Vita snapped her beak at him.

Starlocke headbutted the dueling birds off the cliff and they fell. Vita flew up with an injured wing.

Ultimae burst into a deep red mass of phlasmatic flames. The space distorting sword appeared in his talons, and he flew menacingly above the army. Suriv's legs failed him, and his robotic shell began to take off like a rocket in an effort to flee.

Eve's hands sparked with phlasma, and she whipped her arm around as the lightning formed a sort of lasso. She swung it around Suriv and pulled him down to the ground.

The box shot a laser made of the same stuff as the siege shield at Suriv's mouth plate. The robotic shell opened.

"Deal with him." Eve demanded of Foxtrot and Agro. She turned her attention to Ultimae. "Leave this planet alone!"

"Why?" Ultimae scoffed. "I do not care about this planet... About any planet. Why worry for these beings if all will perish in the end?"

"Because if I have anything to say about it, the Multiverse will continue without you in it."

## ❖ CHAPTER 31 ❖

"Confident." Ultimae scowled. "You would make a good Paradox Master."

Eve spat. Starlocke growled, and Vita landed near them, tending to her wing.

Suriv, the Ilsian within the suit of armor, jumped from the robotic suit and tried to crawl away with what limbs he had remaining.

Foxtrot and Agro shot at him but missed before he reached out for a device that was dislodged from the armor, and he teleported away.

Ultimae slammed his wings together and a massive, dark, shockwave hit the group and pushed them to the floor. Eve struggled to stand, but again Ultimae hit them with another shockwave.

Foxtrot held his wrist as it stung with pain. He thought he was bleeding when a liquid spilled from it, soaking into his suit.

Foxtrot winced in pain and a piercing ring rang in everyone's ears, distracting Ultimae.

Foxtrot shook his head and noticed the liquid spilling from his fingers was a deep purple. He stood up, and Ultimae stared at him with curiosity.

"You used him!" Foxtrot yelled.

"What are you doing?" Eve asked.

"Foxtrot, stand down," Agro whispered loudly.

"You used him!" Foxtrot yelled again. He held his arms up and in an instant Ultimae was suspended in a ball of liquid phlasma.

"Holy—!" Agro exclaimed, surprised and afraid.

"What the!?" Eve stepped away.

Foxtrot twisted his arms and the ball of liquid shifted and twirled Ultimae around in it.

Foxtrot slammed the liquid into the ground, taking Ultimae with it. The liquid splashed and exploded into flames on the quartz.

"Foxtrot!" Agro stammered, "How did you—"

"Canshla chose us for a reason!" Foxtrot yelled. He lifted his arms and the flames dropped and warped into liquid again.

As Ultimae tried to stand up he was swallowed by the liquid again. "Just took me awhile to figure it out!" Foxtrot yelled. He turned to Eve. "Come on!"

Eve lifted her hands and shocked the ball of liquid phlasma with sparks of electricity. The electric ball sparked as it flew through the air with Morty's body splashing in it.

## ❖ CHAPTER 31 ❖

Agro lifted his arms and tried to contribute, but nothing happened. "Come on!" he groaned. "Something!"

Without warning Ultimae burst from the bubble and slammed on the ground. He dropped the sword from his grasps, and without it he swept forward with a wing at Foxtrot. A burst wave of dark phlasma shot from him and knocked Foxtrot down.

Eve clapped her hands together and crystal spikes of phlasma shot from the ground, about to impale Ultimae when he extended his wings and crushed them.

Eve stomped her foot on the ground and a boulder of phlasma shot from the ground behind Ultimae and smashed him into the floor. His body skidded across the quartz to Starlocke.

Starlocke barked and chomped down with his strong jaws around Morty's neck. Ultimae struggled, and with a jab of his talons, and an explosion of phlasma, Starlocke was pushed off the cliff, his body flying like a ragdoll as he whined and whimpered.

"Starlocke!" Eve yelled.

Vita dove off the cliff and flew after him. Not a moment too late, she created a wormhole and sent him back to Camp Vistor, tumbling into the snow. Vita flew over the cliff and skidded across the quartz in front of Ultimae. "Get out of him!" she yelled. "Leave him be!"

Ultimae ruffled his feathers. "And why should I?"

"Because he's my friend," Vita grumbled.

Foxtrot clenched his fist, and a ringing burst of sound blasted in Ultimae's head.

Ultimae collapsed to the floor. His eyes darted to Foxtrot, and intrigue soon colored his face. He closed his eyes.

A whispering voice trailed through Foxtrot's mind. He stumbled like he'd been slapped, and his eyes widened with fear.

Ultimae abruptly opened his eyes again and jumped up, flying into the sky in a spiral. As he flew down, a trail of dark clouds followed him. He landed with a thud, and the darkness clouded Eve's vision. She looked around for him.

The squawking of a Deusaves screeched through the air as bright white light zoomed past Eve in the darkness. More flashes of light flew by, it seemed the rest of the Deusaves were joining the fight.

Eve's eyes glowed and she spread her arms to separate the clouds. Agro was huddled over Foxtrot's barely conscious body, something had happened.

## ❖ CHAPTER 31 ❖

"Keep them safe." Eve told the box. It quickly flashed the two of them away and returned to Eve's side. Eve walked through the gaseous clouds as they parted before her. Deusaves swooped in and out of the cloud, pushing it away and revealing the struggling Ultimae behind flashes of red lightning.

Ultimae got a hold of his sword again and he swept it forward, a blast of energy shot from it and in its line of sight several Deusaves were eviscerated in seconds. Eve held out her hand, and a spike of phlasma extended from her wrist. Ultimae caught sight of her and turned his attention away from the attacking Deusaves. He swept down with the sword, and Eve held up her arm. The blade slammed against the phlasma blade, shaking Eve to her core.

She could feel the reverberations in her bones but she kept a straight face and confident posture. She had been hardened by the stinging pain. She was used to it now. She pushed the blade away and jabbed at Ultimae with her other arm, a blade already extended. Ultimae laughed it off and kicked Eve with his taloned foot, launching her like a flicked bug off of the cliff. Time slowed in Eve's perception as she watched the cliff drift from her line of sight, as she fell over the edge. She could see the burning canyon, and the ember filled sky as the flames consumed the planet.

She was about to close her eyes, for all was lost, when Vita swooped over the edge of the cliff to fly after her. Eve's hopes returned only for a moment before Ultimae followed closely behind. The cliff itself crumbled and fell with Eve.

A sinkhole opened in the ground below Eve, and the flames that blanketed the horizon fell down the sinkhole like a fluid, and Eve fell through. She knew she'd have to do something now, and so she closed her eyes and concentrated.

Sparks shone on her shoulder blades as her electric blue phlasmatic wings sprouted and spread with grace. Vita continued to fly after her, and Ultimae was catching up. Eve launched herself with her wings and flew up, Vita recognized the change in course and flew up as well, but Ultimae had been caught off guard. Time returned to its normal pace as Eve and Vita barreled out of the mouth of the sinkhole. Eve turned around and clasped her hands together. Like sliding doors, walls of phlasma pounded together and sealed the sinkhole shut, but it wasn't enough to stop Ultimae from bursting through the thick barricade.

As he sped toward Eve, she had to decide. She held out her hand and extended her wrist blade again. Ultimae flew right into it, impaling his chest.

## ❖ CHAPTER 31 ❖

Eve flew down and down, pushing Ultimae into the sinkhole he had created until she slammed the body of the Deusaves he had possessed into the quartz ground.

Vita flew in quickly to survey the situation. She landed on Eve's shoulders, and watched. "No." She shook her head. "Ultimae's gone," she deduced.

Morty gasped for breath.

"Morty was right... it wouldn't work... The mortality didn't go to Ultimae, just Morty... Ultimae left his body," Vita determined. "The glow of his eyes... gone."

"Death..." Eve realized what she'd done. "No, no stay with me."

"I'm sorry," He coughed, "To disappoint," His eyes met Vita's. "I could've stopped... him..."

"Don't talk," Vita whispered. "It'll be fine," she promised.

Eve didn't know what to do. If she removed the blade, she feared that Morty may bleed out. She was struck with shock.

"Is this what mortality feels like?" Morty asked. He directed his question to Eve. "Pain?" he asked.

Eve didn't know how else to react but nod. She cried out of sheer guilt. "I'm so sorry..."

"I know you are." Morty closed his eyes, and his head fell limp.

"Morty." Vita stared at him. "Morty…"

"He's gone." Eve retracted the crystal blade. "Vita…"

Before Vita could react, she flew from the sinkhole, and away from the planet.

Eve teleported to the mouth of the hole, surrounded by the flames of the dying planet. Whatever Deusaves remained flew to her side, and stared into the sinkhole. Eve sealed the sinkhole shut with phlasma, and fell to her knees.

"What's going to happen?" a small, pigeon-like Deusaves asked Eve. "Are we safe?"

"No." Eve cried softly. "No, you're not."

"Are we at war?" a grand and old looking eagle-like Deusaves asked.

"Yes," Eve answered.

"Can we win?" another Deusaves asked.

Eve didn't answer. She didn't know, and she wasn't confident in guessing.

When she felt the Deusaves needed an answer, and needed hope, she finally answered, "That's up to you." She flashed away.

❖ Chapter 32 ❖
# Possession

A forest of dark looming vines and a faint ambience of red glowing across the horizon surrounded the injured and suitless Ilsian, Suriv. He sat in the black dirt against a rock in the midst of the purple night on one of Ultimae's hideout planets. "You'll get me the Calcurus for a new suit?" Suriv asked.

"Do not press me for it." Ultimae paced back and forth in front of Suriv. "You are lucky to be alive. In any other circumstance I would have removed you from your pitiful existence."

"Then why do you keep me, huh?" Suriv smiled. He examined his spear-tipped hand.

"You know full well." Ultimae scowled.

"Say it." Suriv clicked his mandibles. "You need me," he teased.

"Only to fulfill a quota, nothing else," Ultimae reasoned.

"Right, right." Suriv laughed. "Now what'd you say about a potential new Emissary you had your eyes on? He's not a replacement for me, is he?" Suriv adjusted his position with one his arms.

"No, but he adds a lot more reason to resurrect this monstrosity." Ultimae held out a weak rêve stone in his hand.

"And as for the other stone?" Suriv asked with a sly smile.

"He has been resurrected." Ultimae continued his pacing.

"Wow. Really?" Suriv seemed genuinely surprised. "Where is he?"

"Collecting himself." Ultimae stopped pacing and looked up at the night sky, something caught his eye. "The beast has been dead awhile, and he thought he was gone for good, and the fact that he is not all the way back does not help. He is just a shadow of his former self."

"But he'll work right?" Suriv asked. "As an Emissary? I mean we don't need him to be around forever, we just need him as a head count, right?"

❖ CHAPTER 32 ❖

"Correct." Ultimae nodded. The galactic shape in his head pulsated. As he stared confusedly at a quickly approaching object in the space above him.

"Man, if the Sentinel were around to see him. I would love to see the horror on her face." Suriv chuckled as he etched something into the dirt with his hand. "The return of—"

Ultimae held out a hand to silence Suriv. He approached the object trailing across the sky. As it came closer it was apparent that it was a spaceship. It began to land like a helicopter, wafting up dust and pushing away the decaying plants. It landed with a soft thud.

A man stumbled from the ship, breathing with quick, short, and sporadic breaths. "You told me you could bring him back?"

"What're we supposed to do?" Nick asked in a somber tone. The Army sat by the fireplace the next morning trying to comprehend what just happened.

"Where's Foxtrot?" Eve asked, noticing a missing member.

"He wasn't here this morning," Agro explained. "Said he'd gone off somewhere, last I heard."

"That doesn't matter." Nick took a sip of tea. "What are we supposed to do? That's what matters."

"Well I don't know if you know, but it turns out that Foxtrot has phlasma powers!" Agro chuckled. "Seems pretty important to me."

Ganto raised his hand. "I do too!"

"*Nosai-oop.*" Vogar slapped Ganto's hand out of the air.

"What matters is not who among us can attack, but who of our people can aid us," Starlocke suggested. "I've been in close contact with Queen Karina, and I can assure all of you that the armies of Amalga-5 are more than willing to help, as are Janistar's. I'm sure the attack on Nidus last night would be more than enough of an incentive to get the Deusaves fighting."

"Tell 'em Strix can't come to help," Ganto said.

"Thought you weren't superstitious?" Starlocke teased.

Ganto chuckled, "I got phlasma coursing through my veins now!" He flexed. "It's kinda like I'm an Original now, I kinda get your dumb religion a bit more."

Starlocke slapped Ganto with his tail. "Show some respect."

"Sure thing, doggy." Ganto chuckled.

## CHAPTER 32

Starlocke growled.

"What can all those regular people do against Ultimae?" Agro questioned. "Guns are useless on him. That's all humans got going for them, anyway."

Starlocke mentioned, "Karina's army employs the use of phlasma-gifted battle mounts. They may aid as a distraction to Ultimae, at the very least."

"Forget the humans," Vita interrupted. She perched herself on a lamp in the far corner, keeping to herself, mostly. "Sorry, Eve and Matrona, but you're the exceptions. I mean the rest. The Originals, we have an intrinsic ability to help us fight back."

"Even then, what good has it done us? Ultimae's hurt us more than we've hurt him," Agro said.

"That's not true." Eve leaned forward in her seat. "He's stopped ending the universe. We're distracting him, he's focused all his efforts on us."

The Army leaned forward in anticipation.

"He doesn't want to show weakness but he's clearly weak, right now at least. If we could exploit that weakness…"

"How?" Vita asked. "He's a god among mortals. What can we do to stop him?"

"Persist. Exist. Fight the good fight. If we can't kill Ultimae, we can be sure to distract him forever. As long as there's an army for him to fight, there's a Multiverse for him to fight them in. He can't end it while we're around."

The Army nodded in silent agreement.

Vita looked down and away. "Sorry to be the pessimist," she spoke up. "But we can't outlive him."

"You're immortal, surely you can," Nick argued.

"So was Morty." Vita looked up. "You say as long as there's an Army, but with every attack Ultimae brings with him death and destruction. The Sentinel, Vaxx, Vistor, Morty… We can't outlive that."

Starlocke drooped his ears in sadness, and lowered his head into his forelegs as he lay on the ground. The Army was without hope again.

"I'm sorry. I'm just trying to be realistic." Vita looked away and huddled herself back in her perch.

Starlocke lifted his head abruptly, his third eye glowing.

The Army knew that wasn't a good sign. "What is it?" Nick asked.

"He's here." Starlocke stood up.

"Ultimae?" Matrona asked fearfully.

## ❖ CHAPTER 32 ❖

"Who else?" Starlocke ran for the door. The Army quickly stood up, ready to fight.

Agro bounced on his toes, hyping himself up. "Alright, you're good. Just do what Foxtrot did, you weren't part of the three for nothing." He ran for the door.

When the Army made it outside, the horrors that awaited them were beyond what they could have imagined. In the sky above, tugging at the gravity of Amalga-5, was the massive Quodstella, Modius.

"Wait a second..." Ganto stared at the frowning face of the distraught Quodstella.

The planet's eyes were glowing a deep red, and in an instant, Eve understood.

"Shit..." She flared her hands.

"What is it?" Nick asked.

"Ultimae possessed Modius..." Eve flared her electric wings to life.

"He's going to destroy Amalga-5..." Nick gasped. "Oh god... We're doomed..."

"You aren't going to fight a planet, are you?" Agro asked Eve.

"I'm going to do my best." Eve launched herself into the sky.

Vita was about to fly after her, but Ganto stopped her. "Wait! Life!" He yelled. "I can help!"

Vita didn't hesitate. She lowered her body and stretched a wing. "Get on," she said, waiting for Ganto to mount up.

Ganto smiled as he jumped onto Vita's back. "Hya!" he yelled as he held onto her feathers. Vita launched herself into the atmosphere after Eve. "Woohoo!" Ganto hollered as they flew into space after Modius.

"Why would he possess a planet?" Vita asked.

"To do that!" Ganto pointed.

Eve watched as Ultimae, using the sheer scale of the body he had possessed, devoured the two halves of New Earth in one massive bite. Eve continued to fly after him regardless. The box struggled to keep up with her and provide her breathable air, so she slowed down. As she slowed, Ultimae opened his mouth, and a massive chunk of what used to be New Earth was sent flying at Eve. She held up her arms defensively. The box lifted its siege shield, allowing for Eve to cut right through the planetary chunk. She turned around, seeing the moon sized piece of Earth being hurdled toward Amalga-5. She turned around and flew after it, passing Vita and Ganto by. They adjusted course and followed after her.

## ❖ CHAPTER 32 ❖

"How are we supposed to stop it!?" Ganto yelled.

"I think I've got something!" Vita responded, "Hang tight." She held her wings to her side and shot forward like a torpedo, zooming past Eve and stopping on the other side of the flying chunk. The piece of Earth was flying right at them.

"What now!?" Ganto looked to Vita, nervously.

Vita spread her wings and closed her eyes. Her feathers dimmed of their light as the tips of her wings seemed to glow brighter. A rip in space sparked itself in front of her, stretching taller and taller, followed by sparks like metal grinding on metal. She flicked her wings outward and the rip spread wide open, tearing a wormhole into the sky so large it swallowed up the entire chunk of Earth. A wormhole opened in the far distance as the chunk of Earth slammed into Modius's face, causing him to flinch as the chunk exploded, shaking the Quodstella to its core.

"Nice!" Ganto cheered, "Now how do we stop him from eating Amalga-5?"

Eve flew past Vita, saying with confidence, "I've got a plan!" Eve turned to the box for help, she didn't quite know how to execute it. "Tell me there's a way I can teleport the whole planet."

"Planetary teleport station. Jungles of Krondico," the box suggested.

"Right!" Eve teleported away.

She appeared above the jungles of Krondico, and slammed into the muddy ground. She stood up and stared at the sky above. She could clearly see Modius, his possessed eyes locked onto Amalga-5. Eve darted her eyes across the sky for a moment and saw Janistar in the distance. A thought popped into her head but she quickly shook it. She ran to the teleport station in the forest. She opened the door and slammed the box into the slot built for it, but she hesitated.

A wormhole opened near her as Vita flew through with Ganto, landing softly in the dirt next to Eve.

"What's the plan?" Vita asked.

"I was gonna teleport Amalga-5 to the opposite side of the sun, keep the same orbit, just far far away from harm, but..." She glanced up at the sky at Janistar. "Janistar doesn't have a planetary teleportation station, does it?"

"No." Ganto shook his head.

"If I teleport Amalga-5 away, Ultimae will still want to do damage with Modius and he'll probably go after Janistar instead... but we can't lose the rift, or this planet... They're all going to die." Eve stared up at Janistar.

## ❖ CHAPTER 32 ❖

Starlocke zoomed into view, pushing up dust as he stopped near Eve. "What is happening here?" he asked. "How are we to stop Modius?"

"Which population is bigger?" Eve asked Starlocke. "Amalga-5 or Janistar?"

"Amalga-5, but not by much," Starlocke said.

Eve shook her head and pinched the bridge of her nose in frustration. "We can move Amalga-5, but we need to evacuate Janistar, there's no saving it."

"We can't just give up on it like that!" Ganto protested the idea. "There are ten billion people living up there! Ilsians, Lorinians, Humans, Andromedans, there's no way we can evacuate all of them!"

"Get them all into ships, fly them out, there's got to be something that can be done!" Eve paced around, holding her hands to back of her neck, sweating.

"Correct me if I'm wrong, isn't there only one way in or out of that planet?" Starlocke reminded all of them, "As of IS-72's colonization after Canada Prime was evacuated, was the planet not surrounded in an impenetrable shield with only a singular gate, for locking in the radiation fields and for protection during the war?"

"How do you know this?" Eve asked.

"Historian," Starlocke answered.

"It's true." Vita nodded.

Eve shook her head before looking up at Modius again. She only looked for a few seconds before she yelled in frustration, slamming the box and teleporting Amalga-5 to the other side of the sun. Eve screamed in frustration, kicking sticks and rocks, pushing up dead leaves. "There has to be something we can do!" she yelled.

"There is!" Ganto yelled "Shady business, my forte, there's a wormhole, permanent fixture, in the capital city. It leads directly from that city to king's square on Ilsose, where my palace is. We just gotta—"

"Syphon ten billion people through an alleyway," Vita finished the statement with a condescending look. "There's no way, especially factoring in the time it would take."

"I can help." Starlocke's ears perked up.

"How?" Eve asked.

Before Starlocke could answer, he zoomed off into space. He ran faster than he'd ever run before. It was funny to him, how quickly people perceived him to travel. Though he was going fast, time from his perspective had slowed. His trip to Janistar in reality had taken him less than a second, but in his perceived time it had been hours. Once he arrived, he bit

## ❖ CHAPTER 32 ❖

the bottom of a citizen's pant leg, and threw them over onto his back. He ran through the wormhole and dropped the person off on Ilsose. He ran back into Janistar, and did this several times over, taking people one by one through the wormhole. There was no way he would be able to carry a Lorinian, or even some humans, through the portal, but he tried his best to get as many people as he could.

As he ran at near the speed of light, and his phlasmatic lightning surrounded him, it gave him time in his relative slowness, to gauge the amount of time he had left before Ultimae, possessing Modius, would consume Janistar whole. He would look up and see ships halfway through their take off, all headed for the one exit on the whole planet.

He watched as Modius drew closer, and all was seeming hopeless, though he knew that even if he could save a handful, it was better than letting them all die.

For a moment he felt alone and helpless in his efforts. Though the lone Dragolupus was soon met with countless others, all doing the same, to aid Starlocke in his mission.

Hundreds of Dragolupus zipped through the streets of Darru Square, saving as many citizens as they could.

Back on Amalga-5, Eve, Vita, and Ganto waited for Starlocke's return. On the other side of the sun, Modius and

Janistar weren't in view. "I can't take this," Eve admitted. She reached out for the box, and flashed off to just outside Camp Vistor, on the platform. Vita and Ganto followed shortly after through a wormhole. They were met with the rest of the Army.

"What's happening?" Nick asked.

"I don't know, but it isn't good. Amalga-5 is safe, but there's no way we can save Janistar."

"Are you absolutely certain?" Agro asked.

Eve nodded with wet eyes, her hand covering her mouth. She walked off for the Freysent, parked nearby. "Ganto, come on."

"What are you doing?" he asked.

"We have to see it," Eve said as she entered the ship. Ganto ran after her and jumped into the pilot seat. The ship took off, and sped out into space. Eve plugged the box into a portion of the panel and the ship flashed away. Outside the cockpit now, they could see Modius and Janistar.

Ganto's claws wrapped around the controls of the panel fiercely. He leaned forward in his seat. They both watched as a few ships made their way out of the planet's singular exit.

Modius' mouth opened wide. The planet began to crack and separate, an orange glow from beneath the crust showed

### ❖ CHAPTER 32 ❖

itself as the planet was pulled by Modius's extreme gravity. A tear came to Ganto's eye.

Modius slammed his jaw down on half of the planet. His mouth was stopped from closing by the shield that surrounded the planet.

Eve clenched her fists.

Starlocke continued to rush people through the portal. Buildings collapsed, pipelines exploded and the ground shifted and cracked. The shield above him flashed with blue energy, sparking as it began to shatter into a million pieces as Modius bit down once more. The blue shards of energy that made of the shield fell slowly in Starlocke's perceived time.

Modius crushed through the shield, and sliced Janistar in half with a crushing bite.

"NO!" Eve screamed, holding out her arm helplessly as she cried over the control panel. "NO! NO!"

Ganto screamed as phlasma flared at his fingertips. He pushed forward on the ship's throttle as it blasted forward.

Modius opened his mouth again as the other half of the planet, now mostly large pieces littered with explosions, fell into his open mouth.

The broken shield spread radiation across Modius' face.

The ancient Quodstella inhaled the noxious gasses. The planet groaned.

Starlocke and his allies continued running, all of this was happening very slowly for him. He pushed through, saving as many people as he could, the chunk of land he stood on was growing smaller. A small infant Lorinian hung from his jaw loosely as he ran to the wormhole. A rock crushed the wormhole ahead of him, even in his relative slowness it happened quickly. He rushed ahead as he tossed the Lorinian into the wormhole, then the rock crushed the wormhole shut. The wormhole had disappeared, and he had saved as many as he possibly could, a mere one hundred and seventy-two Humans, Andromedans, and Ilsians combined, only managing to save a handful Lorinians that could fit through the portal. His job on the planet was done, it was getting out that would be the issue. He bolted through to Modius, jumping from rock to rock until he landed on the Quodstella's surface. He turned his head up and flew off into space.

Ganto stopped the ship as Starlocke approached. He opened an airlock and Starlocke bolted in, slowing down almost instantaneously, out of breath and sparking madly with electricity. The airlock closed with Starlocke fully in the ship.

## ❖ CHAPTER 32 ❖

The three of them watched as the rest of Janistar was swallowed by the massive Quodstella.

"Ultimae..." Starlocke said behind broken breath, panting as he laid down on the cold metal floor of the ship. "Just killed ten *billion* beings in a matter of minutes... He's a monster..."

"How many do you think escaped?" Ganto asked, with a hint of hope in his quavering voice.

"I saved a little over one hundred beings, as much as I could in the time that I had... and as far as the ships that escaped, I'd say a few hundred thousand more survived, maybe. Other Dragolupus came to help. I'm not sure how much they saved, but it couldn't have been many..."

Eve watched with fear as the ships blasted away from Modius as fast as possible. Modius' glowing red eyes soon angled themselves to face the Freysent directly.

"Oh shit..." Ganto wiped an arm across his face. "He's looking at us, isn't he?"

Eve stared into Modius's eyes deeply. In a brief moment, all of the red that signified Ultimae's presence, drained from his eyes. In fact, it seemed, that the life force of Modius himself drained from his eyes.

Starlocke's head shot up as he whimpered. "No..."

"What?" Eve stood up from her seat.

"The radiation field around Janistar..." Starlocke's ears lowered. He tucked his tail under himself and backed away in fear.

"What?" Ganto asked. "What is it?"

"It killed Modius..." Starlocke said.

"And what about Ultimae?" Eve asked.

"Where'd he go?" Ganto looked around.

The red that had drained from Modius' eyes filled the Freysent. Ganto and Eve looked around fearfully as their eyes came back to meet Starlocke.

Starlocke stumbled as he shook. He growled, baring his sharp teeth. His eyes were shut tightly as he fell to the floor and shook violently. He growled and flinched, frothing at the mouth like a ravenous dog.

"Starlocke!" Eve yelled, running to his aid.

Ganto held her back.

The stone in Starlocke's forehead shifted its hue to a deep red, and Starlocke's sporadic movements slowed to a halt.

Eve stopped.

Starlocke opened his once deep purple eyes. They glowed a dark ominous red.

## CHAPTER 32

"No." Ganto said, "Not this."

"Do you understand my capabilities?" Ultimae's voice boomed from Starlocke. "It would be idiotic of you to not fear me, to not surrender."

"LEAVE MY FRIEND ALONE!" Ganto yelled as he jabbed an arm forward, blasting phlasma at Starlocke's face in an attempt to draw Ultimae out.

Eve jumped forward and locked her arms around Starlocke's neck. "Come on!" she yelled. "Ganto, hold him down!"

Starlocke shocked Ganto with a blast of red lightning, flinging him into a wall of the Freysent. He snapped at Eve, flaring his sharp teeth, and drooling on her face.

"I don't want to hurt you!" Eve yelled, not fighting back.

A red energy flung from Starlocke and launched itself into Eve. Ultimae switched bodies.

Starlocke shook his head. "What?"

Eve punched forward with a flaming red fist, flinging Starlocke away with a whimper.

"Eve!?" Starlocke looked up at her.

"RAH!" Eve yelled as icy lightning shot from her eyes, ejecting Ultimae from her. Ultimae transferred to Starlocke again. Starlocke pounced at Eve and bit down on her arm.

"AGH!" Eve groaned.

Ganto looked between his two friends fighting. He didn't know what to do, how to stop them.

Starlocke pinned Eve down. Eve looked away, helpless. Starlocke's forehead stone began to glow an intense red, charging up and preparing for a super-charged laser to shoot into Eve's face.

Eve flinched when the box landed by her side and opened the lime green shield.

Starlocke's laser blasted and bounced off the shield. He shook his head as Ultimae transferred back to Eve.

Eve, possessed, grabbed the box and tossed it across the Freysent, where it landed by Ganto. Eve turned back around and extended a phlasmatic blade from her wrist, ready to stab Starlocke.

Ganto looked between them. He had to do something.

Ganto grabbed the box. He ran between his two battling friends, interrupting Eve's stab forward.

Ultimae began to transition between Eve to Starlocke, but Ganto jumped in the way. Ultimae possessed him instead,

❖ CHAPTER 32 ❖

just as he had teleported away with the box, appearing just outside the spaceship, floating in space.

The box came back and lodged itself into the control panel of the Freysent.

"Ganto!" Starlocke and Eve yelled at the same time.

Ganto, possessed by Ultimae, quickly turned his attention to the ship. He charged at it, ready to transfer possession, just as the ship teleported away and fell into its parking place near Camp Vistor.

Eve and Starlocke stumbled from the ship and stood before the Sentinel's Army.

"What's happening?" Matrona asked, holding her arms out wide. Her voice trembled.

"Where's Ganto?" Vita was quick to ask.

Ultimae had separated himself from Ganto, floating in space ahead of him in his celestial form. The sword appeared in his hands.

"I could kill you. Right now," Ultimae said.

Ganto held his neck. Stranded in space, the empty void started to get the better of him. Breathing was becoming increasingly difficult. He stuttered and said, "Eh, well. I sorta imagined it would go this way…"

"Alone," Ultimae said.

Ganto nodded.

Ultimae lifted his blade.

Ganto closed his eyes.

In a flash of light, a wormhole opened up before Ganto. Vita flung herself from the portal and hit Ultimae in the chest like a torpedo, catching him off guard. Vita swooped around and grabbed Ganto in her talons before she blasted another portal and flew through with Ganto in her clutches just as Ultimae swung his sword at them. The wormhole closed; Ultimae missed.

Vita crash landed into the snow outside of Camp Vistor.

When they gained their bearings, Ganto launched himself at Vita and hugged her.

"*Thank you,*" he said.

Vita patted around him with her wing.

Eve and Starlocke ran to Ganto's side, glad to see him back. But the events that had just occurred ate away at Eve's mind.

She looked up at the sky and said, "Janistar's gone."

## CHAPTER 32

"What do you mean gone?" Vita asked. "That's not-"

"The whole thing's been eaten by Modius. All the life on it too," Starlocke said.

"What are we supposed to do against that?" Agro yelled.

"Ultimae ditched Modius after the radiation from Janistar killed it," Ganto said, "He possessed Starlocke and Eve for a bit and made them fight, then left me to die, but then you saved my ass," Ganto pointed at Vita.

"You're saying we lost Ultimae?" Nick asked.

"Yeah." Eve nodded. "But I don't think he's done with his attack. His target was us, Amalga-5, not Janistar."

"How can we fight back?" Nick asked. "How much time do we have to plan a counterattack, he could be here any second."

Space ripped ahead of the Army atop that platform. Near the Gateway a dark wormhole opened and closed as a figure stepped through. The man pushed his fingers through his white hair, and he blinked his red eyes. "A willing host makes all this so much easier. Makes me so much more powerful." The wormhole closed.

"Foxtrot?" Agro stepped away.

The Army stared at Ultimae's new host in fear.

❖ POSSESSION ❖

"Willing?" Eve asked, stepping away with flared hands.

The space distorting sword appeared in Foxtrot's hands. "He would do anything to get his Arlo back." Ultimae grimaced. "He would even work for me."

"You can't bring Rhey back... You're lying to him!" Agro yelled.

"You underestimate the powers of a god." Ultimae dragged the sword against the platform as he approached them. He swung the sword, sparking it against the phlasma platform. "I..." he swung it again, slicing at a pillar of the Gateway. "Can do..." He pointed the sword at the rift. "*Anything.*"

The rips in space the sword created seemed to reach out like a ghastly hand at the shatter, opening it and spreading it wider. The Gateway started to collapse around it.

Eve leapt at Ultimae with a blade extended from her wrist. Ultimae blocked the jab with his blade.

"I don't want to kill you, Foxtrot," Eve spoke to Foxtrot, trying to break through the possession. "He's tricking you!"

"You don't know that." Foxtrot's conscience broke through for a moment.

### ❖ CHAPTER 32 ❖

"I don't want to hurt you, we don't want to hurt you... and you don't want to hurt us..." Eve pressed forward with her blade, it drew nearer to Foxtrot's chest.

"You hurt him." Foxtrot closed his eyes as he felt a sharp pain. He clenched his wrist, and the Army was pushed back by an invisible sound wave blasting at their ears.

"Look at him!" Ultimae laughed through Foxtrot. "He knows this Multiverse is ruined! He wants to start anew with the man he loved, and I will give that him that luxury!"

"He doesn't care about you!" Starlocke barked. "He wants to fill a quota! He needs you to use you! He will get rid of you the first chance he gets!"

"And yet I will still give him what he wants!" Ultimae chuckled. "That is more than any of you could possibly do for him." Ultimae pushed forward with the sword, blasting the space distorting energy at Eve. Eve dodged the blast and fired a bolt of electricity at Ultimae's ankles, causing him to fall. Eve jumped at him with her blade, attempting to stab him, but again she was blasted with a wave of high pitch sound. Ultimae stood victoriously over the Army too stunned to fight. "I have won!" he declared boastfully. He made his way to the rift.

Nothing could have prepared Ultimae for the flaming blue-green fist of Celestae punching through the rift and into his chest. Ultimae's celestial body was flung from Foxtrot. Before Foxtrot could get out a word, Ultimae clenched his fist and Foxtrot vanished. He leapt at Celestae, and they locked in combat. The two gods dueled in front of the Army.

Celestae held his hand around Ultimae's neck and slammed him against the ground. As Ultimae hit the ground he exploded into dark fiery red flames. The flames shot up into the air and vanished, and Ultimae had run away again. Celestae fell to his knees, and his galactic core jittered.

"What just happened!?" Nick yelled.

"Foxtrot... *lin- masi...*" Terri stuttered in confusion.

"Ultimae can't just... bring Rhey back to life... can he?" Nick asked with a shaky voice.

"I don't think so..." Eve paced around.

"He can." Celestae stood up again. "As long as he has a rêve stone."

"There's no way he'd have one..." Agro shook his head. "Even if he did, Rhey would just be a weak ghost..."

## ❖ CHAPTER 32 ❖

"No." Celestae shook his head. "With a sacrifice of many trapped phlasmatic souls... One can be fully revived. Ultimae collects phlasmatic souls..."

"Foxtrot will come to his senses..." Agro said, looking for any hope in the hopeless situation.

"I hope so." Vita lowered her head in dismay. "With every move, things grow more desperate."

"You're lying to me." Foxtrot sat against a log on the strange planet with a purple sky and dark forest. Ultimae paced around him. Foxtrot needed more convincing after the battle with his former allies.

"You cost me that fight," Ultimae said. "They almost had me, I had to flee. Separate your emotions from them, they will soon be gone."

"You can't bring him back," Foxtrot said. "I shouldn't have come to you."

"Would I lie to you?" Ultimae stood before Foxtrot with a rêve stone in hand.

"Yes." Foxtrot nodded.

"He's right you know," Suriv yelled from afar as he worked on a new robotic shell.

"Do you want me to prove it to you? Because I will prove it to you." Ultimae tossed the stone on the ground. "Will this keep you loyal to my cause?" Ultimae asked before he did anything.

"It's what I've been fighting for," Foxtrot said. "I would do anything to have him back."

Ultimae nodded, then lifted his arms.

Foxtrot stood up straighter in anticipation.

A gaseous black figure formed from the stone. Foxtrot smiled as he watched Arlo come back from the dead, but his smile very quickly faded when he saw the rectangular silhouette of his head take shape. It wasn't Arlo that stood before him when all was said and done, it was Rhey.

"You lied to me!" Foxtrot sprang up from the log. "You said..."

Rhey stared at his hands, confused. The last thing he remembered, the Sentinel had killed him, and Vaxx had died, and he had successfully ripped a hole in the Extraverse. He didn't think that Ultimae would actually follow through with bringing him back. "Aghhh!" Rhey stretched his arms. "It's good to be back," were the first words out of Rhey's speakers.

## ❖ CHAPTER 32 ❖

His shrill voice echoed through the forest. His screen caught sight of Foxtrot, and his animated smile faded. "Foxy? What are you doing here?"

"Arlo?" Foxtrot stepped forward.

"What did I tell you?" Ultimae waved his hand dismissively at Foxtrot. "He is back."

"But it isn't him. Not really," Foxtrot stepped away.

"Picky," Suriv said with a smirk. "Just be happy your boyfriend is back."

"He missed you." Ultimae slyly walked around Rhey. "He called out for you in that stone."

"Arlo." Foxtrot held out a hand.

"Arlo's gone." Rhey stepped away.

Foxtrot hesitated. "I can't do this. I can't work for you. Kill me."

"Unfortunate that you feel this way. We can change that." Ultimae gestured toward a shadowy figure in the woods. The figure emerged, a man that Foxtrot hadn't seen before, but an odd familiarity hung around him. The man held in his arms a Clone Suppressor helmet. He approached Foxtrot.

"No." Foxtrot shook his head and backed away. He tripped over the log and fell on his back in the mud. "Get that away from me!"

"We can finally understand each other, Foxy." Rhey's animated face stretched into a grin.

"Who are you!?" Foxtrot held up his arms, trying to defend himself against the mystery man.

The man pulled up his arms. Foxtrot was trapped on the ground in roots of black gaseous snaking phlasma. The man held out his hand, forcing Foxtrot to keep his head still. He slid the helmet on and backed away. "And to think, I'd be working with you again." He turned to face Ultimae. "Why did you bring me back?" He asked.

"I need you," Ultimae answered easily.

"And you." The man turned to face Rhey. He unclenched his fist and the phlasmatic roots holding Foxtrot down vanished. "You made me kill my own people. My entire purpose for helping—"

"Your people would never have been saved," Ultimae admitted. "They were going to die."

"Then what's in it for me?" The man stepped forward. Dark phlasma spewed from his nostrils as anger brewed in him. "Why should I still work for you?"

"That is your modus operandi, is it not? A thirst for power. You wanted land and I will get you your own universe," Ultimae promised

### ❖ CHAPTER 32 ❖

"I wanted land for my people," the man hissed. "Not myself."

"Who is this?" Foxtrot stood. He held his helmet; his head was searing with a burning pain. "Where am I?"

"Foxtrot!" Rhey ran after him. "Look at this! We're twinsies!"

"What?" Foxtrot groaned. A blue line shook on his screen, simulating his audio output from his speakers on his newly equipped helmet.

"Tell me... how does it *feel*." Rhey held his arm over Foxtrot's shoulder. "Good, huh?"

"I... guess..." Foxtrot looked down at his hands through the screen on his helmet.

"That's how it wants you to feel." Rhey's grim smile shifted to an angry scorn. "Welcome to hell."

"I missed you," Foxtrot admitted. "I know you're in there, Arlo."

"He's not." Rhey looked away. "Don't try to bring him back."

Foxtrot held a hand up to Rhey's screen. "You're here now. That's one step closer than before."

Rhey stared into Foxtrot's screen in silence. They locked eye contact with each other.

"Oi!" Suriv called out. "Enough with the romance, get a room!"

"That is the goal, is it not." Ultimae turned to face Suriv. "We will all have a room when the Extraverse is mine…"

"Dude, it was a joke…" Suriv smiled.

"Because when my time comes!" Ultimae yelled.

"Oh, is it speech time, now?" Suriv turned around in his robotic suit, with only the legs finished.

"And when you all help me achieve what is rightfully mine… rule over the Extraverse. Suriv, you will be the new Paradox Master. Foxtrot and Rhey, our Masters of Life and Death." Ultimae then pointed to the mystery man. The man shifted his form. Wings sprouted from his back as his legs became a dangling reptilian tail. "And the prophecy will be fulfilled, with you on our side. *Rogar*, the new Phlasma Master. And I the ruler of all, the Time Master's *rightful* replacement. When I get my way and the Extraverse is mine… the Multiverse will be reborn in my image, and the Thrones of Time… *will fall.*"

❖ Chapter 33 ❖
# The Calcurus Warriors

"A plan of attack is severely needed. As is defense," Starlocke said. "We cannot keep waiting for Ultimae to come to us. Every time he shows up right beside the Gateway and we are still caught off guard."

The Sentinel's Army met up in the Extraverse to speak with Time and Celestae about a plan. Starlocke paced in front of them, and a guest stood near him.

"Who is this?" Time asked.

"Daughter of Miser and Gnatus, Queen Jane Miser Karina of Canam," Karina bowed, introducing herself. "From one Queen to another, Time, I have to applaud the absolute mess you've created."

"Karina?" Starlocke looked to her with confusion on his face.

Time stepped back a bit.

Karina continued, "None of this would have happened if you had properly dealt with Ultimae when you first had the chance."

"There is no properly dealing with that child," Time insisted.

"Yeah, well. I'll show you how it's done." Karina smirked. "This battle coming up is gonna be hell. I told Eve that she wouldn't need the help of my raptors because, quite frankly it's ridiculous that the Sentinel's Army would have to resort to a bunch of experimentally trained animals. She's got *you* on her side."

"What do you know of this conflict?"

"I know that you're the most powerful being in all of existence. I know that if you fought we'd win."

"Then what do you suggest we do, Karina of Canam? A one-on-one fight to accomplish nothing? Now that is what is truly ridiculous."

Karina explained, "We need a proper attack plan. There's no way to stop Ultimae if he keeps showing up on top of that mountain. There's simply not enough room for the man-power needed to stop him."

"What are you suggesting?" Time asked.

## ❖ CHAPTER 33 ❖

"We need a way for him to show up near the base of the mountain, preferably the plains situated there. Though if we wait for him there, he'll just avoid us all together and go for the Gateway."

"Hm." Time held her hand to her chin. "He hates me. I will be bait."

"Fair enough." Karina paced around. "I heard rumor of Calcurus-B based armor?"

"I can confirm that," Vita said.

"Who's providing it?"

"Krantharnics. Hive Two," Agro said. "But the issue remains that we are in limited supply. We just lost mines of the stuff to Modius. What we have collected should do, but I feel like you're going to ask for more."

"I need to armor my animals."

"Is it just the few raptors?" Eve asked.

"A few hundred Triceratops, and Krondicoraptors, mostly. A scattered few dozen with phlasma abilities."

"Hold on, am I missing something here?" Nick asked. "You domesticated dinosaurs?"

"That's all this planet has in terms of animal life, we have limited domestication options." Karina shrugged.

"So, prepare your army," Time waved her arm at Karina to shoo her away.

"Actually," Eve thought, "If Ultimae knows we're prepared for a full-scale war, then he'll bring more than himself and Suriv. Until now he's been showing up with just himself or his lackeys, but if he shows up and we've got an army he'll bring his."

"Hold on," Agro shook his head. "Ultimae has an army? What for? He's a one-man army himself!"

"He's got an army of undead clones on the back burner…"

"How long were you waiting to tell us this?" Nick asked.

"Oh shit… I forgot about that…" Ganto looked away.

"You knew?" Vita looked at him with a quick turn of her head.

Eve explained, "Like I said, he hasn't been using them. It was Kranthar's army, I think. I don't know that Ultimae ever planned to use them, but if he had too… I feel he might."

"They won't be able to do much without armor," Karina said.

"We'll see what we can do," Agro said.

## ❖ CHAPTER 33 ❖

The Sentinel's Army left the Extraverse and waited in Camp Vistor for their next move.

The allies armored up. The Calcurus-B miners of Janistar were all lost to Modius. It was lucky for the Sentinel's Army that they had mostly moved out of the Pantheon recently, as it turned out that it was a victim of the destruction as well.

The Calcurus they had collected had not been lost, all of it had already been shipped to Amalga-5. Blacksmiths had to deal with what was collected, and so they started getting to work constructing armor. Full suits of knight-like armor were made for the Gars of Woestyn, and Woestondo, what was left of the Deusaves of Nidus, the Dragolupus of Starwynn, even some of the Lorinians from Loron and Ilsose, and various Lorinian countries of Amalga-5.

They had enough Calcurus to provide armor for Karina's human troops and their dinosaur mounts. A special suit of armor was made for Orso, Hive Two's hivemind, and Starlocke, the current Paradox Master.

A while later, Time had called a meeting in the Extraverse with Eve and Starlocke.

"The damage already done to your universe is irreparable, I am sorry to say it," Time admitted. "What has been lost to Ultimae will stay lost. Your universe is smaller now and worlds have ended with the collapse. But recently, it has been halted."

"And so when Ultimae is gone, it'll be fine, right?" Eve asked.

"It has been something I have been meaning to inform you of." Time shifted nervously in her throne. "Upon Ultimae's defeat, the Paradox Master must be a slave to that universe in order to sustain its existence. A sort of life support, as a way you would understand it."

"Forever?" Starlocke asked.

"Yes," Time answered.

Starlocke lowered his head. "When Ultimae is killed, I will be honored to continue being the Paradox Master." Starlocke decided. "The universe will be safe with me."

"That's assuming Ultimae can be killed." Eve looked up at Time, "He can, can't he?"

"No," Time shook her head. "But he can be stopped," she said.

"How?"

"I do not know. But I can assure you that nothing is unstoppable. Even the unbreakable Calcurus can crack when countered correctly."

## ❖ CHAPTER 33 ❖

"He is made of the master element," Celestae spoke up from his nearby throne.

"Okay?" Eve didn't see the relevance, at least not at first. "Wait..." She thought about ways that phlasma could be manipulated. "If I could turn Ultimae into a rêve stone, contain him..."

"He likely wouldn't be able to escape," Starlocke finished the thought. "It's brilliant."

"But how?" Vita ruffled her feathers atop her perch. She stared at Death's empty throne. "You can't just ask him nicely."

"The nature of a Celestial Being complicates things," Time said. "You cannot simply make turn a being of his caliber into a rêve stone. Ultimae knows this very well. It is how his sword functions. He plans to make a stone of us. He cannot do so without the shell of another stone, of another being."

"So, I need the rêve stone of someone else to trap him in?" Eve asked.

"Someone else who is also a phlasma ghost. Someone dead."

Eve looked away, her eyes widening. She knew exactly who, but didn't want to say it, or even think it.

"Where's Ultimae weakest?" Starlocke asked Time. "You should know."

"The closer he is to the Extraverse. He is at his absolute weakest inside it."

"But…" Eve thought to herself, "That's what he wants, to be here. It would be risky because if he won that battle… The Extraverse would be his…"

"It's the only way," Starlocke determined with a glowing stone in his forehead. "It's how it needs to be done."

"Alright." Eve stepped away for the door. "No, I have a plan. This'll all be fine. I can do this," she told herself. "I'm gonna save the Multiverse," she said as she left the Extraverse.

"The Sentinel would be proud." Time leaned back in her throne.

Eve exited through the Extraverse door, which led her through the front door of the log cabin. She walked into the warm fire-lit room, surrounded by the rest of the Army. Ganto sat on the floor showing some sort of instructional cards to Terri and Vogar both. It seemed that he was teaching them English.

Agro sat alone at a table, his head in his arms.

Nick and Matrona conversed with each other on the couch, but quickly turned their attention to Eve.

## ❖ CHAPTER 33 ❖

"Alright." Eve held her hands to her hips. "If we're gonna stop Ultimae, we need to work as a unit. We need to train and learn how to fight together."

Starlocke zoomed into view next to Eve, the door slammed open and closed.

"Starlocke and I are going to train you Ganto."

"But!" Ganto held up a hand.

"Don't deny you need training."

Ganto lowered his hand.

"And as for you Agro." Eve pointed to him. "I know about the Chosen Three, and I know that you were Canshla's top choice originally. If Foxtrot can find his inner phlasma I know we can draw it out of you."

"But where are we gonna train?" Nick asked. "And what about me? I'm just a dude." He gestured to himself.

"Do you want to fight?" Eve asked.

"For the universe, hell yeah." Nick stood from the couch confidently.

"Then you'll train." Eve nodded.

"Where are we gonna train? There's barely any room up here." Ganto asked.

Starlocke zoomed off out of the cabin. Eve held out her hand for Ganto. Ganto took her hand, and Agro, Nick,

Matrona, Terri, and Vogar took one of Ganto's remaining outstretched arms. They all flashed away and appeared next to Starlocke.

Sprawling fields of bright green grass stretched as far the eye could see. Purple-gray stone shone through the patches of missing grass. Large clusters of phlasma crystals were scattered across the ground.

The Army turned their heads to the sky above. The atmosphere was thin and all they could see was deep red and black space and dying stars.

"Welcome to the corpse of Modius." Starlocke paced around. "And the Drakona plains, training grounds of Deusaves and Dragolupus soldiers during the first ever war." Starlocke pointed with nose out behind the Army.

They turned and saw a large temple. Above the temple's entrance was the same carving of the originals as the carvings in the temples of Tornlozor and Illiosopherium. "Drakona's temple built by the Deusaves. Here would be a holy place to train."

"Ah it's all bull anyway." Ganto turned around, disinterested. "Just show me how to use this stuff." He widened his stance as if he were ready to fight Starlocke.

### ❖ CHAPTER 33 ❖

A wormhole opened near Starlocke and from it stepped a Deusaves carrying some sort of sack made of leather. It dragged it behind itself and flapped its wings to land. Karina was with the bird, and her raptor Koda stood by her, alongside another raptor.

"What's this?" Starlocke asked.

"Calcurus armor, for the Paradox Master." The Deusaves lowered his head in a show of respect.

"Thank you." Starlocke bowed back.

"Oh come on!" Ganto complained, losing his battle stance. "That's not fair!"

"They're making armor for you too, all of us," Nick reminded him.

"Oh and he gets preferential treatment just because he's the Paradox Master now?"

"Yes," Starlocke answered clearly. The Army turned their attention back to him. They stared in awe as Agro helped fasten the armor on Starlocke for him. The armor glowed like ancient bronze, accented with a shining reddish copper. The helmet concealed his face, allowing only his glowing purple eyes and stone to shine through.

Red leather sat on the majestic creature's back, like a saddle. The armor covered every part of his body in plates, allowing for mobility. The armor covered his bushy tail and his skinny legs, leaving only his underside even remotely vulnerable. Starlocke posed in a proud way, showing off his shiny new armor.

"Is that a…" Agro stepped back to admire the armor, "Saddle?" he asked.

"Is that a request to ride?" Starlocke lowered his upper body to the ground, allowing for Agro to sit on his back.

"Awesome." Agro mounted the saddle. He took out his rifle and cocked it back.

"Not fair!" Ganto complained. "*I'm* the one that rides Originals into battle!"

"Wait until you see my armor," Vita teased.

"Oh."

"Alright, Starlocke." Eve walked around among the army. "Run between the crystal clusters, weave in and out. Agro, shoot down the crystals as you pass," she instructed, "Vogar, Terri, wrestle each other. Practice fighting and dodging. Just don't kill each other."

Vogar saluted Eve, and Terri tried to replicate the gesture, but his stubby arm couldn't reach his head.

## ❖ CHAPTER 33 ❖

"Vita, I need you to help Nick with his agility. All he needs to be able to do is shoot down Suriv, which he seems capable of, but he needs to be able to dodge hits."

Vita accepted, and she flew to Nick.

"Matrona…" Eve stared into Matrona's eyes. "I…"

"I know." Matrona nodded. "I shouldn't be using my powers. I'm fine watching. Watching training is just as good as training, in my eyes."

"It's not just that…" Eve kept staring. She glanced at the stone in Matrona's chest. "I need to talk with you later."

"Okay?" Matrona examined Eve's expression, confused and worried.

Eve walked up to Karina. "What's with the extra raptor here?" she asked.

"We can't afford normal humans just standing on the battlefield doing nothing but shooting." Karina gestured to Nick. "This raptor's for that guy, like a bodyguard."

"Did I hear that right?" Nick called out. "That dinosaur is for me?"

"Don't get too attached." Karina smiled. She patted the side of the raptor, signaling it to go to Nick.

"Sweet!" Nick chuckled. As the tall beast approached him though, he backed up, somewhat fearfully.

"She doesn't bite!" Karina teased. "Usually."

Eve laughed.

"Thank you, uh, Queen. Ma'am." Nick bowed awkwardly.

"Eh, no. Don't, that's. Wow you look like you're in pain, don't do that. Just Karina is fine."

"Yeah, felt weird," Nick chuckled lightly.

"If there's anything else you need, I'll be here training with Koda," Karina said to Eve.

"Sure thing." Eve nodded, waving as Karina hopped onto Koda and rode off to the temple nearby.

Eve turned her attention down to Ganto. "Ganto." She held up her arms defensively. "Please refrain from ripping my arms off."

"You want me to fight you?" Ganto asked.

Eve taunted Ganto with her hands.

"Woohoo!" Agro shouted from the back of Starlocke as he ran through the fields of Modius. "This is way better than being a pilot!"

"Concentrate Agro!" Starlocke barked.

Agro pointed his rifle at a cluster of crystals that were fast approaching. He knew Starlocke would have to turn eventually, and he saw a clear path to the left of the crystals.

## ❖ CHAPTER 33 ❖

He aimed ahead of the crystals, to the right, anticipating the turn and firing accordingly. He fired, and just as he expected, the crystals burst, a dead-on shot.

"Good shot!" Starlocke commented.

"Come on, give me a challenge. I may have been created as a perfect soldier, but I'm not good enough. Push me!" Agro demanded.

"Alright." Starlocke smiled from underneath his helmet as he sped up, zooming across the plains.

The burst of sparks from Starlocke passed by Vogar and Terri.

Vogar had shapeshifted into the image of Foxtrot, and held his arms out, asking for Terri to headbutt him. Terri's fat hardened into muscle as his legs lengthened and his tail shortened.

Horns sprouted from his head and he stood like a looming bull before Vogar. He crushed his foot through the dirt, preparing to charge.

He ran at Vogar and headbutted him in the chest, pushing him into the stony dirt far far away. When he finally stopped, lying in the dirt next to Nick, he shapeshifted back into his Gar form and gave Terri a thumbs up.

Vogar's plummet into the ground distracted Nick. Nick was slapped across the face by Vita's wing. "Ow!" He complained.

"Do not allow yourself to be distracted! The heat of battle will be terribly busy!" Vita scolded.

"Are you sure you're qualified to train a human?" Nick asked, rubbing his sore cheek.

"I trained rebel Gars that fought with us in the first ever war in the Multiverse."

"I'm not a Gar." Nick gestured toward himself, laughing.

"Neither Gar nor a Human is Deusaves, but I feel that if I am qualified to train one, I can train the less complicated just as easily."

"Wow. Harsh." Nick stepped back, ready to try and dodge again. Vita dove at him, spiraling and flaring her bright white feathers as she darted past him.

Nick successfully dodged and leapt up, landing on the back of his new raptor bodyguard. He withdrew his pistol and fired a blank at Vita's back. Vita turned around and nodded at him.

## ❖ CHAPTER 33 ❖

A blast of electric phlasma shot Ganto between Vita and Nick. Ganto stood up and wiped dirt off of himself. He looked up at Nick. "I'm fine," he asserted.

"Didn't ask." Nick chuckled.

Ganto kicked his jetpack into gear and launched himself at Eve. Eve held out her hand and created a wall of crystal phlasma in front of her.

Ganto continued flying at the wall of crystal. One of his arms became surrounded in crystal phlasma, and he jabbed at the wall to pierce it, cracking through the solid crystal and nearly jabbing at Eve's head. Eve dissolved the wall.

"Good job." She smiled.

"I'm just fighting how I always do except I've got this stuff now…" Ganto stared at his hands as he floated in front of Eve.

"Good." She nodded. "Just use it as an extension of yourself."

"Like my jetpack?" Ganto asked.

"Exactly." Eve watched over the Army, training and having fun doing so. She hoped that it would all be worth it, and that she wouldn't lose this new family like she lost her first.

Starlocke zoomed into view near Eve. A winded and worn out Agro atop of Starlocke slid off. He wiped his brow and separated his rifle into pistols, holstering them on his side.

"Starlocke, would you mind training Ganto for a bit?" Eve asked.

"No problem." Starlocke lowered his head at Ganto. "As long as you're cooperative."

"Yeah, yeah, whatever." Ganto crossed his arms.

"Thanks." Eve approached Matrona, who had been watching. "Hey, so, I need to talk with you…"

"Cool, what about?" Matrona asked.

"Ultimae can't be stopped without a rêve stone to contain him. A stone of someone dead."

Matrona looked away, her hand inadvertently finding its way over the stone in her chest.

"I don't want to sacrifice you, but…"

"But I should." Matrona looked up at Eve. "You know I should."

Eve nodded slowly, not breaking eye contact. "When the time comes… you'd be turned back into a stone."

Matrona stared blankly ahead. "If Ultimae gets trapped in the stone… will he take over my consciousness? Will I finally die?"

### ❖ CHAPTER 33 ❖

"I don't know," Eve answered.

"I guess there's really only one way to find out then, isn't there?" Matrona chuckled with a smile. "You can count on me."

"Hey, Eve check this out!" Ganto yelled from afar.

"Come here!" Starlocke howled.

"Thank you." Eve left Matrona as she walked off to Ganto and Starlocke, "I'd tell Nick," she said before fully turning her attention away. "What's this?" she asked Ganto.

"Vogar bets we can't push him over." Ganto gestured to Vogar, who floated before him, arms outstretched, and awaiting a challenge.

"That's what you brought me here for?" Eve turned around.

"No wait," Ganto held out his hand.

Eve turned. "What?" she laughed.

"He says that if one of us can do it that he'll clean the camp up for the next week."

Eve smiled. "Alright." She rolled up her sleeves, and stood before Vogar, crouching in a pouncing position. "You ready?"

"*Lu-u'r saccin,*" Vogar said with a sly grin.

Eve leapt forward, electricity sparking at her feet as she boosted herself into Vogar's chest, hugging around him and launching forward.

She managed to push Vogar back, but not over. Vogar pushed her off of him and shrugged, laughing. Terri clapped in the distance. Nick, Vita, and Agro had stopped what they were doing to watch. Karina approached atop Koda.

Vogar taunted Eve.

"Okay…" Eve smiled, looking around while the Army watched in anticipation. "Ganto what about you, have you tried?"

"Agh!" Ganto ran forward without further questioning. He launched himself off of a rock and twisted forward like a phlasmatic flaming torpedo as he hit Vogar's chest, dispersing the flames in a flamboyant explosion, pushing Vogar back significantly less than Eve had, while making a bigger deal out of it.

Agro snorted a suppressed chuckle as he held his hand over his mouth. Ganto angrily pointed a finger at him while using the rest of his hands to dust off. Agro looked away. Ganto turned around and yelled at Vogar.

## ❖ CHAPTER 33 ❖

"This isn't fair and you know it! You're floating! There's no leverage to push you over with! You can't use physics to win, that's cheating!"

"Surely you could knock him down, Starlocke," Vita said from a distance. "Do be careful not to kill him."

Starlocke stared Vogar down.

Vogar smiled. "Doggy," he said.

Starlocke growled before launching himself at Vogar with such intense speeds that the flash of light barely registered before the Army could turn their heads to follow his movement.

Starlocke had seemingly missed Vogar all together and crashed into a bundle of phlasma crystals sticking out of the ground.

Vogar had seemingly vanished. The army turned their attention back to where he was, just to see a floating bumblebee, that quickly transformed back into Vogar. He clapped, while laughing.

"How?" Starlocke asked. "How could you perceive my absolute speed?" he asked.

Vogar told him in Garish that he noticed the sparking fur at his feet before he ran forward.

Starlocke growled at him. He ran back to Eve's side. Ganto stood by her as well.

"Anything against all of us trying at once?" Eve asked.

Vogar shook his head and held out his arms, confidently, even going so far as to close his eyes and raise his head up and away, pretending not to care.

Eve looked to either side of her, nodding at both Ganto and Starlocke. They nodded back, knowingly. Eve launched herself forward with a burst of electricity.

Ganto pushed himself forward like a rocket and Starlocke did the same.

Eve hit Vogar in the chest, pushing him back. Just as she did, Starlocke locked his mouth around Vogar's outstretched arm, while Ganto held onto his other.

Starlocke angled himself downward while Ganto pushed down with his jetpack, and Eve kept pushing forward.

The combined pushing downward and forward on Vogar's arms and chest twisted him until his body fell back and he slammed into the ground, pinning him down under Eve, Starlocke, and Ganto combined.

Eve stared down Vogar's face, laughing with accomplishment. She pressed against Vogar's nose with her

### ❖ CHAPTER 33 ❖

finger and said, "Gotcha." A tiny spark shot from her finger and tickled Vogar's nose.

"Mrgm." Vogar brushed himself off and floated up.

"Woo!" Ganto yelled excitedly, high-fiving Eve. "Teamwork, gottem!"

The Army had a laugh over the silly fun but quickly got back to training. They trained well into the night, and as things settled down, Agro approached Eve. Matrona and Nick had a walk to the temple, talking with each other.

"When do we attack?" Agro asked.

"Tomorrow."

"So soon?" Agro looked at Eve with concern. "Don't you think we should train a bit more?"

Eve didn't answer, she just kept watching ahead.

Agro looked ahead too, realizing there wouldn't be a response. "I should have phlasma powers too," he spoke up. "I'm part of the Chosen Three."

Eve looked at him.

"Will you help me find it?" he asked.

"You'll find it when you need it," Eve answered.

"Oh come on." Agro shook his head. Eve stood up, and Agro followed after her. "It could be a huge asset."

"Then you'll find it right on time, won't you?"

"Why won't you help me?" Agro asked.

"Look at Ganto." Eve pointed. "He thinks he's invincible now with his new powers. Look at Nick, he's cautious. I don't want to be the reason you die because of your overconfidence, and that's what I'm worried about with Ganto too. If you draw out your powers in combat, you'll use it to save your life, you'll use it instinctively and wisely, out of fear. Ganto will use it to show off. He'll try and outdo himself and that'll be detrimental to him."

"That's Ganto, I'm—"

"I'm being cautious," Eve reiterated. "If there's a reason I'm alive when so many of us have lost their lives it's so that I can protect anyone else from falling. I'm not losing any more of you. I'm supposed to be a Sentinel after all, I'm supposed to be protecting you." Eve turned to walk away. "Now if you'll excuse me, I need to give Ganto a little speech on overconfidence."

Agro nodded. He understood.

The training continued on into the night, and everyone was well worn out. Karina left for Canam. When the rest of them left for Camp Vistor, they all quickly dozed off in bed, except for Eve.

## ❖ CHAPTER 33 ❖

She stayed awake, staring up at the ceiling, lying on top of her covers. She twiddled her fingers and shook her foot. The box floated by her calmly, casting a dim red light over her.

"Where are we to attack?" the box asked.

"Base of the mountain. Time will draw him out in the morning," Eve answered, still staring at the ceiling, and the rafters that held it up.

She squinted at the rafters, she thought she saw movement. The small beady eyes of a finch stared at her. It saw that she caught a glimpse of it, and it scurried away.

"Box…" Eve spoke with a nervous voice, "What kind of animals are native to Amalga-5?"

"Several species from Earth's late cretaceous, why?"

"Finches?" Eve asked.

"No," the box answered.

"Hm…" Eve wondered, something unsettling sat in her mind.

❖ Chapter 34 ❖
# Doomed

"Rise and shine!" Eve yelled from the living room of the log cabin. She hadn't slept the whole night. "Gear up! Let's go! Let's go!"

Ganto excitedly ran into the living room. "Man, am I ready!"

"Ganto, remember what I told you last night." Eve pointed him down.

"I know, I know."

"What's the plan, Eve?" Nick asked, leaning over the railing of the loft above with Matrona. The rest of the Army was already gathered in the living room.

Eve began, "Nick, Agro, Terri, focus your attacks on Suriv. Go for the legs and the mouth-door thing. Kill the Ilsian inside. Vita, Ganto, Vogar, Starlocke, Matrona all of you will

## ❖ CHAPTER 34 ❖

help me attack Ultimae. We just have to overwhelm him, so he's thinking about too much at once.

"He only has one sword after all. Get it out of his grasp if you can. We need to surround him and trap him down for my plan to work. We can't let him beat us down because…" Eve didn't know how to explain the next part, "We need to lead him into the Gateway. We need to pin him down in the Extraverse so I can turn him into a stone, but if he knocks us out of there… there's no going back in… and we've lost."

"He doesn't have five Emissaries," Starlocke reminded Eve. "He can't do much in there. Not all is lost if we lose the battle."

"But things get harder if we do, so let's not even consider it an option. We have to win." Eve stood tall. "We'll set off as soon as Orso drops off the Calcurus armor that's been made for all of us. Then Karina will send in the armies.

"Ganto, come with me to get the Freysent ready," Eve said as she walked to the door. She put on her scarf and cold-weather gear, then opened the door to the light snowfall outside.

Ganto followed.

"When I see Suriv, don't hold me back. I'm gonna beat the sh—"

Eve held her hand in front of Ganto, stopping his exit from the camp.

Eve stood completely still. Frozen.

The wind howled outside as the snow swirled in front of the tall glowing red figure of Ultimae, standing outside, staring at the door. He held his sword in one hand, the blade lazily tilted downward into the snow. The many stones dangled from the handle. Ultimae's cerebral galaxy shifted as the snow pushed out of his way and flew off into the gray sky.

Matrona glanced outside and saw the glow of red. "Eve?" she stood up.

"What's wrong?" Nick asked, following Matrona as she approached the door.

"Stay inside, Nick," Matrona urged.

The rest of the Sentinel's Army inside came to the door.

"Oh, *fu*..." Agro mumbled under his breath, his jaw dropping.

Eve flicked her hand out. It sparked aflame with phlasma. She flicked her other hand out, and the fire burst. She marched cautiously forward as her hands lit aflame. Then, all at once, the lights in the cabin shut off. Eve's heart jumped and everyone looked around for the source of a quiet static sound.

## ❖ CHAPTER 34 ❖

"What's happening?" Ganto asked.

The lights flickered back on and off. The static noise grew louder. "*It's good to be back,*" a shrill voice called.

Nick and Agro's eyes widened with surprise and an all too familiar fear. Shivers ran down their spines, and the hairs on their necks stood up on end.

"No..." Nick refused to believe it.

"*Yes,*" the voice taunted. "Oh Nick, it's been a while since we last saw each other." The voice moved around the room, and the Army desperately tried to find its source.

There was an odd familiarity about the voice to Eve, but she couldn't quite put her finger on it. The rest of the Army though, they seemed to know, they were certain of what it was, but not where it was, or how it was back.

"There's so much we need to catch up on. Oh, I killed your aunt! That was fun!"

"What!?" Matrona yelled.

"No." Nick stood back. "No no no..."

"But that's old news, what else..." the shrill voice stung at their ears. "I'm alive that's good... in a bit of a relationship, about time... Hm, oh yeah, I'm not the only one that's back, it's a big old party, isn't it!?"

"Show yourself, Rhey!" Nick yelled.

"Rhey?" Eve yelled.

From behind Ultimae, in a flash of light, Rhey and Foxtrot appeared, with suppressor helmets firmly on their heads.

"Honey, I'm home," Rhey chanted. "Foxy, why don't you show 'em what you got?"

Foxtrot lifted a hand.

"Foxtrot?" The Army realized all at once who the man beside him was.

Foxtrot clenched his fist, and the Army fell to the ground after a stinging burst of sound rang in their ears.

"You know, we *were* gonna wait for you to attack us but, a little birdie told me about that, and we decided we should get the upper hand."

"Who?" Eve asked. "Was it the finch?" she pressed.

"Always hard to tell with a Gar."

"Who!?" Nick stepped forward, furious at Rhey's continued existence.

"Everyone put your hands up!" Rhey threw his hands into the air and turned around. "For the one and only! Galactic War veteran and slayer of his own kind!"

"*No.*" Matrona's heart skipped a beat. She knew.

## ❖ CHAPTER 34 ❖

"R-R-*Rogar*!" Rhey bowed with a deep annunciatory voice when a finch perched on the windowsill behind the Army quickly shapeshifted into Rogar, floating before them menacingly.

He furrowed his brow and scowled at them all. Dark phlasma spewed from his nostrils as he roared at them.

Vogar cowered away and fell onto the couch. The Army'sentire plan had been thrown out the window. Ganto flared his fists in preparation to fight back, unafraid. Matrona held her abdomen and fell to the floor, she'd never felt more unprepared for anything.

Eve stumbled to the ground and stood up again, making a run for it to the door. She had just made it outside when Foxtrot snapped his fingers. Her ears burst and she fell into the snow, screaming as blood dripped from her ears and splashed in the snow.

The Army ran after her, pushing past Rhey and Foxtrot, and away from Rogar. The Army stopped in their tracks, staring up at the menacing figure of Ultimae standing in the snow. Suriv landed next to him like a rocket, pushing away snow as he anchored himself with his brand new robotic, Calcurus shielded legs.

"I do not know if you have been counting." Ultimae stepped forward, looming over Eve. "Or if the pain is too overwhelming."

Foxtrot's fists tensed, and Eve convulsed on the floor. Voices swam through her head, whispering, "*I'm sorry.*"

"There are five of us."

Agro whispered in Nick's ear, they were close to each other on the ground, "If you can break Foxtrot's helmet, he'll come to his senses."

"Are you sure?" Nick asked.

Agro silently nodded, not too sure of himself to say anything.

Nick stood up and took aim at Foxtrot's helmet. He didn't hesitate and he fired.

Foxtrot turned around and shot his hand out, his arm shaking. In a near instant the bullet was suspended in a small bubble of purple liquid. Foxtrot let down his hand and the liquid dropped, the bullet dropping with it.

Nick was about to fire again, but Rhey held out his hand. Without so much as a remote to help him, Rhey was able to cause Nick to fall to the ground, screaming for mercy. "MOM!" he screamed. "AELLA!" He writhed around on the floor. "QUINN! *MATRONA!*"

## ❖ CHAPTER 34 ❖

Foxtrot stomped his foot on the ground, causing Nick to flinch and his ears to bleed.

"Don't do this!" Matrona yelled, running forward as her hands flared with dark phlasma.

Eve stood up in front of Ultimae, her fingers sparking. She turned to face the Army. "Do something!" She demanded. Her mind wandered to Andrew. She saw the look of terror and fear in Matrona's eyes. She couldn't let this happen.

The Army was too shocked to do anything. In front of them was Ultimae and Suriv, and behind them Rhey, Foxtrot and Rogar. They didn't know what to do.

"HELP ME!" Nick screamed.

Matrona ran for Nick. Foxtrot lifted a hand.

"*AH!*" Matrona swung her hand across. A lash of flaming black phlasma swung from her fingertips like whips and ripped across Foxtrot.

Foxtrot flinched and retaliated, shooting his arms down and flinging them up.

Liquid phlasma collected around Matrona's feet, then flung her into the air.

She fell into the snow with a thud.

Nick held his head, writhing in pain.

"Don't just stand there! Do something!" Eve begged. She didn't even know how to fight back and yet she expected them to help.

Vogar bowed down to Rogar and muttered in Garish that he surrendered. There was no winning.

"I didn't think there were survivors," Rogar commented of Vogar. "I'm sorry it had to turn out like this." Rogar whipped his tail on the ground, causing a snaking vine of dark phlasma to lash out of the floor underneath Vogar and launch him into the snow.

Terri screamed and charged at Rogar. Rogar coolly lifted an arm as dark phlasmatic roots crawled up Terri, trapping him in place.

"Why fight back when there is clearly no winning?" Ultimae taunted. "I would kill you all now, but that would be a waste of energy I could better use in taking the Extraverse."

"*No.*" Eve limped forward and approached Ultimae as he turned away for the Gateway. "Fight us."

Ultimae chuckled. "Do you really want more of you to die?" He looked around and shrugged. "Very well then. Rhcy." He lowered his head. "Foxtrot."

Nick lifted his gun and fired. The bullet shot through the back of Foxtrot's helmet, and came barreling out of the

## CHAPTER 34

front, then it passed right through Ultimae's head like it was a cloud.

The helmet sparked and smoked up. It had been broken; the effects of the helmet gone. As a result, the army expected Foxtrot to realize the error of his ways, but as Foxtrot took off the helmet, he turned slowly to face Nick. Something about his red eyes seemed empty. His white hair wasn't full of life, instead thick and dirty, lying over his face. He looked like hadn't slept in days. He stared Nick down with a deadly blankness.

Rhey's smile vanished, waiting to see what Foxtrot would do. Foxtrot lifted his arms and Nick was enveloped in liquid phlasma from underneath, until he was trapped in a sphere of pure phlasmatic water. Foxtrot lifted the sphere into the air, and in it, Nick struggled to get his face to the surface for air, but any time he got even close, Foxtrot swiveled his hand to move the liquid and swish Nick around inside it.

"NO!" Matrona yelled. Her entire body flared with dark phlasma.

"Careful, Matrona!" Eve warned.

"Foxtrot! Don't do this!" Agro yelled.

Rhey lifted a hand and slowly closed his fist. Muffled screams emanated from the sphere as Nick's mind was being bombarded by Rhey's emotional torture.

Eve blasted at Foxtrot with a bolt of cold electricity, but it bounced off his thin Calcurus shielding, the same as Rhey's.

Matrona screamed as she ran to Rhey. Suriv fired a laser into the snow. The explosion launched Matrona back.

Nick had dropped the Calcurus revolver. Ganto crawled over to pick it up, but the gun was slapped away from his grasps by Rogar's tail. Ganto tried to jump up at him, but Rogar pinned him down. Starlocke pounced at Rogar and smashed him into a wall.

"*LET HIM GO!*" Matrona shouted, pushing herself up from the snow. "LEAVE HIM ALONE!"

Agro stared into Foxtrot's eyes. The same as his. "*RAAAH!*" Agro yelled as a burst of phlasma exploded at his feet and launched him into the suspended bubble. Once inside the liquid, Agro kicked Nick out of it.

Nick stumbled into the snow and gasped for breath, crying and shivering, shaking violently, eyes bloodshot. Matrona ran to his side and hugged him. A look of relief washed over Eve.

## ❖ CHAPTER 34 ❖

Agro shot his head out of the bubble to catch his breath, but Foxtrot tensed his fists and pulled Agro deeper into the bubble. The bubble closed in on him, shrinking as the liquid pushed through his body.

Foxtrot's eyes flashed with rage.

Agro swished around in the bubble and caught a glimpse of Foxtrot. Their eyes met for a moment as Agro begged for his life with a single look.

For a second a look of regret flashed over Foxtrot's face. The look didn't go unnoticed by Rhey. Rhey screamed and shot his hand outward, blasting the floating liquid with a burst of black lightning, tormenting and shocking Agro's mind.

The screaming from the liquid bubble subsided, and Agro's struggle vanished as his body swished around lifelessly in the phlasma.

"NO!" Ganto called out.

"Rah!" Rhey screamed. "You ruined my plan! And we had to kill a perfectly good clone to do it…"

"You're a monster!" Eve yelled.

"Tell me something I don't know!" Rhey yelled as he flicked his arm at Eve. A bolt of black lightning shot into Eve's head and she fell to the ground with a thud. Her mind swarmed with dark thoughts, being tormented by clouded evil. Nothing specifically targeted her. It wasn't a personal attack; it was simple torture. Rhey wasn't putting much effort into Eve.

With Agro's death, the army burst into a rage-fueled fight. Vogar and Rogar wrestled while Starlocke shot phlasmatic lasers from his stone at Ultimae. Nick struggled to stand and shot at Rhey and Foxtrot. Terri relentlessly headbutted Suriv, trying to push him off the platform. Vita flew around, spewing white hot flames from her wings at Ultimae and trying to disarm him of his sword.

Ganto stood by Eve's side, shaking her awake. "Come on," he encouraged, "Get up."

Eve stood up and readied herself. "Ultimae!" she called out weakly.

Ultimae was distracted for a brief enough moment for Vita to swoop by and steal the sword. Starlocke pounced at him, but Ultimae simply backhanded him away.

"Come and get me," Eve threatened. She ran for the Gateway's rift and jumped into it. Ganto followed after her.

Matrona turned to Nick and said, "Stay here. Stay safe." She grabbed the Calcurus pistol and ran for the Gateway.

## ❖ CHAPTER 34 ❖

"Idiot child," Ultimae whispered to himself as he ignored the battle to crouch under the roof of the Gateway and enter the Extraverse.

The shatter in the Extraverse opened wide as Ultimae stepped in. Time stood from her throne and the galactic spiral in her head pulsated with anger. Celestae readied himself as well. Eve, Ganto and Matrona stepped back, afraid.

Ultimae's form jittered and flickered, he was where he was weakest.

"I do not want to have to do this to you, brother." Ultimae threatened Celestae, "We could recreate the Multiverse together, preserve the sanctity."

"Why do you always try to get people on your side?!" Eve questioned angrily from below, small and insignificant among the Celestial Beings. "Is it because you're too weak on your own!?" Eve asked.

"If I were too weak on my own I would not be here, at my goal, right this moment you incompetent, foolish—"

"Silence." Time outstretched her arm, freezing Ultimae in his place. "I do not want to have to banish you again."

"Go ahead. Try." Ultimae's galaxy shifted and twirled, darkening and distorting itself. He lifted an arm up at Time, despite her freezing him in place, and Time stumbled back.

"You are not fit to rule over my creation." Ultimae struggled to take a step forward, which in turn pushed Time back as well, she too was frozen in place, and Celestae, Ganto, Matrona, and Eve, watched from the sidelines, mortified at Ultimae's power. "Your own creations rebel against mine and they break it. What kind of ruler allows that?"

"I do not seek to control, only to provide," Time struggled to speak.

Ultimae stepped forward again, "Do you not see that that is where you fail?"

Time fell to the floor with a massive thud. She landed next to her throne, and she watched as it was pushed back, and replaced with the empty throne. Ultimae casually sat down and rested his arm on his leg. "Now go. I have no need for you here." Ultimae flicked his wrist and in a near instant Time was flung into the rift and out of the Extraverse.

Celestae leaped forward and held out his hand for Ultimae's head, but with an outstretched arm Ultimae wrapped his hand around Celestae's neck. The galactic shape in Celestae's head expanded and warped as its glow brightened.

Celestae screamed in pain, something Eve never thought a Celestial could do. Ultimae's red phlasma pushed

## ❖ CHAPTER 34 ❖

through Celestae, sending waves of stinging fire through him. And when Ultimae let go, Celestae was thrust through the rift.

Eve and Ganto both flared their hands at the ready, prepared to fight Ultimae.

"What are you going to do?" Ultimae asked. "If the Celestials failed so spectacularly? What could you *possibly* do?"

The rift warped and expanded to let something else in, Eve was hopeful that Time or Celestae had returned, but instead Suriv, followed by Rhey, Foxtrot, and Rogar entered the Extraverse.

Ganto jumped at Foxtrot, enraged, and screaming. Rogar flicked his hand nonchalantly, and Ganto was launched into the rift. Eve ignored the newcomers and instead jumped at Ultimae. She stood on him and pushed her hand against his head. The cold electric phlasma sparked across Ultimae, and for a moment it seemed that she had him stunned. "Matrona get over here!" she yelled.

Matrona stepped back, afraid, crying, and stunned.

Laser fire from Suriv's eye grazed Eve's back. She screamed with shock and fell to the ground. Ultimae shook his head and lifted a hand. In a near instant Matrona was tossed out of the Extraverse. She dropped the Calcurus pistol.

Eve stepped forward. Rhey held out his hand.

A blast of dark electricity shocked Eve in the head.

She flinched.

Rhey turned around. "Do it now!" He blasted Eve again to push her away. She shook her head. The emotional phlasma had done seemingly nothing but push her away.

Ultimae rose from his throne, floating with his arms out by his side… and he clenched his fists.

"NO!" Eve shrieked.

Rhey blasted her one more time with a strong strike of dark lightning that launched her to the floor.

The Extraverse shook. An explosion of light burst through the void. Five thrones crumbled to ash; the projection of the Multiverse faded. The stars in the room died out, one by one.

Darkness.

Darkness, and the empty throne.

Nothing else.

Eve pushed herself up and wiped her arm across her face. She shook her arms and held them up, ready to fight. "This isn't over…"

## ❖ CHAPTER 34 ❖

Ultimae shook his head, disappointed in Eve. Rhey gave her a sly smile. Eve glared at him. Her fists instinctively clenched.

"Child…" Ultimae said, almost with a hint of sadness. "It is."

Eve turned around and opened the Extraverse door, hoping to appear in the cabin.

The white void met her optimistic gaze, and it swiftly killed that optimism.

Eve slammed the door shut and opened it again.

Nothing.

She slammed the door shut with a shriek, grunting as she ripped it open again.

White.

"WHAT DID YOU DO?" she threw herself around and pointed a shaking finger at Ultimae.

Rhey cackled.

Rogar slumped down in his throne.

Ultimae said nothing.

"WHERE ARE MY FRIENDS?" Eve screamed.

"I would say they're dead," Rhey said. "But they're more than that."

Ultimae sat down in his throne.

"No." Eve shook her head. "No." She turned around.

And she ran.

Her legs burned as she ran as fast as she had ever run. She ran away, leaving the thrones behind. As the thrones stretched away into nothingness behind her, the door and Rhey hadn't moved.

She fell, catching herself, not her breath.

She slammed her fist on the ground. "No…" she cried.

Rhey knelt by her. He placed his hand on Eve's back.

She flinched.

"It's okay… It's over now… You can finally rest."

Eve looked up to Rhey, her eyes distraught, her voice shaking. "But I tried so hard…"

"You really should have given up sooner… You knew this was going to happen." Rhey patted her. "You knew you weren't good enough to be a Sentinel."

"*Where are my friends?*" Eve asked in desperation, even though she knew the answer.

"They don't exist anymore, sweetheart. Nothing does."

Eve grimaced, "You're *lying* to me…"

"You can tell yourself that," Rhey's screen jittered. "But deep down you know you're wrong."

## ❖ CHAPTER 34 ❖

Eve stared into Rhey's screen. Was this really how it ended? All she worked for?

"Yes," Rhey answered her thoughts. "A shame, for you, I know. But you should learn from your ancestor, not all stories end happily ever after. Mine does, though." Rhey smiled condescendingly.

Eve cried, but she couldn't feel the full weight. She couldn't understand. The shock persisted.

"I would understand if you welcomed death. Dying is really your only option. Is that what you want?" Rhey asked. "I can give it to you."

Eve nodded slowly as she sniffled and wiped away a tear. She looked down at the reflective floor of the Extraverse, and in it she saw her young self again, staring back at her with tear-filled, lost, hopeless eyes. Rhey's flickering animated face lingered in the reflection over her shoulder.

Rhey held out his hand. "Come on. I can end it for you. Nice and quick. No pain. Like your friends."

Eve looked up at him. His screen seemed strangely welcoming, entrancing. She had forgotten her surroundings. The detail was lost. For a moment she thought, *is this real?*

But as the doubts entered her mind, her hand had already found its way toward Rhey's. She was about to take his hand and accept death.

And then, everything snapped.

"AH!"

Ganto's hand shot through Rhey's abdomen.

Eve shrieked, stepping away. She looked to her hand. She had been holding the Calcurus pistol to her head, her finger over the trigger. She dropped the gun and pushed herself away, shocked, terrified, blindsided. She held her chest and panicked for air.

Ganto tore his hand from Rhey's body and looked to the box, which had shot Rhey with a siege shield blast to weaken his shield and allow Ganto to attack.

Starlocke was in the Extraverse with him.

Foxtrot grabbed Rhey and pulled him aside. He blasted Ganto with a wave of deafening noise.

"Whatever Rhey showed you was merely a hallucination, Eve!" Starlocke barked. "Do not be afraid."

"DO IT!" Rhey groaned to Ultimae.

Ultimae stood up.

"NO!" Eve yelled. "It was real!" she shrieked. "It was real!"

## CHAPTER 34

"We have to get out of here," Ganto grabbed Eve's hand and tried to pull her to the exit.

Ultimae held out his arms.

"NO!" Eve screamed. "DON'T GO! DON'T GO OUT THERE!"

"Eve, come on! We have to go!" Ganto yelled.

Eve screamed, she tugged back, trying with all her strength to *not let go*. She couldn't let Ganto leave the Extraverse. "DON'T GO!"

"Eve!" Starlocke pushed her. "We don't have much time."

"PLEASE, DON'T GO!" Eve bellowed. "PLEASE!"

Foxtrot looked away.

Ultimae was becoming annoyed. He flicked his hand. Starlocke was sent flying out of the Extraverse.

"NO!" Eve screamed with all her might. She cried out, her heart begging to break free from her chest. She fell over and crawled to the Extraverse door.

Suriv looked up to Ultimae. "Get them out of here, I'm sick of this."

"Eve, come on!" Ganto opened the door.

"NOT YOU TOO!" Eve begged. "PLEASE, GANTO, NOT YOU TOO!"

Ultimae blasted Ganto out of the Extraverse.

Eve curled up in a ball, petrified, overwhelmed, destroyed.

Rhey shook his head. "Tsk, tsk…" He crossed his arms. "I wasn't even trying," he boasted. "Look at you." He kicked Eve while she was down. "Ruined."

She flinched. "This isn't real, you're still tricking me!" Eve stuttered.

"Do you know what the beautiful thing is?" Rhey knelt down by Eve.

Eve darted her eyes at Rhey, terrified of his animated smile, but transfixed all the same.

"You'll never know for sure." Rhey smiled. He held up his hand.

Ultimae nodded and flicked his hand.

Eve was cast out of the Extraverse. She tumbled in the snow until stopping in front of the Sentinel's army. Eve stood up, without a second thought, to run after the rift again. She grabbed Ganto's hand and tried to pull him along with her.

"WE HAVE TO GET IN THERE!"

"Eve, no!" Ganto fought back.

## ❖ CHAPTER 34 ❖

Starlocke wrapped around Eve and kept her in place. He looked at Ganto with serious eyes. "What did Rhey show her?" he projected the thought into Ganto.

Ganto responded only with a fearful glance.

The phlasma platform holding up the Gateway and the log cabin cracked.

"What do we do?" Nick panicked.

"They have the Extraverse…" Vita breathed heavily; her wing was severely injured.

Vogar tended to Terri's wounds, he seemed to be missing a stubby arm.

Vita lowered her head over Agro's body. Time and Celestae flickered as if they shouldn't be outside of the Extraverse.

"We have to go," Ganto determined.

"What?" Nick approached him. "What do you mean?"

"Whatever Rhey showed Eve ruined her."

"He's gonna do it…" Eve shook. Starlocke lowered his head to her, like a hug. "I'm sorry… I'm sorry." Tears streamed down Eve's face, with no sign of stopping.

"I think Ultimae is…" The platform shook and cracked again. The surface began to lighten as gaseous energy trailed from it and into the rift. "He's getting rid of the platform," Ganto said. "We have to go. Now."

"But the Extraverse," Vita argued.

"All is lost." Time held her head in her hands. "All is lost…"

"How can you possibly lose hope?" Starlocke asked. "You are Time itself. How could you not fight for your home?"

"Because she's right." Ganto adjusted his jetpack. "There's nothing we can do."

"I'm so sorry." Eve held Ganto's hand.

Vita hesitated before lowering her head in shame, and lifting her wing to Eve's hand. Terri slugged behind Eve and rested his lower arms on her shoulder, while Vogar stayed with Terri. Starlocke approached with Agro's body slouched over his saddle.

Starlocke sniffed at Matrona, crying in the snow. "Come now, child," he beckoned for her. Nick was the last to approach the group.

The box flew into them and teleported them to the base of the mountain.

Time and Celestae appeared near them, and they all looked up and watched as the platform crumbled.

## ❖ CHAPTER 34 ❖

Terri cried violently. "No!" he cried out. "*Vistor!*" he held his stubby arms up at the cabin. Vogar held him close and tried to comfort him. But Vogar couldn't look at Terri's sad face. He looked up at the cabin, far atop the mountain.

He held up his arms and twisted his hands.

The phlasma platform under the camp tore away from the rest of the platform. Flames encircled the chunk of platform torn away. Vogar roared as power surged through him and he led the cabin down the mountain, trying his best to keep it steady. Terri rubbed his eyes and sniffled.

The Gateway crumbled. The rest of the platform fell with it. The mountain shook and an avalanche of rock and snow rushed down the peak.

"Ah!" Vogar pulled away, pulling the camp further from the destruction. A chunk of the gateway lodged itself in the roof as Vogar directed the building down.

His wrist stung with pain, and he held his hand, collapsing to the ground.

Terri hugged him, thankful and teary eyed.

The cabin had almost made it all the way down. It fell into the ground at the base of the mountain with an echoing thud. The structure cracked and shifted, tilting itself, but it was intact. It was all that was left.

The ground shook. The crashing of the rock echoed across the plains as the mountain shook and rumbled.

Red lightning flashed over the mountain, striking the peak and the shatter, flashing in the clouds above.

Eve shook her head, eyes dry, broken. "It's no use. It's gonna happen any second now. I failed. I knew it wasn't me. I failed."

Starlocke looked away.

"We didn't lose, did we?" Nick asked.

Eve let out a small cry. She held onto Ganto, his exoskeleton piercing her skin as she hugged tighter, just to hold him as close as she could.

The stars in the sky shifted. The sky grew dark. A silence prevailed.

"I can't watch this…" Ganto said. "Come on Terri." He pried Eve from him and left her with Starlocke. He led Terri and Vogar inside, to the cabin. "Everything's gonna be okay," he said.

The rest of the Army followed. Starlocke bowed to Eve, leaving her in the grass. Eve and Vita stayed put.

"We can't give up. Is this what the Sentinel would have wanted?" Vita asked as the Army hid in the fallen building.

## ❖ CHAPTER 34 ❖

Eve clenched her fist. She furrowed her shaky brow. Her lip quivered. She flashed away.

Ultimae adjusted himself on his throne, one he hadn't sat in for ages. Rogar, Rhey, Foxtrot, and Suriv stood before him, waiting. Ultimae raised an arm and all the thrones near him exploded in a fiery burst of phlasma, before they vanished. He lowered his arm and new thrones formed.

One beside him formed into a pilot seat from an old Andromedan warship. Foxtrot and Rhey knew it was meant for them. Rhey sat down moments before the throne finished appearing, and he lightly tapped his leg, gesturing for Foxtrot. Foxtrot came over and sat on Rhey's lap, staring into his screen. Rhey lightly caressed Foxtrot's face with the back of his hand.

"I'll make you the best universe." Rhey's animated screen smiled.

"The Andromedan Army. They created clones, and new life." Ultimae gestured to Foxtrot, "And used them to destroy." He gestured to Rhey. "Life and Death."

A throne appeared on the other side of Ultimae's throne. Silver and industrial, it had a perfect outcropping for Suriv's suit. Suriv approached it, and locked his legs in. The Calcurus shielding in the shape of a crystal lowered and exposed the Ilsian within, making his suit the throne itself. "A Paradox alone, how you survived the escape of the Sentinel's attack on the Galactic Jail, it would be fitting that you become the new Paradox Master, as you requested." Ultimae turned his head as a new throne appeared next to Rhey's and Foxtrot's. It was identical to the throne of the Gars that Rogar had stolen from Sogar. "Nothing need be explained, Phlasma Master." Ultimae slowly nodded as Rogar sat.

"What now?" Suriv asked. "Is there a reset button on this thing?"

"Time, there has to be something we can do." Starlocke looked up to her with hope, his ears drooping.

Time hesitated before the galactic shape in her head glowed. She looked to Starlocke and spoke…

## ❖ CHAPTER 34 ❖

"There is." Ultimae lifted his hand, and a projection of the vast and infinite Multiverse appeared before him, overtaking the entire Extraverse. The new Emissaries stared in awe. Rogar seemed uneasy on his throne. Ultimae held out his arms and clenched his fists, expecting to see the universes collapse before him, but nothing. He tried again.

Nothing.

"I have done nothing more than buy us some time," Time explained.

"What have you done?" Celestae asked.

"I let Ultimae cast me out of the Extraverse. Our greatest weakness is that we as non-banished Celestials, are intrinsically linked to the Extraverse itself. I have used our weakness to our advantage."

"Why is nothing happening?" Suriv asked. "Come on I was promised my own universe, what's the hold up?"

"Shut up, you insufferable imbecile." Ultimae stood up

and clenched his fist again, and yet nothing. "AGH!" He yelled. "Curse it all!"

"What is it?" Rhey asked.

"We are not done." Ultimae turned around frustratedly. He grabbed a small floating planet that orbited his throne, and he crushed it in his hands out of anger. "AGH!" He tossed the pieces to the ground.

"I was promised a universe to myself." Suriv rotated his torso to face Ultimae. "If you can't provide that then—" Suriv was cut off in his speech. He struggled to breathe, and he blinked furiously. He lifted an arm to his throat, which was burning with a deep red phlasma.

Ultimae lifted an arm. Suriv's waist was pried from his suit as the deep red phlasma consumed him and lifted him up. His body was torn from his life support, and he floated in the air like a ragdoll. His remaining arms struggled to fight it. Ultimae drew his arm closer and Suriv floated near him.

Rogar snaked down in his throne, looking away.

Rhey smiled.

"I have it under control," Ultimae growled in a deep voice to the choking Suriv. "Questioning my power will be the biggest mistake you make." Ultimae let go and Suriv fell to the ground, gasping for air. "But… It seems that…"

# ❖ CHAPTER 34 ❖

"The Multiverse cannot be destroyed while Celestials are present within it," Time explained. "We need to send the Army in to stop Ultimae, without us. Us being out here is our failsafe."

Vogar asked if there was still hope.

"It is all we have," Celestae answered.

Terri asked how they could find Eve to tell her. The Army didn't know how to answer that.

"How do we stop Time and Celestae then?" Foxtrot spoke up. "They're just like you." Foxtrot gestured to Ultimae. "If you can't be stopped like you say then how do we stop them?" Foxtrot asked.

"Are you questioning my power?" Ultimae threatened.

"No." Foxtrot shook his head.

"I'll stop them," Rogar interjected, looking away from everyone else.

Ultimae laughed, "How will a Gar, who is barely alive, stop Celestials—"

"I'll figure it out, I'll lead them to you." Rogar still didn't make eye contact.

Rhey stared at him suspiciously.

"How?" Ultimae asked.

"I'll get on their side," Rogar answered simply. "I'll trick them into thinking I'm with them, get them to trust me, plan an attack, and lead them here, into a trap." As Rogar spoke, his voice became softer.

"Do you really honestly believe that you could pull that off?"

"Yes." Rogar floated away from his throne quickly. He shapeshifted. Rhey's screen flickered with surprise. Foxtrot flinched at the sight of Rogar's new appearance. Rogar bowed before Ultimae and looked up. His face... *the Sentinel's*. "They will have no reason not to trust me…" Rogar spoke with the Eighth Sentinel's soft voice, fully transformed.

Suriv smiled and laughed. "Always pays to have a shapeshifter on our side." He groaned as he made his way back into his suit. "Let him do it."

"What authority do you think you have?" Ultimae turned to Suriv. "You cannot persuade me!"

## ❖ CHAPTER 34 ❖

"Alright." Suriv shrugged as he locked himself into his suit again.

Ultimae hesitated and adjusted himself on his throne. "Fine. I will allow it."

Suriv chuckled.

Rogar nodded in a half bow, "Thank you." He walked over to the rift. "I won't disappoint."

"I will not bring you back again if you do, Rogar. Not like last time," Ultimae threatened.

"I know." Rogar stepped through the rift, and with that, he was gone.

"Do you think he can pull it off?" Foxtrot asked Rhey.

"He's a dumb lizard-man, but the Sentinel's Army is dumber, and they're desperately in search of hope," Rhey answered. "He can pull it off. And when he does, we'll have a universe all to ourselves."

Foxtrot lowered his head into Rhey's chest, trying to get closer to him. Rhey put his arm over Foxtrot and twirled his fingers through his white hair.

❖ Chapter 35 ❖
# In Search of Hope

Eve appeared somewhere that called to her. She didn't know where she was, or what was calling to her. She didn't know why she was still alive. She thought that the Multiverse would have been reset by now. She assumed that something happened, that there was a reason she was still alive. But she wasn't certain.

A lingering fear told her that Rhey was still tricking her, that maybe they had lost.

Regardless, it didn't matter that she was alive if she was. What mattered is if she would stay that way.

Wherever she had appeared, the air smelled of sulfur, and the ground was cold. A massive brown-tan gas planet with a magnificent ring loomed in the sky above. All around her

## ❖ CHAPTER 35 ❖

rocky hills loomed, and it seemed that the very floor she stood on was nothing but a brownish lake, frozen over.

"Hello?" Eve called out, expecting someone to be there. For some strange reason it felt as though she was called to that place.

She stared ahead and her eyes met a figure atop a hill.

"Hello!?" she called to it. "I'm Eve. Eve Sanchez," she said. "Evelyn," she elaborated. "I think this place was calling out to me. Was it you?" she asked with a shaky voice. She cleared her throat and asked, "Am I dead?"

The figure's long hair floated and flowed in the windless atmosphere of the planet. The figure emitted a ghostly aura, glowing but with an air of darkness about it. Eve trekked up the hill and approached the figure. As she neared the top of the hill, and studied the back of the figure's head, she noticed that she was a woman. The woman stared at the massive planet above, ignoring Eve's footsteps as if she didn't hear, or didn't care. Her flowing ghostly dress floated idly.

"Excuse me..." Eve spoke up.

"Why are you here?" the woman spoke with a soft voice. "Leave me alone."

"Who are you?" Eve asked.

The woman turned around, and Eve was suddenly struck with a sense of familiarity. She stepped back out of awe. Her mind played memories back to her like a flashback, trying to prove herself wrong but doing nothing but reinforcing the thought.

"I'm dead," Eve said. "It happened. This can't be happening, this isn't real. Rhey better not still be messing with me, because this is too far. I saw you disappear," Eve stammered. "You died. You're supposed to be dead!"

"Trust me, I wish I was," the woman whispered.

"Why didn't you help us!? You're the *Sentinel*!" Eve yelled, her voice carried a tone of almost anger though the ghostly figure could feel that it was produced by sadness, betrayal almost.

"Death never told me what really happens after a phlasma ghost is reduced to nothing. I don't wish this form of resurrection on anyone, even Rogar."

"What do you mean?" Eve paced around the figure, trying to judge her reality. The Sentinel followed her pace with the turn of her body, her legs barely moving as if she were just a hovering ghost.

"I'll be like this forever," she held out a hand to Eve.

## ❖ CHAPTER 35 ❖

Eve stopped pacing and stared at the hand. She held out her hand, slowly, to reach out for hers. When their fingers were about to touch, Eve's hand simply passed through the ghost's like nothing. "You aren't real?" Eve asked.

"If only this were just some nightmare." The ghost chuckled. "I can't do anything. I might as well be not real. I'm useless. All I can do is be conscious, I can't even sleep. I'm hungry. But I can't eat. I can't dream, or feel the cold. I'm numb. I just exist." She stared at her own hands, rubbing her ring finger, missing something. "If you could call it that…"

"Why are you here then? Wherever this is." Eve looked around.

"Titan. It's a moon of Saturn. Where my wife said…" the ghostly Sentinel choked on her own words, "Where she said she fell in love." The Sentinel took a deep breath and looked up toward Saturn. "I'm just holding out hope that maybe… if she's out there… it'd be here."

"She doesn't have a phlasma ghost," Eve struggled to swallow a lump in her throat.

"I know… *I know*." The Sentinel looked away. Her eyes were dry, but they were the eyes of a broken woman. "Just let me hope."

"I can't leave you like this." Eve stared into the Sentinel's eyes.

"You have to."

"Your Army needs you now more than ever. You can help, I know you can. Tomas told me that phlasma ghosts can interact with Celestial Beings, that's gotta account for something! Ultimae, he—"

"They need you, Eve. Not me. What can I do?"

"Be there at least. Just let them hope."

The Sentinel looked down at Eve. Eve could tell that she wanted to hug her, but knew she couldn't, not as a ghost like this. "I envy the Paradox Master. He got his peace. He got his time with you…"

"Then come with me, we can make up for lost time."

"I don't want to go back. I can't. This hurts enough. You can do this Eve; I know you can."

"I'm sorry but you're wrong." Eve stepped back. "I failed. And I'm not you."

"When have I ever been wrong?" the Sentinel asked.

"From what I hear, a lot, actually."

"When have I ever been wrong about you?"

"You never knew me." Eve shook her head.

## ❖ CHAPTER 35 ❖

"Then I've never been wrong about you. Let's see you show me that I'm right. Just this once. Remind Ultimae of who you are. Remind the Army of who you are. You're my daughter. Don't let them forget that."

"How do you know about me?" Eve asked.

A flash of light appeared near the Sentinel. Vaxx's purple replica of the box floated by her.

"I've been keeping watch. I know what's happening."

"Then why didn't you come help?" Eve asked.

"I can't leave here, in case—"

"She isn't coming."

"You don't know that!" the Sentinel yelled.

"I do. They never come back. Not really."

The Sentinel understood. She sat down on the cold ground of Titan. The purple box floated closer to the Sentinel, trying to nudge her, but it passed right through her. "Sit with me."

"I don't understand what we're looking for," Ganto complained.

Time elaborated, "Ganto, you Terri and Vogar will get on your ship in search of Eve."

"She could be anywhere! How do we even know she's in this time period!?"

Time lowered her head, even without a face Ganto understood she was giving him a condescending look.

"Right, okay."

Time continued, "Paradox Master, Nick, you two split off and search as well." Time gestured to Starlocke and Nick. She then turned her attention to Vita, "Life Master, I am sure you will be fine looking on your own."

Vita nodded.

"And as for you, Tempus girl," Time looked to Matrona, "You may stay with us, to stay safe."

Matrona nodded silently, sitting down next to Time.

"And what're you idiots doing?" Ganto asked Time and Celestae. "Sitting around doing nothing?"

"Ensuring the safety of the Multiverse," Time answered.

"So yes," Celestae agreed. "Sitting around doing nothing."

"At least one of you is honest," Ganto scoffed. "Alright crew, let's get a move on." Ganto gestured for Terri and Vogar.

## ❖ CHAPTER 35 ❖

Nick mounted Starlocke's saddle as Vita flew off through a wormhole she created. "Where do we look first?" Nick asked Starlocke.

"I'm getting distress signals from Illiosopherium 2," Starlocke answered.

"Okay." Nick patted the fur on Starlocke's neck, then lowered his head, ready to go.

"Nick!" Matrona called out.

Nick looked to her.

"Be careful," she said.

Nick nodded. Starlocke zoomed off into space like a lightning bolt. He and Nick quickly appeared on the surface of Illiosopherium 2, in the middle of all the pirate markets and stalls. "I don't see why Eve would be here," Nick commented with a hint of nervousness in his voice.

Starlocke walked around, his head making quick jolts back and forth, scanning his surroundings. His ears shot up at the same time as his tail. He lifted his front leg and pointed his nose forward in the distance. Though the stalls of the vast market spread as far as the eye could see, the pattern of tarps and poorly constructed shacks was interrupted by a large, destroyed building. The building was covered in tarps and surrounded heavily by stalls. It was covered almost as if to turn heads away from it, like it was supposed to be hidden, to hide the planet's past in plain sight, but Starlocke sensed something from within it.

"That's the Temple of Rogar," Starlocke recognized the deteriorated building even from underneath all the tarp and from behind all the stalls.

"Why would Eve be there?" Nick questioned.

Starlocke walked his way over, cautiously and slowly.

"*Onso esny lootk* Ilsose," Terri suggested to Ganto as the Freysent left Amalga-5's atmosphere.

"Why would we check Ilsose? Do you really think Eve's gone off to party right now? She isn't the Sentinel, get your head straight."

"*Menhal elle-iouln l'e-on Amalga-Sanon*," Vogar suggested.

"Vogar, we just left Amalga-5, are you suggesting we turn around?" Ganto complained.

Vogar shrugged. "*Menhal.*"

"I need more than a maybe." Ganto didn't turn around.

"Oo! Oo!" Terri raised his hand.

## CHAPTER 35

"Terri you don't have to raise your hand, just say it." Ganto saw him in a mirror on his dash.

"*Amar esny bie ilincacto oni* Modius!"

"Now that's a thought." Ganto smiled. "It would make sense if she were training there to be able to fight back, that seems like Eve."

"*Ore-elle-usj onno beyogon. Antintricano-es unt.*"

Ganto didn't respond to Vogar's input, still flying off towards Modius. Terri looked out the window, he knew better than to argue. "She wouldn't just run away," Ganto whispered.

"*U-exta kkar aboot elle. Lu-u nont?*" Vogar asked.

"Of course I care about her," Ganto answered. "She's my friend."

"*I ragno* Ilsians *did trie kar. Ethnout antilsia,*" Terri mumbled under his breath.

"Ilsians don't care, you're right." Ganto sped up the ship. "But I'm not like the other Ilsians, not anymore. I don't think I ever was. I'm not like Suriv, I care. I have emotions, why else do you think you guys are my friends."

"*Terno?*" Terri asked.

"Shut up, Terri, of course you're my friends." Ganto smiled. "You stupid idiots." The Freysent began to land on Modius.

Vita appeared somewhere else. She wasn't looking for Eve. She flew across the flat ground of Sanzi and landed near a pit. She waited for the ground to rumble and for Orso, Hive Two's hivemind, to resurface. When she did, she lowered her head to it in a show of respect.

"What brings you here, Master of Life?" Orso asked.

"How's the armor coming along?" Vita asked.

Orso smiled behind her chitin faceplate. She nodded as her five eyes closed. "Ah yes yes, very good. Very good indeed."

"We're going to need them very soon." Vita spoke nervously.

"I understand the urgency, but I can't make my drones work much faster. I can assure you though that the Sentinel's Army will be the first to be armored."

"Thank you." Vita bowed. "Have you seen Eve?" Vita asked.

"No." Orso shook her head, "Is she missing?"

Vita's silence answered Orso's question.

"Hmm. Well, I'll keep an eye out," Orso assured her.

"Thank you." Vita nodded and vanished.

## ❖ CHAPTER 35 ❖

Eve and the Sentinel sat, staring at Saturn in the distance. They had been sitting in silence for a while when the Sentinel broke it.

"I couldn't have asked for a better daughter."

"What?" Eve asked.

"But you really do underestimate yourself. You can do better than me. I know you can. But I can't leave this place, I'm sorry."

"Do I tell the others?" Eve asked.

"About what? That I'm still around? No. I don't want to give them false hope. There's nothing I can do."

"Sometimes it seems like there's nothing you can't do," Eve argued. "Just because you can't do anything doesn't mean…" Eve struggled with her words, "You can't… do anything…"

"Eloquently put," The Sentinel remarked, chuckling sarcastically.

"You know what I mean." Eve looked down and away.

"Goodbye, Eve." The Sentinel looked up at her.

"You're leaving?" Eve asked.

"You are. My Army needs you." The Sentinel stood up with Eve. "I'd hug you but…"

"You're a ghost."

"Yeah." The Sentinel smiled.

"Oh, and Sentinel, one more thing. Maybe reconsider staying here. Come back and spend some time with your daughters. Both of them." Eve stepped back and reached out for the box. "Goodbye."

The Sentinel smiled, "*Au revoir.*" She flicked her hand out in an awkward mix of a wave and a salute.

Eve smiled and flashed away.

Starlocke approached the old and destroyed remnants of Rogar's temple.

"What're you sensing?" Nick asked.

"Not Eve." Starlocke growled as he snuck into the building. "Show yourself!" Starlocke barked.

"Starlocke," a voice snaked around the temple. "An Original, nice to see."

"Show yourself." Starlocke shot his head up.

## CHAPTER 35

Rogar emerged from the shadows of the destroyed temple. "Don't get aggressive. I'm here peacefully." He floated before them menacingly, holding his arms up.

Starlocke lowered his head and growled, widening his stance. The stone in his forehead glowed brightly and shrieked with a charging beam of laser phlasma, ready to strike. Nick reached for his pistol and pointed it at Rogar with shaky hands.

Rogar held out his hands, "No no! What did I *just* say!"

"Why should we trust you!?" Nick yelled.

"Hey! Hey!" Rogar yelled. "Calm down! Hear me out!"

Starlocke barked.

"Relax!" Rogar yelled.

Starlocke paced around the room. Nick didn't lower his pistol.

"Hear me out." Rogar lowered his hands. "From the very beginning I set out to control land and expand my reign for my people. For the Gars."

"And you killed people in the process." Nick raised the pistol.

"Hey! The Sentinel fought in the same war I did, he did too. Listen! Let me finish!" Rogar held out his hands.

Nick lowered his pistol, ever so slightly. He knew where Rogar was coming from. Before Quinn, Nick was highly critical of the Sentinel. Maybe Rogar had a point.

"Ultimae came to me, promising me infinite land, infinite power. My own universe. He said I needed to kill the Sentinel and acquire the human harboring Time. When I slacked... Rhey came, and he... He made me slaughter my people. I thought I had killed them all, my entire purpose... and I couldn't stray from Ultimae now, I was in too deep. It became a fight for survival after that. I fight to keep at least the last Gar alive," Rogar gestured to himself.

Nick scanned Rogar's face, trying to tell if he was lying. Starlocke's forehead stone glowed.

"I want to redeem myself. I saw the Gar on your side..."

"Vogar," Nick elaborated.

"Yes, and I... *My people are alive.*" Rogar stuttered, on the verge of tears. "I want to redeem myself in my people's eyes. The Gars have spread across the lands of Amalga-5... across the lands born of Illiosopherium's corpse. The Sentinel fulfilled my own purpose, now I must fulfill his. I want to fight against Rhey, kill the man who tricked me into committing the

## ❖ CHAPTER 35 ❖

highest crime. The man who tricked me into slaughtering my people. And the Celestial Being who instructed that he do so."

"How do we know if you're lying?" Nick asked.

"I can't prove it to you by saying anything. You need to let me help you."

"I'm not the one you need to convince," Nick holstered his pistol.

"She's not here." Ganto stood out in the middle of a field on Modius. "This was a stupid idea."

"*Masi u,*" Terri spoke up.

"I don't care if I said it was a good idea, Terri! I changed my mind." Ganto crossed his arms.

Vogar stayed in the Freysent to keep track of the communication units. An incoming message beeped over the ship. "Calling the Freysent, we have an emergency, come to the mountain base." Vita's voice cut out and the ship hummed on.

"Ganto!" Vogar stuck his head out. "*Wu-ooo l'u git jnick!*"

"Why!?" Ganto yelled. "Did they find her!"

"*Wu-ooo l'u-y!*"

622

"Alright alright!" Ganto ran back to the ship and got into the pilot seat. Terri slugged along and crawled in just as the ship took off. The Freysent sped to the base of the mountain in Doxland, and landed right by Time and Celestae, standing outside the camp. Starlocke was there with Nick, standing before Rogar. Vita stood behind Starlocke for safety. Matrona cowered behind Time, her brow shaking and her face red with anger, her body shivering with fear. Ganto, Terri, and Vogar got out of the ship and ran up to the group. Ganto's hands were flared with phlasma, as were Vogar's.

"No, wait!" Nick turned around. "He's with us."

"*WHAT!?*" Ganto yelled. "Are you? What's-? *Huh?*"

Nick calmed everyone down and allowed Rogar to explain his situation again to everyone. Though the Army was suspicious, they needed any help they could get.

"How are we supposed to tell Eve this?" Vita asked.

"I know." Eve flashed into view. "The box told me what he said. I don't trust him."

"Why not?" Ganto asked.

"That may or may not be the single most stupid question you have ever asked me." Eve stared Ganto down. Eve looked up at Rogar. "I know Rogar's past."

"You killed me!" Matrona called out.

## ❖ CHAPTER 35 ❖

"I've never met you before." Rogar floated back.

"No. You have. Look into my eyes." Matrona stepped forward, away from Time, swallowing her fear, and standing strong before Rogar.

Rogar recognized almost immediately. "Matrona..."

"See? You do remember me."

"It was a tactical decision." Rogar held his arms up.

"You killed Kogar too, was that tactical!? How was I a strategic target? To traumatize the Sentinel? You're a monster!"

"I KNOW WHAT I AM!" Rogar roared, dark phlasma spewing from his nostrils. "This is not what I meant to be... I was mislead... I just wanted peace..."

The Army waited as Rogar caught his breath.

He continued, "As a deteriorating phlasma ghost I *am* going to die. I to die as a hero to my people. I want to redeem myself in the eyes of the Sentinel. Though he isn't here, the most I can do is redeem myself in the eyes of his daughter."

"*WHY!? Why do you care?*" Matrona stepped forward, her hands flaring with dark phlasma.

"*SARRANITH!*" Rogar yelled.

Eve stepped forward. She summoned a strike of lightning to silence the crowd. She looked up into Rogar's eyes. "She's alive. The Sentinel's ghost is alive."

"What?" The Sentinel's Army collectively asked.

Rogar's eyes widened. "*What...*"

"Well not... *alive* alive, but..." Eve shook her head and pinched the bridge of her nose. The Sentinel told her not to tell.

"I need to speak with her..." Rogar mumbled under his breath. "Let me fix this. Please," Rogar begged.

In the silence that followed, Time spoke up, "You can trust Rogar."

"Why would you have any reason to vouch for me?" Rogar asked. "You know my crimes."

"Though your means of protecting your people were strange, and your trusts misplaced, you had an innate drive to protect. Why is it that you needed land for the Gars?"

Rogar stuttered, "With all of the Gars in one place like that... Sogar threatened war with the Dragolupus... My people were in danger of a swift attack to take them all out. We needed to spread out... far... so we could persist. Earth was a prime target, and I regret that. But Ultimae pointed me in that direction and when I locked on, he wouldn't let me turn away.

## ❖ CHAPTER 35 ❖

I had to, for my people. And when my people perished, I had to survive."

"Rogar... have you wondered of your parentage..." Time asked.

"Often." Rogar nodded.

"Have you heard the rumors of the Sarran?"

Eve glanced at Time before turning her full attention to Rogar. Her eyes widened with realization.

"Of course I have," Rogar said.

Time nodded. "Your drive to protect does not fail you, not even after death. You are a Sarran. Eve," Time looked down at Eve. "You can trust this Gar, this Sarran, your family by phlasmatic blood, with your life."

"If you turn against us." Eve approached Rogar and held a pointed finger up to his face. "I will not hesitate to end your life."

"Deal." Rogar held out his bird like hand. Eve didn't hesitate to take it in hers and shake on it. Rogar looked around at the Sentinel's army, who were still eyeing him down and giving him nasty, untrusting looks. He looked to Eve. "Where is the Sentinel?"

"Titan," Eve answered.

Rogar nodded. He tossed out a portal sphere and stepped through.

"What now?" Nick asked.

Vita lowered her head as her feathers glowed.

From the skies above hundreds of Terror drones flew down, carrying Calcurus armor in their tentacles. They flew by and dropped off the armor for the army and flew away. One of the Terror drones remained.

"Thank you, Orso." Vita bowed.

"Good luck." the Terror blinked before flying off.

## ❖ Chapter 36 ❖
# Reunion of Ghosts

Titan was cold, even for a ghost. Rogar floated through the portal, and he appeared right by the Sentinel's side. He took a deep breath, not ready to see his old foe again.

"Rogar," the Sentinel greeted her former enemy with a calmness that could only be achieved by a woman with nothing left to lose. "I'm tortured enough, *why* are you here?" The Sentinel seemed to groan in a way that exuded *'of course.'* "Are you here to kill me?" she asked. "Once and for all? I don't blame you. I would welcome it, if we're being honest with ourselves. I'd thank you for it. You're a ghost, you have the ability to rip me from this universe before it collapses. You have the power to relieve me from this prison."

"I'm not here for that..." Rogar said.

"I get it, I'm a captive audience. You're here to laugh at me, then?" the Sentinel asked. "Because I didn't believe you. You said it yourself when you died, that if you died all this wouldn't be over. That I would be stopped and that the Extraverse would fall to the banished god. You came to say I told you so."

"You remembered?" Rogar asked.

"I didn't," the Sentinel said. "Not until I watched my wife die in front of me in the Extraverse. Before reality shattered and all hope was lost. When I came back from the dead that first time, I didn't want to think it but... My immediate thought... the very *first* thing that came to mind..." The Sentinel looked up at Rogar.

Rogar floated back a bit.

"It wasn't that Amara could be saved... that Matrona could be saved... That Kogar or anyone else could have a second chance... No. My first thought was *you*. It was just a brief flicker of fear... That you were right... That you could still be out there. So what? You aren't here to kill me?"

Rogar hesitated, staring into the Sentinel's hopeless eyes. He had never seen the Sentinel like this before, without hope. This wasn't the Sentinel he knew.

## ❖ CHAPTER 36 ❖

"No." Rogar said. "I'm here to fulfill my prophecy. I'm here to betray my boss. To get revenge. To set things right. To be the Gar I was meant to be from the start. I told Ultimae that I would use your image to trick your army into trusting me... I need you on that battlefield."

The Sentinel turned around. Her eyes black as the starry sky. "Why would I bend to your will? After all you've done..."

"Sentinel... you and I are the last Sarran. The two of us. We're dead. But our cursed existence serves us well. We have one more chance to be what we were meant to be."

"What?" The Sentinel sat up straighter.

"We, Time's secret children, were destined to protect this universe from her banished child, we were created for it. She needs us now more than ever. I need you, Sentinel. Help me correct my wrongs."

The purple box that floated by the Sentinel's side twirled over to Rogar and nudged into his shoulder.

The Sentinel stood up. Her ghostly dress flowed around her. She floated around Rogar. Slowly, she lifted her hand, and poked him.

She could actually feel it.

"Ghosts can interact with ghosts, no matter how weak or strong," Rogar said.

The Sentinel pressed her hand against Rogar. Rogar snaked his head back.

"Sorry…" the Sentinel took her hand away and shook it, holding her wrist. "I just… haven't felt anything in a long time…" It took every fiber of the Sentinel's being not to hug Rogar. She craved touch, from anything. She was starved of life.

She glanced at Rogar with conflicted eyes. Rogar floated away slightly. He held his wrist and wondered. He wondered how terrible it must be. To lose everything. *Everything.*

Vaxx's purple time machine bumped into Rogar again. Rogar looked down at it. "What is the meaning of this?"

"The speakers were damaged," the Sentinel said. "It can't explain itself. I think it's malfunctioned or something."

Rogar grabbed the box. It glowed. A panel opened.

The Sentinel flinched when Rogar took hold of the box, but continued, "Look, Rogar, I know we're in a weird place right now… But I can't trust you that easily. I can't throw away all that history we have and ignore it because the Multiverse is at stake. I want to protect it, I do, but I'm a

## ❖ CHAPTER 36 ❖

realistic person. I want nothing more than to protect what's left of this universe, but I know when my efforts are ill placed. I know when hope is lost. I know when we've lost. This is it. I'm not going to watch the Multiverse die knowing I died with it fighting alongside my enemy. I can't do that."

Rogar stared into Vaxx's time machine with an intense focus and curiosity. He looked up at the Sentinel. "Is there anything I could do to gain your trust? Anything?"

"I have nothing left," the Sentinel said.

Rogar shoved his hand into the box and quickly pulled something out with a clenched fist.

"Don't touch that! What are you doing!" The Sentinel stepped forward and punched Rogar in the arm. "That box is all I have left of her!"

Rogar opened his palm. In it... sat a rêve stone.

The Sentinel stepped back. "What... *No*... There's no way..."

"Is this what I think it is?" Rogar asked.

The box floated away from Rogar and spun toward the Sentinel. The Sentinel stared at it.

"Way back then, I made this box for Vaxx... I programmed it to save her life... whenever it could... at all costs... to keep her alive..." The Sentinel looked up at the stone in Rogar's hands.

"This is her, isn't it?" Rogar asked.

A ghostly tear dripped down the Sentinel's face. She shook her head and held her wrist. She rubbed her fingers over her ring finger. She stared at the stone and thought hard. She looked down at her translucent hand, staring through it. "I don't want to curse her with this existence..." she said.

"You'd rather her relive her dying moments forever in this stone?" Rogar asked. "This invention of yours has cursed her regardless. You have the option to free her from this curse and bring her into your realm," Rogar explained.

"You talk about this like you can do it," the Sentinel looked up to Rogar. "But you can't... Can you...?"

Rogar smiled. He closed his eyes and his bushy brows softened, curling in a sorry expression. Regret colored his reptilian face.

"I'm sorry, Sentinel. For everything I've done. I owe you my life, and more. Rhey wronged us both. This is the absolute least I can give you." Rogar bowed down. The stone in his hand glowed a bright white.

Ghostly tears collected in the Sentinel's eyes.

## ❖ CHAPTER 36 ❖

A phlasmatic white figure formed before her eyes. Sacrificing a brand-new body and solid existence like Rogar, an old familiar form appeared before the Sentinel, flickering weakly, just like her.

A starry phlasmatic dress covered the ghostly body of the revived Vaxx, who fell into the Sentinel's arms the moment she opened her eyes. She gasped for air, tears flowing down her face, her arms shaking with fear. "No!" she cried. "Make it stop! *I'm sorry...*" she muttered. "I'm so sorry, Sentinel. I'm sorry..." she cried. She looked around, fearfully. Her eyes darted back and forth and her whole image flickered and shivered.

The Sentinel hugged her arms around Vaxx with the strongest grip she had ever held. She clasped her hand behind her head and pushed her fingers through her hair. *She could feel.*

The Sentinel held her close and cried into her shoulder, "*Don't.*" she said. *"Don't you dare be sorry."*

Vaxx cried into the Sentinel's shoulder, holding her close. "*I'm so sorry... I didn't mean to... he made me...*"

"I know, Vaxx, I know," the Sentinel closed her eyes, pushing out a tear. She hugged harder, never wanting to let go.

"He's gone now," the Sentinel said. "You can rest, he's gone… I'm here Vaxx… I'm here…"

Rogar turned away and tossed down his portal sphere to leave Titan.

"Rogar, wait," the Sentinel looked up.

Vaxx turned around. Things were already confusing. She could barely see through the phantom tears floating in her eyes like they were trapped in space.

She had just lived through the torturous reign of Rhey on repeat in that stone.

Her mind bombarded with hatred and unrelenting sadness. And she was back, with the love of her life, her wife, the Sentinel, who was also dead.

They were both ghosts, and here stood before her the foe that once haunted them. The evil catalyst for the Galactic War. Also, dead.

Three ghosts, alone on Titan.

Vaxx stared. "What's happening?" she asked. "Are we dead? Is this…" she looked around. "This isn't Hell, is it?" she asked.

Rogar looked at them both. The tip of his rugged mouth turned up in a smirk.

## ❖ CHAPTER 36 ❖

Of all the times the Sentinel and Vaxx had seen Rogar smile, it was sly, cunning, dangerous. It induced fear, it meant something bad was bound to happen.

But this smile was different. This smile was joy.

The Sentinel smiled. "No," she said. "We're back." The Sentinel held Vaxx close. She glanced at her one more time before she looked back to Rogar. "We'll fight. Together."

Rogar nodded. "Let's do it right this time."

"Thank you," the Sentinel whispered.

Rogar floated through the portal as it closed.

Vaxx and the Sentinel were alone on Titan.

They stared into each other's eyes. The Sentinel held her hand to Vaxx's face.

They were dead. They were ghosts of their former selves. Her face was cold to the touch, but the Sentinel could feel it. She could feel her.

That's all that mattered.

Vaxx's mouth was kept agape in confusion, fear, shock and awe. She stared at the Sentinel with the widest eyes one could manage.

"You weren't supposed to die," Vaxx said.

The Sentinel laughed and closed her eyes. She pulled her head closer to hers and leaned her forehead against hers. "Neither were you."

"This is what Death meant by 'poof', right?" Vaxx asked.

"Yeah…" the Sentinel nodded.

Vaxx looked around. She twirled her fingers through the Sentinel's hair and smiled.

She glanced up at the imposing presence of Saturn in the sky above. The stars twinkled in her teary eyes as she looked back down at the Sentinel.

"Ah, well. We've got each other. It could be worse."

The Sentinel smiled. Vaxx wiped a tear off the Sentinel's cheek with her shaky hand. "I love you."

The Sentinel pulled Vaxx close, and they embraced in a kiss.

The two ghosts twirled around over the glassy ice of the Titan hills, dancing under the light of Saturn and the distant stars.

They were dead, but they were whole again.

❖ Chapter 37 ❖
# Before the Storm

Passive buzzing droned through the open fields at the base of the mountain.

Eve sat on a rock outside of the battle-damaged Camp Vistor. She stared blankly over the fields, admiring the sun getting low in the sky. Large prehistoric bugs buzzed by from time to time. In any other circumstance Eve would be entranced, or awed. Her mind was too clouded.

Fear lingered.

Andrew might want to brag about touching one of those bugs. They were huge.

Eve cried.

Soft pats followed Starlocke's paws as they pressed into the grass. He plopped down next to Eve and stared ahead with her.

♦ BEFORE THE STORM ♦

Ganto stood at the open door of the cabin.

Starlocke looked down to Eve.

"What are we looking at?"

She didn't respond.

Starlocke read her mind. He looked back out at the sun. He sighed and lowered himself to the ground, stretching his forelegs out in front of him and resting his head between them. He drooped his ears. "We'll get to see the sun again. I promise."

Ganto sat by Eve's other side.

"Karina said all the troops should be here by tomorrow," Ganto said. "I don't know how well they'll do against Ultimae, but I mean…"

"I don't want to talk about that right now," Eve said.

Ganto nodded.

He looked ahead out at the sun.

The three of them sat in silence.

Eve broke it, saying, "I don't think I've had a conversation that didn't have to do with all this fighting since before I had anything to do with it."

"That's how it goes with these things," Ganto said. "But it'll be over soon, one way or another."

The silence prevailed. Ganto slouched.

## CHAPTER 37

"I was a historian," Starlocke said. "I chronicled histories of many planets. I learned about their wars. I never anticipated that I'd be part of history."

"Let's hope our future has the privilege of being history someday," Ganto said.

Eve was still frozen in place, eyes locked ahead.

She said, "I think I need a hug."

Starlocke's ears perked up. He lifted his head.

Ganto looked at Eve.

She wiped away a tear. "It's been too long." Her voice wavered as if suppressing a bout of crying.

Starlocke stood up and walked in front of Eve. He lowered his head into her. She wrapped her arms around his fluffy mane and closed her eyes. Her tears were absorbed by his phlasmatic fur. A warmth surged through Eve as her muscles relaxed. She felt less tense. She chuckled behind a tear.

"Starlocke, are your hugs magic? Is there some sort of phlasma psychic power that makes me feel better?" Eve cried.

"It's called affection, Eve," Starlocke said. "The benefits you describe are common side effects among mammals."

Eve squeezed Starlocke.

Ganto held out his arms for a hug too. "I want in on whatever this affection stuff is."

"Ganto, I appreciate it," Eve sniffled as she wiped away a tear. "But your hugs are uncomfortable. You're a sharp little guy."

"Oh, that's okay!" Ganto smiled. He turned around and ran for the cabin, flinging his arms behind him. "I'll put on a sweater!"

Eve chuckled.

Starlocke pulled away. "Come on, let's get inside where it's cooler. You need rest for tomorrow."

"We all do."

Vita and Nick were out patrolling the perimeter of the mountain. They returned to camp when the sun had set. Nick opened the door, and Vita glided in with a quiet grace.

"Aw," Vita tilted her head. "Nick, look," she whispered.

Nick quietly closed the door.

Eve was asleep on the couch. Starlocke was curled up next to her, resting his head on her shoulder. Ganto's arms and

## ❖ CHAPTER 37 ❖

legs were spread out all over the place. He snored, buried under a very puffy blue sweater.

"Oh, that's precious," Nick smiled. He walked with quiet steps past them as Vita followed. "Ganto always looks ridiculous in his sweaters, though."

"I think it's cute," Vita said.

"The sweaters or Ganto?" Nick teased.

"Oh, shut up, Nick." Vita clicked her beak. She glanced back at the three of them asleep on the couch.

"Why are you staring, weirdo?" Nick asked.

Vita slouched a bit with her response, "Just in case," she said.

"In case what?"

"I don't get to see them again."

❖ Chapter 38 ❖
# Thrones of Time

Eve and the Sentinel's Army sat in a temporary camp at the base of Doxland mountain. The morning sun cast a radiant light on the dewy grass of the plains surrounding the mountain. Time and Celestae stood at the base of the mountain, waiting to draw Ultimae out. It would be any moment now before he would attack. Before he would attempt to apprehend his fellow Celestial Beings in order to wipe the Multiverse clean and start anew.

Armies from around Amalga-5, and allied planets, came to the mountain's base to aid the Sentinel's army. Help came in the form of Lorinian armies from as near as Ilsindi and as far as Misendi.

Ganto called upon the armies of Ilsose to aid in the fight, he called anyone with weapons, gangs from the city

## ❖ CHAPTER 38 ❖

underbelly, militias from rebel groups, and the cloud battalion floating above the city. Anyone with a fighting spirit followed their new King into battle.

Deusaves flew from across the galaxy to aid in reclaiming the Extraverse and ensuring the safety of the Multiverse. Every Dragolupus in the universe appeared, ready for the fight. Gars from around Amalga-5 came to their aid. It wasn't long in the day until Karina's army would show.

In the distance, over a hill, Karina showed herself, riding atop her raptor, Koda. Koda's intelligent, piercing yellow eyes watched over the army. It ticked its massive killing claw on the ground.

From behind Karina and her beast, hundreds of human-mounted Triceratops cleared the hill, honking and making their presence known. Their heads were heavily armored with a large plate protecting their neck and extending outward like a frill, each armed with three protruding horns and a sharp beak. Their bulky bodies swayed side to side like heavy organic tanks. Their short tails swung, and they dug their stocky legs into the ground, readying themselves.

Throughout the day, the armies were armored up in Calcurus-B, specially made for them by Orso's Terror drones, and a battle plan was set in place.

Karina and Nick planned a formation with the help of leaders from the various armies that came to help, occasionally checking in with Eve, Ganto and Starlocke for confirmation. Eve trusted their combined experience enough.

Some of the armies dug trenches. They set up turrets, called in tanks, and marked landing spots for Andromedan helicopter-like airships.

A nervousness bubbled in Eve's stomach. Sweat beaded down her forehead, and as the day marched on so too did her queasiness. Matrona stayed by her side. She knew what was to happen to her when the time came.

It wasn't long before night fell, though to Eve it felt as though an eternity had passed.

Orso sat curled like a massive snake around the camp, acting as a wall. She watched over the Army with her five eyes, keeping them safe.

The Army sat around a campfire, armored in their Calcurus garb. Eve rested her arm on her medieval styled helmet, leaning back on a rock and watching the fire smolder.

A large hadrosaur thigh turned over the fire as Ganto cooked it, wearing a self-made apron over his armor. Vita stood by his side, watching curiously, periodically fanning the flames.

## ❖ CHAPTER 38 ❖

Starlocke sat in the grass by Nick like a large, tired dog. Nick tousled Starlocke's fur, sliding his fingers on his head, calming him.

Terri slugged along among the army men. He wore an apron and a chef's hat and carried with him several trays of cookies. Vogar floated by him and helped him distribute the treats among the armies.

The armies of Nidus, Woestyn, Starwynn, Ilsose, and various Lorinian inhabited countries of Amalga-5; Deusaves, Dragolupus, Gars and Lorinians alike, all stood guard around the border Orso created. They stood by in their armor, protected by a wall of Orso's Terror drones, floating idly by, ready to strike, and Karina's dinosaurs, watching like obedient guard dogs.

Fireflies floated in the still night sky, blending in with the floating embers of the roaring fire. The relative calm of the night didn't mesh well with the feeling of dread in each member of the Army.

Eve looked up from her trancelike state staring into the fire because of the sound of Time and Celestae stomping their feet on the ground as the massive beings walked by and sat down in the grass.

The simple gesture made Eve smile. Seeing these godlike beings without their thrones resorting to sitting in the wet grass of a planet the Sentinel created, sitting calmly before a fire as their galactic faces were transfixed on the flame, an element that represented the most basic of inferno, the embers that flew up to meet the stars that they created. It put things into perspective, and Matrona sitting by her, seemed to have the same idea. They looked at each other, and chuckled.

"Why are you laughing?" a deep rumbling voice spoke beside them.

"Oh my god!" Matrona held her hand over her chest.

Eve jumped slightly, turning to see Rogar curled like a serpent by their side. He had returned from Titan the previous day, alone.

"Sorry, I didn't mean to—" he stuttered.

"No, I get it." Eve nodded. She couldn't keep eye contact with him. Her eyes drifted down to his hands. His fingers were folded in each other, he twiddled them nervously.

"Are you alright?" Matrona asked Rogar.

Eve looked at her strangely.

"Me?" Rogar darted his eyes at her.

"Who else?" Matrona asked with a smile.

### ❖ CHAPTER 38 ❖

"Why would you care about me? I killed you." Rogar looked away.

"Hey, water under the bridge." Matrona smiled.

"Why? I don't think you should forgive me. I'm not like the rest of you. I'm not good, I'm not—"

Eve interrupted, saying to Rogar, "Look at Ganto." She pointed ahead. Ganto lifted the cooked thigh from the fire and slammed it onto a plate. Vita nodded at him and pointed at the thigh with her wing, saying something to him about it that made him laugh. Eve continued, "A bounty hunter. A killer. He doesn't think twice before killing if it's for a good price. I don't even know how many he's killed."

"But," Rogar argued.

"And what about Agro?" Matrona added, looking away, saddened. "He was a clone that was the right-hand man to Canshla. He went on tons of missions against the Sentinel. He was part of a war that killed innocent people."

"I wasn't part of a war." Rogar shook his head. "I was the war."

"But look at you now." Matrona smiled and gestured to him. "You can't undo the things you've done, that's true, but you've realized, just like Ganto, and just like Agro did, what the right thing to do is."

Rogar couldn't keep eye contact with Eve or Matrona. "Right," he mumbled under his breath. "I hope so."

"Plus," Matrona continued, "I'm not about to die holding a grudge. Especially since you're here to fight for us. With us."

The sound of a horn blasted in the distance. It sounded two more times, drawing the attention of the entire army. Orso lifted her heavy head, her centipede like legs twitched. Matrona stood up. Rogar flapped his wings and the spikes on his head shot up. Eve clenched her fists.

### · BATTLE OF DOXLAND ·

Far across the battlefield stood a single Triceratops, and a man mounting it.

"What is it?" Karina yelled across the battlefield.

"A disturbance, Ma'am! The space here, it's—" before the man could finish his statement, a bright red phlasmatic crystal shot up from the ground and impaled the dinosaur that he mounted.

The creature let out a drawn-out groan, and the man atop the beast screamed, leaping off of the creature and trying to run away, unable to do so as a bolt of deeply red lightning

## ❖ CHAPTER 38 ❖

shot out from seemingly nowhere, and solidified in an instant, shooting through his body, and pinning him to the ground.

The space in front of him ripped and warped, shaking and sparking with energy as it opened like a portal.

The armies stood at the ready. In the frontlines, a wall of Krondicoraptors stood. Karina ran to her position. Behind them, Triceratops at the ready. Behind them, Lorinians and Gars stood at the ready. The Lorinians all shifted into their battle-ready, beastly forms. The Gars flared their hands to life with phlasma. Rogar quickly shapeshifted to match the appearance of the Sentinel. The Army was clued in on his plan to trick Ultimae into thinking he was betraying the Army.

Behind them a row of Terror drones sparked their tentacles at the ready, flanked on all sides by Dragolupus and hovering Deusaves.

Orso snaked between the armies in the forefront and the Sentinel's Army behind, waiting for the call to action.

The portal stretched open wide with a massive shockwave blast, tearing the sky before them. Ultimae crouched through the thin portal, his arms held out wide. Behind him hundreds of thousands of undead clones donning the Suppressor Helmets stepped forward, all armed with seemingly modified Andromedan weaponry. Ultimae's sword formed in his grip.

"I see you have brought a challenge for me today!" Ultimae announced. "What a surprise. Though you are not the only one with an army." Ultimae paced back and forth as more undead clones made their way from the portal.

Old, repurposed Galaxy War era Scorlions limped from the tear in space-time.

Suriv's tiny drone bots swarmed from the rift like angry spiders. Bigger ones joined them, stomping their metallic blade like legs into the ground. They differed from Suriv in their amped up artillery and bulkier build. Their aperture eyes readied themselves for laser fire.

"You are outnumbered," Ultimae announced.

Nervousness got the better of Eve. She had time to think since Rogar arrived. She changed her mind. Eve looked to Rogar. "Rogar. I need to turn you into a stone."

"What?" Rogar asked. "Why?"

"So that I can trap Ultimae in it. Only works if you're a ghost."

"Wait, Eve." Matrona held Eve's shoulder. "What are you doing?"

## ❖ CHAPTER 38 ❖

"I can't let you do this…" Eve stared into Matrona's eyes. "We're like sisters… You're what little family I have left… And I can't let Nick lose his sister twice."

"Eve, Rogar is a Sarran. You need him. I've already come to terms with my death. Let me do my part." Matrona grabbed Eve's hand and moved it over the stone in her chest. "Let me have a death that means something."

Nick was near them, mounted on his raptor, Starlocke by his side. Nick looked at Matrona, grief in his eyes. "Matrona…"

"Goodbye, Nick. Stay safe. Fight hard."

"I will." Nick nodded.

A tear dropped down Eve's cheek as she said, "I had fun, while it lasted."

Matrona laughed, looking away for a moment before she locked eyes with Eve. "I did too," she said with a smile.

Eve closed her eyes and concentrated, quickly turning Matrona into a rêve stone that now rested in her palm. She closed her hand over it tightly and turned her attention back to Ultimae.

Nick secured a Calcurus helmet on his raptor, then himself. He wiped away a tear and shook himself. His face was stone cold, serious.

Starlocke ran to the edge of a small ledge and howled. "Dragolupus! Attack position!"

Thousands of Dragolupus stood at the ready.

Ganto secured himself on a saddle over Vita's back. Vita launched herself into the air, cawing and screeching as she swooped back down to the ground, flying low with the terrain. Thousands of Deusaves followed behind her.

Hundreds of Gars' fists flared at the ready as they charged. Human soldiers lowered themselves into the trenches and manned the turrets. Ilsians and Lorinians joined them.

Celestae looked to Time fearfully. "We cannot let him get us into the Extraverse."

"How could he?" Time asked.

"Do not underestimate him," Celestae warned. "He has the means to trap us in stones. Do not engage."

"Are you suggesting we do not fight?" Time rose from her sitting position. "And here I thought you were the aggressive one."

"Please, stand down."

"The Sentinel's Army cannot handle this on their own," Time argued.

"Then you underestimate their power as well," Celestae said.

## ❖ CHAPTER 38 ❖

"Eve!" Rogar darted his head to her. "Good luck."

"Show him who you really are." Eve nodded, her eyes sparking with ice cold electricity. She ran as fast as she could ahead. Orso flapped her wings as she lifted from the ground, pushing air underneath her, pushing away the embers of the fire and snuffing out the flame.

"*ALLER!*" Karina yelled as a battle cry. The stampeding beasts rushed forward. The raptors sped ahead, zigzagging between each other. The Triceratops kicked up dust as they lowered their heads, aiming their spikes at the undead clones. The leading beasts' spikes glowed a deep purple as phlasma flowed through them.

In the darkness of the night the only light came from the lightning sparking at the feet of the dimly purple glowing Dragolupus that sped past the dinosaurs, and the dimly lit screens of the clones' helmets. The trailing white flames of the Deusaves were nothing compared to the ambient glow of the Celestial Beings themselves. Eve pushed herself into the air with strong blasts of electricity.

Wings formed at her shoulders and soon she flew alongside Orso, Rogar disguised as the Eighth Sentinel, and Ganto on the back of Vita. Airships flew alongside them.

Raptors leapt over the trenches.

Ultimae's Army stood ground, bracing for impact.

A Suriv drone fired the first shot, which exploded a Sentinel's Army turret.

Then fire rained.

The turrets bombarded Ultimae's army. The armed trench warriors fired away. The airships launched missiles. The Triceratops blasted phlasma from their horns, the raptors breathed phlasmatic flames like dragons as they quickly approached the undead clone army.

Eve's wings folded as she fell to the ground with her arm raised in the air, like she was winding up a punch. Solid phlasma formed around her fist as she neared the ground. Her feet hit the grass as her fist flung forward into the screen of a clone's helmet.

Vita flipped upside down as Ganto jumped from the saddle and launched himself at two clones, his hands impaling both of them. Vita's wings outstretched as beams of bright white inferno spiraled from them, burning clones on impact.

As the first clones perished, it was evident that something was not quite right. Dark phlasma trailed from their bodies as they died for a second time.

Rogar shapeshifted into a finch as to not be seen by Ultimae. He flew between the ranks of undead soldiers as if he

## ❖ CHAPTER 38 ❖

were in slow motion, dodging laser fire and jabs. He swooped between Ultimae's legs and landed on the ground behind him. He quickly shapeshifted back into the Eighth Sentinel. He locked eyes with Ultimae.

Ultimae saw him. "You have gained their trust?" Ultimae asked.

Rogar silently nodded.

"Betray them..." Ultimae ordered.

Orso hugged her wings to the side of her body as she dove to the ground, crashing between a large group of clones, burying them into the ground as she burrowed deep.

The rest of the Sentinel's army caught up. Dragolupus charged and leapt at clones, biting down on their necks and arms, and pushing them to the ground.

Explosions burst across the battlefield as airships fired away at Suriv drones.

A large Suriv drone folded its legs and launched itself at an airship like a rocket, then blasted through it, sending it falling to the ground.

That same Suriv drone landed in a trench.

"Fall back! Fall back!" an army man roared.

The drone fired lasers into the trench as a swarm of smaller drones filled in the trench and tore at the flesh of the army men with their knife-like legs.

Ganto rampaged, spewing phlasmatic flames every direction. He heard the screaming from the trench and jumped in to help. Starlocke zigzagged between the ranks, running over clones as he zoomed around.

Nick rode his raptor alongside Starlocke, firing off multiple shots from atop his mount.

Vita swooped in and out, slicing her wings against clones left and right.

Gars charged in and swept their tails underneath clones, knocking them off balance before bombarding them with flames, or sweeping them up in their mouths and chomping them in half.

Lorinians rampaged among the tanky dinosaurs and tossed clones around like ragdolls, pushing them into the air or stomping them into the ground.

Mounted and unmounted raptors alike pounced at Scorlions, imbedding their large sickle claws into their machinery. Some opened their mouths and breathed phlasma upon the battlefield, blanketing it with heat.

## ❖ CHAPTER 38 ❖

Karina's raptor charged at a group of clones intending to sideswipe them but was quickly caught off guard when one of Suriv's drones turned and fired a laser at the raptor, striking it in the chest.

It fell forward, and Karina stumbled from the beast, landing on the ground. She struggled to stand before the robots surrounded her with laser fire, and swiftly ended her life. Her screams echoed through the battlefield, and the Sentinel's army heard it, sending shivers up their spines.

The first major loss of the Sentinel's army was known.

Terri roared in his beastly form as Orso burst from the ground near him, diving over the clone army like a whale out of the ocean before slamming her body on top of the clones.

Deusaves fell from the sky and Gars phazed or died trying. Explosions from Calcurus grenades sent swaths of Dragolupus flying. Terror drones didn't last long in the heat of battle against the clones who had switched their rifles to stun.

The Calcurus armor was penetrated more easily than imagined by blasts of the same material from Suriv's robots, and soldiers were dying.

Ganto was sent flying through the air by an explosion. As he rolled across the burnt grass, a falling piece of ship debris crushed one of his legs.

"RAH!" he yelled.

Clones swarmed around him.

He blasted at them with all the phlasma he could muster, flinching as he did. He tried to pull his leg out from under the rubble, but it was well and truly stuck. The clones closed in. He couldn't stave off the laser blasts for long.

He lifted his arms and raised a wall of phlasma.

He tried to pull his leg from the debris.

A clone burst through the phlasma wall and pointed his rifle at Ganto.

"AH!" Ganto lifted an arm. A crystalline phlasmatic blade extended from it and he sliced down, cutting his leg from his body. "AHHH! *SHIT*!" he roared in pain as he rolled over and dodged a laser blast. He ripped the leg from the debris and threw it at the clone, distracting him for just a moment before he blasted at him with a fire ball. Vita swooped in and picked Ganto up, flying him away from the clones.

Starlocke stopped mid-battle to help a fellow Dragolupus stand.

"Come on," he said. "Don't give up."

"We can't stop him…" the Dragolupus groaned.

Starlocke shook his head. "Not with that attitude."

## ❖ CHAPTER 38 ❖

A Scorlion tail shot past Starlocke and impaled the heart of the injured Dragolupus.

Starlocke growled and snapped his head around, a fire burning in his eyes. He blasted the Scorlion with a concentrated phlasmatic laser. The Scorlion retaliated with a tail strike. Starlocke did his best to dodge, but the tail spike lodged itself in his ribs.

Starlocke howled in pain. He bit down on the tail and tore it from the Scorlion's robotic body. He ripped it from his flesh and sent a burning blue electricity through the metal. He swung his head around and stabbed the metal beast in the neck with its own spike. The electricity infused in the tail spike shut the beast down. Starlocke limped away.

"I'm injured," he projected the thought into Eve's mind.

Eve ran between the death and destruction, watching as beasts were torn to shreds by dark phlasma, as clones killed themselves in the heat of ripping raptors to shreds with their phlasma, or shooting at a charging Lorinian even seconds before it headbutted them.

Eve shook her head, and kept running. "Walk it off," she said as she continued running.

Starlocke heard her voice, even across the battlefield. He closed his eyes as he lowered his head. "I'm afraid it's bad." He looked to the wound. A trickle of light blue blood dampened his fur.

"Don't die on me," Eve said as she kept running toward Ultimae.

"I'll try not to," Starlocke said. He lifted his head, and opened his eyes. They glowed with fierce phlasmatic power. "And if I do…"

Eve ran ahead, tears in her eyes. The battlefield was too much.

Starlocke opened his mouth and panted like a dog. "I'll walk it off." He zoomed forward and tackled a clone, killing it instantly.

Eve smiled, but stopped dead in her tracks when a ghostly aura passed her by. "Wait a minute…" she mumbled.

The clones weren't dying. They were becoming true phlasma ghosts.

Their phlasma ghosts were floating over the battlefield, headed directly for Time and Celestae.

Eve held out her hand and blasted at a passing ghost clone with a burst of phlasma, but the ghost passed by unaffected.

## ❖ CHAPTER 38 ❖

They can't interact with the living world, and the living world can't interact with them. But they could harm other ghosts... or beings similar in structure... like the Celestial Beings; Time, and Celestae. They were in danger.

"Time!" Eve called out.

Time punched forward with her fist and crushed a ghostly clone as it approached her. But more swarmed in.

The more clones the Sentinel's Army killed, the more they lost, but the more they let live... the more they lost.

In the distance, the glowing red of Ultimae's body signified Eve's true target. If she could stop him now, they could worry about the ghosts later. Matrona's stone glowed in her closed fist. She ran faster, cold lightning sparking at her feet as she did. She needed to be faster. Clones had begun firing at her and she couldn't escape it.

An armored raptor ran by her side, rider already mounted. She outstretched her arm and swung herself onto it, speeding ahead at Ultimae. Nick was the rider, leading the raptor to Ultimae.

"Eve?" Nick turned to see his new passenger.

"Just ride!" Eve yelled.

The raptor dodged laser fire, and as it approached a clone, snapped down on its helmet, crushing it and the head within, then kept running. A downed Lorinian tumbled in the grass ahead of Eve, sliding before the raptor. In a quick course correction, the raptor held out its winged arms and used them to make a quick sharp turn, avoiding the tumbling corpse of the massive beast, and continued running after Ultimae. The raptor stopped before Ultimae. Eve jumped from the raptor and stood before him.

"Stand down!" she yelled.

Ultimae chuckled and stopped fighting as the war raged on around him. A Deusaves dove to his head. With the snap of Ultimae's finger, a red bolt of electricity shot from the galactic shape in his head and struck the Deusaves down in an instant.

"Do you think war is a foreign concept to me? That the battleground is not painfully familiar? I have destroyed cities in an afternoon." Ultimae rose his arm as a spike burst from the ground.

Eve jumped out of the way. Nick's raptor ducked down and closed its eyes, summoning a crystal phlasma wall to protect itself and Nick. Eve looked up, fear in her eyes.

"I was in a freshly comparable situation to this before, child." Ultimae reached out his hand and grabbed Eve by the neck, raising her up into the air.

## CHAPTER 38

"Eve!" Nick reached his hand out. He couldn't do anything.

"*Ultimae—*" Eve choked on her words. She grasped Matrona's stone in her hand like her life depended on it, not letting go. She held her hands up to her throat to try to catch one more breath. It was hard to keep her fist closed, but she had to.

"Say my name." The galactic spiral in Ultimae's head wavered and glowed with anger. "Every galactic cluster with the misfortune of holding life in it has had a guardian to protect it." Ultimae tightened his grip. Eve's vision blurred, her breathing grew painful, she knew she only had moments left to live. Her hand loosened its grip, Matrona's stone started to slip. But just then, a mechanical flash.

"None of them fortunate enough to have the help of *me!*" A dark flaming fist struck Ultimae in the face.

He let go of Eve. She fell to the floor and turned around, grasping the stone in both her hands. Floating before Ultimae, above Eve, was hope.

The Sentinel, and Vaxx.

"*No…*" Ultimae stepped back.

Vaxx and the Sentinel charged forward with flaming fists and struck Ultimae in the face. The galaxy in his head flickered.

"Sentinel!" Eve yelled.

Ultimae stumbled and pointed at the Sentinel and Vaxx. "*Destroy them!*" he instructed his clones.

The ghostly clones charged after the Sentinel and Vaxx.

They stood together, back-to-back, fists aflame. Vaxx turned her head to the Sentinel. "Whatever happens, I love you."

"I'm not losing you again," the Sentinel said.

An army of ghostly clones closed in on the Sentinel and Vaxx. They fought off the first few, but soon were buried under a pile of the clones.

Time and Celestae saw what was happening. Time stepped forward. Celestae grabbed her by the arm. "No. It is not worth the risk."

Time turned around. "I know what must be done. We cannot lose the Sentinel again. Karina of Canam was right. I am the strongest being in existence. I should fight. We could win." Time pulled away from Celestae and charged at Ultimae.

"TIME!" Celestae jumped forward.

## CHAPTER 38

Time charged into the fray, and with a swing of her arm, she launched a mass of ghostly clones off of the Sentinel and Vaxx. Her glowing blue fist flung forward and struck Ultimae in his face, flinging him to the floor. Eve rolled out of the way and watched in awe. She remembered her place, and stood up to join the action.

Ultimae launched himself back to a standing position. Ignoring Eve, he launched his hand forward and tried to grab Time's head. Time dodged and pushed her hand into his back. Her arm shifted with its blue phlasmatic form and shot through Ultimae like a fluid blade. He groaned in pain, but pushed through, stepping back with red flaming hands.

A blast of black electric phlasma pushed Ultimae back. The Sentinel floated over Time's shoulder. A bright burning white concentrated beam of phlasma blasted from Vaxx's palm as she pushed Ultimae back too.

Time lifted her hand and retaliated with a wave of blue fire.

Starlocke zoomed in and lowered his head. A laser blasted from his forehead and struck Ultimae in the knee, pushing him to the ground. Ultimae held out his hand in front of his head to stave off the intense fire he was under. Terror drones surrounded Ultimae and shocked him with lightning.

Ganto and Vita swooped in and blasted Ultimae with fireballs. Vogar roared his phlasma breath down upon the Celestial Being. Celestae helped from afar, raining fire down upon Ultimae.

Eve rose and held out her arms. Cold lightning shot through the ground and up through Ultimae's arms and legs, tying him to the ground and keeping him in place. The galaxy in his head flickered.

The Sentinel and Vaxx floated down to either side of Eve.

"You can do this," the Sentinel said.

The bombardment of beams, flame, and electricity stopped. Ultimae shook himself. His image flickered.

Time lifted her arms, shifting her fists into spikes. She jabbed forward, stabbing through Ultimae's head, causing his galactic shape to flicker more intensely. Ultimae kicked forward, pushing Time back. He stood up and swung forward with a punch, at the same moment that Time did. Their fists collided and a shockwave burst around them, pushing over clones and Sentinel's Army's allies alike.

Thunder blasted in the mountains and bright blue and red lightning struck down in the battlefield of chaos. The bolts fought for dominance in the night sky. Time held Ultimae's

## CHAPTER 38

shoulders and kneed him in the face, pushing him back and holding out her hand, bombarding him with bright blue crystal shards that shot through his body and head, pinning him down into the ground.

"Go, Eve! Now!" Time yelled.

Eve ran ahead, launching herself into the air, and holding out Matrona's stone in her hand. Before she could reach Ultimae, he outstretched his hand. A shockwave of invisible energy rippled over the battlefield. Eve froze in midair. Ultimae's sword appeared in his other hand.

"Eve, no!" Time yelled. She lunged forward, passing through Eve, now standing before her. Time held out her hands and was about to send a wave of time freezing energy to stop Ultimae in his tracks, but she was too late.

Ultimae shoved his sword forward, stabbing the blade through Time's head. The tip of the sword lay mere inches before Eve's head as she floated there. She watched as the galaxy in Time's face flickered and and was absorbed into the blade.

"No... NO!" Eve yelled, her whole body flaring with phlasma. She was helplessly trapped suspended in air. She could do nothing more than watch.

"Oh god…" Vaxx floated back. She held her hand over her mouth. The Sentinel held her close.

The crystals pinning Ultimae down disappeared just as Time's body did, absorbing into the blade of the sword, causing it to glow a deep blue.

The Army stopped its fighting and stared in awe as Time's body vanished, and a bright blue rêve stone formed at the end of Ultimae's sword.

A silence fell over the battlefield. A bright white Deusaves flew overhead, screeching. It's one metal wing shone in the night sky, and it turned its owl face to Eve with sorry eyes. The Deusaves was Strix, the Bird Before Death.

Eve stayed floating in air, helpless and afraid, shaking and trying desperately to break free. Her fingers sparked with electricity; her eyes flared with a purple flame. She screamed and screamed, her veins popping, trying desperately to move.

Ultimae rose from the ground, admiring his sword, and Time's stone dangling from its handle. The stone shook and pulsated, swinging around as if Time were trying to break free from within. It sparked with tiny electric bolts. The stone wouldn't hold her for long, but for the moment, Time was trapped.

## ❖ CHAPTER 38 ❖

The clones lifted their weapons as the armies surrendered, and the Sentinel's Army raised their hands and lowered their weapons.

An army of ghostly clones surrounded Vaxx and the Sentinel.

The dinosaurs and their human riders were far and few between. The Lorinians numbers severely cut. The Deusaves and Dragolupus stood by hopelessly, and the Gars were near gone.

"Brother!" Celestae yelled.

"Stand down!" Ultimae yelled back across the battlefield.

Rogar lifted his hidden form and shifted back into his Garish self. He slithered his way to Ultimae.

Eve gave him a look of confusion, bordering on hatred, when she caught a glimpse from him that she couldn't shake. He was afraid.

"Traitorous bastard!" Ganto yelled at him.

"Ganto!" Eve snapped. She tried to hush him.

"I'll kill you!" Ganto limped forward, then kicked his jetpack into gear and launched himself at Rogar. Ultimae lifted his hand and turned his head toward Ganto.

"Ganto!" Eve clenched her fist and blasted Ganto with a short burst of phlasma, pushing him to the ground. Her blast pushed him out of the way of a devastating, strangely silent, red lighting burst from Ultimae, that instead hit the ground.

Eve gasped for air as she was freed of her time freeze, and fell to the ground with a thud.

The bolt of red lighting didn't act normally. Instead of fading away and leaving a burn mark in the ground, it stayed, almost frozen in time. Eve stared at it in fear. Ultimae snapped his head to look back at Celestae.

"Brother do you not see what you have done!?" Celestae yelled. "Without a master over time what will keep the Multiverse in check!?"

"Do you forget my purpose!? I will break the Multiverse by any means! And when it is gone and replaced, there *will* be a master over time, and it will be *me*!"

The blasting sound from the lighting strike echoed through the air, much later than the strike occurred.

"You have broken time." Celestae shook his head in disappointment.

The red lightning bolt reappeared, and absorbed itself. The battlefield shook as time reversed.

## ❖ CHAPTER 38 ❖

"Do you forget my purpose!? I will break the Multiverse by any means! And when it is gone and replaced, there *will* be a master over time, and it will be *me*!" Ultimae repeated himself.

"And break it you have," Celestae shook his head. He perceived the redoing of time.

"What the…" Eve looked down at her hands.

"You will not make it to the Extraverse," Celestae said with a somber tone. "You cannot."

"What makes you say that?" Ultimae asked. Time froze and reversed slightly. "What makes you say that?" he asked, again.

Celestae gestured his head forward. "Them."

Ultimae turned around and was faced with the entire Army pointing their weapons or standing in an attack stance toward him.

Eve, the Sentinel, and Vaxx, stared him down, their eyes glowing.

Suriv, Foxtrot, and Rhey sat in the Extraverse waiting for Ultimae and Rogar to return. Foxtrot and Rhey had been discussing what they would do with the new Multiverse, how they would use their universes and all the fun they could have. Suriv was getting annoyed and hoping for Ultimae's swift arrival when he noticed something.

"Oh great," he grumbled to himself. The Calcurus armor that usually covered him was lowered, and his mangled Ilsian self was visible, staring into a dark cloud hovering before him.

"What is it?" Foxtrot asked, adjusting his position in his and Rhey's throne.

"Ultimae just turned Time into a rêve stone and I think... broke time itself?"

Rhey shot up in his seat, startling Foxtrot. "Sorry," he comforted him, and turned his attention back to Suriv. "That's our shot then? He's going to win, there's no way he won't."

"What's Rogar up to?" Foxtrot asked suspiciously.

"He's fighting by Ultimae's side, he's betrayed them already," Suriv observed.

"Who's he fighting?" Foxtrot asked, admiring his hands. "The Sentinel's Army? Or the nobody warriors tagging along?"

"Does it matter?" Suriv asked. "What are you getting at?"

## ❖ CHAPTER 38 ❖

Foxtrot slid off of Rhey's lap and walked over to the floating dark cloud. Rhey's animated face shifted to one of curiosity, and he got off his throne to follow Foxtrot.

"What're you thinking, Foxy?" Rhey asked him.

Foxtrot stared into the cloud with judging eyes. "He's avoiding core members of the Army," he took note, "And watch... do you really think the face of the Galactic War would struggle in a fight? That he wouldn't kill with ease? Look at him get pinned down by a Dragolupus just long enough to push him off of him and then not go for the kill... He's stalling..."

"Should we let Ultimae know?" Rhey asked.

"Let him come back. I want to see how Ultimae deals with him." Suriv shrugged. "Could be interesting."

"Get the stone!" Eve yelled to Starlocke as he ran past her. Ganto was busy tearing clones to shreds while Orso commanded her drones to swoop in and aid in the fight. "We need Time back!"

"On it!" Starlocke barked. He leapt at Ultimae, instantly regretting the decision when he saw his massive red hand coming in for a backhand slap. Starlocke tucked himself in for a roll when the hand swept past him.

"Starlocke!" Nick called out. He turned his raptor to run toward Starlocke for aid, but with a blast of red lightning cutting off his path, an explosion launched him from his raptor.

Nick went flying.

"NICK!" The Sentinel swooped in to catch Nick, but he passed right through her.

His body hit the floor rolling as Starlocke locked his jaw around the handle of Ultimae's sword, tearing it from his grip. He skidded across the grass and turned his attention to Nick's limp body on the ground. "Nick!" he yelled, running after him.

Nick groaned.

Ultimae leaned forward and grabbed Starlocke by his tail, flinging him far off into the sky and retrieving his sword.

"Vita!" Ganto yelled to get her attention. Vita swooped in and picked Ganto up, slinging him onto the saddle. She flew off toward Starlocke.

Ultimae pointed his sword at Eve.

Eve held up her arms as her hands sparked with electricity. She directed the bolts toward Ultimae, but they didn't make it far before freezing in place. Time seemed to be

## ❖ CHAPTER 38 ❖

getting more unstable as the battle waged on. Vaxx swooped in and tackled Ultimae's wrist, pinning his arm to the ground.

"Eve get the sword!" Vaxx yelled.

Eve stumbled back as time pushed through her. Her eyes rolled back into her head as a sort of vision seemed to play itself out. She witnessed Vaxx, holding onto Ultimae's wrist with impressive strength, only to be grabbed by his other hand and disintegrated. Her eyes rolled forward again as she stumbled.

She looked at the Sentinel with fear in her eyes. The Sentinel had seen it too. The Sentinel pushed forward with a blast of phlasma that knocked Vaxx off of Ultimae's arm.

Just then, Ultimae swung forward with his arm to grab his own wrist, missing Vaxx. Red phlasmatic energy disintegrated his own hand.

"Agh!" Ultimae groaned. He stumbled back and his hand grew back.

"What…" Vaxx rose from the floor, breathing heavily, eyes wide with fear.

"You cannot do anything to stop me!" Ultimae roared. He turned to face Celestae watching from afar. "Is this what you wanted?!" he yelled, "The only way to stop me is to fight me yourself!"

"Don't do it!" Eve yelled. "That's what he wants!"

"I know!" Celestae acknowledged. "I am truly sorry."

"What?" Eve whispered to herself, not knowing what Celestae would do.

Celestae's form shifted from a humanoid figure into a floating orb containing his galactic spiral. He spun around and flew up the mountain toward the Gateway.

Ultimae shifted his focus from Eve and to the Gateway.

"Celestae don't!" Eve protested. "He'll win!"

Ultimae's sword vanished as he too became an orb of energy and followed after Celestae.

Rogar saw his boss fly away and he turned from the battle to follow after him.

Thousands of thoughts flooded Eve's mind. She didn't know what to do. Her phlasma powers barely worked with time being broken, she couldn't think straight, and all seemed lost.

"Eve watch out!" Nick groaned from afar.

Eve turned around and was met with the end of an Andromedan rifle pointed at her face. Her hands flared. The clone fired and the blast exploded in her face. Just then, time reversed, and Eve had remembered. She dodged before the clone could fire. She reached for the gun and snapped it out of

## CHAPTER 38

the clone's hands. She pushed forward with the butt of the rifle into the clone's Suppressor Helmet screen, shattering it.

The clone, now stunned, couldn't fight back when Eve swept her leg behind his and knocked him to the floor. She split the rifle into two pistols and fired rapidly at the clone before she tossed the pistols aside and swung her arm up and with the clench of a fist, caused a sharp rock of phlasma to shoot from the ground and through the clone's chest.

The ghost of the clone was launched from the corpse when the crystal burst through, but it was swiftly taken care of by a blast from Vaxx.

Eve ran to Nick, who had been groaning on the ground for some time. "Are you alright?" Eve asked as the Sentinel and Vaxx floated to her side.

"Yeah." Nick grimaced. "I think my legs are broken, I'll be fine." His raptor lowered its head to Nick, inspecting him. It pushed its snout to Nick's head, clicking its mouth open and closed like a bird, concerned.

"I'll get you out of here." Eve reached for the box floating by her shoulder and held it to Nick's chest, attempting to flash away.

"I'm afraid I can't do that," the box chimed.

"Why not?" Eve asked.

"Time traveling now would be like driving a car over a road that's on fire. Time is broken," the box explained. "It wouldn't be safe." The box shivered a bit as a tiny shockwave flooded the battlefield. "Time is broken," the box repeated itself. "It wouldn't be safe."

"Dammit." Eve stood up. "Orso!" Eve yelled. "Get him to safety!"

Terror drones swooped in and surrounded Nick.

"No, I can help," Nick argued, "Let me help, please."

"I'm not letting more of the Army die because of me." Eve shook her head.

The Terrors slid their tentacles underneath Nick and used their mind manipulation to keep him calm as they lifted him into the sky.

"If you let the Multiverse die, I'll kill you!" Nick joked as he was lifted into the sky. His raptor ran underneath and followed him.

"Yeah have fun trying that!" Eve smiled. She looked up at the peak of Doxland's mountain and had a troubling thought.

She turned around and looked at Vaxx and the Sentinel floating before her.

## ❖ CHAPTER 38 ❖

"Stay here. Don't help us fight. You guys deserve time with each other."

"Eve..." the Sentinel floated in. "We have to fight. If you lose, the Multiverse is destroyed. We would die anyway. We might as well die doing something useful."

"And together," Vaxx added. "Though, I would like to not die again."

"Are you sure you're gonna be okay?" Eve asked.

"I'm the Sentinel," the Sentinel assured her.

"But Rhey is up there."

Vaxx stumbled back, gasping. She held her head and fell to the ground. The Sentinel caught her and held her face, trying to calm her. "Vaxx! Are you okay?"

"He's supposed to dead!" Vaxx growled, shivering and shaking with anger and fear.

The Sentinel held Vaxx close. "We can't go up there," she said.

"No." Vaxx stood up. "We're going up there. And I'm gonna kill that son-of-a-bitch."

Starlocke zipped into view near her as Vita swooped in with Ganto clinging to her back. Terri stomped his way over to the group as Vogar slithered in. They all looked up at the mountain ahead of them.

Red lighting crashed in the night sky, the stars burned red, and the shatter glowed, enticing them to come and fight the decisive battle. One last go.

Eve patted Starlocke on his helmet and mounted his saddle. Starlocke flinched as his armor pushed into his wound, but he shook his head and looked up with a determined face. They were off to climb the mountain, while remaining Dragolupus, Gars, Deusaves, Lorinians, and Orso fought off the dwindling clone army.

## · BATTLE FOR THE THRONES ·

When Ultimae and Rogar arrived at the mountain's peak Celestae was nowhere to be seen. Frustrated, Ultimae shifted back into a humanoid form and summoned his sword, swinging it around angrily and smashing it into the snow and nearby boulders.

"Sir," Rogar spoke up.

The shattered boulders reformed themselves as local time reversed.

"I am so close!" Ultimae bellowed, "And yet he keeps me from what I want. Every time."

## ❖ CHAPTER 38 ❖

"We could wait in the Extraverse for him. He can't be out for too long, and soon the lack of functional time will take its toll and they will come to us, to the Extraverse, timeless, where it is stable."

"You may be right," Ultimae admitted. He made his way to the Gateway and stepped through the pulsating shatter. Rogar hesitated before slithering in.

"Well, if it isn't the lizard man himself." Rhey's screen lit up brighter as the smile stretched. "Did you enjoy your vacation?" he said with a sly voice.

Foxtrot stared at Rogar suspiciously as he floated behind their throne.

"So, what's the plan, man?" Suriv casually asked Ultimae.

"We wait for them to come to us. With Time as a stone and Celestae in the Extraverse I will have free reign to restart the Multiverse, no matter the number of Emissaries I have so long as the headcount in the Extraverse meets five. You can die if you so please," Ultimae plucked Time's jittering stone from the sword and admired it in his hands as it desperately shook, "Though I have a feeling we need that Eve girl and her allies dead before we can get some peace and quiet to do what we must. And to make matters worse… The Sentinel and her wife have joined in the battle against my ghosts, which has proven to be quite the annoyance."

Foxtrot sat up straighter. A shiver ran up his spine. "The Sentinel and Vaxx are alive?"

"No, though they are not much better dead," Ultimae grumbled.

Foxtrot looked to Rhey. His face lost what little color it had, his eyes wide and his palms clammy.

"What?" Rhey asked, confused about Foxtrot's sudden shift in mood.

"But I will rid this Multiverse of their presence when Celestae enters this realm. We need not kill their army, only hold them off until my plan can be executed, then they will have no choice but to surrender." Ultimae slouched down on his throne. "Now we simply wait."

Foxtrot's head stiffened. He felt his ear and squinted, "They're here." He shook his head and slid off Rhey's lap.

Starlocke stood in front of the Gateway with Eve on his back while Terri, Vogar, Ganto, and Vita watched from in front of them. Terror drones had escorted them up the

## ❖ CHAPTER 38 ❖

mountain, and they now floated around them, watching for threats.

One of the drones flew by Eve and spoke, "Ultimae's Army is dwindling in numbers. Should I send you some back-up?"

Eve nodded, "On my word, you can send in the armies."

The Terror drone acknowledged and floated back.

Vaxx and the Sentinel stood off, conversing with themselves. They were happy to be able to touch and feel. They may be dead, but they had one another. They held their hands, floating across from each other. The Sentinel looked into Vaxx's eyes.

"One more chance. That's all we have."

"It's all we need." Vaxx smiled.

The Sentinel looked to Eve and nodded. They were ready.

Eve smiled. She had no family left. But as she looked around at the remaining Sentinel's Army, she knew she had a reason to fight. A return to normalcy was out of the question, but she had a family in the Sentinel's Army. She had found a strange new normal. She had to do anything to maintain that.

Eve held her helmet in her arms, and straightened her posture, clearing her throat. "When we go in there," she exclaimed, pointing to the Gateway, "some of us may die. But I saw what losing looks like. I felt what our loss could bring.

"We are not fighting for any of your planets, or your people, not for the galaxy – not for the galactic cluster even – not even the universe. We are fighting for every single living thing in every universe spanning the entire Multiverse. There are beings living out there in this universe, and others, that don't even know that they're in danger. They don't know that we're about to save them. But we will, and they will know about us. They will hear what the Sentinel's Army accomplished to save them, and they will immortalize us.

"I will let it be known, that *we* were the saviors of the Extraverse. Vita, the Deusaves from Nidus. Starlocke, the Dragolupus from Modius." Eve patted Starlocke's neck, "Vogar, the Gar from Illiosopherium. Terri, the Lorinian from Loron. Ganto, the Ilsian from Ilsose, Orso, the hivemind of the Krantharnic's second Hive." Eve looked at the Sentinel and smiled. "The Sentinel, from New York. Vaxx, from Canada Prime, and Matrona," Eve held up Matrona's stone, "and *me*... The Sentinel's daughters."

### ❖ CHAPTER 38 ❖

"And for those who helped us along the way," Ganto added. "Vistor, the King of Ilsose. For Andrew and Laura."

"For the Tempus family." Eve put on her helmet.

"For Modius," Starlocke bowed his head, "The last Quodstella."

"For Janistar and its people," Ganto added.

"For Morty." Vita bowed, "The Death Master and my friend."

"For the Sentinel, and everyone that died for the Sentinel's Army." Eve nodded.

The Sentinel looked away and held Vaxx close to her, closing her eyes as she lowered her head on hers.

"Let's go."

Starlocke turned around and jumped through the rift, Vita with Ganto on her back, Terri, and Vogar followed. The Terrors floated around the Gateway to protect it. The Terror drones bowed as the Sentinel and Vaxx floated through the rift.

"How can you tell?" Rhey asked Foxtrot how he knew the Sentinel's Army arrived. He looked to the rift for answers.

"I hear them." Foxtrot answered. "If they kill you again, I'm gonna be pissed."

"They won't." Rhey comforted Foxtrot. "I'll make them feel pain beyond suffering. We can watch them die together. It'll be fun. We'll make an evening out of it." Rhey stood up and massaged Foxtrot's shoulders. "They can't touch us, not now. We're a powerhouse, you and I."

"Yeah." Foxtrot stared ahead at the rift.

"Are you wishing you accepted my offer to join me all those years ago?" Rhey asked.

"A little," Foxtrot admitted.

Rhey chuckled.

The rift warped itself. Suriv formed the shell of his suit around himself and stood from his throne, ready to fight. Ultimae sat up straighter.

Starlocke shot through the rift and skidded across the Extraverse floor, positioning himself and Eve directly in front of Ultimae's throne.

Eve and Rogar shared a glance with each other.

Vita, Ganto, the Sentinel, Vaxx, Terri, and Vogar came through the rift and took their places around Eve and Starlocke.

## ❖ CHAPTER 38 ❖

Vaxx caught a glimpse of Rhey that shook her to her core, but when she saw Foxtrot, a different feeling overcame her.

"Fox?" Vaxx yelled.

Foxtrot couldn't look Vaxx in the eye.

"What are you doing here?"

"He's with me now, hon. You're a married gal, you shouldn't be jealous," Rhey said.

"I'm sorry," Foxtrot said. "I didn't know you would come back."

"We were friends..." Vaxx whispered. The Sentinel squeezed her hand and tried to pull her away. "How dare you?" Vaxx pushed out her words behind gritted teeth.

Foxtrot didn't say a word.

"We can make this easy, Ultimae," Eve interrupted the tension and addressed Ultimae. "Cut to the inevitable, or you could make it a fight."

Ultimae stepped from his throne. "Can you not see that I have already won?" He held out his arms to gesture to the entire Extraverse. "You would have to be blind."

"Time isn't dead!" Eve yelled. "You can't kill a Celestial Being, we can bring her back!"

"Did *she* tell you that?" Ultimae laughed, gesturing toward the stone in his hand. "You *can* kill them... but she would never kill me. She is not that harsh."

"You're lying." Eve shook her head.

"Am I?" Ultimae's galactic spiral glowed as a portal opened up behind him. The brightest light Eve had ever seen shone through the portal.

The Sentinel's Army stumbled back.

Ultimae held Time's stone in the air.

"What is that?" Eve asked of the portal.

Vita answered, "A portal to Black Star 7, a phlasmatic star."

"A what?" Eve asked.

"A core of phlasma that can destroy even the most perfect rêve stone."

Ultimae held the shaking stone in his hands. Blue light seeped through his glowing red fingers as Time tried to break free from her shackles. Ultimae flicked his fingers, tossing the stone like flipping a coin.

"No!" Eve held out her hand. Time slowed down to a near complete halt as the stone left Ultimae's fingers and flew through the air.

"Eve, no!" Starlocke barked.

### ❖ CHAPTER 38 ❖

Eve jumped forward, fingers sparking. Phlasma extended from her arm almost like an extension of her being, trying to grasp onto the stone. Wings spread at Eve's back as she launched herself toward the stone.

Ultimae reached out and clasped his hand around Eve's waist. Eve's hand wrapped around Time's stone. She grabbed it. Her hand was through the portal, scorched by the proximity of Black Star 7's licking flames. Ultimae started to pull her away.

The portal closed.

A flash of light exploded and flooded the Extraverse with white. The portal snapping shut blasted a shrieking sound through the void as it sliced Eve's arm clean off, taking Time's stone with it, and disintegrating both into the fires of the burning star.

A blue shockwave burst through the Extraverse. Ultimae tossed Eve away from where the portal once was. She collapsed onto the ground, rolling across the floor of the Extraverse.

She stopped and leaned on her knee, throwing her helmet from her head, tossing it aside as it clanked across the Extraverse. She held what was left of her arm above the elbow with her hand. Bright white and blue flames from the star lingered on her wound. Eve groaned, crying in pain as what was left of her arm was consumed in bright burning flames. In her remaining hand, she kept a tight grip on Matrona's stone.

The shockwave that pushed through the Extraverse pushed everyone back. A ripple of blue sent shivers up their spines. A deafening silence followed as realization fell upon the Sentinel's Army.

Rogar flinched, ashamed.

The Sentinel covered her mouth in shock, fear, and realization.

Ultimae felt a burning sensation in his head, his galactic spiral spun wildly and pulsated. Flames burst from his body, and he screamed with anger.

Celestae stood outside the Extraverse, where he fell to his knees by the shatter, surrounded by Terrors. He too felt the pain burning in his head, and blue-green flames burst from his back and hands. He looked up. "No…" The galaxy in his head twirled and shifted with anger as his body darkened.

Back in the Extraverse, Ultimae clenched his fists and inhaled deeply, the flames subsided and the galactic shape in his head slowed back to normal, he shook his head. "Ahh," he sighed, "I can *feel* the freedom. *Time is dead. I* am the Time Master now. No longer will the Thrones of Time reign, say hello to the Thrones of Ultimae, and witness the Multiverse... *reborn.*"

The Sentinel's army backed away.

Eve looked up, tears in her eyes. Her curly hair covered her face, dripped in sweat. Ganto held himself up with his arms by Eve's side, holding her close. Starlocke limped in front of her, protecting her. Eve's eyes flared with hatred. She breathed heavily, holding herself up with her one remaining arm. Resting on her knees, she pushed herself up. Matrona's stone glowed furiously in her hand.

Ganto held onto her, "Don't push it, Eve."

"Agh!" Eve groaned. She stumbled, standing up all the way. She looked up at Ultimae.

Outside the Extraverse, Celestae weighed his options. If he were to step in and help, he would run the risk of allowing Ultimae to restart the Multiverse with him in the Extraverse. He conjured a surveillance cloud before him and watched the inside of the Extraverse.

A tear streamed down Eve's face. She held tightly onto Matrona's stone. She stood straight and lifted her chin up, closing her eyes and taking a deep breath. The pain stabbed through her whole body and mind... but she was used to the pain.

She looked at Ultimae. Her hand sparked with cold electricity as Starlocke's eyes glowed.

All six of Ganto's hands burst into flames as Vita's feathers flared themselves.

Terri widened his stance and showed off his beastly muscles and horns, growling at Ultimae. Vogar's spikes shot up threateningly as his eyes glowed.

"You are merely minor obstacles in the way of my guaranteed success," Ultimae said confidently. He was waiting for Eve to bring in Celestae, not knowing that she wouldn't.

Eve took in a few deep breaths, then looked to the nearest Terror drone. She pushed through the pain, saying behind gritted teeth, "Send in back-up."

The rift struggled to open enough to allow in what was left of the armies of Deusaves, Gars, Terrors, and Dragolupus pouring into the Extraverse.

"Nothing to a god." Ultimae widened his stance, ready to fight. The blade of the sword appeared in his grasp.

Rogar closed his eyes. It was his time to strike. Rogar yelled. His tail flared with phlasma that quickly solidified itself into crystal. He jabbed his tail forward as it shot itself through Rhey's helmet, splattering blood onto himself and Foxtrot.

## ❖ CHAPTER 38 ❖

"NO!" Foxtrot yelled as if he had been struck by Rogar's tail himself.

"Rogar?" Ultimae turned his attention.

Rogar slid the tail out of the helmet and shook it off. Rhey stumbled forward.

"YOU MONSTER!" Foxtrot screamed, his voice cracking. Starlocke charged ahead toward Suriv. Eve leaped and her wings blazed as she flew toward Ultimae. Her one hand tightened into a fist that surrounded itself with hardened crystal phlasma, sparking with electric ice.

Starlocke bit down on Suriv's legs as Terri headbutted Suriv over and over trying to knock him down. Vogar charged at Ultimae to help Eve. Vita flew up into the air as Ganto spewed flames down from above over the thrones, surrounding Ultimae. The armies bombarded him with everything they had.

Several Gars flew after Ultimae's throne. They ripped it apart, tearing it to the ground. While the Gars ripped the thrones to shreds Rogar turned his attention to Foxtrot.

Rhey's helmet had shattered, falling to the ground. His head was visible, Rogar's tail had only scraped his scalp. Foxtrot could see the stitches holding Rhey's head to his neck. Rogar stared into Rhey's white, cloudy eyes.

Rhey whipped his arm forward and held his other hand to his head. Black lightning shot from his fingertips and wrapped around Rogar's head.

"GAH!" Rogar groaned as he fell to the ground. His vision faded as his memory played back to him. All of his people, slaughtered by his own hand, cannibalized and betrayed by their leader, and behind it all, Rhey. Rogar shook his head as the lightning bounced back to Rhey. Rhey shook his hand in confusion. Rogar roared and stared Rhey down with glowing yellow eyes. "You've made a mistake... angering me."

The Sentinel and Vaxx floated to Rogar's sides. They stared Rhey down, eyes glowing with anger.

Rhey stumbled back, staring at his hands. "I win," he said. "There's no undoing what I've done. You might as well succumb to Ultimae now, It's your only chance of survival."

"I don't want to live with what I've done. What you made me do," Rogar growled. "And you're wrong. My people are alive, they persist. The most I can do is ensure their survival, and your demise."

"Arlo, move!" Foxtrot pushed Rhey out of the way as Rogar flicked his tail outward, impaling Foxtrot in his chest with his crystal black phlasma encrusted tail.

## ❖ CHAPTER 38 ❖

Rhey held out his hand to Rogar once more and screamed with so much pain and anger, it seemed for once that something actually had affected him. He was in genuine pain, for once in his life as Rhey, Arlo shone through. "HOW DARE YOU!" Rhey screamed.

Rogar rose from the floor and snapped his arm forward. Rogar's outstretched clawed hand quickly impaled Rhey's chest. He watched as the life drained from his eyes. Quickly, however, Rogar realized Rhey wouldn't die so easily.

His phlasma ghost shot from his lifeless corpse, and it passed right through Rogar, making its way to Vaxx and the Sentinel.

Rhey held out his hand. Black lightning burst at his fingertips, but Vaxx was too fast.

"RAH!" Vaxx shot her hand out. Ghostly, gaseous, white phlasmatic flames twirled around her arms and coalesced into a blade that shot through Rhey and curled around him like a snake.

The Sentinel held out her hand, pointing it at Rhey like finger guns. She fired away with phlasmatic lasers, bombarding his ghost with black fire and death.

Rogar watched, the reflection of the light twinkling in his eyes. He was mesmerized.

"AHHH!" Vaxx screamed. Her back flared white as phlasma wings sprouted from her shoulders. Her hair floated in a ghostly tangle as she pushed forward with all her might, her eyes, bright twinkling stars.

The Sentinel shot out a similar blade of phlasma, black as night, her eyes darkened, wings sprouted from her back as she pushed forward with all her might.

Rhey's ghost burst, and faded away into nothing as it was ripped to shreds.

Vaxx and the Sentinel calmed down, and looked at each other.

"We did it…" Vaxx smiled.

"You got the wings." The Sentinel smiled ear to ear with delight.

Suriv rotated his chamber toward Rogar and blasted at him with a laser. A Dragolupus from the army jumped in front of the laser and took the hit, stumbling to the ground.

With the distraction to Suriv, Terri successfully knocked over the massive suit. Hundreds of Deusaves flew in to hold Suriv down and keep him from getting back up. "You bumbling buffoon!" Suriv yelled. He shot out a leg from his suit, impaling Terri.

## ❖ CHAPTER 38 ❖

Ganto turned his head as quickly as Vogar had. "NO!" they yelled.

Ganto and Vogar saw the downed Ilsian and charged at him without a second thought, ready to break through the armor and rip the Ilsian inside to shreds without any hesitation.

Dragolupus surrounded Ultimae at his feet as Eve flew before him. The plan was for the Dragolupus to keep him still as Eve reached for his forehead to turn him into a stone, but Eve hadn't anticipated the extent of Ultimae's power.

Ultimae's body glowed with a bright aura, when his body condensed into nothing more than a glowing red sphere surrounding the galactic shape in his head. He flew past Eve, the dark red phlasma trailing behind him like the tail of a comet as he did. He stopped across the Extraverse, away from the armies, as he returned to his normal form. "You cannot contain me!" Ultimae yelled. "You fool!"

The Dragolupus charged across the Extraverse to attack Ultimae again, not giving up. Ultimae kicked at the Dragolupus attacking his feet. He raised his sword and swung at the Gars flying in to attack. He raised the blade and sent bolts of red lighting blasting at the Deusaves holding Suriv down.

Eve raised her arm and shocked Ultimae's fist, breaking his grip on his sword.

"AH!" Ultimae exclaimed as he swung a fist at Eve, launching her down to the floor.

Deusaves fell from above and littered the Extraverse. Rogar, Ganto, Starlocke, Vita, as well as Terror drones that had just entered, and the rest of the Army desperately tried to stop Suriv and penetrate his layered Calcurus shielding.

The sword that Eve had disarmed from Ultimae vanished, only to reappear in Ultimae's hand. He lifted it above Eve, "Nothing you can do can stop me. NOTHING!" Ultimae yelled as the blade flared with the space ripping flame.

A blast of lightning shocked Ultimae in the face. The Sentinel and Vaxx floated up to him, ready to attack.

Ultimae quickly turned around and lifted an arm and blasted the Sentinel with a beam of concentrated red phlasma. The Sentinel vanished in a puff of black smoke, which trailed along like a flying snake through the air, between Ultimae's legs, then reappearing behind him.

The Sentinel and Vaxx attacked Ultimae with opposite beams of phlasma on either side of him.

Suriv was knocked to the ground again as his legs collapsed. He fell near the rift, and suddenly, the head of Orso

## ❖ CHAPTER 38 ❖

popped through the rift, and smashed itself onto Suriv. Calcurus armor hitting Calcurus armor chipped Suriv's casing enough to drop the mouth door. Vogar flew by and grabbed the Ilsian from within and dropped him to the floor.

Suriv seemed to have built cybernetic legs for himself so that he could stand outside of the suit. He lifted his remaining arms to fight. Ganto slid off of Vita's back, and landed in front of Suriv. His antlers sparked like electricity, now appearing as a tree of lightning, seemingly frozen in place. Ganto stood on his arms and one remaining leg. He glanced at Terri, who was bleeding out beside him.

Terri nodded. He opened his mouth to speak, barely managing to say, "*Len ino...* F- Friend..." The life drained from his eyes.

"You killed my king, and my friend," Ganto muttered behind tears before he charged forward. Suriv and Ganto interlocked antlers.

The Army switched their focus to Ultimae as Ganto and Suriv fought.

Ultimae retaliated with a wall of red fire. He transformed into an orb again, using the wall of fire as cover to swiftly eject himself from the Sentinel and Vaxx's advancements.

He reformed himself into his standing form, reaching out his arm as he transformed, just in time to grab hold of Rogar's tail. He slammed him into Rogar's own throne, smashing it. "You betrayed me!" Ultimae yelled. "How dare you!" As Ultimae yelled, the galactic shape in his head flickered. The fighting had weakened him.

The Sentinel and Vaxx skidded next to Eve.

"You betrayed me." Rogar spat. "You had it coming."

"I will not hesitate to kill you."

"Do it." Rogar smiled with broken teeth. "And hey, maybe the prophecy was right after all, huh, Ultimae?" he hissed. "The Gar that cheats death *will* fall on the winning side in the end."

"AHH!" Ultimae screamed as he lifted his sword.

The Sentinel raised her hand, and a burst of ghost-like energy, similar to the puff of smoke that Death once used to grant immortality, passed through Rogar, and the wave of energy pushed Ultimae away, causing him to drop his sword. Vaxx flew by and absorbed the energy that blasted out of Rogar.

Ultimae turned around and faced Eve.

Rogar gave the Sentinel a look of confusion and gratitude. The Sentinel nodded.

## ❖ CHAPTER 38 ❖

Ganto flung his head up, launching Suriv away, smacking him into his armor. Vita swooped in and ripped one of Suriv's mechanical legs from his body. She tossed it at Ganto. She then wrapped her talons around Suriv's body and threw him into the air.

With a swift raise of Ganto's arms, a phlasmatic lightning bolt appeared in the air above Suriv, and slammed into him, launching him into his Calcurus suit, and impaling him on the same leg that killed Terri.

"Ha!" Ganto yelled. He spit on Suriv. He held up his mechanical leg that Vita has tossed him. He nodded at Vita.

The armies that had come to help were mostly dead, but those who remained stood around Ultimae angrily.

Rogar lifted from the ground, staring at his hands.

The remaining Dragolupus, Deusaves, Gars and Terrors fought Ultimae off with the help of Eve and the Sentinel's Army. Rogar continued staring at his hands. He looked up.

They couldn't win this on fighting alone. Ultimae was too strong.

Vogar had the same idea. He approached Rogar and whispered something in Garish in his ear. Rogar looked up at him.

"A distraction won't work," he said, in Garish.

Vogar nodded. "This one will," he responded in their native tongue. "Trust me."

Rogar closed his eyes and took in a deep breath. "*Make him think he's won...*" Rogar whispered, almost as if convincing himself the plan would work.

The Sentinel floated behind Eve as Ultimae drew his attention to them. The Sentinel stood by her side, encouraging her, "You're so close."

Ultimae held out his arm and blasted the Sentinel with a concentrated beam of red phlasma, catching her off guard. As the beam subsided however, the Sentinel remained. Ultimae stumbled back in confusion.

The Sentinel's eyes were closed. She held her arm over her head in a last-ditch effort to protect herself. She opened her eyes to see that a green shield surrounded her. Tomas' old orange box had shown up to protect her.

"What!?" Ultimae yelled.

With the distraction, Vogar slapped his tail behind Ultimae's knees, knocking him off balance.

Eve held out the stone, but she wasn't ready.

A blue-green fist punched Ultimae across face.

Celestae stood in the Extraverse.

"No..." Eve stood back.

## ❖ CHAPTER 38 ❖

"You killed Mother!" Celestae yelled. "How could you!"

Fear covered the Sentinel's face. "CELESTAE, *NO*!"

Ultimae turned around, withdrawing his sword. "AH!" he yelled, swinging it down, just missing Celestae's head.

"Celestae, what are you thinking!?" Vita yelled.

The Sentinel and Vaxx flew up to Celestae and pushed at his shoulders. "GET OUT!" Vaxx yelled.

"WE'RE SO CLOSE!" the Sentinel screamed.

"AH!" Celestae pushed forward. He turned into an orb and passed by the Sentinel and Vaxx. He reformed and punched Ultimae in the face.

Ultimae kicked him back, then held his hands together and pushed out, and in a quick blast he froze Celestae in place. "WATCH ME, BROTHER!" he yelled. "Watch as I wipe the slate clean!" Ultimae floated up, his feet lifted from the ground and he held out his arms.

Vogar glanced at Eve, he lifted his bushy brows. He gestured Ultimae, then mimicked his pose and nodded furiously, dically pointing to himself.

Eve ed to Ganto and Starlocke by her side, dread in her eyes.

Starlocke and Ganto caught a glimpse of Vogar and looked back at Eve, nodding in agreement.

"After all this time!" Ultimae yelled. "I can finally have what I want!" He raised his arms further, and a projection of the vast Multiverse formed in front of him.

The armies stared in fear at Ultimae, waiting for the final blow that would mean their demise.

Before he clenched his fist and destroyed every universe, he turned to face Celestae. "Thank you, brother, for allowing me to win. I will favor you greatly when the work is done. We will rule together."

Celestae struggled to lift his head, but as he did, he said, "You're welcome. I'm just doing what's right." As he spoke, his form shifted. It wasn't Celestae. Rogar took his place, with a sly toothy smile stretching across his face. "*Sarrinith*," he hissed.

"What?" Ultimae snapped his head back to the projection.

"NOW!" Eve yelled. She launched herself forward, pushing herself up with a burst of electricity.

Ganto blasted himself from the ground at the same time Starlocke did, the both of them locking onto Ultimae's arms. Eve pushed into his chest with her legs, flapping her electric

### ❖ CHAPTER 38 ❖

wings to continue her momentum, pushing forward as Ganto and Starlocke pushed down, knocking Ultimae to the floor, and crashing him into his throne.

Eve held her only arm out, pushing Matrona's stone to his forehead. Her wings flapped constantly to keep her balance and push her down, keeping Ultimae on the floor.

They all struggled to keep Ultimae down while Eve's hand and Matrona's stone glowed on his forehead.

"AGH!" Eve and Ultimae both screamed, Ultimae's red phlasma fusing with Eve's sparking blue cold electricity.

Ultimae thrust his arms forward, launching Starlocke and Ganto into the air. They landed far off in the Extraverse, rolling over. Eve stumbled over, unable to balance on her one arm. Matrona's stone was stuck in Ultimae's head. He lifted his hand to rip the stone out.

Tendrils of red phlasma protruded from Ultimae's chest and wrapped around Eve's arm, tying her to his body, and stopping her from lifting her hand to his head.

Eve's wings vanished as she used all her strength to try to pry herself from Ultimae.

Vaxx and the Sentinel flew in, pinning down Ultimae's arms, stopping him from grabbing the stone and keeping him down.

"You can do this!" the Sentinel yelled.

"Go, Eve!" Vaxx said, pushing with all her might.

Vogar helped Starlocke and Ganto up, and they ran to Ultimae to keep him down.

Vita flew in and pushed against Ultimae's legs. It took the might of the Army to keep him down.

Eve's arm was still restrained. She couldn't reach out for the stone.

Cold, stinging electric ice stung at the burnt remnants of her missing arm. A blue starry phlasma as bright as Time's extended from her severed arm.

A ghostly phlasmatic arm reached out.

Ultimae's galaxy pulsated and brightened like a frantic beating heart.

Eve reached her blue burning phlasmatic hand out and slammed it down on the stone.

The phlasmatic fingers pushed into Ultimae's glowing red head as his galactic spiral shattered and flickered. Eve screamed with a final push, her eyes glowing with a bright blue intensity. Her arm fused with Ultimae's being as red snaked through the phlasmatic arm, taking over the bright blue as Ultimae fought back with what little spark he had left in him.

## ❖ CHAPTER 38 ❖

Blue ice-cold lightning crackled from Eve's eyes and shot into Ultimae's head, fighting with his pitiful counter barrage of red sparks.

Eve's fingers pushed through Ultimae and wrapped around the stone lodged in his head. She pushed her phlasmatic fist through his head, into the center, holding the stone inside his galaxy. She screamed. Ultimae flickered and jolted with a flinch.

With a bright flash of light an explosion shattered the very air of the Extraverse. Like broken glass the stars fell, leaving the Extraverse pitch black.

A silence suffocated the room.

Chaos vanished.

Eve fell to the floor, her phlasmatic arm flickered as it grasped a stone. She tried to hold herself up with it, but it vanished in a cloud of purple, letting the stone fall to the floor, just as she did.

The Sentinel and Vaxx floated to her, unable to hold her and help her up. Rogar fell from his time freeze. He floated over to them, nodding knowingly, then helped Eve up. Starlocke and Ganto ran to her side and helped her stand.

"Are you okay?" Ganto asked. "Eve?" His voice wavered.

The silence prevailed.

Eve could hear nothing but her own breathing and heartbeat. A few silent sparks lingered at her fingertips and at her scarred severed arm. Her heart pounded in her chest faster than she believed possible. She blinked; her eyes calmed as the electricity dissipated. She breathed out when she laid eyes on the stone that fell from her ghostly arm.

A single, dark red, glowing rêve stone lay on the ground. It pulsated angrily, shaking on the ground like an upturned beetle. Cold electricity lingered on the stone.

Eve sighed and held her chest. Her eyes rolled back into her head, and she collapsed.

"Eve?" Ganto limped to her and held her.

The Sentinel's Army all turned their attention to the flickering, shaking stone, and Eve on the floor.

Starlocke's third eye glowed. "The pain consumed her. Her body can't take it."

One of Orso's Terror drones flew by and touched a tentacle to Eve's head. It used mind manipulation to calm Eve, and reduce her pain, easing her awake.

The shatter in the Extraverse warped as Celestae stepped through. A surveillance cloud floated by him. He

## CHAPTER 38

dissipated it and looked at Rogar. He gave him a quick knowing nod.

Rogar smiled.

It took only a brief moment for the armies to realize that they'd done it. Those who survived didn't know what to think. Celestae stared at the stone, and he knew. Eve had done it.

They won.

"Is this it?" Starlocke asked.

Tears streamed down Eve's face and she shook her head. She pushed herself up. The Terror had calmed her, but her heart was still pounding, her head with it, she couldn't process that it was over.

It was finally over.

Celestae knelt down on his knees. He reached for Ultimae's stone and held it in his hand. "My mother and brother…"

Eve wiped her tears and looked quizzically at Celestae.

"Gone…" Celestae whispered.

The Army stood by, silent.

"What will you do with Ultimae's stone?" the Sentinel asked.

Celestae looked to Eve. "Matrona wanted to die for a cause. To rid existence of Ultimae."

Eve nodded, wiping away a tear. "Let her be free. Kill him."

Celestae clenched Ultimae's stone in his hand. Celestae stood up. His galactic spiral shifted and glowed as a portal opened up next to him. He held Ultimae's stone in his hand, staring at it.

The Army waited in anticipation.

A glowing starry tear dripped from Celestae's face. His image darkened.

"I'm sorry," Eve said. "Can you do it?" she asked.

Celestae knelt down and presented the stone to Eve. "Please," he said.

Eve stared at the shaking stone for just a moment. A brief hesitation had lingered in her mind. She tossed the stone into Black Star 7, and the portal closed.

A red shockwave burst across the Extraverse. Members of the Army stumbled, but did not fall.

Celestae shifted with red energy just for a second. He held his hand to his chest and declared, "He is dead... And... I guess he got part of what he wanted... A new Extraverse is born."

## ❖ CHAPTER 38 ❖

The Dragolupus that remained lowered their heads, their forehead stones glowing, before they raised their heads and howled in unison, their voices swimming through the air and intertwining in an angelic chorus.

Starlocke joined them.

The Deusaves and Vita sang too, like distant songbirds.

Vogar, Rogar and the rest of the Gars hummed in a deep growl.

Orso closed her eyes as the Terror drones that remained glowed and shone like distant stars, humming passively. Gars escorted their dead from the Extraverse. Deusaves flew theirs out too.

Rogar, the Sentinel, Vaxx, Ganto and Starlocke, escorted Eve out of the Extraverse. She limped out, flinching, and wincing at the pain of her severed arm. They held her and let her rest on Starlocke's back.

"Rest now, child," Starlocke said.

Eve closed her eyes.

"Rest now, for history will forever remember you."

❖ Chapter 39 ❖

# The Empty Throne

Starlocke walked across the golden grassy beach of Starwynn, with Eve by his side. She limped; her whole body ached. A glowing blue arm swung by her side, replacing what was once there. Red twirled around like snaking vines in the blue. Eve held her remaining arm. It was scarred with patterns of interlacing lightning. The scars left trails of ghostly bleached skin.

The box floated by her side.

Starlocke's side was bandaged heavily, and he walked alongside Eve with a subtle limp. Though he held his head high with pride.

Ganto wore a blue knitted sweater, with 'Time' sewed onto the front, alongside a little galaxy. He rode on Starlocke's

## ❖ CHAPTER 39 ❖

back, and Vita was perched just behind him, resting her tired head on his shoulder. She wore a knitted scarf.

Ganto's leg had been replaced, using the leg he had stolen from Suriv. Etched into the metal of the leg were the words, 'Vistor and Terri, may they rest in Lorinian heaven, or whatever.' He straightened the crown on his head and sighed.

Nick sat in a wheelchair that he controlled. His raptor walked alongside him. It would occasionally lower its head to check in on Nick, making sure he was okay.

The Sentinel and Vaxx floated just behind Eve, hand in hand, and Celestae marched behind them, with Rogar floating calmly at his side.

Pterosaurs soared through the sky, cawing like birds. The sun was rising, casting a golden orange light over the tall golden-brown grass and tan sandy beach.

"So, the Extraverse isn't in a very stable place right now, huh?" Eve asked Celestae. "It's just you, Vita, and Starlocke now, left to clean up the mess."

"We need five Emissaries," Celestae said. "Before things grow too unstable."

"I guess now would be the time to let you know that I'm stepping down, then," Vita announced. "If you would be so kind as to allow me."

"What?" the Sentinel looked to her.

"Birdie over here needs to get a life," Ganto said. "She's been missing out on a whole Multiverse of fun. I thought I'd show her around."

"That brings you down to two Emissaries, then?" Eve turned around and walked backwards. She looked up at Celestae's towering figure.

Celestae looked around at the heroes that surrounded him. "All of you changed everything. You saved us all. I am eternally grateful for your sacrifices, and your contributions." Celestae looked to Eve. "You have shown unprecedented amounts of power, Evelyn." Celestae knelt down in the grass. The galaxy in his head pulsated ever so slightly. "Will you join us in protecting the Multiverse, as Phlasma Master?"

"Isn't that your job?" Eve asked.

"I now carry the burden of Time Master."

Eve looked away. She didn't know how she felt about taking on another huge responsibility. But with the largest threat to the Multiverse eliminated, it seemed like a safe, secure bet to take. She looked up to Celestae.

"While we're on the subject of making changes..." Eve glanced at Starlocke. "I don't think it's fair that my friend here

## ❖ CHAPTER 39 ❖

has to stay a slave to keeping the Multiverse alive. He shouldn't be reduced to glorified life support."

"You have a suggestion for a replacement then?" Celestae asked.

"Rogar," Eve said.

"What?" the Sentinel looked to her.

Rogar straightened his posture as his brow twitched.

"He did the right thing in the end but that doesn't change all the wrong that he did. He should pay for his past in the only way I think works. Make Rogar the new Paradox Master."

Celestae stood up and turned around with a slow and elegant grace. His looming figure towered over Rogar, casting a shadow over his figure.

Rogar bowed, willingly accepting his fate. "It would be an honor."

Celestae nodded slowly, with understanding. "I have a vision for this new Extraverse."

The group of them returned to the Extraverse. The five thrones were new.

In order, the throne of a Gar, a throne of ever shifting gold, a log throne built in the style of Camp Vistor, with phlasma cloth cushions in the seat, and beside it, a pilot's seat, and a throne of rock and dirt, covered in prehistoric ferns and flowers.

"That's…" Vaxx mumbled, "That's the pilot seat of the Riptide."

"That's a piece of Amalga-5," the Sentinel said. "What is this?" she asked Celestae.

"Rogar, the new Paradox Master." Celestae paced around the thrones. "I, the new Time Master. Evelyn Garcia Sanchez, the new Phlasma Master. Vaxx and A.J. Perrier… the Masters of Life and Death."

Vaxx and the Sentinel looked to each other, then back at Celestae.

"Do you accept?" Celestae asked.

"I do," Vaxx and the Sentinel said together, to each other, and to Celestae.

The new Emissaries took their place on their thrones and looked over those who would leave the Extraverse; Ganto, Vita, Starlocke, and Nick.

"It was nice meeting you again, A.J." Starlocke bowed to the Sentinel. "Perhaps in another life we would have been friends for longer."

"This isn't goodbye, Star," the Sentinel laughed. "Please, come visit. I missed you."

## ❖ CHAPTER 39 ❖

Starlocke smiled and panted like a dog.

"I'm gonna miss you guys," Eve said. "Go, have fun."

"Where to first?" Ganto asked Vita.

The group of them headed for the door.

Vaxx's purple box and the Sentinel's orange one twirled around each other.

Eve looked down at the white and gray box in her hands and sighed.

"What's up, Eve?" Vaxx leaned in and asked.

"I wish my Mom and my brother knew I was okay. I wish they knew what I'd done."

"I'm sorry," the Sentinel chimed in. "They would've been proud. I know I am."

Eve looked up at Vaxx and the Sentinel. Their glowing ghostly auras surrounded them and shone them in a light that beamed hope.

Eve smiled. She looked down at her time machine and leaned forward.

"Box. Tell our story. Let the worlds fortunate enough to lack a Sentinel know of our sacrifices. Let the universes we saved know. *We won...*" Eve whispered.

"Affirmative." The box glowed, and it flashed away.

Eve stood up. She looked at Celestae. "Do I have to be here all the time?" she asked.

"No. Just make sure to check in," Celestae said.

"Alright." Eve smiled. She ran for the door.

"Where's she going?" Vaxx asked the Sentinel.

"To live the life she never got."

"Ganto, Star, wait up!"

The door to the Extraverse closed, and the group vanished, off to go on adventures together, without a worry in the world. Vaxx smiled with a chuckle. She looked over at the Sentinel.

The Sentinel shuffled, trying to sit in the throne she couldn't feel, then looked up at Vaxx. The Sentinel held her hand out. Vaxx took it in hers. They held each other's hands. That, they could feel. They smiled.

They had each other.

Rogar looked over a surveillance cloud that displayed the entire Multiverse before him. He twiddled his fingers in the cloud, moving parts, and watching over others, making sure that the complete system didn't fall apart. He watched peacefully over the Gars, prospering in this new era.

Celestae took a deep breath, calm for the first time.

All was well.

❖ CHAPTER 39 ❖

And so, our story ends. It's all I know. And as the box, the time machine that traveled with the Multiverse's saviors, it's all I've ever known.

The story of how the Extraverse was restored, and the Multiverse with all of its universes, including the very universe *you*, the reader, live in, was saved. The story of the generations of Sentinels, and their family.

The story of the dueling Paradox Masters. Of the Broken Universe that vexed the banished god, and the throne he left behind. The story of the Paradox Child dueling against the Paradox Master child of Time, a once powerful god reduced to ash. The story of how the Thrones of Time were saved and restored.

You now know what the future holds. But do not fear it. You can rest assured knowing the Extraverse will be in safe hands, with the new Emissaries sitting in those thrones. They will watch over you, the eternal guardians, the Emissaries of the Extraverse: Rogar, Celestae, Vaxx, the Sentinel, and Eve's *empty throne.*

## THE END

*Special thanks to:*

*The Nova League*

*Jaylinn Rivas and Disneiruby Parra*

### ***Randy Avina***
*For helping develop the story and keeping me up when I was down – being there for when life got weird. For reading along as I wrote and being an inspiration to keep on writing. For making fun of my work and having fun with it. Without you, the story would not have gone in the direction it did.*

*And to my parents. Without them, this story would have never been made a reality.*

*To Everyone.*
*Thank You.*

Made in the USA
Middletown, DE
22 June 2023

33234800R00435